$aturday's ¢hild

$aturday's ¢hild

Gayle Jackson Sloan

Writer's Showcase
San Jose New York Lincoln Shanghai

$aturday's ¢hild

Writer's Showcase
an imprint of iUniverse.com, Inc.

For information address:
iUniverse.com, Inc.
5220 S 16th, Ste. 200
Lincoln, NE 68512
www.iuniverse.com

ISBN: 0-595-18744-7

Printed in the United States of America

This book is dedicated in loving memory to my mother, Nannett A. Jackson, who is my guardian; to my husband Ronald Sloan, who is my rock, and to my daughter, Rachel Jackson-Worrell, who is my pride.

Acknowledgements

I want to first and foremost, thank my mother Nannett A. Jackson, who is no longer with us: I did it Mom! Thank you for all of your words of wisdom over the years and the words of encouragement, no matter what I was into. You always knew me better than any one. *"Mama, you know I love you!…You're love is like tears from the stars!…Loving you is like food to my soul."* God, how I miss talking to you! You were always my best friend and staunchest supporter. *"Yes, our lives are better left to chance. I could have missed the pain, but I'd have had to miss the dance."* Not a day goes by that I don't talk to you in my mind. I miss you, Lady, and I will always, *always* love you.

To my father, Charles Jackson: I hope I finally made you proud of me Dad! The last couple of years without Mom have been hell, but the bonus has been that at long last, we have a relationship based on mutual respect and yes, love. I love you Daddy!

To my husband Ronnie, who has always been the wind beneath my wings: I did it baby, I finally finished something! Thank you for allowing me to let the housework go and not paying you enough attention when I was trying to finish this. Next to Mom, you have always been my biggest fan. You are my strength, my rock, the one true love of my life. I can't begin to make you realize just how much I love you baby!

To my daughter Rachel: I love you sweetie, even when I tend to criticize too much. *"If I could, I would cry your tears."* I knew you were my child when you wouldn't take your daily naps unless you were listening to Earth Wind and Fire! YOU have always been the best thing I have ever done. You will always be my "Shining Star." I love you and I only want you to be happy. You gave me three beautiful grandchildren. I ain't mad at you!

To my sister Charlotte: I love you sis! You told me I could do it and I did. The last couple of years have been crazy, but I learned that I don't just have a sister; I have discovered the most wonderful friend. You are so special!

To Barbara: What would I have done without all those Sunday dinners? You feed my soul as well as my stomach! There's not another kinder, gentler soul on this earth. You're one of God's true angels and I thank Him for bringing you into my life. Saying I love you doesn't seem like enough.

To Reda: I want to thank you for being my sister-friend all of these years. Even when we didn't talk as often as we'd have liked, you have always in my heart. I hope you know how much I love and cherish our friendship. Not only that, you have the BEST family I've ever had the pleasure of knowing. You're what I want to be when I grow up!

To Lanie: Girl, how could I have ever gotten through this without you? Thank you for your editing, direction and encouragement. You pushed, bullied, harassed and encouraged me every step of the way. If it hadn't been for you, there would be no book. I love you gurl!

To my stepchildren, Ronnie and Rhonda: I know I haven't always been the easiest person to live with, but I hope you have always known how much I love your father and how much I love you! Rhonda: You are so special, love yourself *first*; Ronnie: If I'd had a natural born son, *you* would be what I would wish for! I am so proud of you both!

To my grandchildren, Keturah, Robert, Ashley, Travis, Nicholas and Kiersten: Let's say it all together: Nana is a Diva!

To Craig: I couldn't have wished for a better godchild if I tried. Your love and dedication to Ronnie is a beautiful thing to see.

To Vanessa, Eddie, Glynette, Kwanna, and the rest of the crew: Poconos forever!

To Kenny, Louie, Johnny, Robert, Wayne, Andre, Derrick, KiKi, Bruce, Lisa, Venus, Michael, Carol, Michelle, Tracy, all the Stevans in the family, Dennis, Lori, Jean, Sherry, yes, even you Sherry (Mom would smack you if she was still here), Mikala, Maya, David, Renaldo and the rest of the family on both sides: I love you all!

To Andre: May your tortured soul finally rest in peace.

To Kym: Girl, with talent like that, you are sure to go far! Thanks for the FANTASTIC cover!

To Shanna: You're going to make Reda and Michael even more proud one day. Always believe in yourself, and you'll be fine, sweetie.

To Richard Seidel (the best boss EVER!), Stuart Agins (who gives GREAT PARTIES!) and Richard Haaz (You da MAN!): How will you guys ever be able to deal with me after this???

To Joe, JuanTia, Jeanne, Cheryl and the rest of 1604 crew: Thanks for being the BEST co-workers and your many words of faith and encouragement.

To anyone I may have missed: Thank you for all the encouragement I have received over the years. I may not have mentioned your name, but I hope you know you're in my heart.

Thanks y'all. MUCH LOVE. *Keep Your Head to the Sky!* Peace out!

Chapter One

What's love got to do with it? Not a damn thing, as far as I can see. If a man can't do more for me than I can do for myself, I don't need him. I mean, seriously, I'm getting out here busting my ass every day, trying to make ends meet. I can't support *my* dreams let alone anyone else's. I don't have time for 'if I coulda, woulda, shoulda's. I also don't have time for love. I've tried it a few times, and while it's very nice in the beginning, it doesn't stay that way. Maybe because I've always loved them more than they loved me, if they ever loved me at all. I've been in love and I've been in lust. I'll take lust any day of the week. You can get your groove on and send them on their way, which at this point in my life, is just fine with me. If they want to give a sistah a little some-something to help out, I don't have a problem with that either. I'm only trying to survive. And whatever I have to do to facilitate that, short of selling drugs, I think I can live with. I don't need love, nor do I *want* love. It just complicates shit. Being in love means you leave yourself open to get hurt; used and abused. Been there, done that.

I also don't want a man to give me anything and think that now he has a say over me either. I'd rather do without, thank you very much. I don't want to be beholden to anyone. I don't want to need, depend or expect anything from anybody other than myself. It's been my experience that when you do, you're almost always guaranteed to be disappointed, let down or generally fucked over.

Sorry, but my life has been reduced to making the rent and trying to keep my utilities on. Like I said, I've don't have time for dreams, mine or anyone else's. I've finally come to the realization that finding my soul mate, my one true love, is something that will probably never happen for me. No white knights in my future.

No, I've been cursed to work. I have a job, not a career. Careers are for those who have graduated college. The rest of us have a job. And all of this because I happened to be born on a Saturday. Thanks a hell of a lot. Whoever made up that little ditty that Saturday's child has to work for its living should be shot. Drawn and quartered then revived and beat down like they stole something from you.

Who sat down one day and decided that what day you were born on would affect the rest of your life? Asshole. I mean, really, give me a break. I had never even heard of that damn poem until my daughter was born. Someone had given me a plaque of the poem for her room because she had been born on a Sunday. It's funny how insidious things can be. I read it, dismissed it, read it again and then I started thinking. Did this mean that I was doomed to spend the rest of my life working and never really getting anywhere? What a totally depressing thought. I guess I should be grateful that I wasn't born on a Wednesday. My sister Zoe *must* have been born on a Wednesday. She had more tales of woe than the law should allow.

You know the poem I'm talking about. Monday's child is fair of face; Tuesday's child is full of grace; Wednesday's child is full of woe; Thursday's child has far to go; Friday's child is loving and giving; *Saturday's child has to work for its living*. But the child that's born on the Sabbath day is loving and wise, happy and gay. Or at least it goes something like that.

Anyway, when I first heard that, I didn't think much about it. I figured it really didn't apply to me. So I happened to be born on a Saturday. No big deal. What felt like an eternity ago, when I had been in high school, I had decided that all I had to do was go to college, maybe start a career, meet Mr. Wonderful, or at least Mr. Very Well Professionally Employed and just get married. Then I'd be that fabled housewife with maybe a 'girl' who came in a few times a week, freeing me, with my husband's blessing and unlimited gold cards, to shop and lunch whenever I felt like it. Was I living in a fantasy or what? I had even gotten a full scholarship to Ohio State for my college education. The good Lord knew my parents couldn't afford to send me to college. So much for the best laid plans and fantasies when I got pregnant in the twelfth grade. Once I found out I was pregnant, I just let the scholarship go. Okay, so it was stupid and I should have had my hormones more under control. At least maybe one of us should have considered some kind of contraception. Well, actually, we were using rubbers, but I hated the way they felt so I made him stop using them. Then stupid me got caught. Another statistic, but hey, no problem. A minor setback. Of course you know the jive-ass niggah left my pregnant ass in a heartbeat. So much for his declarations of true love. What's worse, he had some other chick pregnant at the same time and, would you believe it, he married her. And we had been together way before he even met her ass. Ain't that some shit? To add insult to injury, she had the nerve to be bulldog ugly, and he left me for that; talk about embarrassing. Everybody was looking at me like what was wrong with me that he threw me over for some ugly chick. That's when I found out that the best friend I had in this world was my mother when everybody else suddenly stopped speaking to me.

At the time, we were living in small-ass Akron, Ohio and that's what folks did back then. All of a sudden, if you got pregnant, you became a social outcast, like last weeks garbage. Neighbors would look at you like they were smelling something bad. Mothers who had thought you were such a nice girl suddenly thought you would contaminate their little Precious, Peaches or Candy, who was probably getting it on with more guys than you would ever think about doing. The only difference between them and me was that I had gotten caught and they hadn't. Yet.

Sometimes I still look back and laugh, because no one could believe that me, little quiet-ass Sara Livingston had been doing the wild thing. Everybody figured I was just a bookworm. Even bookworms like to get their groove on every now and then. Besides, he was my steady boyfriend. As I said, stupid me thought we were in *love*. Nobody should have their heart smashed to smithereens at seventeen.

Anyway, my mother told me to hold my head up and to *keep* it up. That I wasn't the first woman to get pregnant out of wedlock and I damn sure wouldn't be the last. To this day, whenever I hear Earth Wind and Fire's *Keep Your Head to the Sky* I think of my mother's words and I smile. And I won't even talk about the many times during my pregnancy when I would go to my mother's closed bedroom door, my hand poised to knock to ask for something or another and would stop dead in my tracks, listening to her quietly weeping on the other side, forcing me to realize that even though she didn't say it, I had greatly disappointed her. I guess she figured all the dreams she had for me would never come true. Looking back, I guess she was right. However, to her credit, the face she always showed me was one of love, concern and undeniable support.

As for my baby's daddy, as they say nowadays, so what if he broke my heart? We all know broken hearts do heal; eventually. It had only taken me three years to recover, but hey, I'm just fine now. I had even gotten over the last time we saw each other.

I remember we passed each other in the street like we were strangers and there had never been a time when we were intimate, or even speaking to each other. My pride refused to let him see how hurt I was. I had gone home, cried my heart out, gotten drunk and then I got mad. That was when I put him out of my heart and out of my mind and I never looked back. Looking back felt like when you had a toothache. You know what I mean. You probe and prod the area that hurts with your tongue, even though you know you shouldn't. Well, he was my toothache, or more appropriately, my heartache. As long as I didn't bother the memories, they didn't bother me, let alone hurt me.

In the meantime, I had a mouth to feed that wasn't just mine. But I was young and pretty good looking with light caramel colored skin, hair just past my shoulders and warm brown eyes. You know the color; sort of like whiskey when you have it in a glass and hold it up to the light. As long as you didn't look in them directly, you'd never know I was one of the walking wounded. Built okay. Maybe not as thin as I'd like, but okay; full-busted, small waist, a black woman's hips and behind. I don't care how much I diet or exercise; those hips aren't going anywhere. I've finally stopped trying to fight genetics and the legacy of the queens who have gone before me. Even after I had the baby, brothas were still rappin' tough. Black men, unlike white men, like a woman with some hips. They even like them with a little meat on their bones. Thank goodness and God Bless them! I could never figure out what some men found attractive about a woman with an iron-board ass. What do they have to hold on to? And don't all those bones hurt? Go figure. Me, I was built for a nice comfortable ride. Or so I've been told. My mother always told me my best feature, though, are my legs. Who was I to argue with my mother? I do have to agree with her; I do have great legs. So I had it going on, at least in the looks department.

Anyway, I went to business school and got my secretarial degree, then got a job during the day and continued to go to college at night. Still, I'm thinking I'm going to find me a Mr.-Do-Right man. Wrong. It seems like I was forever finding losers and no-account-can't-get-a-job niggahs with no more goals in life than to spend my little bit of money and busting a nut, thinking they were doing something. To tell the truth, sometimes I probably could have done a better job getting me off by myself, if you get my drift, and I don't even have anything battery operated. Don't act like you're so shocked. You know we've all gone there on more than one occasion, so don't even try it.

So after a couple of stops and starts, I dropped out of college to take a legal secretarial job at a big law firm and here I sit, with these damn Dictaphone earphones stuck in my ears, wishing I could hear anything else but this woman droning on and on in my ear about some boring ass case that no one really gives a shit about. So instead, I keep stomping my foot on the pedal like I can't understand what she's saying when I'm really daydreaming and trying to figure out where it all went so horribly wrong. Not just my life, but this last relationship I was in. Relationship? Who was I kidding beside myself? Again. I had thought my dog-antennae had been fully functioning. I guess the batteries had died and I had been blissfully unaware.

I had thought for a minute that Keith was going to be the one. But I mean, really, I should, and do, know better. You would think with all the other drama I've been through I would have seen him coming at a hundred paces. Yeah, right. First of all, never think some guy you meet at a nightclub is going to turn out to be Mr. Right. Fat chance. Wait. Let me add an addendum to that. *Most* times you can't find anybody worthwhile in a club. My sistah-friend, Lela, is the one in a hundred million exception.

At one time I had lived in Washington, D.C., among other places, and we used to go to this club for Thursday lunchtime disco. Seriously. I can't remember the name of the club, but anyway, she met this great guy there. When she first met him, she didn't even want to be bothered and had even asked me if I wanted him. I had told her I would love to, but any fool could see that he only had eyes for her. Now they are married, have this bad ass house in the suburbs, and a little girl who is like some kind of child prodigy. Lela is one of those women who seems destined to always have everything in life go right for her. She'd done everything by the book. She'd gone to, and finished, college. She met and married a great guy, then had a child. Somehow, she'd ended up living my fantasy. She, unlike me, had waited before becoming a mother, and legally at that. I love my daughter and could never imagine my life without her. I just wish I had waited like everyone had told me to and maybe my life could have gone more like Lela's. Don't get me wrong. I love her like a sister, and there were times I loved her more, since my own sisters were forever putting me down, but sometimes I can't help but wish my life could go at least a little bit as smoothly as hers. I mean come on. How many women do you know who have it going on so tough that their hairdresser comes to *them?* You heard me right. Sister-girl doesn't even have to go to a shop. He comes to her house once a week to do her 'do. I guess I was standing in the wrong line when they were handing out charmed lives.

I met a guy in the same club. His name was Michael, and he was tall, dark and handsome. We ended up living together for a while. One day I came home from work a little early and just missed him and some hoochie in the final act of doing the wild thing in our bed. Looking back, I should have known that something was up. I had chosen to ignore the funk I smelled when I first stepped into the living room where my sofa-bed was. I even chose to not question why it was open that time of the day. After all, I reasoned, it was his day off from work and maybe he had just been extra tired and had lounged around in bed all day. However, when he forced me to go down on him, I didn't want to believe what I was smelling and tasting was what I was smelling and tasting. After I threw him out, he broke back into my apartment and stole a bunch of my stuff that he held for ransom until *I* paid *him* to get my stuff back. Now ain't *that* some shit! Chile please.

Anyway, getting back to that loser Keith. I should have known that the man was just too damn smooth for his own damn good, but more importantly, for *my* own good. I mean he was so slick, it's a wonder they didn't have to strap him in bed at night to keep him from slithering out. No good son of a bit——oh, sorry. Forgot myself for a minute. But you know the worst part? I married that sorry piece of work. Don't ask me what bit of insanity had taken over the rational part of my brain when I made *that* move. I guess 'cause everybody around me was getting married and I was feeling a little desperate. More like a whole lot of stupid.

I couldn't see past that pretty face and fantastic body. I soon found out, however, that from eight to eighty, he was tossing them left and right. He had even had the nerve, the *temerity*, to bring one of his sluts home and do her in *my* bed that I had bought and paid for! And don't even get me started on Keith and his work habits. He couldn't keep a job to save his sorry life.

I remember when we first started living together. I'd come home from work and find a hot bubble bath, dinner fixed, clothes already ironed and hung up for work the next day. Then I'd get a sumptuous meal, a great body massage and better than other times sex. Sounds like heaven, right? Yeah, right. I soon learned that was when he was getting ready to tell me he'd lost another job, needed money for this or that, or had generally fucked up somehow. Six months into it I knew I had made a major mistake, especially after I discovered he'd sold the diamond ring my grandmother had given me for Christmas when I was twelve, and the one my mother had given me for my twenty-first birthday. Six more months, endless phone calls from anonymous females and the telltale funky smell of sex on him when he would finally deign to come home, *again*, and we were splitsville. Thanks to Keith, I discovered that I was in arrears for the rent, gas, electric and telephone. All the bills he had sworn were being paid. Hey, I can do bad all by my damn self. Thank God for my credit union. Otherwise, Bethany and I would have been living on the street.

Now its three years later and I'm pretending it never happened even though we are still lawfully wedded. I have no idea where he is and not especially interested in knowing. I'm just glad not to have to deal with all the stupid drama that Keith always seemed to attract. I can't afford to get a divorce at the moment, so it really doesn't matter. As long as he's not knocking at my door, even though occasionally I dream about what a good fuck he was. Actually, he wasn't that great, but he could do magical things with his tongue. I guess so if you've got a forked one, since he was a liar and a snake! But after the appetizer, you really do need a good piece of meat and his just wasn't all there. Now, I'm not saying that I need something that hangs down to the knees, but I should at least be able to feel it when he puts in! But good head ain't everything. There's a whole lot to be said about having some sanity and peace of mind in your life. Whenever I start to get a little soft and fuzzy about Keith, I remember the debt he left me in and the feeling quickly evaporates. If I can give you one piece of advice, it's this: never marry a man whose last name you don't like. Trust me on this one. His was *Horsestetter* for God's sake. Horseshit would have been more apropos.

Before I could slide into a deeper funk thinking about the unfairness of life in general and my state of affairs, or lack thereof, specifically, my girlfriend, Brenda Bodell, came boppin' up to my desk and pulled me out of reverie.

Brenda and I have been friends for about six years. Brenda's full name was Brenda Starr Bodell. She hated it. Yes, she was named after the comic strip. It used to be her mothers' favorite one. It didn't help that she had those big eyes like the comic strip, right down to the unbeliev-ably long eyelashes. She almost never told anyone what the "S" in her name stood for because, of course, when she did, they would always say 'Brenda Starr? Wasn't that a comic strip?' and then laugh until they real-ized that she was not amused. Every now and then, just to tease her, I would call her 'Starr' instead of 'Brenda.'

We both started at the law firm on the same day, in the same depart-ment and have been friends ever since. Brenda was a little taller than my five feet three inches, with smooth golden brown skin, huge, almond shaped, sparkling black eyes and a head full of unruly, wavy hair that refused to do whatever she was trying to do with it. She had a pretty, expressive face that never left you wondering what she was thinking; it was always clear exactly what was on her mind. Thank goodness we were friends because walking down the street with Brenda would be intimidating for any woman who wasn't comfortable with herself. With the way she was built, her name could have been Shanaynay and it wouldn't have mattered. Brenda always made sure she dressed in a fashion that showed those curves off to the fullest, which at times just bordered on hoochie mama chic. However, since she had no children, outside of her bills, most of Brenda's money went into her closet. And don't even get me started on her shoe and boot collection. My only regret was that we were not the same shoe size.

The first time most men saw her, they found themselves rendered either totally speechless, or behaving like idiots. Brenda could put an hour glass to shame and she reveled in the attention. For the last few months, though, I had started to worry about my girl. She'd been missing a lot of time from work and sometimes, when she didn't know I was watching her, she seemed so sad, lacking her usual spark. That in itself was puzzling because my girl was always quick with a laugh, a joke or smart remark, and she was sho'nuff always ready for a good time. She said it came from coming from such a huge family. You had to be quick on your feet with a ready comeback. Whenever I would ask her about her sadness, though, she'd just laugh or shrug it off and move onto another subject, forcing a false animation back into her conversation. Unless that subject was her boyfriend Terrell; she would really go mum then, which I found totally bewildering because I usually couldn't shut her up about whoever she was digging at the moment. I couldn't believe I hadn't met him yet. But she kept making up excuses and finally, I had gotten the hint and just let it go.

"Wanna catch a smoke?"

"Yeah, sounds good to me. I could use some air to clear my head and I truly *need* to stop listening to this bullshit in my ear."

"Dave got you bogged down with tapes today?"

"Chile, please. Not Dave, it's that damn Eloise. I hate working for women. I swear to God, I'm ready to break that damn recorder of hers. I don't know how many times I've asked her not tape when she's on the damn train or worse, when she's eating or chewing gum. Every time I say something to her, she just gives me that phony-ass smile of hers and say 'Oh, I'm sorry!' then turns around and does it again! I know she just does it on purpose to get on my nerves."

By this time we had descended the forty-three floors to the lobby. I guess they thought if we were up high enough, we'd think twice about getting a smoke and being away from our desk too long. Wrong. It only made me want to smoke more. Okay, so I know it's a filthy habit. What can I say? I'll stop one day, like when life quits throwing dumb shit my way and I could take a deep breath and not wonder where next month's rent was gonna come from. Or how I was going to pay the gas, electric, phone, buy food, go to the Laundromat, have transportation money and pay for my daughter's Catholic school tuition. Even though the public schools where we lived were pretty good, I believed that she deserved the same type of education my mother had given me. I said I had made stupid choices, not that I was educationally stupid. Let's not get the two confused! Where was I? Oh yeah. And forget about groceries. If I never see another box of that cheap-ass macaroni and cheese that some store always has for three boxes for a dollar and Spam will be just fine with me. Don't believe the commercials, it ain't that good. I get so tired of telling my daughter before we go to the store to not ask for any extras because we can't afford them. It really hurt my feelings the day my six-year old child told me that oft-repeated sentence before I could finish telling her. That was four years ago and she still knew the shopping rules.

And I won't even talk about how many times I'd scrape some kind of dinner together for her and I just drank coffee. When she'd ask why I wasn't eating, I'd lie and say I wasn't hungry. That's one way to stay slim. That shit can seriously work your nerves. So I smoke. At least I'm not an alcoholic. Yet.

"So," Brenda's saying to me, "are you going to meet my uncle or not?"

Brenda has been on my back for six months to meet her widowed uncle. Please. The man was *old*. At least forty-something and I was only in my damn twenties! So I just gave her this 'girl-will-you-leave-me-alone?' look.

"Look, he has his own business, lives in Wyncote, and has this bumpin' house. Gurl, he even has an in-ground *heated* pool!"

"You never said anything about all that before! Besides, what's that got to do with me anyway?"

"Well, I wanted you to meet him for him, not for what he has," she said, all indignant-like. "As for what it has to do with you, well, nothing, I guess. But who knows? At least you know he's not a broke ass scrub."

"So what's wrong with him? Why does he want to meet me?"

"He doesn't know he wants to meet you, yet."

"Humph. So why would I want to meet somebody who doesn't even know I exist?"

"Well, I don't know. Like I said, I just think y'all might click, you know?"

"No, I don't know, and I don't think I want to meet this uncle of yours either," I told her. I mean, *damn*, I don't know how many times I'd told this girl the same damn thing over and over. I've had my share of bad blind dates and don't want anymore, thank you very much. I guess she decided that she had been buggin' me enough because she changed the subject.

"So, what are you doing this weekend?"

"Same as any other weekend, nothing, other than laundry, grocery shopping, cleaning, you know. Same ole, same ole."

"Isn't your daughter coming home soon? And you've done nothing but sit up in that place weekend after weekend. Why don't you meet me on Saturday and we'll go down to South Street and stroll around and maybe break over to Penn's Landing."

"Chile, please. That costs money, something which I don't have."

"Just train fare. Everything else will be my treat. I mean, damn, Sara, you've done nothing all summer. What's the point in not having a child around if you don't get out sometime?"

"It means free day care since she's with my mom. I couldn't afford a babysitter. I don't even know how I'm going to get her. I guess I'll have to suffer through that eight-hour bus ride. You'd think one of my self-ish-ass sisters could take me, but I guess that's too much like right!"

For the last three summers, I'd been sending my daughter to my parents for the summer. My parents lived in upstate Pennsylvania in a teeny, tiny town called Athens. I guess if you liked being in the country, it was an okay place. It was in a valley surrounded by densely treed mountains. No matter where you were in the town, when you were outside, wherever you looked, you were surrounded by those mountains. It was quite pretty in the fall actually, with the mountains bursting with all the vibrant hues and shades of Autumn. It was also bordered by two rivers, the names of which I can never remember, something Indian-sounding I think. If you blinked while passing through, you'd miss the whole place. However, in the last couple of years, Main Street had extended to include an Ames and a Walmart, along with few other stores, including an Aldi's and a Wendy's, further out on the highway. I guess they were trying to be progressive. It just wasn't my cup of tea. Ambler was a small town, but it at least looked more modern than that place. Athens looked like something out of a 1950's movie set; a picture postcard for Small Town, USA, with its Painted Lady Victorians, cape cods, quasi-modern ranches, farmhouse style houses and log cabin inspired homes. They even had an ice cream parlor in town. Don't ask me what black folks were doing living in a one-ass-horse town like that, but that was where my father grew up and had returned to after his mother died to take care of his mean-ass father. My mother hated it. So did I. And being up there had nothing to do with feeling like I was able to breathe easier and feel more relaxed in the slower-moving environment. It wasn't those damn mountains at all. It was being with my mother and having her fuss over me and baby me. That's all. I really did hate being up there. Really. I visited as infrequently as I could. However, since I didn't have anyone to watch my daughter during the summers, it had gotten to be routine for the last few years to have my daughter spend summers with my parents. My mother loved having her. She got to spend time with her favorite grandchild and was guaranteed two visits from me: dropping Bethany off and picking Bethany up.

"When is she coming home?"

"Three weeks."

"Three weeks! Okay, that's it. You are meeting me tomorrow and we are hanging out. I don't want to hear any if, ands or buts about it. All that other stuff can wait. You've been putting me off all summer and I'm not taking no for an answer anymore. I heard about this bumpin' party down in the projects and that cousin of Terrell's wanted to meet you face-to-face anyway."

"Franklin? He wants to meet me, huh? He does look good in that picture I saw of him. Just too damn pretty! Can't trust those pretty niggahs. All they want to do is play a sistah. So I'll finally get to meet the elusive Terrell, huh? Oh what the hell. I'll call you and let you know what time my train gets in." I told her as my thoughts bumped and collided into each other, tripping off my tongue as I thought about it out loud.

"Cool! Glad you're finally getting out of the house," Brenda said, grinning from ear to ear.

I should have known something was up. She was just too damn happy about spending a day hanging out with another female.

Chapter Two

Well *damn!* I thought Franklin Santiago looked good in the picture Brenda had showed me. But the camera really hadn't done him any justice at all. Chile, this brother was beyond fine. Over six feet tall, body sculpted by Michelangelo, jet-black wavy hair that almost begged you to run your fingers through it, smooth, deep chocolate skin with deep, almost black, brown eyes, with silky black brows that were perfectly arched over his eyes and the longest lashes I'd ever seen on a man. Damn! It couldn't get any better than this. So now I'm wondering what's wrong with him; besides living in the worst projects the good City of Philadelphia had to offer. But the place was hooked up; I'll give him that. Once you walked in the door, you would think you were in a Chestnut Hill townhouse. The living and dining room beyond, both had soft yellow walls, hardwood floors, thick beams in the ceiling and classy white furniture. That was a plus. The fact that the furniture was all shrink-wrapped in plastic was a big minus. Under the dining room table was what looked like an antique oriental patterned rug. There was a matching one in the living room which was under the square oak cocktail table with a beautiful burgundy, green, off-white and yellow dried and silk floral arrangement in the center. The dining room furniture was an ornate, almost Baroque in style, done in an antique white finish with jewel colored striped seats that matched the window treatments over lacy cream-colored sheers. Next to the dining room was the kitchen beyond which I couldn't see at first. As we stepped further into the living room, and I picked up strains of some obscene rapper spewing his spiel from unseen speakers, I could see the kitchen had very nice raised paneled white cabinets and a faux green marble counter top in a space that looked small, but spotless, with cheerful green and white plaid curtains at the small window above the stainless steel sink. These were not the standard project-issue cabinets or counters. Somebody had put their own money into making the place more like home.

"Nice place," I told him, surprise evident in my voice.

"Yeah, my Moms did a nice job with this place," Franklin answered, checking me out from head to toe.

"Your mother did this for you? Wow. Her place must really be something."

"This is her place."

"Her and your dad?"

"No, just her; and now me. They've been divorced for years."

I looked at Brenda with raised eyebrows and she just shrugged.

Brenda's boyfriend Terrell Kingston, a thick, brown-skinned, no-neck brother about five eight who looked like he spent all of his spare time working out, asked if everybody was ready to leave for some cook-out we're supposed to be going to, cause he's ready to do some serious grubbing. I guess he was all right looking if you liked the type. You know what I mean, okay looking with small dark eyes, a broad nose, thick lips and an out of style fade that looked really tired and in desperate need of a shape up. It was hard to believe that he and the Adonis I had just met were even remotely related. Judging from the last name, and his looks, Franklin's mom must have went south of the border for a minute. Terrell just looked sneaky and kind of mean to me. I hated him on sight. He kept looking at me like he was seeing me without my clothes on or envisioning a kinky threesome or something equally strange. He was seriously giving me the creeps.

Anyway, there was also some talk about going to a party later tonight. I asked where the bathroom was and dragged Brenda's ass in with me. I was so angry with her I barely noticed the black and bronze faux marbled walls with a black sink, tub and toilet. As soon as the door closed, I laid into her.

"Girl, you didn't tell me he lived with his *mama*. What kind of shit is that?"

"I didn't know! Swear to God. Terrell just said he was a nice guy. I mean where else would he live, just getting out of jail and all?" Then she clapped her hand over her mouth.

"Jail! Jail! Did you just say jail? Now I *know* you done lost your mind. I am so out of here," I snapped as I tried to get past her to snatch open the warped bathroom door. I was positive that my girl had lost the last bit of sense she had been born with. Who did she think she was tryin' to play?

"Sara, wait! Please don't leave. Terrell will be pissed with me for telling you. He wanted me to let Franklin tell you. Please Sara, don't leave! Please? Let's just go to the cookout and you never have to see him again. Terrell's going to kill me if he finds out I told you."

I'm looking at her, pissed off big time, but vaguely wondering why she's practically in tears. Something is up, but I'm too pissed to really care what it is.

"Yeah, well, I thought we was down, Brenda, and that's some ugly shit to keep from me. What was he in jail for anyway?"

"Armed robbery, I think."

"I knew I should have kept my ass at home. I thought we were going to Penn's Landing and South Street. What happened to that?"

"Plans change?" she asked weakly.

"Yeah, right. Look, I'll go to the picnic, but I am *not* going to any damn party with his criminal ass. You got that?"

"Thanks, gurl. I'm really sorry about this. It seemed like a good idea at the time. But his ass is fine though, isn't he?" Brenda asked hopefully as she refreshed her blood red lipstick and adjusted her black and white polka dot halter top she's sporting over her black Daisy Dukes and white ankle strap sandals. I almost didn't even notice her bright red fingernails and toenails. Obviously, girlfriend went to a shop to get hers done. I'm hoping nobody notices my homemade efforts on my toes and nails. I had worn a pair of comfortable jeans, a hot pink tank top and pink strappy, flat sandals.

"I don't care how fine his broke-ass, living-at-home-with-his-mama is! I can do bad all by my-damn-self. Shit, a niggah be looking for some place to move into. Guess what, it won't be my spot!"

"Yo! What y'all bitches doing in there? Let's go. *Now*."

"We're coming, baby. One sec," Brenda answers, all nervous and motioning for me to hurry up.

"Was that Terrell?" At her slow nod I asked, "Who is Terrell calling a bitch? Girl, you let him talk to you like that?"

"He doesn't mean anything by it," she answers, shifting her eyes away from mine.

"That might be fine for you. But he's not getting away with calling me a bitch," I tell her as I finally snatch open the warped bathroom door. Brenda tried to grab me but I jerked my arm away as I marched out and asked Terrell, "Why you have to call us all out our names?"

"What are you talking about?"

And I'm thinking to myself, "*Where in the world did Brenda find this loser?*"

"I'm talking about you calling us bitches. Who you calling a bitch?" And yes, the neck thing was going on; BIG time.

Franklin jumps in when he sees that I'm getting a little warm and Terrell's looking like he's ready to go off.

"Yo, my sistah. Chill, okay? He wasn't raised right. Some men don't know how to treat a lady," he says with a chuckle, trying to defuse the situation. Brenda's standing to the side looking scared and I'm looking at her wondering why she hasn't jumped into her man's shit. Instead, she suddenly springs into action, grabbing her purse and mine and pushing me toward the front door and Terrell's hoopty. Oh yeah, this is looking like its going to be a fun date. Yeah, right.

Twenty minutes later we are in Fairmont Park, near the Philadelphia Zoo, surrounded by people I've never seen in my life and I'm feeling the beginning of a raging headache starting. First of all, I'm pissed about even being here. Second, I'm not too happy that Franklin and Terrell had imbibed in illegal narcotics on the way over here. In case you don't know what I'm talking about, they smoked a joint. I had been shocked when they passed it back to Brenda and me in the back seat and she had taken a long and satisfying drag on it before passing it back up front after I shook of my head in the negative when she offered it to me.

Drugs have never been my cup of tea. I'm from the old school and yes, I actually believed those nuns when they said that drugs were the final step into hell. Give me a drink any day of the week. Hey, I never *said* I was perfect, okay? Given the family genetics, I could probably drink any man under the table. And I'm not an alcoholic. At least, I'm not admitting that I'm one, okay? But drugs? Please. And how dare this man who I just met presume to think that it's okay to do drugs in front of me. I guess he wasn't worried about making a good impression. Between the smoke and the obscene rap blasting out of speakers that probably cost more than the whole damn car, my head was starting to feel like it was five times bigger than usual. Oh this is fun.

Anyway , the men were looking like they all wanted to talk to me and Brenda, and the women were looking like they'd like to cheerfully slit our throats. Come to find out, they were some of Terrell's, and I guess Frankie's, people. I didn't want anything to eat because I didn't know who cooked what, let alone what their kitchens looked like. If their kitchens looked as bad as Terrell's head, no thank you. Call me snobby if you want to, I don't care. That's just the way I am. If I don't know the person, I ain't eating shit, okay? I don't know how clean they may or may not be. So I stick to the safe things, like corn on the cob or fruit that I pour water on from the bottled water in the cooler. It's a little hard to fuck up some corn and fruit.

Finally, I couldn't take sitting around anymore, and I got up to take a walk. Besides being bored to death, I was finding it hard to keep biting my tongue, given the way Terrell was talking to Brenda.

I had been appalled, listening to the way he ordered her around, and when she didn't move fast enough, how he would curse her out and say stuff like, "You simple bitch, can't you do shit right? How many times have I told you how I like things done? Huh? Damn! You'd think even a *dumb* bitch could follow directions!" That would make his people sniggle even more, and only made him puff up with more nonexistent self-importance. She had to fix his plate, then get him more food, and then repeatedly get up to get him more beer, then some desert and just generally fuss over him. And the whole time, she was 'baby this' and 'baby that.' It was nauseating. I saw cut her eyes over to me a couple of times to see if I was watching and when she found that I was, she would quickly avert her eyes away from mine like she was ashamed for me to see her in such a subservient way.

Sucking my teeth in disgust, after I figured out that she wasn't going to tell him where to get off, I just started walking away from the picnic site as fast as I could, while Franklin ran to catch up with me.

"Mind if I join you?" He asked me in that rich deep voice of his. It really was a shame he had so many minuses against him. Different circumstances, he might have been nice to know. But I decided to act like I had some manners.

"No, I don't mind," I finally answer. We walked in silence for a while, no particular destination in mind as we wandered around, taking in the beauty of the sunny day and enjoying the unexpected wildflowers growing in abundance at the base of many of the huge trees in the park. Finally, we came to a shady spot near a merry little brook. The noise of the water rushing over the rocks and the cool shade were a welcome retreat from the smoke and noise of the cookout and almost immediately chilled me out. Almost.

"I'm sorry you don't seem to be enjoying yourself."

"Don't worry about it; it's not your problem."

"You don't like me do you?"

"I don't know you well enough to say whether I do or I don't, Franklin."

"Call me Frankie, please. Only my Moms calls me Franklin," he said with a small smile, and I caught a flash of his pearly whites winking at me.

He continued with, "Well, I'm glad I got to meet you today, Sara. Please, don't judge me by my obnoxious cousin." At my surprised look he chuckled.

"I was checking it out too. I can't believe that he treats his woman that way. I don't know Brenda that well, but she seems like a nice lady. How she got hooked up with Terrell, I'll never know. But as I said earlier, he wasn't raised right."

"I don't care how he was raised. There's no excuse for the way he talks to her. Worse, there's no excuse for her taking it."

"You're right. I would never treat my woman like that." His voice dropping even deeper, he said, "I would never treat *you* like that."

"You don't even know me. How can you say that? But to a certain degree, you're right. You wouldn't talk to me like that because I wouldn't put up with it!"

"You're right. And I don't know you, but I would like to know you like that. Look, I want to see you again, but I think you need to know something first," prompting me to look up at him from the damp, moss-covered rock I was sitting on.

"And what would that be?"

"I've been debating whether to say anything or not, but I want to be honest with you," he said then stopped like he's struggling to get the words out.

"Honest about what?"

"I just got out of prison about two months ago."

"Prison?" I said, faking surprise. "What were you in for?"

"Armed robbery. It was a stupid mistake I made when I was a kid. But I was old enough to know better. But I served my time and I finished school while I was in there. I didn't just sit around working out like some guys do." As I let my eyes obviously travel over his sculpted body, he laughed and said, "Okay, I did my share of working out too, but I took some Continuing Ed classes and I'm trying to find a job and maybe finally do something to make my mother proud of me. To make me proud of myself. I just wanted to let you know. I hope it doesn't make a difference now that you do. I'd like to see you again. You're feisty. I like that in a woman."

"You do, huh?" I smiled in spite of myself.

"Yeah, I do," he smiled back, flashing those perfect teeth again. I inanely wondered how somebody who'd been in prison could have such beautiful teeth. I guess it was some more of our taxpayers' dollars at work.

However, the brother was not exactly what I had dismissed him to be. I could feel some compassion swelling somewhere inside. The problem was, I didn't want to feel compassion. I didn't want to feel anything for anybody. I just wanted to get the hell out of there and go home to my little corner of the world. I had been down this road more times than I wanted to remember. Now was not a good time in my life to be taking in any more wounded birds, six-two and gorgeous or not. So when he asked if it made a difference, why did I say, "No, it doesn't make any difference?" I knew damn well it made a difference. I guess I would have to figure out a way later to blow him off. However, the smile of relief that came over his face, together with his seemingly genuine openness, made me smile again in return.

For a while we were quiet, each lost in thought and then we both seemed to try to turn the conversation to less intense topics. After a while, our conversation became easier, less stilted. As we were talking, I was struck by how cultured his manner of speech was. Finally, I felt compelled to comment on it.

"No offense, but you don't sound like the typical North Philly kind of guy. What's up with that?"

For a minute he didn't answer, just looked at me. I thought maybe I had said something wrong and he was going to go off on me.

Finally he said, "You're right. I guess I don't sound like a lot of the people around here. I may be an ex-con Sara, but that doesn't mean that I'm ignorant." I had the grace to flush in embarrassment.

"My Moms always wanted a better life for me. So even though we lived in the projects, she skimped, begged, borrowed and practically stole to send me to private school. Chestnut Hill Academy, actually. But don't get me wrong, I can slip into the vernacular of the neighborhood whenever I want. I like to think of myself as bilingual," he said with a small laugh.

"Private school? So how did you end up in prison? That doesn't make any sense," I said, shocked, ignoring the last part of his not so funny comment.

"You're right. It doesn't make any sense. But trying to be accepted by the guys in my neighborhood, trying to fit in, is what landed me in prison." At my bewildered look, he went on to say, "I was working at a bank through a program at my school. Some of the guys in the neighborhood found out, and let's just say, being stupid, I got caught up. I also got caught. I suppose I could have gotten off had I given names, but in my neighborhood, you learn early that you don't talk. Nobody wants to be known as a rat. My mother begged me to tell, but I wouldn't. She thought I was being stupid and stubborn."

"It was stupid!" I said, outraged. "Didn't you want to get out and go to college?"

"Actually, I had already been accepted into Hampton, Georgetown and Moorehouse. No, it was being safe. I had been told that if I talked, well, let's just say my mother might not have continued to enjoy her good health."

I could only look at him, amazed at his resigned attitude. Not wanting to pursue the conversation any longer, I punked out and didn't pry any further. However, once again, we managed to move onto other less intense discussions. By the time Brenda and Terrell found us, we were laughing and splashing each other with our feet that had found their way into the cool, refreshing water.

"Gurl, I've been looking all over for you. Ready to go? I told Terrell to drop us over my mother's house. I almost forgot that she wanted me to come over to help her with my sister's bad-ass kids today. Why didn't you remind me?" she asked, telling the lie we had worked out earlier so we wouldn't have to go to the party with Terrell and Frankie. At this point, I was almost reluctant to go along with it, but Brenda had that strange pleading look in her eyes I'd seen earlier. So instead, I said, "Oh, I'm sorry Starr! I forgot all about the time. I hadn't even noticed it's getting dark. Sure, I'm ready to go, we can roll," I said with false cheerfulness.

"Starr? Who's Starr?" Frankie asked, puzzled.

"Private joke. Don't even worry about it," I smirked as Brenda threw me a furious look.

Chapter Three

"Where are we going now?" I shout over the music blasting out of the six speakers in Brenda's mother's gold and creme Camry, feeling the bass pulsating through my body, as she recklessly swung in and out of traffic. This time, being in the front seat, and relieved to be away from Terrell's boorish ass, I didn't mind the volume, especially since it was WDAS we were jamming to.

Brenda had been going north on Broad Street to Cheltenham Avenue, but was now twisting and turning on streets I didn't know the names of as we cut through Cheltenham, then Elkins Park and then headed for Wyncote.

"I have to make a run for a minute. Don't worry about it. Enjoy the ride," she hollered back before cranking the music even louder, both of us bouncing with the beat. With the music being so loud, I couldn't ask her about her relationship with Terrell. I decided that I'd try to find out what the deal was later. In the meantime, it was a hot Saturday evening and we were feeling good and having some flirtatious fun with the honeys we zoomed past. Any other time, I might have been scared to death with my girlfriend's lead foot, but today I was feeling adventurous after that so-called picnic with Terrell and Frankie. But most of all, I was enjoying being out of the house for a change and doing something other than my usual routine of cleaning and watching television.

Before I knew it, we were pulling into a driveway, at the end of a cul-de-sac, of a really nice soft pink brick house with a manicured, jewel-green lawn that sparkled in the dappled light from the watering it had obviously just received. A profusion of bright flowers in random borders surrounded the lawn. Tall, leafy trees dotted the front yard, whose leaves played and danced with the early evening light.

"Whose house is this? This is *sharp*," I told Brenda, looking around. Glancing into the backyard, I could see a spacious yard and what looked like a sliding board disappearing into a shimmering pool. I also noticed the almost new silver Lincoln Navigator, with roof rack, running boards, fierce wheel rims, and every other goody you could think of, parked in the driveway next to the walkway to the house. *Very* nice.

"Uh, my Uncle Theo's house," Brenda told me with a big grin on her face.

"*Oh no you didn't*! I'll wait out here in the car," I huffed.

"No, you won't either. Come on. My mom asked me to pick up something for her. I really didn't plan this, Sara."

"Yeah, right," I grumbled as we walked along a meandering path bordered by more flower beds bursting with a rainbow of Impatiens, hot pink, lemon-scented Martha Washington begonias, lavender geraniums and waxy leaf white and salmon pink begonias toward the front door. Purple and white Alyssum spilled from the edge of the borders onto the sidewalk, letting their sweet freshness perfume the hot, moist, evening air as we brushed by it. Looking toward the street in front of the house, I noted how deep the front yard was. A tree I couldn't identify near the street caught my eye. It was huge with a black trunk and many twisting Medusa-like branches overhead and had two curved wrought iron benches, nested in a bed of pachysandra, situated around the base of the tree. I could just picture Bethany and I curled up together, each of us on a bench, engrossed in whatever we were reading, doing or thinking, but enjoying each other's company. Sighing wistfully, I turned around and looking back at the house, I noticed that the windows on either side of the front door were huge twin bays. The front of the house had an open porch with four white ionic columns supporting the extended roofline. Unlike a lot of the homes in Philly, where it seemed like everyone kept the shades or curtains tightly drawn, these windows had swags running across the tops of them and drapes on either side with light filmy sheers over them, probably allowing the light to flood the rooms within. *Dag.* I would love a place like this. The way my life was going, I doubted I would ever be in anything other than a small-ass apartment. Hell, I might end up in a damn cardboard box on Market Street if things kept going the way they were. By this time we were at the front door and Brenda was laying on the bell.

"Damn, give a person a chance to answer the damn door!" her uncle was grumbling when he snatched the door open.

"Sorry Uncle Theo. I wasn't sure you were home."

"You knew damn well I was home. Didn't your mother tell you to come here to pick up the crab pot?"

"That doesn't mean you would still be here. You know how you get in the wind sometimes."

"Who's that with you?" he asked, ignoring her comment as he looked past Brenda to me.

"Well if you'd let us in the door, I could introduce you," Brenda laughed as he moved aside to let us in.

As soon as we stepped in the door, I noticed the dramatic black and white ceramic floor tiles set on an angle to look like a diamond pattern instead of straight squares. The entire spacious foyer was done with these tiles. The walls in this area were papered a creamy eggshell with pale blue and yellow stripes, with a blue, yellow and green border at the top of the walls. Stark black and white photos of Billie Holiday, Louis Armstrong and Miles Davis graced the walls leading to the rear of the house. Moving further into the foyer, I forgot the manners I had been raised with and proceeded to check his house out, practically rubber-necking in order to see everything. I noted that to the left of the foyer was the living room, and to the right, the dining room. Both of these rooms were carpeted with a pale blue plush carpet that complimented the ultra-pale yellow walls. The dining room furnishings were deep mahogany in color, while the living room furniture, what I could see of it, looked like faux French Provincial, in a pale green and was upholstered in pastel multicolored stripes, arranged around a large rectangular cream Aubusson rug. The material on the furniture looked like it might have been polished cotton. The stairs to the upstairs were set back from the door in the entryway and carpeted in the same pale blue. Looking behind us, I noticed the small white deacon's bench with a mirror over it to the right of the double front doors. The hallway/entryway we were standing in appeared to run back to what I assumed was the kitchen. Surreptitiously peeking into the living and dining rooms, I noticed that the rooms appeared to be spacious and neat. I could just barely see what looked like still life art work in the dining room and beautiful landscapes on the walls in the living room. This house made Frankie's look like a shack.

"This is my friend from work, Sara Livingston. Sara, this is my Uncle Theodosius Watkins, but everybody just calls him Theo."

"Nice to meet you," I said.

"Yeah, you too," he answered as he held my hands a little longer than necessary.

"Nice hands," he murmured, as his thumb lightly stroked the back of my hand.

"Thanks," I answered shyly, shocked at the heat radiating from his palm, causing my body to involuntarily tingle before I looked up into the most incredible green eyes I had ever seen. They weren't exactly a pure green; they had flecks of golden brown in them. A face that was a smooth chestnut brown framed those intense eyes, with dark, curly lashes making the color all the more shocking and intense. His hair was curly brown and he was sporting a close beard that defined his jaw line, but was fuller than that Miami Vice shadow bullshit that had been so popular a few years back.

Standing in front of him I noticed that I came to about the middle of his chest, so I had to look up at him to see his face. For a man in his forties, he was built pretty damn well, which was easy to assess since he was wearing a short-sleeved red polo shirt that molded itself to his thick chest and muscled biceps, tucked into a pair of khakis. It was obvious that he took care of himself. He may not have been as physically fit as Frankie, but he still looked good; at least to me he did. To my mortification, I found myself blushing. Damn. I hadn't blushed in *years*.

He was still holding my hand and I know it sounds stupid, but I swear I could feel a current running from his hand to mine. As I said, I noticed that he had the most incredibly warm hands I had ever felt in my life. Most people's hands were either cold or normal body temperature. His were almost hot. I also noticed that they were rough-smooth in texture. I hate it when a man's hands are as soft as mine. I like a man who uses his hands for more than picking up a fork or the remote control. Or a man who calls somebody every time something needs to be fixed. Ever notice when you shake a business man, doctor or lawyers hand how it feels like your holding onto a dead fish? Especially those limp, damp handshakes. Yuck! I hate that feeling. I always find a way to wipe my hand on my pants or skirt. Anyway, I had started to slowly pull my hand back when he seemed to reluctantly let it go. During this exchange, Brenda's standing there with this self-satisfied, stupid-ass grin on her face.

Laughing slightly, Brenda reminded her uncle, "Ah, Uncle Theo, the crab pot? Or are we going to stand in the foyer all night while you two admire each other?"

"Sure, come on in. I was in the kitchen cooking. Would you ladies like something to eat or drink?" he asked, but he was looking at me, ignoring Brenda's comment again.

"Hey, I'm down, but I'm with her. Don't you have to get this pot back to your mother right away?" I asked looking at Brenda, and giving her a withering look for her unnecessary remark.

"Naw, my mom won't need it till later. Something sure smells good. Whatcha cooking, Uncle T?" she asked Theo, smiling broadly as she ignored my look.

As we walked toward the kitchen, I looked into the living room, and sure enough, I could see the light flooding the room, making it seem even bigger than it was. Of course, to my eyes, the room looked huge compared to my little house.

My apartment consisted of a decent sized kitchen, which was big enough to have a small square table with four chairs, a lot of empty cabinets and an even more empty pantry that was really a closet for laundry waiting to be ironed; an ugly brown paneled living room with a stereo, television and a broken down, second hand sofa that had seen better days, but had to do for now. Upstairs, I had two okay sized bedrooms and an antiquated bathroom. Faithfully, however, I vacuumed and dusted it every weekend. I might not have had much, but I made sure that it was always clean and neat. My mother had given me little knick-knacks to make it a little more homey. My art collection were cheap prints of either flowers or woodland scenes that I'd either picked up from Kmart or garage sales. However, it had seemed like a palace after the place Bethany and I had lived in before. Besides having only one bedroom, a rat that lived in the kitchen and bathroom that was a joke, it had also came with neighbors who got the spirit at one o'clock in the morning and liked to make a joyful noise on their stereo, at its highest decibel, until about five o'clock in the morning. I was thinking that both my kitchen and living room would easily fit into this man's living room.

By now we were in a kitchen I know my mother would have killed for. Almost the entire room was ringed with cabinets and counter space. In the middle of the floor was a butcher block-topped island with stools on one side of it. Off to one side was an eating area in front of sliding glass doors to the outside patio. Beyond that was the family room. At one end of the family was a stone fireplace with a rough wooden mantle. The furniture in that room was all brown leather, with wood and wrought iron tables.

Pulling myself from my observations, I heard Brenda's uncle say, "Just some steaks with onions and peppers, rice and gravy and string beans. Little T was supposed to be home, but I he called right before you got here to say he wanted to spend the night over Carol's house."

"Aunt Carol is my mother's other sister and Uncle Theo's twin." Brenda explained.

"Oh, I never met a twin before. Cool."

"Yeah, I call her my other half."

"You've got to meet her, Sara. She is so cool. Not to mention drop dead gorgeous."

"I see it runs in the family," I smiled into Theo's eyes. Oh yeah. There were some *serious* currents flowing back and forth.

"Is that Billie Holiday I hear playing?" I asked, cocking my head to one side, listening to the music coming from the family room.

"Yeah. How did you know?" he asked, surprise evident in his voice.

"My parents, my mother especially, have always been fans of hers. My mother told me she met her once. She had a cousin that was a singer and they were on the same bill. Ever since then she's loved her music. I grew up listening to her," I laughed.

"Well I'm impressed that a woman your age would know good music when she hears it. Not that Diana Ross bullshit that everyone heard in that movie. Don't get me wrong, Diana can sing, but *nobody* can do Billie but Billie."

"I agree," I said as we smiled into each others eyes.

"Daddy! Daddy! You back there?"

"Yo! In the kitchen," Theo called out, breaking the spell as a young lady strolled into the kitchen. She was about nineteen or twenty, cappuccino brown, with a small face, killer cheek bones, the same hazel green eyes and hair flowing down her back almost to her behind. She was really pretty and built like the proverbial brick you-know-what, especially with that Dolly Parton chest on such a small frame. She looked so sweet and innocent; until she opened her mouth.

"Hey Daddy. Hey Brenda! What you doin' here? Who's this?"

"Damn, slow down Chelsea! Hello to you too. This is my friend Sara. Sara, Theo's big mouth daughter, Chelsea."

"Nice to meet you." Looking me over from head to toe she asked, "Brenda bring you here for my father?" she asked bluntly.

I was a little taken aback. What did that mean? Like I was some prostitute bought and paid for to help the recovering widow get his groove on. Recovering I said, "I don't *think* so! I just happened to be with her when she came to pick up a pot for her mother."

"Chelsea. Mind your manners. You know I raised you better than that."

"I just asked a question. Dag! Every other niece you got has been parading them through here like it's a damn pageant or something. Mom's only been dead a year, okay? Excuse me if I'm a little sensitive," she huffed.

I looked at Brenda with a what's-up-with-that? look. She just shrugged and kind of waved her hands in an I'll-tell-you-later kind of way.

Theo saved the moment by asking, rather impatiently, "What do you want, Chelsea?"

"Dag! Can't a daughter come by to check on her pops?"

"Yes, she can. But you usually don't unless you want something," he told her, his eyes twinkling.

"Can you baby-sit Aisha tonight?"

"No, I can't," he told her brusquely as he checked his steaks in the wall oven broiler.

"Aw come on, Daddy! What else you got to do beside sit around the house?"

"None of your business what I may have to do. I'm not babysitting and that's that. Where are you going anyway?"

"To a party down on Broad Street at the Stinger."

"Again? That's all you do is party. You need to spend more time with your child and get more into your books. There will be plenty of time for partying after you get your nursing degree," he told her tiredly, like he'd said it all before.

"It's the weekend, Daddy. I'm tired of sitting up in the apartment by myself. I need to get out and boogie a little."

"Getting out boogieing a little is how you got Aisha," he told her roughly.

"Are we going to go down that road again? I'm sick of hearing it. Forget it. Never mind. You never do anything for me. Ever since Mom died, it's like I don't even exist. You never want to see your own grand-daughter and the only person that matters is Little T and you don't even seem to have time for him. He's always down Grandmommy's or Aunt Carol's. I guess you want to take another one of your midnight rides looking for God only knows what. Why can't you ever do anything for me?" "That's enough, Chelsea. I'm not going into this with you in front of company. I actually have plans for tonight or I would watch Aisha. Why can't her father watch her or Rita?"

"I hate to ask ReRe again to watch her. She's trying to take over Aisha as it is."

"If you started acting more like the child's mother instead of a babysitter your damn self, you wouldn't have that problem," Theo told his daughter scathingly.

"Never mind. Dag. You don't ever do anything for me. If Mommy were still here, wouldn't be no thing."

"But she's not, and stop trying to use your mother as a weapon against me. You did that shit the entire time she was alive and now you are trying to use her memory as a weapon. I ain't having it. If that's all you have to say, goodbye," he told her as he abruptly turned his back and went back to checking the steaks in the oven.

Chelsea sucked her teeth, and mumbling goodbye, left in a huff.

"I apologize for my daughter's bad manners," Theo said as he turned around with the sizzling steaks on the broiler pan in his oven-mitted hand.

"Her mother always spoiled her outrageously. I love her to death, but I won't put up with her selfishness," he said, sounding tired.

"Your daughter is really beautiful," I offered.

"That's her whole damn problem. People have always catered to her because of her looks. Especially her mother," he said, sounding slightly bitter.

An uncomfortable silence descended until Brenda piped in with, "So, let's eat some of that steak Uncle Theo. Damn! I'm staved."

Theo gave an indulgent, albeit uneasy, laugh, as he began fixing our plates with steak, rice and gravy, string beans and salad. After that, the time passed in easy banter, and I felt like I had known this man forever.

The entire time through our meal, sparks were flying between us. Both of us kept peeping the other out. Rather than making me happy, it disturbed the hell out of me. This was not somebody I wanted to get involved with. He probably had more baggage than I did. So why was I feeling so attracted to him?

After eating, we sat out on his patio, sipping glasses of iced tea. It was so quiet and peaceful, and I was really enjoying myself. Soon, however, Brenda said that we had to go. We thanked Theo for his hospitality and took our leave.

"See. I told you my uncle was a nice guy. Go ahead, cuss me out for tricking you and then you can tell me thanks," she laughed.

I had to laugh myself. She was right, he did seem like a really nice guy and I had enjoyed meeting him.

"Yeah, he was nice, but you didn't tell me how fine he was Brenda. Damn! If I had known that, I would have agreed to meeting him a long time ago," I said.

"That was my surprise. Anyway, the rest is up to y'all. I've got a feeling he's going to be calling me and asking for your telephone number."

"Yeah, right." But I was hoping he would.

Turning down the music, I asked her, "So what's the story with you and Terrell?"

Shrugging, she said, "No story. He takes care of me. I haven't had to pay any rent since I met him. He takes me to expensive places and we have fun."

"Uh huh. So how come you seem so scared of him? And does he always talk to you like that?"

"I am not scared of him! And I resent you saying that. How dare you say something like that! And no, he doesn't. He was just showing off today. No big deal."

"Okay, okay. Chill. Dag. My bad, but you just seemed a little jumpy around him, that's all. I'm just trying to look out for you gurl."

"We're fine, Sara. Terrell just has a temper and sometimes he does get a little rambunctious, and I just don't want to rock my gravy boat, okay?"

"If you say so, girlfriend. I didn't mean to get you upset, Brenda. I'm just concerned, that's all." I told her gently.

"I know, girl. And I appreciate it. But I can look out for myself, okay? Trust me. Everything is fine."

"Okay. But you know I'm here for you, right?"

"I know, girl," she answered reaching over to squeeze my hand in hers.

Frankly, I didn't believe her, but I let it drop. I figured when she was ready to talk, she would. At least I hoped she knew I was there for her. Changing the subject I asked, "What was all that with Chelsea? Is she always so, I don't know, blunt?"

"Yeah, she is. Chelsea has no problem speaking her mind. She and her mother were very close. She's very protective, not so much of her father, as she is her mother's memory. I think she thinks he's never supposed to even look at another woman."

"Humph. Well, she has to realize, he's a man who has needs just like she does."

"As far as Chelsea is concerned, he's just 'Daddy,' and not really a man. She has a lot of growing up to do. Her mother made her think her shit didn't stink, and she thinks everybody else is supposed to treat her the same way."

"Yeah, well, everybody ain't her mama. When she realizes that, her feelings are really going to be hurt," I said before reaching over as I fiddled with the radio dial until a bumpin' song came on, then I cranked the music up, with both of us saying, "That's my jam!" as we burst out laughing.

Later that night, we hooked up with some girlfriends of Brenda's that had stopped by, and after piling into one of the girl's car, whose name I never quite caught, we hung out at a couple of nondescript neighborhood bars. We kicked it out, big time. These were places where being dressed to the nines wasn't necessary so I didn't feel uncomfortable in my casual gear. They might have been dead when we walked in, but weren't by the time we left. At a couple of spots, folks were asking Brenda where Terrell was. She just played it off, finished her drink and suggested we leave to check out another spot. I got the impression she didn't want to stay too long in any place where she and Terrell were known as a couple.

We got our drink on, picked up a couple of numbers, which we promptly threw away when we left, and moved onto the next spot.

When it came time to take me home, however, we had a problem. After we got dropped off at Brenda's mother's house, we discovered that Brenda's brother had taken their mother's car, and it was anybody's guess when he'd be back home and the buses and trains had long since stopped running to Ambler, a suburb outside of Philly, where I lived.

"Well I guess I'll have to stay over your house then Brenda."

"Girl, we can't stay at my house. My spot is being exterminated. That's why I'm crashing here at my mom's."

"What? Then what the hell am I supposed to do Brenda, sleep on the damn porch? I knew I should have kept my ass at home. At least I'd be sleeping in my own damn bed," I fussed. I was feeling more than a little bit tipsy and I wasn't in the mood for any dumb shit.

"Give me a minute to think. I'll figure something out." Suddenly snapping her fingers, she ran into the kitchen and grabbed the phone. I couldn't hear what she was saying but every time I thought about not having a way to get home, I sucked my teeth. I was almost mad enough at Brenda to hit her. I was prowling around her mother's postage stamp living room, getting madder by the minute.

To tell you the truth, I didn't want to stay here either. Ms. Sadie was a very nice lady. However, her home left a lot to be desired. In short, the house was a pigsty and was the last place I wanted to lay my head. The porch was starting to look pretty damn good.

"Okay, it's all taken care of. I have some place for you to sleep."

"Where?"

"You'll see," she laughed mysteriously.

Chapter Four

"Did you sleep well last night? I hope you're hungry. I made some waffles, sausage, bacon, scrapple, home fries, toast and eggs. I didn't know what you might like. I've also got coffee, but I can make you some tea if you'd prefer, and I have orange and apple juice."

"That's what woke me up! I thought I was dreaming when I smelled the onions and peppers. That's how my mother used to get us up when we were teenagers. She'd fry a mess of onions and peppers and before long everyone would rush the kitchen, starved. Then she'd put us to work before we actually got to eat anything. No matter how many times she did it, we always fell for it!" I chuckled at the memory, and Theo just grinned.

"But really, you didn't have to go to all this trouble, Theo. I really don't want anything," I told him, still rubbing the sleep out of my eyes. At his crestfallen look, I relented and told him I'd take some waffles, a little bit of home fries, bacon and a piece of toast. I also had some coffee and apple juice.

I was feeling a little scroungy, considering I didn't have a toothbrush and was still wearing the same pair of panties from the day before.

After Brenda had said there was no place for me to sleep at her house, she had asked her uncle if I could stay at his house. Actually, she had asked him if he would mind taking me home first. Theo had said flat out that he wasn't driving to Ambler at that time of night because he had worked that day and was too tired. So he told Brenda to put me in a cab and he'd pay for it when I got to his house. I told her that there was no way in hell I was spending the night at somebody's house I had just met and to bring her ass on with me. She had bitched and moaned, but when she saw I was serious, she had finally given in and agreed to come with me.

Once we arrived, Theo had graciously offered us his bedroom said he would sleep on the couch. He said would have put us in his son's room but it was too messy for us to sleep in there and his daughter's old room was piled up with a lot of stuff. Both rooms only had twin beds anyway. He also told us that even though there was a bathroom in his room, it wasn't working because he was having some plumbing work done and the water was shut off in there so we'd have to use the bathroom in the hall. We were putting him out and he apologized for inconveniencing us! Amazing. He had even lent me a pair of his pajamas that were miles too big on me when Brenda forgot to bring an extra pair for me. Forgive the female in me, but I kind of liked the idea of leaving the scent of my Chloe, my current favorite perfume, behind in his pajamas.

Brenda had given me a really nice gift set of the perfume the month before as an early birthday present, so I had been wearing it every day. She'd called it a 'get happy' gift. She was always doing stuff like that and when she wasn't being a smart ass and I wasn't pissed off big time at her, I loved her for it.

Once when I hadn't had any money to buy my daughter a birthday gift, she'd gone out and bought her a complete outfit, including underwear and shoes, and had made me promise not to tell her it was from her but from me. To make sure that I told Bethany it was from me, she had gone home with me so she could hear me tell my daughter the outrageous lie. It had stuck like cement in my throat. I had been so ashamed that I couldn't afford a birthday gift for her. Brenda told me to get over it. Since she had no children of her own, she had adopted Bethany as her godchild and loved to spoil her. Then she'd turned around and bought Bethany another gift and presented it as her gift. Talk about being a true friend.

Anyway, I could just picture a man who had been without a woman for over a year holding his pajama shirt in his hands and deeply inhaling my scent and maybe getting a woody in the process. That's some twisted thinking, isn't it? I didn't want him creeping into bed with me, but I didn't mind him getting a woody thinking about me. Go figure.

At the moment, however, I was trying not to talk too much because I didn't have a toothbrush to use and even though I had done the toothpaste on the washcloth thing, I still didn't feel like my mouth was clean enough. I didn't have any makeup with me, and I hated having to wear the same thing that I had been in all day the day before. Brenda might have been my girl, but right about now I was ready to cuss her ass out; again. I hated not being in control, and nothing she could say would convince me that she hadn't done this shit on purpose.

However, on the other hand, the night, which had started out feeling uncomfortable, hadn't been that bad. Almost as soon as we got to Theo's house, Brenda had gotten a snack and then headed up to his bedroom and the phone. I assumed to call that jerk of a boyfriend of hers. I had elected to stay up with Theo rather than listen to that drivel. We were sitting in his family room, with only the light from his floor model television, watching an old Barbra Streisand movie, "*On a Clear Day You can See Forever*," which I had never seen before.

I don't like being in a dark room, and don't particularly care for darkness in general. I even slept with the TV on because I have always found total darkness to be suffocating, like I was in a coffin or something. I always figured I'd be in enough darkness when I died, so while I have control over it, I like having some kind of light. Same thing goes for silence. I always have a TV or the stereo on. I guess to drown out the things in my head that I didn't want to think about, let alone remember the things I was always fighting so hard to forget.

Anyway, to my surprise, I loved the movie and I didn't feel as uncomfortable about the darkness as I usually did. Maybe because I wasn't in the dark by myself for a change. But I didn't want to think about that, either. While we were watching the movie, with me on the love seat the furthest away from the sofa he was laying on, Theo had told me quite a bit about his life with his deceased wife and his life since her death. Apparently, they had been together since she was sixteen years old. They had been married since a week after her eighteenth birthday. She was thirty-eight when she died of complications during surgery to reconstruct her breast that had been removed because of cancer. He told me that he was still trying to come to terms with her death. He just couldn't understand how a woman that young could die. Something to do with the hospital giving her the wrong anesthesia. He said that in all those years, he'd never cheated once. Wow. How rare is that? A man who didn't believe in cheating. At least that's what he *said*.

He even talked about how one of his other nieces had tried to hook him up with one of her skeezer friends. He told me about how they had went out to dinner a couple of times and he realized that she really wasn't his type. Especially when he'd gone to pick her up for a date and her boyfriend was sitting up in her house. After that, he'd stopped seeing her. But it had made him realize that he was ready to rejoin the land of the living instead of wallowing in the pain of his recent past. He said he still grieved for his wife, but it was getting easier. Since I had never lost anyone that close to me, I really had no point of reference, but I did make sympathetic noises to let him know I was feeling him. I, in turn, told him a little about Bethany's father and my loser husband. I guess I just wanted to make sure he knew I was married. Not that it mattered, really.

What I really remembered the most about last night was that, as his voice floated to me in the semi-darkness, were the little jolts I kept feeling. Sort of like those feelings that you get when you get a sudden chill, or what the old folks used to say was somebody walking over your grave. But it wasn't a cold, forbidding chill; more like a pleasant, warm sensation. I know I'm not making any sense, but if I can't explain it to myself, how can I explain it to anyone else? Anyway, these jolts, or chills, were zapping me left and right and throwing me into total confusion. I suppose deep down inside, I had a pretty good idea what it meant, but I didn't want to know. I don't want to feel anything for anybody. And I certainly don't want to be attracted to somebody who, as I said before, probably has more baggage than I do. I just don't want to *feel*. Feeling leads to hurting, and damn it, I'd been hurt enough. Besides, anybody who I'm even remotely attracted to must have something wrong with him. So there must be something really wrong with this guy whose voice is zapping me all over the place. Maybe that was what I was feeling. Yeah, that had to be it. A warning to get the hell away from him before it was too late. Maybe this time my dog antenna was actually working.

Finally, I couldn't take it anymore, and I told him I was dead on my feet and was going to sleep. I finally fell into an exhausted sleep and as tired as I was, he could have come in and ravished me and I probably wouldn't have even known it. Of course, with his niece right there in the bed with me, I guess that would have been a little kinky, and Theo didn't strike as that kind of guy. But hey, you just never know!

So here I am, so tired I felt hung over, I surreptitiously watched him when I thought he wasn't looking, trying to figure out if what I was feeling last night was from being tired or what.

"By the way, where is Brenda? I've looked everywhere for her. I thought maybe she was in down here in the kitchen with you when I woke up."

"She left early this morning. She said she'd call you later to hook up if you still needed a ride home. I told her not to worry about it, that I'd take you home."

"Oh. Well, thanks, but I don't want to put you out. I hate being so much trouble."

"No trouble at all," he smiled into my eyes.

"Yo, Pop! I'm home!" A young man I assumed to be his son said as he came bopping into the kitchen. He was about thirteen, tall, skinny, penny brown, with tightly curled black hair and huge black eyes. Although he didn't look anything like Theo, he was really cute. I assumed he looked like his mother.

"Whoa!" he said as he stopped short when he spotted me.

Unfazed, his father said, "Theo, this is Sara. She's a friend of Brenda's. Sara, this is T.J, short for Theo, Jr."

That's it. That's all he said like it was an everyday occurrence for his son to come home and find a strange woman in his house.

"Nice to meet you," I smiled as he reluctantly shook my hand.

"Hi," he mumbled, questions in his eyes.

I looked at Theo, but he turned his back, fixing an unasked for plate for his son. Feeling compelled to explain, I said, "I missed my train last night and your father was kind enough to let Brenda and me stay here." He seemed to brighten up some then and a little of the frost seemed to leave his eyes.

"Oh, ok."

"So, I'm ready to go whenever you are," I told him.

"Actually, my sister called this morning and everybody wants to go Wildwood. Want to go?"

"Really? I would love it, but I don't even have a pair of shorts with me. Not to mention a toothbrush," I laughed.

"Don't worry about it. I've got some extra toothbrushes upstairs in the hall closet. I'm sorry, I forgot to give you one last night. As for the shorts, just roll your pants up. You'll be fine."

In the middle of thinking up excuses not to go, I thought, '*Why the hell not?*' I hadn't been to the shore in years. It would be a pleasant change from my usual dreary Sunday of laundry and ironing. The hell with it. I'd iron whatever I needed for work tomorrow.

"Sure. As long as you don't mind me tagging along."

"I wouldn't have asked you if I didn't want you to come," he told me quietly.

And there went another one of those zaps.

Chapter Five

Lord that air felt good! I thought as the hot ocean breezes caressed my body. Taking a deep breath, I inhaled the salty tang of the air as I let the deafening rumble of the surf hitting the shore soothe my tired spirit. I listened to the screech of the ever hungry sea gulls swooping and diving overhead. The hot, moist sand I had been letting sift through my fingers felt coarse but good. Scooting a little further down the blanket, I buried my feet a little deeper into the sun heated sand. Looking up at the sky, I smiled as the fluffy white clouds meandered across an azure blue sky. Every now and then, a plane would skim across with an advertisement or a proposal of marriage. Small boats lazily drifted along the horizon. Small children dashed in and out of the teasing surf, laughing and squealing in delight and big children and grown ups challenged the oncoming, never ending foamy waves.

I would have burned to a crisp, but thankfully, Theo had bought a green and white striped umbrella that was shading our little piece of heaven. Looking up and down the beach, I noted how packed it was. Apparently, a lot of people had felt the need to commune with the ocean and sand today.

Of course, there were the beautiful people, men and women so cut they made you sick to look at them. They were a refreshing diversion, however, from the people who felt it was okay to just let it all hang out. I mean come on. Some of these women should have been ashamed to parade along the beach with some of the stomachs I saw hanging out, stretch marks and all. With men, you kind of expect it, but some of these women really should have known better. I saw one woman who had to be no less than a size 22 in a *two-piece* bikini! What the hell had she been thinking? I mean, *damn!* I was beginning to think I was pretty damn tight compared to some of the bodies I was seeing down here. Go figure.

But through it all, was the caressing breeze, the salty smell of the ocean, the hypnotic sound of the surf hitting the beach and the screech of the sea gulls overhead.

This had been just what I needed. The day had been perfect. Theo's family had treated me with, at first curiosity, and then, almost like a member of the family, joking with and teasing me. They really teased him as the day went on whenever they would catch him watching me. I was sure they were wildly curious. I got the feeling they were happy to see their uncle so relaxed. I could tell that they all seemed to care about this man a lot. I had never felt so comfortable in my life among strangers.

I have always been a person to keep to myself. My sisters Zoe and Gina were the social butterflies. Stephanie was the militant, but still more social than me. I was the bookworm. Meeting new people had never been my thing. And being in a group of people I had never met was totally unheard of. Zoe could walk into any bar or party in the world she wanted to. Me? Please. I would have had to be under a gun to do such a thing. I've never gone to a party, bar, club or even alone to a restaurant to eat by myself. I have always felt too self-conscious. The only thing I have ever done by myself was gone on a job interview, but that was business and totally different. And now, here I was, surrounded by people I'd never seen before in my life. At least I had met Theo first, so maybe that was why I wasn't feeling completely out of place. Theo and I had ended up being the only adults. His sister Carol had opted to stay at home. I think she appreciated having the house free of all her kids for a change. And Brenda, bless her traitorous soul, had bailed on me, saying she had some pressing business with Terrell.

To my complete surprise, I found myself enjoying the company of all these exuberant young adults. I laughed out loud when one of his nephews, Mark, I think his name was, I still couldn't get them all straight, packed his sister Shelly's swimsuit with sand until it looked like she had a load of you-know-what dragging behind her. All the people on the beach, black and white, had fallen out laughing with their antics.

I had rolled up my pants as far as they would go and had even flirted with the surf for a while. Theo and I played in the water and I squealed in mock fright when he splashed water on me as we ran along the water's edge.

At the moment, I was reclining on my elbows on the blanket, my head thrown back as I allowed the sun and salt laden wind to kiss whatever exposed areas it could find, my eyes closed, listening to the surf and birds and people as they drifted past my space and I tried not to think about how hungry all this fresh air was making me. There was a cooler of sodas, chips and such, but no real food. I tried to stay away from soda and chips because they tended to break me out. Theo had disappeared, but I wasn't that concerned. I figured he was in the surf somewhere and I just hadn't spotted him yet.

"Here you go. You should have told me sooner that you were hungry," Theo said as he handed me a hot dog loaded with everything, some boardwalk fries and a large juice.

"I noticed you didn't seem to want any soda, so I hope the juice is okay."

"Thanks. I try not to drink soda, it breaks me out too much," surprised because I hadn't seen him walk toward the boardwalk.

"So that's why you have such pretty skin," he said as his eyes roamed over my face.

"I didn't want to impose," I told him, as I felt an embarrassing blush and let his comment pass without a reaction.

"We didn't bring any real food because Carol will have a huge dinner waiting when we get back. I'm afraid we stayed a little longer than originally anticipated."

"That's okay. I've enjoyed myself. I just hadn't realized how hungry I was. I guess I should have eaten more of that great breakfast you had made."

"Thank goodness I was sitting close enough to hear your stomach growling," he laughed.

I felt my cheeks burning even more. I had been mortified when I heard my stomach grumble in protest. It was worse when I realized that he had heard it also. I hadn't said anything sooner because I was flat broke. I hadn't brought any money with me because I hadn't stopped at an ATM, mainly because there wasn't anything to get out from the ATM. I had just enough at home to pay for my train tickets the following week and already knew it was going to be soft pretzels and juice for lunch all week.

Gratefully I chomped on the hot dog and fries. I was also enjoying the wonderful eye candy his nephews were providing. Chile, I have never seen so many good-looking men in one place in my life. They were like Philadelphia's best-kept secret.

When we had pulled up to his sister's West Philadelphia house, my jaw had all but dropped to the floor of the car. The woman had seven sons and two daughters. Each male that fell out of the house was better looking than the last one. I couldn't believe it. I was like, *DAY-UM!* He thought I was surprised to see so many people coming out of one house. It was that, true, but DAAAY-UM. How could one woman produce so many examples of fine black-manship? Talk about your rainbow coalition. I mean, these brothers went from café au lait to smooth dark chocolate, and from slim-goodies to muscle-bound hunks. I later found out that they all had the same father except for her oldest son. But after I met her, I could understand how she did it. She reminded me of pictures I'd seen of Dorothy Dandridge. I quickly learned, however, that it was not her looks that drew people to her. It was her calm and pleasant personality. She instantly made me feel welcome and soon we were laughing almost like old friends. Still, I caught a couple of questioning looks that she was sending to her twin. When she had hustled him upstairs, I could just imagine the conversation they were having.

"So, does a pretty young thing like you have a boyfriend?" Theo was asking me, pulling me out of my revelry.

"Nope. Not even a fuck buddy," I said, trying to shock him. I was the one surprised when he came back with, "Is that suppose to shock me?" he laughed, his eyes twinkling. I noticed they did that a lot. Especially being around his nieces and nephews. He acted more like a proud papa, than an indulgent uncle.

Now I was disconcerted. I had called myself being flip and cute. Changing the subject, I nodded toward his family and said, "You seem to be very close to your nieces and nephews. My family is so distant, and I'm not used to seeing that."

"I helped to raise most of my twin sister's kids. Their father was in and out, and coming from a large family myself, it was no big deal. It was a little more difficult when my wife and I moved to Wyncote, but until then, we had lived in the same house with Carol, her kids, my two kids and my parents."

"Jesus! That would have driven me crazy. For as long as I can remember, I've always had my own room, then my own apartments. I guess I'm not used to sharing my personal space like that."

Shrugging, he said, "You get used to it. I come from a family of thirteen, so I've never had a room of my own," he chuckled. "I went from sharing a bed with my brothers to sharing one with my wife. Until she died, I don't think I have ever slept by myself. That was the hardest thing to get used to, I guess," he said as he looked off toward the waves rolling to shore. For a moment, the roar of the ocean filled the empty space between us.

"Thirteen! Damn! Your father must have just looked at your mother hard and she'd end up pregnant," I said jokingly, but slightly appalled.

Laughing, he turned back to me and said, "Yeah, I guess. I never really thought about it."

"My mother had always wanted a big family like that. I never did. My poor daughter has been begging me for years to have another baby. She hates being an only child."

"Tell me about your daughter."

"Bethany? She's a great kid. Too bad she has me for a mother," I said.

"Why would you say that?"

"Because I'm always so overwhelmed by life, I'm afraid I don't make enough time for her. And I'm probably too hard on her. But it's all I know. My mother was hard on me and I don't think I'm any worse for it. And I adore my mother. She's my best friend. I know if no one else in this world loves me, she does; without judgment and without fault," I finished feeling a little embarrassed.

"Sounds like you and your mother are close. Do you feel that way about your daughter?"

"We are, and yes, I absolutely feel that way about Bethany! My problem is in trying to learn to let Bethy be her own person, instead of a miniature me. My mother keeps telling me to stop trying to make her walk in my footprints. But having my daughter has taught me that I have more strength of character than I thought I did."

"What do you mean?"

"There were a lot of times when I would have just given up, when things have been really bad, but I knew I couldn't because I had to provide for her. My sisters are always telling me to grow up and to not be so selfish. They have no idea how much I have sacrificed for my daughter. I just want a better life for my daughter. Come hell or high water, I'm going to see that she gets it. I just haven't figured out how yet," I laughed, trying to lighten my mood.

Changing the subject I asked, "Can we talk about something else? Isn't it time to go? I hate to be a party pooper, but I've got to be at work by eight-thirty tomorrow and I really want to go home and chill at my own house."

"Sure, no problem. I was just getting ready to get everybody together anyway," he said as he stood up and dusted the sand off his shapely legs, as he called to his family that it was time to go. Theo in swimming trunks was a nice sight to behold. I had to make myself stop looking at that line of hair that went from his chest, down his taunt stomach and disappeared into his trunks. Nice legs, *great* butt. It had taken all of my self control not to run my hands through that hairy chest. I don't know what it is, but a hairy chest really turns me on. I think my nipples had been standing at attention all day, and the ocean breeze had nothing to do with it. Keeping my hands and eyes off that chest had been an exercise in self-control all day. I was exhausted!

When we got back to Philly, of course everyone insisted that I stay a little longer and eat dinner. I have to admit that it was really good. Carol even insisted that I take a plate home with me. These people were really into food.

When I finally got home that night, and after a relaxing, hot shower, that did nothing to dissipate my horniness, my last thought before drifting off to sleep was, who is this man and why did he get to me so?

Chapter Six

"Hey sexy lady. How was your day today?" This deep silky voice purred over the phone line.

"Who is this?" I asked, having just gotten in the door from work.

"Oh, now you don't know me. You got that many men calling you up you can't tell one from the other?"

"Maybe, maybe not. For all I know, this could be a new tactic from a bill collector," I snapped, not really in a guess-who mood.

"Whoa, baby! I guess I caught you at a bad time. It's me, Franklin. Maybe I should talk to you at another time."

"Oh. Frankie. Sorry 'bout that. Yeah, you did catch me at a bad time. I just walked in the door from work. I haven't even had a chance to put my purse down," I told him, trying to at least sound apologetic. I hated to get phone calls as soon as I walked in the door. Just cause his ass was sittin' around his mama's house all damn day doing nothing didn't mean I had been doing the same thing.

"I was calling you because I wanted to see if you wanted to maybe catch a movie or something."

"On a *Wednesday?* I don't do weekday dates. I have to get up at six o'clock in order to be at work by eight-thirty. With SEPTA being the way it is, you never know if the train will be running on time or not. It doesn't matter how many times I stay late to help out or to get something done. Hell, I could stay half an hour, an hour or even longer.

There's never any comment about that. But be late a couple of minutes and there's a whole lot of shit said."

"Damn, that's rough, baby. But I was hoping we could get together. I enjoyed the cookout and I've been thinking about you a lot since then. Tell you what. Have you eaten yet?" At my negative comment he continued with, "No? How about I pick up some ribs and stuff from the Rib Crib and bring dinner to you? I promise I won't stay long. You shouldn't have to cook after a rough day at work."

"You got a car?" I asked, surprised.

"I can use my mom's, I don't think she's going anywhere anytime soon."

"Oh," I said, not really impressed. I don't have a car, but I just think there is something pitiful about a grown-ass man having to borrow his mama's car.

"So, how about it?"

I'm looking at my empty refrigerator and thinking, hey, free grub. Not a hard decision.

"Sure, as long as you know that you really can't stay long. As I said, I have to get up early."

"No problem babe. Give me directions and I'll be there directly."

Directly? What, is he from the south too? Next I guess he was going to tell me he just wanted to *conversate* a little. And God, help me, didn't he say exactly that!

"Okay, I'll be there soon. We can eat a little, conversate a little, and get to know each other better over some good food," he said cheerfully, like he had just something brilliant.

I was just thinking about my rumbling stomach, tired feet and empty fridge. However, I am still a female. So I raced upstairs, jumped in the shower, squeezed out a little of my favorite perfume and tried to find something comfortable that wasn't too frumpy looking, but not too provocative, to put on. Racing back downstairs, I quickly straightened up my living room and kitchen.

As I had said, my place is what a realtor would call "cozy," which is really a euphemism for tiny. The kitchen, while large enough for my table and chairs, had these ugly-ass green cabinets with oatmeal colored counters. Right off from the kitchen was my fake wood paneled living room, with the broken down gold velour sofa my sister had picked up from a neighbor, my stereo, end table and beige ginger jar lamp and a small stand and television in the corner near the door. Actually, the whole damn house was paneled. Dark brown in the living room, up the stairs and hallway. Honey brown in my room and white-washed in Bethany's room. The whole house was carpeted in gold sculpted carpet that had seen better days about ten years ago. The only rooms not paneled were the kitchen and bathroom. The bathroom was plain white walls with a claw-footed tub that had been rigged with a shower so that you had to close the shower curtain around the metal bar that ran around the inside of the tub. It was really an apartment, but having two floors made it seem more like a house. It was one of four places that must have been divided up from what had been one huge house in a prior life.

With Bethany not there, my place stayed a lot neater than usual. At least I'm not tripping over a Barbie doll ever time I turn around. Ever step on one of those tiny fuck-me pumps of Barbie's in the middle of the night? Chile please. Have you cussing for days. It was a constant battle of wills between us trying to get her to learn to clean up behind herself. Just about the time I was satisfied that all was in order, I heard a knock at my door.

"Any trouble finding my place?" I asked casually as I let him in.

"Naw, baby. Your directions were good. Never been to Ambler before. Nice little place here. I have never seen streets this clean before."

"It's okay, but the people out here are strange. Didn't you notice how everybody turned and looked as you came down the street? I don't know how they know when somebody not from around here hits town, but they do."

"Yeah, I did notice that. What's up with that? It was kind of creepy."

Laughing, I told him, "You get used to it. Just ignore it. Damn, whatever you have in those bags sure smells good!"

Grinning, he began pulling out ribs, hot wings, potato salad, baked beans, greens, cornbread and a large container of cherry soda.

"Damn! Is somebody else coming to dinner that I don't know about?" I asked, my mouth watering.

"I didn't know what you might or might not like baby, so I figured I'd get a little bit of everything."

Baby? Hhmm. Not saying anything, I got two plates and glasses out and helped myself to a little bit of everything. Hey, I never said I didn't like to eat! Sister-girl could throw down with the best of them, okay?

Obviously he noticed too, because he said jokingly, "Oh I see you appreciate a good meal. I like that in a woman."

"What is that?" I asked around a rib bone.

"A woman with a good appetite. You know they say one good appetite is indicative of another," he murmured in that sexy voice of his.

I almost choked on my food. Oh *shit!* Now why did he have to go *there*? The atmosphere in the room had changed, and it was suddenly charged with a sexual tension I wasn't ready to deal with. My appetite fled and I became suddenly nervous. I mean, it had been quite I while since I'd had me some. But I didn't think I was ready for that. I certainly wasn't ready for brother-man to come out like that. He must have noticed my discomfiture, because he said, "I'm sorry, baby, I didn't mean to make you uncomfortable. But damn! I think you are one sexy woman. But I didn't mean to disrespect you, baby-girl. Please. Forgive my breach."

Shrugging nonchalantly, I said, "No biggie. And you are right, I do have a health appetite. In all things."

Now it was my turn to watch him choke. Hey, I could give as good as I got. Trust me, I have always held my own. Before things could get too heavy, the phone rang. Wondering who could be calling, I hesitated before picking up the phone, expecting one of my many bill collectors, and I didn't want him to witness an embarrassing phone call. Still I couldn't just let the damn thing ring and not answer it. Sighing, I slowly lifted the receiver.

"Hello, Sara? It's me, Theo. I hope you don't mind, but I talked Brenda into giving me your phone number."

Trying not to say any names, and in relief, I answered, "Hi! No, I don't mind. Um, I was just sitting down to eat. Can I call you back later?" I asked casually as I glanced at Frankie and could almost see his ears straining to pick up the callers voice.

"I'm not at home. I was calling to see if I could drop by on my way home. Just wanted to check and make sure you were okay."

"That's so nice of you. But really, I had a dog of a day. You know my boss, the one I told you about, well, she's getting ready for her first trial, and has been like a maniac." As I started to tell Theo about my day, I had almost forgotten about Frankie until I glanced around and caught that none too pleased look on his face. *Shit!* I quickly got off the phone and explained to Frankie, "A friend. Sorry about that."

"Sounded like more than a friend to me."

"Really? Hhmm. Can you pass me a piece of that chicken?" I asked, refusing to discuss it any further.

After we finished our meal, I was surprised when Frankie offered to help me with the dishes. As he washed and I dried, he told me that he had a lead on a job.

"Terrell says that it's pretty much a shoe-in, but I've learned not to take anything for granted."

"Well I hope you get it. I can only imagine how hard it must be, having a record and all."

"Tell me about it. It doesn't matter that I did my time, that I was young and stupid. All they can see is another black man who they can legally kick to the curb."

"Hhmm." I didn't say anything because young or not, I felt that he had been old enough to know better and I get tired of brothers always trying to blame all of their problems on society in general, and the white man specifically. Things had been hard for our fathers and grand-fathers, but they had somehow managed. What was wrong with this generation? Expecting everybody else to hand them something. How come black *women* could always get out there and find a job but they couldn't? I found myself comparing Frankie to Theo. Theo had found a way. He'd started his own business doing what he liked to do, working on cars. From the looks of his house, he apparently was very successful at what he did. Brenda had told me that he'd started his business when he was in his early twenties, working out of a rented garage and had built it into what he had today; a full service shop that did body work as well as detailing, painting, rust proofing and repairs.

Thinking about Theo prompted me to ask Frankie, "Ever thought about starting your own business?"

"And who is going to give me a loan? Come on, Sara, let's not even go there."

"You could try. You never know."

"Yeah, right. Let me get this job first, baby, before you have me being an entrepreneur. But it's something to think about. Yeah. Maybe if this construction gig works out, I could save up enough to open a health food store or something."

At least he was willing to think of other options. It was a start.

Not wanting to be impolite and kick him out almost as soon as we'd finished eating, I invited him to stay for a while. We listened to some music and told each other a little more about ourselves. We were sitting on my old lumpy sofa that seemed determined to make us keep falling into each other. Tired of fighting the sofa, I jumped up and exclaimed, "Will you look at the time! I hadn't realized it was so late. I hate to be rude, but I do have to get up early tomorrow."

"No problem. I enjoyed your company tonight, Sara. I hope we can do this again sometime," he said as I walked him to the door. We stood awkwardly looking at each other before he gently pulled me to him. Bending down, he lightly brushed his pillow soft lips over mine before suddenly crushing me to him in a passionate kiss. Taken by surprise, I opened my mouth to protest but was cut off by his tongue plunging into my mouth. At first, I gave in to his kiss, but then something started to bug me. His lips were soft, his tongue skillful, but it did nothing for me. Beginning to feel suffocated, I pushed against his chest with all of my might, finally breaking us apart. Making up some excuse, I hustled him out of there with a quickness. It wasn't that I had been repulsed. I just hadn't been exactly turned on either. That in itself puzzled me. And then it hit me. The entire time he had been kissing me, in the back of my mind, I kept seeing a pair of twinkling golden-flecked green eyes smiling into mine.

Chapter Seven

TGIF! If Friday hadn't gotten here, I might have cheerfully killed my boss and blamed it on PMS. The man had driven me crazy all week! As a third-year associate, he was assisting the partner he worked with on an upcoming trial. So of course, he had to do most of the grunt work. Preparing the jury questions, making sure the exhibits were in order, scheduling last minute depositions and any, and every, damn things else that needed to be done. You would think this was his first big trial, the way he was acting like he was losing his mind. And of course, shit rolls downhill, so he was taking all of his anxieties out on little ole me.

Then there was the other attorney who I worked for, Eloise. She was also in the process of preparing for trial. Unfortunately, she and Dave couldn't stand each other. I thought they were going to come to blows about whose work was going to get done first. They had gotten into a shouting match that half the floor must have heard. Dave might get on my nerves, but I preferred doing his work over hers. Especially after the time when I had been on the phone with Bethany, who had been home by herself on a school holiday.

I didn't have anyone to watch her, and at the time, being nine years old, she was scared to death. She had called me because she thought she heard something or someone in the house. While I had been on the phone with her, trying to calm her down, this bitch told me her work was more important than a scared child. I almost lost my job behind that one. In no uncertain terms I had told her what she could do with her work. Fortunately for me, my secretarial supervisor and the personnel director had agreed with me and had let me leave early. Every since then, things have been tense between us.

As for her fight with Dave, he won out and her work had ended up with the overflow pool.

Brenda and I had laughed all through lunch when I had described the fight to her. Being on the other side of the floor, she had missed it.

"Girl, you should have seen her. I think if she'd had a gun, she would have cheerfully shot Dave! She was so red, she was almost purple. She saw the big grin Dave and I exchanged too. I'm going to have to pay for that, I'm sure."

"Yeah, I've heard she's a mean one. You better watch your back with her girl." Changing the subject, she asked, "So, have you talked to my uncle this week?" she asked slyly.

"I should tell you it's none of your business," I threatened. At her crestfallen look, I relented.

"As a matter of fact, I have. We've talked almost every night this week. I'm beginning to feel like a teenager. We talked a couple of nights until almost one o'clock in the morning!"

"Talk about what?"

"I don't know. Anything. Everything. He's nice. I like him," I told her, not wanting to get into specifics.

"Mm-hmm. See I told you y'all would hit it off."

"Yeah, yeah, whatever," I waved it off. The fact of the matter was, we *had* hit it off; big time. I found myself looking forward to those phone calls. I just wasn't willing to share that yet, even if Brenda was the one responsible for me meeting Theo.

"And what about Frankie? Have you talked to him?"

"Yeah. But not as much. He's usually pretty beat after getting home from work. He's so happy Terrell got him that job. Speaking of Terrell, how are things with you guys?" I asked her, turning the conversation away from me.

"The same. Okay, I guess. My bills are still getting paid. What else is there to say?"

"Brenda, what do you see in that guy, besides his fat wallet?"

"Is there anything else? I mean if a man can't do for you, what's the point?"

"That's it? That's all you look for in a man? Girl you need to get grip. Doesn't he have any other redeeming qualities?"

"He's a good fuck?" she jokingly asked.

"Please. Sometimes that's not even worth it."

"Maybe, but hey, I'm gettin' laid and gettin' paid," she laughed. "Besides, aren't you the one always talking about a man doing more for you than you can do for yourself?"

"So maybe I have to rethink that one."

"Yeah, right. But forget the money for a minute. Don't nothing beat a good piece, girl."

"Can't argue with that. Been so long since I had a good piece, I'm almost ready to settle for a bad one!"

"Girl, stop! A bad one ain't even worth the trouble. Hold out for that good one. All that a bad one will do is leave you pissed and even more frustrated."

"Yeah, I guess you're right. I've waited this long, a little longer can't hurt," I laughed. Once again, without volition, I was thinking of Theo.

"Seriously Brenda. You need to check yourself. There's more to a relationship than what you seem to have with Terrell. You might be gettin' paid, but what price are *you* paying in the long run?"

"Chile, please." What else could she say? She didn't want to hear it. And until my girl figured out that she was just prostituting herself, nothing I could say would make a difference. Don't get me wrong. I know quite a few of us have been there. Willing to do whatever it took to get a man to give up those bucks. I've been there a few times myself. I had even thought about it where Theo was concerned. Brother man had it goin' on. So what that he was so much older than me? I could get used to that. He was at least good looking, had a good body and what looked like plenty of money. However, in the short time that we'd know each other, and from our many long and intimate conversations, I found that I genuinely *liked* Theo. I found myself wanting more than a relationship where I would just be playing him. I was finding that Theo was touching a place somewhere deep inside that I had thought had died a long time ago. I can't say that I was completely happy about that, but I was finding it wildly interesting.

And then there was Frankie. At least he was working now, and not sitting around his mama's house. He was also good looking, built, reasonably intelligent and was trying to get his shit together. However, try as I might though, my feelings for Frankie remained ambivalent. He seemed like a nice enough guy, but he didn't elicit the feelings in me that Theo did. But on some level, I enjoyed his conversation and occasionally his company.

I ended up having a hard time for the rest of the day trying to stay focused on my work and not my love life. For months I had been without any male companionship at all. Now here I was with two men vying for my attention.

Needless to say, the rest of my day went by in a blur and if you held a gun to my head, I couldn't tell you what I did. I had been so busy thinking about Theo and Frankie that I had gotten through the rest of the day on automatic pilot. It wasn't that the job was that easy, I was just that good, even if I do say so myself! Seriously, though, what Dave and I had to accomplish, I was able to do with little thought. I was glad to finally see five o'clock roll around. You would have thought somebody had a rocket tied to my butt, I got out of there so fast.

Anyway, I'm just glad to be home with my shoes off, a little vintage Earth, Wind and Fire on the stereo, a rum and coke in my hand and the weekend stretched out in front of me There are only a couple more weekends before Bethany would be coming home and I planned on enjoying them! This weekend, for sure, Brenda and I had made plans to go to Penns Landing and South Street and I was really looking forward to it. And if she finagled to have her uncle there, I really wouldn't be mad at her. As for any other worries and concerns, I'd decided to put them to rest until later. For now I was just enjoying my moment of peace. And then I started thinking about Bethany and getting her home.

All week I had been agonizing on how I was going to be able to bring my child home. I was still trying to decide which bill wasn't going to get paid this month so I could afford the two bus tickets. And I didn't even want to think about that awful bus ride. But that was just one more problem I wasn't in the mood to deal with at the moment. I was thinking about making a tuna sandwich, getting my clothes together for my outing with Brenda tomorrow and then curling up with a good book before heading to bed when I heard a frantic knocking at my door.

"I think you'd better come with me," Frankie said as he burst through my kitchen door I had just opened.

"Why? What's wrong? What are you doing here?" I asked, sensing that something was up.

"Terrell has lost his mind and is threatening to kill Brenda," he told me.

"*What?* What the hell are you talking about?" I asked in a rising panic.

"I'll explain on the way," Frankie told me, hustling me out of the door, barely giving me time to grab my purse and cigarettes.

On the way down to Brenda's house he told me that Brenda had called him hysterical that Terrell had come over all drunk and they had gotten into an argument and then he had proceeded to beat the shit out of her. I was stunned. Apparently, it wasn't the first time it had happened. Brenda had never said a word to me. I wanted to know when had all this started.

"I don't know," he told me shaking his head, "she just said it had been going on for a while."

All of a sudden, all the missed days at work, the unexplained bruises, the fearful look in her eyes the day of the cookout all made sense.

"Shit!" I spat. "I thought Brenda had more sense than to get caught up like that. *Shit!*" The rest of the ride was made in silence.

The car had barely stopped before I was out of it and up the steps to her place. I had barely noticed the police cars outside in my haste to get to Brenda. However, I skidded to a halt when I rushed through the door and almost ran over a cop.

"Excuse me Miss, you can't come in here," this beefy white cop with a unibrow said as he tried to grab me.

"The hell I can't! Brenda, tell this idiot to let me in," I yelled across to her from the door.

"It's okay, officer," she said through bruised, swollen lips.

"Oh my God! What the hell did he do to you?" I asked as I looked at the black and purple pulp that was her face. Her bottom lip was bloody and looked five times its normal size on one side, her eyes were almost shut they were so swollen and her left jaw was bruised and still swelling. Glancing around her apartment, I was appalled at the chaos. Furniture was overturned, lamps broken. It looked like a small war had been waged in there.

"It looks worse than it is. Really. I'll be okay," she struggled to say as tears flowed down her mangled face.

When I went to hug her, she winced and that was when I noticed her bruised arms.

"The ambulance is here, Miss. Are you ready to go to the hospital?" Unibrow asked. He didn't sound that sympathetic. More like disgusted, as if her ass kicking had been *her* fault.

"Officer, it this really necessary?" Brenda asked, like she was really thinking about not going.

"You could have some broken ribs, Miss. I think you should be checked out. I really don't like how your jaw is looking either." Unibrow told her. Maybe he was human after all.

"Look, Brenda, you have to go. It'll help your case if you have all this documented," I told her, trying to make her see reason.

"What case? I can't press charges, Sara. Terrell would get into too much trouble," she said, sounding scared again.

"Fuck him! He should have thought about that shit before he put his fuckin' hands on you!" I told her, thinking she had lost her mind *not* to press charges. But I could see she was getting upset, so I told her, "Look, just get in the ambulance and go to the hospital so they can fix you up. You don't have to make any decisions right now. Come on, girl, you know you have to be at work Monday."

For some reason that seemed to motivate her, even though I knew there was no way she was going to work Monday. By then, she'd probably look worse than she did right now.

"I'd better call your mom and Theo, huh?"

"No! Please, Sara! Promise me you won't call them. Jesus Christ, there wouldn't be a hole in all of Philadelphia that Terrell could hide in, especially if my crazy-ass brothers decided to go after him!"

Personally, I thought that might be a good thing, but in order to keep her calm, I promised not to call her mother, Miss Sadie, or Theo. I hadn't known Theo that long, but I could tell that he probably wasn't the type to play and I vaguely remembered seeing a gun case in his bedroom when I had stayed there, full of rifles. He told me that he hunted deer, but I bet if I called, he'd be hunting some Terrell. Frankie had been standing by the front door talking with Unibrow and hadn't heard anything that Brenda had said. I planned on asking him just where the hell his triflin' cousin was.

After eight hours of agonizing waiting in the emergency room at Albert Einstein Medical Center, a doctor finally came and told Frankie and me that they were keeping Brenda. She had two broken ribs, multiple contusions, a fractured arm and they had to wire her jaw back together.

When they finally let me in to see her, I just sat for a while next to her, thinking to myself, *how could she let some no account niggah do her like that?* I was pissed and I had nowhere to direct my anger. I think after looking at the mess that was suppose to be my friend, I could have cheerfully killed Terrell with my bare hands. I mean, how *dare* some muthafucka do that to a woman he claimed to *love!* I knew this story only to well. I violently pushed the memories away from me. I didn't want to think about it now. The memories always filled me with such impotent fury. I'd always sworn to myself that I would never, *ever* allow any man to put his hands on me.

Keith had tried it once. He'd ended up with the biggest knife I could find against his jugular. I remember that fight very clearly. Keith had come home, late again, and had had the nerve to throw his keys, wallet and some picture of some big tooth bitch up on the bookcase. I had gone off. We ended up tussling and he hit me, but not before I had tried to rip all the skin off his face and neck. After I had picked myself up off the floor when he had called himself pimp slapping me, I had calmly walked into the kitchen, quietly pulled the biggest knife I could find out of the drawer and had it behind my back as I walked back into the living room. I had sat down on his lap, and before he could blink, I had the knife point under his chin. I had started out talking very quietly. By the time I was finished, I was screaming at the top of my lungs, and with each word, his head had gone further and further back and before I knew it, I watched, fascinated, as a single drop of his blood had slid down the knife in my hand. I had cheerfully promised to cut him from ear to ear before I'd let him put his hands on me again. That had truly been the end of our marriage. But that had nothing to do the dreams and memories that I was always fighting so hard to forget.

As for Terrell, I don't care how deep his pockets are. Brenda would have been better off by herself. She didn't need a man that damn bad. There wasn't that much dick in the world. Can we say vibrator?

I guess I must have dosed off, because I felt a soft touch on my head, jerking me awake.

"You still here?" Brenda whispered-slurred though her wired jaw and medication.

I had pulled my chair up to the side of her bed and had fallen asleep with my head on the side of her bed. Frankie was sprawled out in the only other chair in the room by the drafty window, fighting to keep his head from crashing through the window.

"Yeah, girl," I whispered back. "I wanted to make sure you were okay. You know you're going home with me when you get out of here."

"I can't impose like that, Sara. You have enough to deal with and Bethany will be coming home come soon, I can't bring this shit to your house. I'll be okay at home."

"Bullshit! I said you're coming to my house and that's that."

"We'll talk about it later, okay? I'm just so tired," she sighed as she slipped back into a drug-induced sleep.

I stayed for a while longer to make sure she was sleeping, then I slipped out of her room, motioning for Frankie to follow me out.

"Let me take you home, Sara. You look beat," he said, concern evident in his face.

"No, Brenda looks *beat*, Frankie," I hissed. Furiously I continued, "So where is that motherfucker? I hope they throw his sorry ass under the damn jail! Trust me, he'd be safer there than if I get my hands on him. Oh, and we won't even talk about Brenda's brothers, Jeff and Romeo. Either one would shoot you as well as look at you. And from what Brenda tells me, she's got a lot of cousins who are the same. Is that man crazy? Doesn't he know what kind of family Brenda comes from?"

"Let's hope it won't come to that. I mean Terrell's got some crazy asses in his family too. It would end up being a war. The last I heard, he'd been arrested and is down at the Round House. I was going to drop you off then go down there."

"For what? I hope you're not planning on bailing his sorry ass out," I said, incredulous that he would even consider something that stupid.

"Well, yeah, I was. I mean he's my boy and he's done nothing but help me since I got out. He just hooked me up with a construction job. I can't just leave him in there. Let's not forget, Sara, he is my cousin."

"Do you see what that girl's face looks like in there? Do you? Have you lost your fucking mind?" I was furious. It was all I could do not to slug him. I couldn't believe he was really serious.

"Sara, look, you have to understand. I don't have a choice. I have to help my cousin out."

"Fuck your cousin and fuck you too. I don't care if he is your cousin. Look, I'll find my own damn way home. Go help your boy. Do what you have to do, and so will I," I sneered at him. He stood there looking at me, trying to decide if he should leave me or not.

"Go! Just get the hell out," I told him.

I know I was being unreasonable, but I was pissed and I was dog tired. I had been at the hospital all damn night, with nothing to eat and hardly any sleep. I was also scared. Scared for Brenda. What would happen if Terrell were back on the street? Would he come after her again? I guess Frankie decided that I was serious because he turned to leave.

"Hey, before you go. You better tell your 'boy' to stay the hell away from my friend. And he better enjoy his freedom while he can. When we get done with him, he'll be gone for awhile. Count on it!" I told him with false bravado before I turned in the opposite direction, heading for the bank of phones down the hall. I turned back once more and hollered down the hall to him, "Oh. And one more thing, don't call me again, okay? I don't think we have anything more to talk about." He just looked at me for a long moment before turning back around and walking away.

I know Brenda didn't want to press charges, but I was going to do all I could to convince her that she should. But first, I was calling Theo since I had no one I could call. My sister Stephanie didn't have a car,

Gina was in DC with her kids and Zoe and Vaughn had gone down to the shore for the week. I felt a little guilty because I knew Brenda hadn't wanted me to call him or her mother, but I felt she was being unreasonable. As usual, it was just one more thing I'd deal with later.

Chapter Eight

"Is there anything else you need?" Theo asked as we exited the Cheltenham Square mall.

"No, I'm fine, I think I have everything I need. I promise I'll pay you back on my next payday," I told him as I juggled my packages before Theo reached over and took most of them from me.

"And I'm telling you again, don't worry about. Is everything a battle with you?" he laughed.

"No!" At his skeptical look, I conceded, "Well, maybe. Sorry. Force of habit." He just laughed at me again.

Theo had picked me up from the hospital and taken me right to the mall so that I could buy a change of clothes, underwear and toiletries. We had gotten into a contest of wills in the store when I had tried to purchase what I needed myself. He had gently, but firmly taken everything from me and quietly insisted on paying for them. I'd finally given up. Especially after I happen to look up and see the cashier looking at me like I was crazy for turning him down.

I was going to go to his house, shower, eat, get some sleep and go back to the hospital and then home once I checked in on Brenda. The hospital had told me before I left that they would be keeping her for a couple of days.

"Don't worry about it. It was no problem. I was glad to help. I just hope your friend will be okay."

I looked away, feeling guilty. I had only told Theo that a friend of mine had been hurt in an accident. So I had managed to keep Brenda's secret anyway, but that didn't mean that I liked it. I thought that Theo should know the truth.

"Yeah, me too," I mumbled, not wanting to talk about it, fearful that I might blurt out the truth.

To change the subject I said, "I can't wait to get into the shower! And I won't even talk about how much I'm looking forward to one of your breakfast specials! Is T.J. home?" I asked as we pulled into his driveway.

"No, he's down Carol's house with his cousins. While you shower, I'll start breakfast," he told me, as I headed for the bathroom with my packages. Theo told me that the shower in his room was still not working, so I used the hall bathroom.

Lord that shower felt good. I dried off and was about to get dress when I realized that I had left my underwear and lotion in Theo's bedroom. I thought I had remembered to bring everything into the bathroom. Damn! I didn't even bother to finish drying off. I figured I'd run down the hall to his room, grab my stuff and slip back into the hall bathroom to finish dressing. Or I could lock his door and finish dressing in his room. Yeah, that would be better. At least I'd have more room. I gathered my toiletries, wrapped the towel around me and was headed for his bedroom when I ran right into him.

For a minute he just stood there looking at me, as I struggled to keep the towel covering all my important parts. Not an easy task with my breast practically spilling over the top of the skimpy towel and the bottom was barely covering my you-know-what. Trying to hold the towel and my toiletries was no easy task. I was thinking if we were still friends by Christmas, I was going to buy this man some large towels.

After thoroughly inspecting me from head to foot, he said, "Uh, the food's ready. I was just coming to tell you to hurry up while it's hot."

I was tempted to let the towel drop, just to see what he would do. But I didn't want to be responsible for giving the poor man a heart attack.

And with my friend, his niece no less, in the hospital, how could I possibly be thinking about seducing this really nice guy? Just because he was sexy as hell and had those incredible green, gold-flecked eyes and probably hadn't had any in over a year was no reason to lose my mind. Was it?

Or just because his voice sent chills down my spine ever time he opened his mouth or those hands of his made me weak every time he casually touched me was no reason to just want to let that thin towel flutter to the floor. Was it?

Thankfully, my stomach made the decision for me. My hunger for food overruled my hunger for other things. I caught a whiff of those onions and peppers in the home fries and I was done.

"I'll be right there. I left something in your room or I'd be dressed by now. I'll be just a hot minute," I told him as I hustled down the hallway to get dressed, to put on my new shorts and halter top.

Looking greatly disappointed, he mumbled an okay and turned to go back down the stairs to the kitchen but not before I noticed the raging woody he was sporting. Nice. *Very* nice. I was almost tempted to change my mind and let that towel drop just to see what would happen.

Sighing to myself, I decided it was probably too soon. As attracted as I was to him, I thought it best to wait. So what if visions of him had been dancing in my head when I had been kissing another man. I needed to eat, get some sleep and then see about my girl.

After eating, and enjoying a much-needed cup of coffee, I was practically falling out of my chair from lack of sleep. I barely remembered Theo taking the cup from my hands, pulling me up and gently pushing me up the stairs in the direction of his room with orders to go to sleep.

Five hours later, Theo gently shook me awake.

"Hey sleepy head. You told me to wake you up an hour ago, but you were sleeping so soundly, I didn't have the heart to wake you up sooner.

"What time is it? Damn, I feel like I could sleep another twelve hours," I said as I stretched and yawned. As tired as I was, I didn't miss

Theo's eyes on my breast as they pressed against the thin material of my halter top as I stretched.

"Ah, it's almost five," he stammered, trying to act like he wasn't staring.

"Almost five! Jesus, I should have been at the hospital hours ago! Brenda's going to kill me!" I blurted out then clapped my hand over my mouth.

"Brenda," he said frowning. "My niece Brenda? What is she doing in the hospital?"

When I didn't answer right away, he grabbed me by my shoulders and asked again, "What is she doing in the hospital, Sara? Tell me now," he said with force.

"She doesn't want you, her mother or anyone in your family, for that matter, to know. I can't tell you. I promised," I said, hoping he would drop it.

"It's that sorry ass nigger she's dealing with, isn't it? What did he do to her, Sara? He kicked her ass again, didn't he?" he asked.

I looked at him, wide-eyed that he could be so on the money.

"Why would you say that?" I asked, hedging.

"Because he's done it before. You didn't know?"

"No, I didn't. A mutual friend came and got me and told me what had happened. She begged me not to call you or her mom, Ms. Sadie. I wanted to tell you, Theo, honestly I did, but I promised I wouldn't," I told him as I felt the tears slipping down my face as I thought about what my friend had looked like when I had last seen her.

"Don't cry, Sara. You gave your word," he said has he wiped my tears away and pulled me closer. That only made it worse and made me cry more.

The next thing I knew, I was looking up at him and then he was kissing me. Saying he made my toes curl is an understatement. How different was his kiss from Frankie's. Where Frankie's kiss had made me feel suffocated, Theo's made me want more.

Reluctantly pulling away, I told him, "I have to get to the hospital. Brenda will be wondering what's going on. I told her I would be there when she woke up. I'm sure she's been awake for hours."

"Call her. See how she's feeling and find out if she's even up to having any company." "I guess I could do that. If she's not it, I could just go home."

"Or you could stay here," he said quietly.

"I can't do that, Theo. I've imposed enough as it is. Besides, you don't want to have to keep buying me clothes," I joked.

"How are you going to tell me what I can and can't do, Sara? What makes you think I don't want to do things for you? What makes you think I don't want you to be here? Look, Sara, I'm too old for games. I like you and I want to spend more time with you. I'm sorry for what happened to my niece, but I'm glad it made you call me. I'm glad it helped us to spend more time together." Running his hand through his hair, he continued with, "This last year has been hell. I have never been so lonely in my life. When my wife died, I wished that I had died too. I never thought that I'd ever be attracted to another woman. I didn't want to be. I didn't want to be in a position to be hurt again. Now, I don't know if we will work out or not, but I know that I'd like to try. You intrigue me. Not to mention, I think you are sexy as hell, and I would really like to get with you."

Well damn. How was I supposed to answer that? I couldn't, so I seized on his last statement. "Get with me? What exactly does that mean? Are you saying you want to have sex with me, Theo?" I asked, trying to make light of the situation.

"Hell yeah, I'd like to have sex with you, Sara. Look at you! You're a very beautiful woman. Any man in his right mind would want to sleep with you."

Okay. Now I'm shocked into silence. No one has ever said that to me. I mean I have never thought of myself as beautiful. Never. Kinda, sorta cute, but never beautiful, let alone sexy. My sister Zoe was always considered the beautiful one in the family. I am considered the smart mouth one, Gina is the intellectual one and Stephanie, the oldest, was the bossy one.

I suppose every person is assigned a certain place in a family and that is usually where they stay and how they think of themselves. And here was this man pulling me out of my box, my place. It may sound silly to you, but it was mind-blowing to me. So I blurted out the first thing that came to my mind, "I'm not beautiful! My sister Zoe is the beautiful one. She's tall and thin and everybody says that she's beautiful."

"Maybe she is, I can't say because I haven't met her yet. But what makes you think that you aren't, Sara?"

I was quiet for a while I thought back to all the years of torment I had gone through, always trying to be like my older sister. Zoe with the long hair, fair skin, gray flecked eyes, straight nose and thin lips. Zoe looked like our father. I was my mother all over again. Me, with my light, whisky-brown eyes, pug nose and oval face. I was light-skinned, but not as fair as Zoe. At least I had small ears. I had always been inordinately proud of my small ears. It was the one thing I could tease Zoe about, considering the size of her ears. Which was probably why she always wore her hair long. At the moment I was sporting a really short, curly 'do. No perms, no curlers, or frying my hair for me.

Pulling myself out of my memories, I told Theo, "When we were kids, my sister, who is almost seven years older than me, whenever she came to my school and the other kids would see her, they would look at her then look at me and say, 'That's *your* sister? She's so pretty, what happened to *you*?' It used to hurt my feelings, but after awhile I would tell them off and I learned to accept it. I was kind of a chubby kid and she was always so thin and beautiful, with the voice of an angel. People used to stop singing in church to turn around and listen to her. I was always so proud of her then. But I never, ever, forgot what those kids used to say to me. And it wasn't just the kids at school. My cousins used to say it all the time. I guess if you hear something often enough, you believe it," I told him, my voice trailing off.

"You're beautiful to me, Sara, and I don't know what mirrors you have been looking in, but you obviously are not seeing what I see," he said, cupping my chin in his hand, forcing me to look into those beautiful, incredible eyes of his. Eyes that had turned a deep smoky green and that I felt that I could lose myself in. Wordlessly, hardly breathing, we stared at each other, as he leaned in and gently brushed his lips against mine.

And there went another zap, straight to my heart.

Chapter Nine

"Are you sure you don't need anything before I go?" I asked Brenda, who had been comfortably settled into Theo's daughter's old bedroom. I had stopped by one day after work to help Theo clean and air out the room.

"I'm fine, girl. Will you stop worrying? I hate all of this fuss. I could have gone home. But y'all wouldn't let me," she huffed, tugging on the soft pink floral bedspread that was faded but soft from many years of use and washing. I was trying not to laugh at the sight of grown-ass Brenda in Chelsea's old frilly, little girl's canopied twin bed.

It had been decided that it would be better for Brenda to stay at Theo's house instead of mine. Theo had insisted that she stay there instead of her coming out to Ambler. I think he was thinking that if Terrell wanted to start some shit, he would think twice about having to deal with a man rather than a woman. I was a little pissed about that, but in the end I had agreed. I also think Theo did it as a way to get me to come to his house more often. He'd acted all innocent when I had questioned him about it.

"I think Uncle T did this just so you could come by here so he could see you," Brenda said slyly, voicing my thoughts.

"You're trippin', Brenda. Get a grip. Your uncle was only concerned with your safety," I told her as I refolded her things to slip into the dresser drawers.

"Yeah right. So how come he's been around here grinning and humming since you've been coming by?"

I didn't have an answer for that, but secretly, I was glad to hear it. However, I wouldn't admit that to Brenda. With my back to her, she didn't see my pleased smile. Turning around to face her I said, "I have no idea. Maybe he's just glad that you're okay and happy to have you here."

"Uh-huh."

"Really!"

"Uh-huh. I think my uncle is sweet on you Sara, and as quiet as it's kept, I think you like him too."

"Please. I don't even know the man. I was just concerned about you, my friend, and wanted to make sure you were okay."

"Uh-huh."

"Really."

"Who are you trying to convince, Sara? Me or yourself?"

Thank goodness her jaw was wired. Otherwise, I could have cheerfully smacked her.

In all honesty though, things between us did seem to be moving at warp speed and that was truly scaring the shit out of me. Here was a man that every mama wished for her daughter. He was kind, gentle, settled and a whole lot of sexy. I guess I'd find out soon enough what my mother thought about him. He had volunteered to take me to pick up Bethany the following week.

During one of our many midnight conversations, I had mentioned that I was dreading the bus ride to pick up my daughter. He had volunteered. I had protested. He had insisted. I had caved in, secretly relieved to not have to endure that bus ride from hell.

In the meantime, he'd finally met my sisters. I, who have *no* sense of direction, had told him that I thought my sister Gina might know the way since she, as a social worker, may have placed clients up that way. Sure enough, Gina did know the fastest way for us to get there. We had agreed to meet at Zoe's house in East Oak Lane so they could go over the map together.

They all seemed to love him on sight. I wasn't too sure I liked that. I mean, I had always picked guys that I knew my sisters would hate. Take my ex-husband Keith for example. They had hated him the first time they met him. Of course, Keith really did nothing to help his case. As soon as he opened his mouth he was doomed as far as my sisters were concerned. Perfect. Him being white, actually Jewish and Italian had been a bonus. Actually I think him being Jewish and Italian was what was wrong with him. He was sexy but felt guilty about it. Surprised? Didn't I mention before that he was white? Oops. Sorry 'bout that. And don't go tripping on me because I was married to a white man. Hell, I thought his ass was Puerto Rican when I met him with all that nappy-looking hair he had. Well if you didn't look at the balding spot. But really, he had been sexy as hell, with a body to make you drool. I've always been a sucker for a hairy chest. His had been broad, well defined and had a covering of curly black hair. I used to love to rub my face in it. Sue me. I don't care. I thought it was sexy and exotic. How many real black men do you meet with a hairy chest? Not many. And if they do have hair, it's like little tight, hard peas. Not exactly my idea of sexy. As I said, don't start. Everybody has their idea of sexy. Anyway, looking back, I could actually blame my interfering sisters for the fiasco with Keith.

When I had met Keith, I was so sick of my sisters always trying to tell me what to do. Just because I was the youngest, you would think I had four mothers instead of one. And if I had to hear "Sara, will you grow up!" one damn more time, I was going to scream. This was from the same women who had spoiled me outrageously. All of a sudden they wanted to cut it off. Too late. I was the baby sister used to being the family darling. Once I realized they no longer wanted to spoil and coddle me, it seemed like I had made it my mission in life to find men who I knew would irritate the hell out of my sisters. I never stopped to think that maybe I was hurting me more than them.

Anyway, when I had called Zoe and told her that this guy was going to take me to pick up Bethany, she was all over me like the FBI. She wanted to know everything. So I told her. I figured if I told her, I wouldn't have to repeat it two more times. She would just pass it onto the other two. When she found it that he was Brenda's uncle, she became even more curious. My sisters had known Brenda almost as long as I had. But at least knowing that he was her uncle convinced my sister that maybe he wasn't an axe murderer in disguise.

However, I had neglected to tell them that he was so much older than I was. That had been my little zinger, watching them trying to recover from the shock.

Of course, when we went to Zoe's house, a really nice twin in East Oak Lane, to meet with Gina for directions, Stephanie just *happened* to show up. Gina and Theo had been going over the map he had open on Zoe's dining room table.

Let me digress for a moment, as Tavis Smiley would say, and tell you a little bit about my sisters.

First, there is Stephanie, the oldest. Steph is five feet three inches of issues. She on the full figured side and still wears an afro. She's still waiting for the revolution to kick off. Steph has never been married, has an opinion about anything and thinks she knows everything. She is mouth almighty. When you are absolutely sure that there is somebody you never wanted to speak to again in life and thereafter, you sic Steph on them.

She will call you every night and tell you all about everyone she has ever met and people you don't know, much less care about, and bore you to death on the phone, and then get offended when you don't remember who Miss Hignafoster's brother's wife's cousin's sister is. It's a family joke on the ways to either avoid or get Steph off the phone. Stephanie has never been married and has no children. As a result, everybody's child thinks Aunt Stephanie is God's gift to aunthood. She spoils them outrageously, and slyly pits them against their parents, her other sisters, in an effort to come off as the 'great, wise one'.

Next in line is my sister Gina. Gina was actually adopted. She and Stephanie were classmates when one day Stephanie saw Gina's mother attempt to push her off a subway platform. Long story short, somehow she ended up in foster care, my mother got her, and she's been my sister ever since. Gina is tall and willowy and has a great sense of style. She can throw anything together and look like she walked off the pages of *Vogue.* Gina is sort of an earth mother type. She believes in crystals and mysticism and other lives. She has two children, Rebecca and Sean. She is currently divorcing her second husband, who she recently found out was having an affair with a white co-worker and is involved with her soon to be third husband. We used to call her second husband, Stanley, the 'Grinch Who Stole Holidays' because guaranteed, Stanley would pick a fight with Gina right before a family gathering or party and have Gina all upset and depressed. No one in the family will be sad to see Stanley go. Her first husband? After he pistol-whipped her, he was history. The only problem was that Rebecca still thought her father was a knight in shining armor and blamed her mother for that divorce. Gina and Rebecca are working through their 'issues.'

Then there was my sister Zoe. Zoe is considered the family beauty. She is about five feet four, thin, and always well turned out. Zoe doesn't put the trash out unless her makeup is picture perfect. When I was younger, Zoe was my idol. I lived to be just like her. Then one day I got pissed off when I realized that no matter how hard I tried, I could never have it together like that. It was just too much work. As a result, I went in the opposite direction and tried to do everything that she wouldn't. However, I have to admit, I have makeup issues like Zoe. It's rare that you ever see my bare face. In that respect, Zoe and I are very much alike. Vain to the bone. And my clothing style, when I can afford it, can best be described as eclectic. I've been told it's very cutting edge, which a nice way of saying it can get pretty wild. Zoe is more suburban chic. Anyway, it doesn't help that every time Steph and I got into a fight, and there have been plenty, Zoe always seems to take Steph's side.

Zoe was also on her second marriage. She had figured out it was time to leave her first husband when after finally getting tired of his infidelities, she had sat in a chair opposite her front door and when she heard the key turn in the lock, proceeded to fire a 9mm, repeatedly. Somehow, her first husband had survived and she had not been charged. When she decided to leave him, she had been seven months pregnant with their second son. Their sons were Christopher and Jonathan, respectively. This shooting incident had happened in California. When she returned to Philadelphia, after meeting many losers, and to hear her tell it, some great lovers, she had met and married Vaughn Knight, a police officer, after filing a complaint against an over-zealous ex-lover. They had a daughter, Shanice.

Since I lived for so long in Ohio, my other three sisters have actually been together longer without me than with me, since they all lived together in Philadelphia. So they have this rapport that I have always felt excluded from. They even had this language and tags that I was excluded from, Steph was 'Big Sis,' Gina was 'Sis,' and Zoe, because she is so slim, was 'little sis.' Whenever we were all together and they would start calling each other by these pet names, I always felt like I was on the outside looking in, like I just didn't count. There was no pet name for me. I was just plain ole 'Sara.' I couldn't help but to think, *I should have been 'little sis,'* after all, I *am* the youngest.

Which brings us to Zoe and Vaughn's house. Even though I may never have told her, I love Zoe's house. As I said, it was a twin, or semi-detached, as some people called it. She had this great backyard with a lot of perennial flowers she had planted herself and an above ground pool. The living and dining rooms where very spacious, with an eclectic mix of furniture, but mostly traditional, including several leather-topped tables. The walls were a soft floral pattern on an even softer pale apple green background.

I really loved Christmas at Zoe's when the fireplace would be blazing all day with a cheery fire, her designer inspired tree and unique and beautiful decorations filling all of the downstairs rooms, including the powder rooms in the basement and first floor. Off from her dining room was a large galley style kitchen with a small breakfast area with a round table, four chairs and television that could be viewed anywhere in the kitchen. Upstairs, she had three generous sized bedrooms, one with bunk beds for Chris and Jon and one really girly room, in shades of pink and complete with canopy bed, for Shanice, and two bathrooms, one of which was off from her bedroom. I couldn't begin to fathom how nice it would be to have my own bathroom in my room. I really like my sister's bedroom, now. Before, it had been a black and white nightmare. At least now, papered in soft pink and white peonies, it was softer, more feminine and inviting. Before it had looked like somebody's house of horrors or at the very least, an S & M nightmare. I didn't even want to think about what my sister and her husband might have been into. Before, every time I went in there, I kept expecting to find whips and chains hanging on the walls. Throughout the years, Zoe and Vaughn's style had gone from Contemporary to Traditional to Eclectic.

Downstairs was a finished basement with a bar, a powder room and a huge sectional, along with the requisite wide screen television and serious stereo system. Zoe and Vaughn had eliminated the garage so that they had one area that was like a family room, which is where the furniture and television were. The other side was like a night club. That was where the bar and dance floor were. We had brought more than a few New Year's in in Zoe's basement. She and Vaughn gave some fierce barbeques in the summer and bumpin' parties in the winter. A party at their house was always a guaranteed good time.

However, Vaughn just knew he was a decorator and when Zoe had finally gotten tired of him being the only one making the designing decisions, she had put her foot down and now the house finally had a nice cozy, family atmosphere. Before, it had been pretty, but uncomfort-able. It had gone from ghetto fabulous to suburban chic.

Anyway, Steph came breezing in like the Queen of Sheba, walked right up to Theo and says, "Hi, I'm Stephanie, the oldest. Well, let's see how long you last, cause my sister doesn't have the sense she was born with. She proved that when she married that loser, Keith. She also neglected to tell us how old you were. But maybe that will settle her fast ass down."

I have never been so embarrassed in my life! But Theo, bless him, took it all in rather calmly. He simply said, with raised eyebrows, "Nice to meet you, too," before turning back to Gina to finish discussing the best way to get my parents' house, effectively dissing my sister. Zoe and I looked at each other, trying to keep from laughing.

Once Gina and Theo were done, my sisters found a way to hustle me up to Gina and Vaughn's bedroom.

"I like him. He seems really nice, not to mention he's fine as hell." That was Zoe.

"You didn't tell us he was so much older than you." That was Gina.

"Try not to fuck this one up, okay?" Who else? Stephanie.

"You said he has kids. What are they like?" Zoe.

"Kids? You didn't tell us he had *kids!*" Stephanie.

"*And* a grandchild, right?" Zoe.

"Damn. How old is his ass?" Stephanie.

"Yeah, but didn't somebody tell me he had his own business?" Gina.

"Yeah, he does. And a house in Wyncote with a pool." Zoe.

"Humph. Oh he really sounds too good to be true. Good looking, settled, and he has his own business. Now I know she's going to find a way to fuck this up." Stephanie.

"Look. We are just friends, okay? Damn, why are y'all tripping? We haven't even slept together."

"Uh-huh." All three of them. In stereo.

"What? Y'all need to stop."

"She's going to fuck it up."

"Fuck you Stephanie."

"I love you too, Sara," she said cheerfully.

Chapter Ten

"Hey lady, how are you?" a familiar voice asked over the phone line. I was standing at my kitchen door, gazing across the empty lot next door, watching two of the neighborhood toughs square off for yet another fight. I had been on my way upstairs to throw a few last minute remembered things into my overnight bag.

"Franklin?" *Shit!* The last person I wanted to talk to. I knew I should have just let the phone ring.

"Yeah. You sure have been hard to catch up too."

"Why are you calling me? I thought I had made myself clear," I snapped, not in a mood for this conversation.

"Aw, come on, Sara. Don't tell me you're going to let what happened between Brenda and Terrell come between us," he said, sounding surprised.

"What us? What us, Frankie? There is no us. You're presuming a lot, aren't you?" I asked as I paced around my kitchen. I couldn't believe he actually had the nerve to call me after bailing that sorry-assed Terrell out of jail. Not wanting to be bothered anymore, I told him, "Look, I'm on my way out the door. I think it would be best if you just didn't call me anymore, okay? I told you at the hospital, you had to do what you had to, and so did I. Good luck with your life, okay?" I said before preparing to hang up.

"Sara! Damn girl, give a brother a chance. Look, I know you are upset with me, but damn it, what choice did I have?"

"There are always choices, Frankie. You know as well as I do that what he did was wrong. And deep down inside, you know you should have left his ass in jail. But no! Under some misguided loyalty, you had to help 'your boy' out. I don't give a shit if he is your cousin. Let me tell you about your 'boy.' He's done nothing but harass Brenda's family all week looking for her. He's begged, cajoled and finally threatened. He even showed up at her uncle's house and threatened his *thirteen-year-old* son. Some big man, huh? The only thing that made him stop was Theo's promise to blow his head off if he came within fifty yards of his house. Theo was totally pissed about it, too."

"How come you know so much about this Theo?"

"Please. Don't even worry about it. The point is, had you left his ass in jail, none of this drama would have had to happen. If anything happens to Brenda, I am holding *you* personally responsible. So we have nothing to talk about. Ever." Then I did hang up. Immediately after, my phone started ringing. I just let it go. Running upstairs, I threw the extra things I needed into my overnight bag and was just coming back down when Theo was knocking at my door.

"Ready? Damn, baby, I like that sundress you're wearing," Theo told me as his eyes roamed over my pale yellow dress that skimmed my thighs, causing me to blush.

"Thank you. Is it too short?" I fretted. "I can run back upstairs and change."

"Oh no, baby. Please don't. I like you just the way you are," he murmured, still appreciatively checking me out, and I was secretly glad I had chosen to wear it. Every woman likes to see such appreciation in a man's eye. I hadn't done it on purpose. Or had I?

"Anyway, I'm ready. I just came back down. Are you sure you don't mind me staying at your house? Brenda looked like she was going stir crazy, and needed some company."

"She is. Poor T.J. She's talked his ear off all week," he said, chuckling.

"I know. I could hardly get any work done with her calling me all day. My boss was starting to get a little impatient. Wouldn't ¯ ᵕu know every time she called happened to be when he was at my desk? And I got a feeling something is up at work, too. Every time I turned around, Sandy was either running in and out of Dave's office or was calling Dave to come to his office. That's all I need is to lose my job," I told him as we sped down Route 309. However, every now and then, I'd catch him checking out my bare thighs as I continued trying to tug the edge of my dress down a little lower.

"Guess you'd better brush that resume up, just in case, huh?" he asked, pulling his eyes away from my legs.

"Please, I don't even want to think about it. Anyway, I think I've finally convinced her it's in her best interest to press charges. She seemed very reluctant, but I told her she'd be crazy not to."

"I've been trying to tell her that myself all week. I find it hard to believe that she agreed with you. It's been like talking to a brick wall."

"I know, but I had to keep trying. Anyway, she finally said that she would yesterday. That's one of the reasons I wanted to come down this weekend, to keep her from changing her mind. Also, it's the weekend and I've got one week before my daughter comes home. After I spend some time with Brenda today, I'm going to run over to Value City at Cheltenham Square and pick up the rest of Bethany's school supplies, and pay some more on her layaway." "Layaway? For what?"

"Her clothes. My mom says she's grown so much, and I'm trying to get a jump-start on getting her winter wardrobe together."

"Hmm, I know what you mean," he said thoughtfully as he took the Paper Mill exit off the highway. Taking the back way, we soon arrived at Theo's house. I had been there enough times to find that I really liked the neighborhood that consisted of split levels, colonial and a few ranch style homes. Theo had told me that his house originally had a small kitchen and no family room at all to speak of; just a small den. He had expanded the whole back of his house about six years earlier, and still had a spacious back yard. He had added the pool about three years earlier. When he had first moved in the first thing he had added was a small basketball court. He said with all the males in his family, it was well used.

Cutting through the garage, we entered the house through the kitchen. Walking down the short hallway to the steps near the front door, I bounded up the steps and went toward the bedroom in the back, where Brenda was staying. When I entered, I saw that she wasn't there. Checking all of the bedrooms and bathrooms, I ran back to the kitchen.

"She's gone!" I breathlessly told him.

"I know. I found this note on the counter," he told me, shaking his head.

"What does it say? Is she coming back?"

"Nope. She just said thanks and she's sorry for putting me out, but she's going back home. And back to Terrell."

"Aw hell no! You can't be serious," I stormed. "Take me over there, right now. I've got to talk some sense into that girl's head. Has she lost her mind? I thought she had finally agreed to press charges. What the hell happened between yesterday and now?"

"I had a feeling this was going to happen. I think she's been talking to him all week. This is why I hate to get in the middle of this kind of shit. What's the point when they always go back? Her mother is going to go seriously off," he said as he grabbed his keys and we went back out through the garage to the car.

Fifteen minutes later we were knocking on Brenda's door at her Linwood Gardens apartment.

"Hey girl, what are you doing here?" she asked when she opened the door with her one good hand. The other arm was still in a soft cast from being fractured. Like this was just an ordinary visit. Her face and body still had bruises, for God's sake! How could she think about going back to the person responsible for that? I could see Terrell in the living room, hovering not that far away from her, like he was afraid of letting her out of his sight. I hated the self-satisfied smirk on his face. When he noticed Theo, he started to act like he wanted to get in his face, but before he could get a word out, Theo told him, "Don't even try it, man. This is my niece and not you or anybody else is going to stop me for coming in here."

"It's okay, Terrell. Don't y'all start nothin' okay?" she pleaded, looking nervous that some shit was going to jump off.

Terrell just grunted and flopped down on the sofa, watching Theo with a malevolent stare.

"Are you okay?" I asked, ignoring Terrell's ignorant ass, wanting to make sure my girl was all right.

"I'm fine, Sara. I just wanted to come home."

"To *him*? Girl, have you lost your mind? Look, can I talk to you for a minute? Can you step outside?"

"Wait, come on in. Look what Terrell did, Sara. He went out and bought me all new furniture. Wasn't that sweet?"

"Yeah, it's nice," I said as I maneuvered her into the kitchen away from him. Actually, it looked like that cheap-ass furniture I despised. Black pleather living room set, black wanna-be lacquer dining room set and one of those cheap octagon glass-topped tables with the chairs that you always have to throw out after six months of use. I shot him another nasty look on the way through the apartment, though.

"Brenda, are you crazy or what? Have you looked in the mirror? Your face is still jacked up, you just got your mouth unwired yesterday and your arm is still in a cast. I thought you were gonna press charges," I told her angrily.

"I can't Sara. He didn't mean it. Really, Sara. He told me he's sorry, and he proved it by doing all of this," she said, waving her arms to encompass the apartment. "I mean, he *cried*, Sara. A man doesn't cry unless he's really sorry for what he's done."

"Girl, get real! Brenda, you need a reality check. If he's hit you before, then he'll do it again," I said, desperate to make her understand.

"That's enough, Sara! I've made up my mind. You just don't understand. Nobody does. He's a good man. He's just under a lot of pressure from his job. How can I make you see? There's just something about him that makes me melt. Just hearing his voice makes me vibrate. I love him, Sara. I can't just walk away. And I know he really loves me too. Things are just, I don't know, complicated right now. He's got so much on him. Plus, his wife is always making demands for his money and stuff. But he loves me, Sara. He really does."

"His wife? You mean to tell me that fool is married?" I asked, horrified.

"They've been separated for two years now. He just hasn't figured out how to get a divorce without her taking all of his money," she said defensively.

I looked at her like she was a circus sideshow. I didn't even want to hear all that other shit she was talking about. I can't understand it. How could the sound of somebody's voice make you vibrate? Please. She needed to get a grip. Quick, fast and in a hurry. I couldn't believe that a grown-ass woman could be this stupid.

"I'm out, Brenda. I think I'd better leave before I say something I can't take back," I told her, pissed, waving her off when she tried to call me back.

"Let's go," I said to Theo as I stormed out of the apartment.

The ride back to Theo's house was in total silence. I sat with my arms crossed, wondering if he could see the steam coming out of my ears.

When we got to his house, I stomped into the kitchen and slumped in the nearest kitchen chair.

Finally, I said, "*Shit!* I need a drink."

"I think I could use one too," he said as he went to the mini bar in the family room.

"What'll you have?"

"Rum and coke," I said as I sat at the table drumming my fingers on the table. I couldn't believe I had just had that conversation with Brenda. What made women go back? I have never understood that. What made what appeared to normal, well-adjusted, intelligent women fall for abusive men?

I'm sorry, there isn't a dick in this world worth me putting up with getting my ass kicked. I have had good dick and are-you-serious, what-the-hell-was-that dick. Then there is the make your toes curl, pull the sheets off the bed, slap your mama, I-can't-believe-I'm-crying dick. And even that kind is not worth me getting my assed kicked, okay? And love? Humph. Like Tina said, what's love got to do with it? Shit, put your hands on me and I'm picking up the closest thing I can grab and I will have to whale on your ass like you stole something from me. Stole something like my self-respect. My peace of mind. My joy. My dignity. My *pride*. No one has the right to take that from you; at least not with me. *No one*. I hated seeing women in that position. I never understood it. Women like my mother who had stayed. Where was their self-worth? I loved my mother so much, but sometimes, I had to admit to myself that I hated her for putting up with the bullshit my father had thrown her way. The only thing I had learned from that was what I *didn't* and *wouldn't* put up with in a relationship. It had taught me to hurt them before they could hurt me.

I was so caught up in my thoughts, I didn't even realize that I had drained the drink that Theo had given me until he asked if I wanted another one. Mutely I nodded yes. By the third one, I was starting to calm down, and finally noticed that we were sitting on his patio.

"Want to talk about it?" he asked when I finally looked his way.

"No. I don't. But I think I'd like another drink," I said, noticing that my tongue was feeling a little thick.

"You've had three almost right in a row, Sara. Don't you think you've had enough?"

"How many have you had?" I asked, indignant.

"Three. But I'm a man. I can handle mine better," he said.

"What are you drinking anyway?"

"Gordon's gin and tonic."

"Well I'd like another one, if you don't mind. And then I think I'd like some thing to eat."

"Whatever the lady wants, the lady gets," he grinned as he went through the patio door to the family room bar to fix me another drink. My head was already swimming. I knew I really didn't need that drink, but I have always hated for anyone to tell me what I do or don't need. After the little drama with Brenda, I was feeling pretty damn mutinous.

"Hey, I could use a hand here," Theo said as he stood at the door with my glass and a tray of meat and vegetables.

"Dag, what is all of that?" I asked looking over the tray as I slid the door open and grabbed the tray.

"Chicken, hamburgers and some veggies. Ever have grilled vegetables? No? You'll love them, trust me," he grinned as he fired up the grill. Soon there were mouth-watering aromas wafting from the huge grill he had in his yard.

While he tended the grill, I went into the kitchen and made a salad after rummaging through his refrigerator and finding all the fixings. As I mixed the salad, I found myself wondering if this is what it felt like to be truly married and happy. Not like that farce I'd had with Keith where he was gone more than home. I was really enjoying myself, now that I had decided to put Brenda and her problems from my mind. This felt like so Carol and Mike Brady-ish. Me in the kitchen, him at the grill. I had to stop myself from looking around for Scooter, or whatever that damn dog's name was on the show. Instead, there was King, Theo's German Sheppard. Just as good I supposed.

After that delicious dinner, we just chilled on the patio for a while before it became too buggy to stay outside. After I helped him to clean up from our impromptu cookout, we moved our private party to the family room.

"Where is your son?" I asked, noting finally that I hadn't seen him all day.

"He's spending the night over Carol's house. He usually likes to spend his weekends down there with his cousins." For a while he was quiet. Then he said, "After my wife died, I couldn't stand being in this house. Too many memories. So a lot of nights I would get up and just drive around the city for hours. When she first died, Chelsea had moved back home, so I knew he wouldn't be here by himself. On the weekends, he wanted to go to Carol's house. The weekends were the worse. I've been spending twelve to fourteen hours a day at the shop. Some days I'm in before seven and I don't leave until almost ten. For the last few months, on weekends I tend to work both Saturday and Sunday, just to give myself a way to fill up the day. For both of us, it's become a familiar habit; me to spend time at the shop and him to spend his weekends at his aunt's house. He's become more used to being away from home than being at home," he said, sounding regretful.

"Do you know this is first time in I don't know how long that I haven't worked on a Saturday? I guess I have you to thank for that," he said as he turned toward me. We were sitting on the sofa, smooth jazz wafting around the room from the invisible speakers. Both of us were feeling pretty mellow from all the drinks we'd had.

"You're welcome, I guess," I told him shyly, refusing to look into those hypnotic eyes of his.

Tipping my face up to look at him, making me look in those eyes anyway, he said in that husky whisper of his, "Common sense tells me I should leave you alone, Sara. I'm way too old for you, but I can't seem to stay away from you. I've never met anyone like you. What are you tryin' to do to me girl?"

Before I could answer, he leaned in and I felt his lips softly brush mine. I could feel my heart beating in triple time like it was trying to burst out of my chest. Ever so gently I felt the increased pressure of his lips on mine and then his tongue slipping into my mouth. His kiss was slow, gentle and very erotic in its gentleness, as he moved his tongue in and out of my mouth in a simulation of something else more basic and powerful. Finally he pulled back and both of us were breathing heavily.

I felt like I was ready to slide off the sofa I was so moist. Before I could catch my breath, he was kissing me again, and I felt his hand drift from my throat to my breast. Before I knew it, the top of my dress was around my waist and Lord, the wonderful things he was during to my breasts and nipples with just his *fingers*. Either it had been too long since somebody had sexed me up, or this man was good! If his fingers felt this good, God help me when he actually used his mouth on my nipples. I swear to God that I felt like I was on the brink of coming. It was pure torture. It was wonderful. It was almost a relief, and a pity, when he stopped kissing me and playing with my nipples.

When I finally caught my breath I said, "It's really getting late. Maybe I should be leaving," I said as I tried to pull myself and my clothes together with fingers that had suddenly grown clumsy.

When he said in a voice husky and thick with lust, "Don't go Sara. Stay with me tonight," I was lost. I suppose I could have insisted that he take me home, but, damn it, I wanted him as much as he wanted me. I have never been one to wait for anything. I hate waiting. When I want something, I want it now, and right this minute, I wanted Theo. I could feel myself vibrating with want. Forget moist, I was white-hot rapids waiting to be ridden.

Wordlessly, I got up and shuffled through his CD collection. Slipping a couple into the stereo, I waited for the music to start. When the first song on Maxwell's *"Urban Hang Suite"* CD started, I started to dance for him. As the music played, I proceeded to do a strip tease. I wanted this to be a night neither one of us would ever forget. As I stood in the semi-darkness, I seduced him as I made love to him across the room and to myself. I had never felt so sensual, so powerful. As one song blended into the next, I changed my movements with the rhythms. Soon, I was as naked as the day I was born, and I displayed my gifts with abandon and pride.

As I danced for him, I came closer and closer to him until I was doing a lap dance on him. I didn't recognize myself. I have no idea what came over me. I pulled him to his feet and proceeded to undress him. I felt like I was a flame, consumed by the heat of our desire. And oh, what a magnificent sight he was naked! What I thought I had felt in my hesitant explorations on the sofa couldn't begin to measure up to the actuality of Theo in all his glory. He was long and thick and throbbing in anticipation.

Grabbing me by my shoulders, he practically threw me down on the sofa. He kissed me deeply as his hands explored my body. I could feel my body arch of its own accord as his fingers dipped into my slick wetness. Soon his mouth was blazing a trail of hot wet kisses to my ear and throat. Down to my breast eagerly awaiting his kisses.

He worshiped each one with his tongue and then returned to my left breast. Slowly he sucked my nipple into his mouth that felt like it was a hundred and ten degrees as his fingers played with me. And then the first climax hit with the force of a storm. I didn't think I could spread my legs any wider as I convulsed around his fingers, a sound coming from deep inside of me forcing its way past my lips. By now, I couldn't wait any longer and I begged him to please take me. Now. Right this minute. I wanted to feel the magnificent length and breath of him deep inside of me.

As he pulled me to the edge of the sofa, he used his penis to further torture me as he rubbed the head of his penis up and down my clitoris and vagina, never quite letting it penetrate me. Frantically, I clawed at his ass and tried to move around to catch the thing that I wanted so desperately.

Finally, he took pity on me and in one exquisite thrust, he penetrated not only me, but also seemingly all my defenses. Oh, yessss! This was one of those make your toes-curl, pull the sheet off (even though there are no sheets) slap-your-mama-cause-it-feels-so-good kind of fucks. With a patience I wouldn't have thought a man who hadn't had any sex in over a year could display, he ever so slowly stroked me. Endlessly stroked me. Made me climax over and over stroked me. Had me cursing and calling to Jesus stoked me. He turned me every which way but loose stroked me. And I came. And came. And came. And came some more. And finally, thankfully, and regretfully, so did he.

Sometime during the night we moved into his bedroom. And two more times, before the dawn stole across our exhausted bodies, we made love. We screwed. We fucked. And each time was better than the last. It was more than a meeting of bodies. It was a meeting of the minds. And I felt that somewhere, some how, there was no turning back. That I was his and he was mine, and things would never be the same ever again, for either of us. I felt connected. I felt safe and that finally, I belonged. I felt like I had been on an endless journey and was finally home.

And then and there, went the deepest zap I have ever felt in my life.

Chapter Eleven

It was a beautiful day for traveling. The sun was just starting to come over the horizon and the weatherman on the radio promised that it was going to be a hot one. At the moment, however, there was still a moist coolness from the newness of dawn.

Theo and I had left at six in the morning to go to my parents to pick up Bethany. He had decided it would be easier to leave from my house since I was closer to the Ft. Washington turnpike on-ramp than him. I didn't argue. It really didn't matter whose bed we slept in as long as we slept together. At the moment, I was grooving to the Phat Cat Players CD Theo had just slipped in. I had laughed when I heard the cut "*Sundress.*" Theo had said when he'd first heard it, it had reminded him of my dress and our first night together so he just had to buy it and that every time he played it, it gave him a hard-on.

The past week had passed in a haze of lust and mind-bending sex. Mostly at my house since there wasn't anyone there but me. Usually his son was home, so Theo would stop by in the evening on his way home from work.

I swear the man was seducing me with food. He said I had the emptiest refrigerator and cupboard he had ever seen. So every time he came by, he came with bags of groceries. He had asked what were Bethany's favorite snacks and *viola*, he came with a bag of every treat she had ever liked. My freezer, that vast place of emptiness that had been so empty there was an echo in it, was now packed. I couldn't get another thing in there if I tried.

The dreaded Spam and boxed macaroni and cheese had been pushed so far in the back of the cupboard that I couldn't even see it. It may not seem like a big deal to you, buy hey, it was major to me. I have never had a full refrigerator or cupboard. I've never had the luxury of trying to decide what I wanted for dinner. At least, not in a very long time, anyway. And that layaway I had for Bethany? He had even gotten that out, along with every possible needed school supply, a new winter coat and boots and even more clothes than I had picked out once he found out what her size was. I had fussed, cussed and protested and he had told me to get a grip. Secretly, however, I was glad that she would be coming home to a lot of new clothes and school things. But I still planned on paying him back.

So for the past week, we had fallen into the habit of me rushing home to fix dinner to share with Theo when he came by. And there was more. I kept finding money all over my house. When I would ask him about it, he would deny any knowledge of it. For the first time in like forever, I was starting to pay bills that hadn't been paid in months. I guess to a certain degree, I could understand how Brenda felt. Every woman likes to feel taken care of. However, I didn't have a man kicking my butt for the price of a bill payment. If that had been the case, I would have rather done without his assistance. I wished things could be for Brenda like they were starting to be for me.

And the sex? Chile, the sex was all of that and a bag of chips. I was walking around in a constant state of arousal and anticipation. Anticipation to hear his voice on the phone. Anticipation to see him come through my door. Anticipation to touch him and feel him touch me. That it could be anything more than lust, I refused to think about, let alone discuss, so let's just drop it, okay?

At least I wouldn't have to think about that fool Frankie for a few hours. That niggah was trippin'. After the fantastic weekend Theo and I had shared, I had been floating on a cloud. After Theo had left me on Sunday evening, I had been in the process of getting my stuff together for the upcoming work week. Maxwell was taking me back on the stereo as I floated around my spot. It came rudely and abruptly to a halt when I heard this obnoxious banging at my door.

"Where the hell have you been all weekend," was the first thing I heard when I opened my door.

"Excuse you? Who do you think you're talking to?"

"And who was that mu'fucka who dropped you off, Sara?" So much for the refined speech.

"Excuse you?" I asked again, incredulous.

"Yeah, I've been sitting out here every since you hung up on me. So I want to know who you been with all damn weekend that your ass couldn't come the fuck home," Frankie spat, furious.

"Wait one minute, asshole. Back that shit up, okay? First of all, who I'm with and where I've been, is none of your fuckin' business. We aren't all of *that*, okay? And just who the hell do you think you are jumping in my face? *Shit.* I don't owe you any damn explanations, so you just better chill with this stupid shit, okay? What, you think you gonna come up in here and beat me down like Terrell did Brenda? If you do, you better make sure the first one is a good one, cause the next time you'll draw back a fuckin' nub. What, I'm supposed to be scared of you? Oh, I don't think so! Baby you got the wrong one! Today is not the day, and I damn sure am not the one," I told him, getting really pissed, as I moved around my kitchen to my knife drawer. "Now try me and see if I'm play-ing," I told him as I pulled out the biggest knife in my drawer.

I guess he realized that I wasn't playing because he backed the hell up and calmed himself down.

"It's not even like that, baby. I was worried about you. Then when I saw you come home with some other guy, I felt like I had been played."

"Played? Played? Why would you think that? There wasn't anything between us to play. We weren't all of that Frankie. We might have been, but, hey, you took care of that. You made your choice. I made mine. End of story. End of us. End of discussion."

"It's because of my record, isn't it? That's the real reason you don't want to deal with me," he said, sounding angry again.

"Will you get real? Your record doesn't have damn thing to do with it, and you know it. Stop trying to hide behind your record and take responsibility for what you did, Frankie. You helped that shithead get out of jail. And while we're talking about his sorry ass, why didn't you tell me he was married?"

"I thought you knew. I thought Brenda was your girl and would have told you."

"Well she didn't. I found out when I went over to her place and found that asshole happily ensconced there, like he's the king of the damn castle. When I questioned her about going back to him, she let it slip out. I thought she had more sense than that. But that's neither here nor there. The point of *this* discussion is that you don't have any rights as far as 'we' are concerned, because there is no 'we,' and as far as I can see, there never will be. Got that? Now get the fuck out," I told him, tired of talking to him.

He looked at me for a long moment, hesitating. I wasn't sure if he was getting ready to go off on me or what. I was holding my breath and shaking inside, but I refused to let him see how scared I really was. I hated confrontations of any kind. But I'm not going to just take somebody else's shit without a fight either.

Finally, he turned to go. Before he left he said, "I really wished things could have been different between us Sara. I really felt that we could have had something special," looking all hurt.

"Yeah, well, whatever. You made the choice, Frankie. Not me. You think what you did was right and I don't. I'm sorry, but I can't forgive that."

With one last lingering look, he left. I sagged against the counter in relief, as I flung the knife I had been clutching into the sink. I couldn't believe that I had just gone through all of that drama.

Now, as Theo's car ate up the miles, it felt like somebody else had gone through that. I hadn't told Theo about what had happened. I just wanted to forget it. All I could think about now was seeing my daughter after being separated all summer. I was looking forward to seeing my mom also. I couldn't wait to see what she thought about Theo. I hadn't told her a whole lot about him, just that he was a little older than I was. I wanted her to draw her own conclusions. And I wanted to hear what those opinions were without my input. My mother was very astute at reading people and I really valued her opinion.

We talked about inconsequential things as the miles comfortably sped by in his Lincoln Navigator and I acted as his copilot, though all I did was change the CDs. We'd stopped for breakfast and I couldn't help but to think how nice it was to have a man take over and pay for everything. I'd pinched pennies for so long, they squeaked in protest. I could get used to this. Yeah.

Finally, we turned down the familiar street to my grandparent's house, the house that was now my parents. The car had barely rolled to a stop before I was out of it and bounding up the back porch and in the house. An empty house.

"I guess they must have made a run out. I didn't tell my mother what time to expect me. Maybe they went to the store," I said, as I looked around the house. We had come in through the kitchen and I was walking into the dining room. Next to that was a room that I guess was sort of like a parlor and beside that was the living room. As I passed through all of the rooms out to the front porch, I noted all of the things my mother had done to make the house her own. From the handmade lace doilies to her needlepoint-covered foot stool near the sofa and jewel-toned, floral needlepoint pillows on either side of the sofa. Then there were the magnificent detailed hand-knitted pastel-colored throws she had on the back of Dad's favorite chair and another solid cream one on the back of the sofa. On the cocktail table in front of the sofa was her arrangement of dried flowers from ones she'd grown last summer in a leaded crystal vase, along with her collection of miniature doll tea sets. On the bottom shelf of the television stand were a few of her porcelain dolls in their freshly iron and starched pinafores. My mother changed their clothes with the seasons, usually with dresses that had belonged to my sisters and I as babies. She didn't through anything away and always believed that almost anything could be used in another way at another time.

I was out on the front porch with its two rocking chairs, and a table in between for holding glasses of iced tea or Mom's tart lemonade and oval shaped rag rug that she had made herself, I looked up the street to see if I could spot my dad's car yet. At the other end of the street was the high river bank, and if you climbed up it, you could see the river below. It was an old-fashioned house, with all of the original mahogany wood-work that people would kill for today.

Upstairs was my parent's bedroom at the front of the house and across the short hallway was a small bedroom with twin beds, which was where Bethany and I stayed whenever we came up. There was also an open area that you had to pass through to get to a back bedroom and the bathroom, after going down two steps. I guess it was sort of an upstairs parlor.

Going back through the house, I went back into the kitchen that still had white metal cabinets and an old-fashioned sink, the kind old folks used to call a 'zinc.'

"No problem. We've got time. It's early. So whenever they get back, just tell me when you want to leave," Theo said with an indulgent smile, as he pulled me into his arms for a soul-burning kiss.

"Keep that up, and my parents may come back to find me in a com-promising position. I don't think that would make too good of an impression!" I laughed, reluctantly moving out of his embrace.

"I guess it would be hard to explain," he chuckled.

"So, your father grew up here, huh?"

"Yeah, my grandfather bought my grandmother here as a blushing bride. When my grandmother died, my father sold his awning business and my parents moved from Ohio up here to take care of my grandfather. Only problem was, he was mean as shit. My mother was never made to feel welcome. At one time, my grandfather wouldn't even let us call her, and we were paying for the damn call! I finally had to call my uncle in New Jersey, my father's youngest brother, and tell him he'd better do something about his father. We heard he told Granddad that he couldn't keep us from calling our mother.

Once, when my mother went to take the trash out, in the winter mind you, that mean son of a bitch locked her out of the house. She had to sit outside all day until my father came home. She didn't know anyone and was too embarrassed to ask to sit in someone else's house. He died a couple of years ago. I'm sorry to say, but I really wasn't that upset about it. After the way he treated my mother, I hated him.

Same thing for a cousin I have. She called when there was a major fight going on after he died, between my father and his brothers. She called my mother a bitch. I have been waiting for *years* to catch her skinny ass. She might be my favorite uncle's daughter, but if I ever catch her, her ass belongs to me! *Nobody* talks to my mother like that. Nobody. It might take me years, but trust me, if I ever see her again, she's going to wish I hadn't."

"Feisty, aren't you? And you seem so quiet," Theo teased, trying to calm me down.

"I guess," I said, letting it go. "I'm going to check upstairs and see if Bethany's stuff is all packed. Make yourself at home," I told him needlessly. Theo always seemed to be at home wherever he was. He had already gotten some juice from the fridge, after washing his hands of course.

I noticed that he never touched any food or anything from the refrigerator without washing his hands first. I liked that. I had also found out that he always washed his hands after using the bathroom. I hate it when men use the bathroom and don't wash their hands. And don't let me know that you just went and then have the nerve to go in the refrigerator. Yuck.

Anyway, I went upstairs and checked out the room Bethany had occupied for the summer. I saw that my mother had all of her things together. I decided I might as well bring her things down and was on the stairway when I saw my dad's car swing into the driveway. As I flew out the front door, I was surprised to see Theo sitting on the front porch, sipping his juice like he owned the place.

Like me, Bethany was out of the car before it had come to a full stop. I don't know if I flew into her arms or she into mine. I was shocked at how much my daughter had grown during the summer. She was tanned to a nut brown and I barely recognized her.

"Bethy! Look how you've grown," I told her, feeling my eyes well up.

"Mommy! I'm so glad to see you. I had so much fun this summer! Pop-pop took me fishing almost every day, and bowling and for walks down to the river and Grandmom and I made cookies and she taught me how to do some cooking and knitting and crocheting, and how to plant flowers and lots of stuff!" she said in one breath.

I looked over my daughter's head to my mother's beaming face and my father's indulgent one. And as glad as I was that my daughter had a nice summer, I couldn't help but to feel a stab of something I couldn't define at all the things that my father had done with my daughter. He had never done those things with me. He never had had time for me. Maybe he was trying to make up for it with his granddaughter. For Bethany's sake, I hoped so.

Disentangling myself from Bethany, I gave my mother a huge hug and a quick, shallow one to my father. I noticed my mother looking past me with questioning eyes to Theo as he came around to the driveway.

I introduced my parents, Amanda and Phillip Livingston to Theo, and then introduced him to my daughter, holding my breath as Bethany scrutinized Theo.

At first she didn't say anything and then I noticed a shy smile.

"What should I call you?" she asked bluntly.

"Whatever you want. How about Theo?" he asked her.

"Oh no. I'm not allowed to ever call a grownup by their first name. Mommy says I have to put a handle on it. So what should I call you, Mr. Theo?"

"Well why don't we wait until we get to know each other better and then you can decide what you want to call me, okay?"

"Okay. I'll think about it. Are you going to marry my mom?"

"Well I don't know Bethany. We haven't talked about it, but if we decide to do that, I'll talk to you about it first, okay?"

She studied him for a long moment, and then a smile as bright as sunshine broke across her face.

"I think that maybe you are a very nice man. I think I like you," she told him as she skipped into the house.

I didn't realize I'd been holding my breath until it came out in a *whish*. I'm sure that I must have blushed to the roots of my hair.

"Sharp kid," he laughed.

"That she is," I told him weakly, as we all moved into the house.

"So you're Theo. My daughter didn't tell me how handsome you were," my mother smiled at him.

"Why thank you, ma'am. And she didn't tell me what a fox her mother was either. I can see now where Sara gets her looks," he told her with a smile.

"Gon' now," my mother said, blushing.

I couldn't believe it. He was charming my mother out of her shoes. She was giggling and blushing like a young girl. I watched the whole thing with a smile on my face. First my daughter, now my mother.

By this time my father had made his way into the living room and his precious television and of course there was a baseball game on.

My father could watch sports twenty-four seven if you let him. I hate sports. When I was growing up and we only had one television, he used to monopolize the television with nothing but sports.

As the man of the house, we had to watch what he watched. No wonder I read so much. It had been a happy day when my father had bought a television for him and Mom's bedroom. Hallelujah! Mom and I got to watch movies on the weekend in the living room and he, when he was home, watched his precious sports upstairs in their bedroom. The only drawback was having to take him his meals upstairs on a tray, though. He couldn't even eat downstairs with us. We had to take him his food upstairs. And forget him bringing the damn tray downstairs. Oh no, that would have been too much like right. No, his highness would leave it at the top of the stairs for somebody else to come get. Sometimes when he'd been drinking, if he didn't like what was on the tray, he'd throw it back down the steps and guess who had to clean the mess up? Then my mother would have to quickly cook something else or face the consequences.

As soon as Theo was out of hearing range, my mother said, "I like your friend. When we were coming down the street, and I saw him sitting on the porch like he belonged there, I was thinking 'who is that man sitting on my porch?' And I liked him right away. I liked that he seemed to feel so comfortable here. He seems like a good man, Sara. You two look good together," she said, her eyes full of questions.

I could tell she wanted to know if we'd slept together yet, but was being too polite to ask. My mother never asked anything outright, but in a roundabout sort of way.

I think my blushing probably told her all she wanted to know. She kind of nodded her head and smiled. I hated that she could read me so easily, but I smiled back in silent answer.

However, I did say, "He is a good man, Mom. Do you know, he never comes by the house unless he has a bag of groceries? I swear the man is trying to woo me with food!"

"Oh yeah? Is it working?" she laughed.

"Yeah. I think it is," I told her in wonder. I walked over to the kitchen screen door and looked out not seeing what was out of the door, but seeing instead Theo coming through my kitchen door, time and time again with his simple offerings. Some men woo you with promises and lies. Some with jewelry and money. This one was wooing me with food. But I didn't need the promises and lies, or the jewelry. I did, however, need the food and the money. But it wasn't that simple. It was that he understood how hard things were for me and his trying to help ease my burdens was what was so touching.

Turning back into the room I told my mother, "You know he's met the Witches of Eastwick," my pet name for my sisters.

"I told you to stop calling them that. They mean well," she said in their defense.

"Now tell me that each and every one didn't call you with the 4-1-1?"

"Well, yeah, they did," she conceded. But she rushed on with, "But they only had good things to say about him."

"Yeah, right," I snorted. "I can just hear Stephanie, 'watch, she's gonna fudge it up because he's too damn nice to handle her fast ass.'"

"How do you all do that? Each of you can always imitate each other so well. Damn, you sound just like her. And that was exactly what she said," she said, laughing softly.

"Cause we know each other so well, unfortunately. My sisters are convinced that I can't do anything right. And up until now, they've pretty much been right. But I'm older now and damn it, I think I deserve some respect for my decisions and choices. I mean, really, who are they to judge me? One has never been married, has no kids but thinks she can tell everybody how they should be raised, one is on her second marriage trying to pretend she's living the American Dream and the other is on her third, for heaven's sake!"

"They only mean well, Sara. It's hard for them not to keep thinking of you as the baby," she said, trying, as usual, to give everyone the benefit of the doubt.

"That's bull. They have always thought that I was spoiled because I was the youngest."

"You were spoiled."

"Gee, thanks Ma."

"You're welcome dear. Hungry?" she asked as she bustled around the kitchen.

I smiled in spite of myself. My mother always thought everything could be fixed with food.

Too soon, however, it was time to go. For the first time ever, I found that I had actually enjoyed my visit to my parents. I was sorry to be leaving so soon. To my surprise, Theo promised to bring us back soon for a longer visit. I looked at him in shock. My mother looked at me and winked. My father hugged me and whispered, "I like him," to my surprise.

My mother, of course, cried as Bethany got in the car. I knew she was going to miss her terribly. At least while Bethany had been there, she'd had someone to talk to. Trying to get two words out of my father was like pulling hens' teeth. To my surprise, I even felt a little weepy myself. Usually, I was so anxious to get out of there, and I had never thought about how it might be for them. And I had never thought that maybe one day they wouldn't be there, but for some undefined reason, this time I did.

For a while, our ride back was quiet; each of us lost in our own thoughts. Finally, I asked Bethany to tell me about her summer. Lord! I had forgotten how much that child could talk. As she chattered on, I found myself glancing at Theo, hoping he wasn't regretting his decision to make this trip. He just smiled and engaged Bethany in more conversation.

After a while she settled down and went to sleep. I was just drifting off myself when I felt Theo take my hand and give it a squeeze. I glanced over and he just nodded and smiled.

"What?" I asked him, smiling myself.

"I liked your parents, especially your mother. She reminded me of my grandmother."

"How so?"

"Soft, motherly, loving, but with an inner strength like a steel magnolia. The kind they used to describe back in the day as not taking tea for the fever."

"Yup. That's my mother. Her only weak spot has always been my father. No way would I have put up with his shit if I had been in her shoes. I guess that's why I'm so hard on men. I never wanted to be like that. Waiting on a man hand and foot. Having to put up with his womanizing, and other things."

"What things?"

"I'd rather not say," I said, glancing into the back seat as if I didn't want to talk around Bethany.

"Some other time, when we're alone," he said.

"Maybe," I said, turning my head to look out the passenger side window. My smile had faded as unpleasant memories flooded my mind.

Memories of sounds in the night, and me cowering and crying in my bed and Zoe being mad as hell, and having the guts to stand toe-to-toe against our father. Memories of my mother trying not to cry and trying to whisper soothing words to me through bleeding and swollen lips. Telling me he didn't mean it.

With an effort, I choked back an unexpected sob and blinked furiously to keep unwanted tears from running down my face. I didn't want to have to explain to Theo the reasons for it. I was practically biting a hole in my lip to keep it in. Again. I always found a way to keep it in. With an effort, I pushed the demons away one more time, and with false brightness, turned to Theo and asked, "So what do you think of my daughter?" hoping he wouldn't notice the unnatural sheen to my eyes.

Luckily, he had his eyes on the road, and said, "She seems like a great kid. A real little lady. Nice manners, too."

"Thanks. I try. It's not always easy being a single mom."

"What happened with her father? Is he around at all?"

"Please. He bit the dust about a month after I told him I was pregnant. Afraid of what his daddy would do if he found out that he had not one, but two girls pregnant at the same time. Mind you, I didn't find out I was pregnant until I was almost four months gone. Anyway, my mother, who used to adore him, did as he asked and gave him time to tell his parents himself. In the meantime, the other girl's mother stormed into his father's office and raised all holy hell. Well, Junior got spooked and was afraid to tell him. I didn't even know about the other chick until he had no choice but to tell me before somebody else in our crowd did. I felt like the proverbial wife, the last to know. To add insult to injury, he told his father that the baby wasn't his. We had been together for almost a year. Stupid me loved his sorry ass. Up until then, I believed him when he said he loved me and we were going to get married. Ha! What a joke that was. Instead, he married the other chick. His father bought them a house, furnished it and everything. Bought Junior into the family electrical business and life was good for them. Meanwhile, I'm struggling on welfare, trying to go to school and take care of a baby. Thank God for my mother. Without her, I don't know what I would have done.

After Bethany was born, I was going to take him to court for child support until I heard that his father offered to pay his friends to say that they had slept with me to cast doubt on Bethany's paternity if I took him to court. I knew that it wasn't true, but we were living in a small town, and I didn't want my daughter to be touched by that. I was too upset and hurt to pursue it, so I let it go. It took me almost three years to get over him. But I have *never* forgiven him and I doubt that I ever will. At the time we had been living in Akron, Ohio. I felt that it wasn't big enough for the both of us, so I left. We moved to Pittsburgh, then Washington, D.C. and finally Philly. I cut off all my ties with everyone I knew in high school and never looked back.

I called him once though, when Bethany was around three. She was asking about her father and I felt I owed it to her to give her a chance to know her sorry-ass father. He asked me what I was calling for. Said we didn't have anything to talk about. I told him since he felt like that, to go fuck himself."

"Damn, baby. You have had it rough, huh?"

"I survived," I said, feeling a bitter twist pass my lips.

"Does she ever ask about him?"

"Sometimes."

"And what do you tell her?"

"The truth. My oldest sister Steph had a different father than Zoe and I, because my mother was married before. Anyway, Ma used to always sugarcoat the truth for my sister, even though her father was an asshole and his mother was even worse. When they were together, she used to treat my mother like shit. The result? My sister adored her father and treated my mother like shit. Uh-uh. I ain't havin' it. I'll be damn if I'll let her put a man who is beneath contempt on a pedestal."

"Damn. That's rough."

"Tell me about it."

Further discussion came to an end when we heard Bethany yawn and stretch and announce that she was *starved.*

After stopping for dinner, we got back on the road and the rest of the ride was filled with silly car games and chatter until we got to my house.

Theo didn't stay long, figuring correctly that my daughter and I needed the time to get reacquainted. She flipped when she saw all the goodies in the freezer and pantry, not to mention all her new clothes. We pigged out on ice cream and cookies and snuggled in my bed while we watched some television before she finally passed out from exhaustion.

It was nice to feel her head on my shoulder again and her warm little body next to mine. I fell asleep that night with a smile on my face, glad to have my little girl back home with me, and grateful to the man who had made it possible.

Chapter Twelve

"Sara, could you come into my office, please?" my boss, David Klein, asked after I picked up his buzz on the intercom.

When I walked into his office he said, "Close the door, and have a seat."

Uh-oh. Shit. What did I do now? I'm wracking my brain trying to remember if there was something with a file I forgot to do. Couldn't have been anything about the trial. That had gone off without a hitch, with a million-plus dollar settlement to boot. I didn't have to guess for long, however.

"I'm sure you must have noticed that Sandy and I have been meeting a lot lately. It would be a little hard for you not to know, sitting right outside my door. Anyway, we have decided to leave the firm and start one of our own, with another friend of ours. Are you interested in going with me?"

"Really? I mean about starting your own firm. Wow. That's deep. And you want me to go with you? Gee, I don't know, Dave. I'd have to think about it. What are you offering?"

"What you're making here, plus three weeks vacation, and one week sick leave, the usual holidays, and after a year, a pension plan."

"Where?"

"Where what?"

"Where is the office going to be?"

"We think we've found a great spot near Rittenhouse Square, a really nice space in a brownstone."

"You can't do any better on the salary?"

"What are you looking for?"

"Six thousand more a year."

"How about thirty-five hundred and a healthy Christmas bonus?"

"Health insurance?"

"Yup and dental, and as I said, profit sharing."

"Guess you get to keep me," I smiled broadly as I leaned over his desk to shake his hand.

"Keep this to yourself, until we let the firm know."

"No problem. HALLELUIAH! No more Eloise! That in itself is worth it! I'd like to be able to finally tell her what I think of her."

"Sara, be nice."

"You don't like her any more than I do."

"I know, but it wouldn't be very professional."

"Whatever. Is Sandy taking his secretary too?"

"I don't know yet if Pricilla will be going with him. They've been together for years, so I would imagine she would."

"Hhmm. I don't know her that well, since they are on the other side of the floor. She's seems okay I guess. Anyway, when are you looking to make this move?"

"Shortly, probably within the next few weeks."

"That soon? Dag. Well, let me know. And thanks Dave," I told him before returning to my desk. I couldn't wait until Theo picked me up after work. Was he going to be surprised. At least now I could stop worrying about losing my job. Hell, things had just greatly improved. I was excited for the guys as well as myself. It would be a nice change, being in a smaller, more intimate firm than just being a faceless number of the support staff like you tend to be with the large firms. And the extra money and vacation time was nice too. I was only getting two weeks at the firm I was at now.

Things between Theo and I had been moving at a pretty fast pace. It had been a couple of months since we had picked up Bethany, and things between Theo and I had been going great. It was scary just how great they were going.

We had continued having dinner almost every night, only now with Bethany, and sometimes with T.J., either at my house or his. Bethany adored him and I felt like T.J. kind of liked me too, even though he was rather reserved and quiet. Bethany, however, got on his nerves. He was a few years older than she was and her following him around worked his nerves. There had been a couple of times when his little attitude had worked *my* nerves.

We had gone to a pumpkin farm out in Bucks County and T.J. had insisted on his cousins Slim and Angie going. That was fine, but no matter how hard Bethany tried to join in the conversation or activities, the three of them would just freeze her out. I could tell from her face that she wanted to cry but was valiantly trying not too. A couple of other times we had gone to different places and the same thing had happened. The next time we were scheduled for an outing, Bethany had said that she didn't want to go. When I had questioned her, she had reluctantly admitted that she was tired of feeling like the outsider. I had confronted Theo and we had had a few words about it. I felt that their treatment was mean and uncalled for. So either he could do something about it, or Bethany and I could go back to staying at home and doing our own thing. Finally, it was decided that T.J. could take Slim and Bethany could bring either one of her cousins or one of her girlfriends. T.J. had been pissed. I didn't care. I wasn't going to let anybody just hurt my daughter's feeling like that.

Then there were the times that it was just Theo and I. One Sunday morning, he surprised me by taking me to Zanzibar Blue for the WJJZ Sunday Brunch. Bethany had spent the night over Zoe's, T.J. at Carol's and Theo at my house. It was such a pleasant surprise and change from my usual Sunday. I really enjoyed myself. I had been living in

Philadelphia for years and hadn't been anywhere. Theo made me feel like a tourist in my own city. He seemed to delight in taking me to new places and sharing new experiences with me.

One of our favorite things to do was to go to Warm Daddies for dinner and then to one of the jazz clubs around South Street afterward. If we weren't in the mood for music, we'd go to the Laff House on South Street.

All in all, Theo and I were spending a lot of time together. And except for the problems between our children, we were enjoying getting to know each other.

During that time, Theo's mother died. I was sorry that I never got a chance to meet her. She died about a week after we had picked Bethany up. Dave was in the middle of the trial and I couldn't go to the funeral. I heard later from Brenda and Theo that his brothers had teased him unmercifully about his 'young chippy,' and told him he was going to die with a smile on his face and that it cost extra to get the smile off. Brenda had told me that he had just smiled and let them tease him without a word. Chelsea, she said, hadn't been amused at all.

Chelsea was not happy about her father moving on with his life. She was polite to me but she still seemed reserved. Strangely, she took to Bethany right away, treating her like a little sister.

Anyway, I was still reeling from Dave's news when Brenda came to my desk, her eyes puffy from crying.

"What's wrong?" I asked her, alarmed.

"Nothing. Wanna go for a smoke?"

"Yeah, sure," I told her, grabbing my pack, wanting to get her away from the curious eyes of people passing by in the hallway. Anybody looking at her could see she was upset, and they were trying to peep her out without looking like they were looking. One thing about a big law firm, they loved drama. Sometimes it could be worse than a damn soap opera. And as large as the place was, everybody knew everyone else's business. Who was sleeping with whom, who was pregnant, who was getting divorced, almost divorced, engaged, getting ready to get fired, whatever.

And don't even get me started on the Christmas party. Monday morning after the party was better than the actual party. That's when you found out who got discovered in some pretty compromising positions. I don't know why some of these young female associates think that's going to get them faster promotions by submitting to some drunken partner. But like clockwork, every year, some silly female got caught. Next thing you knew, she wouldn't be working there anymore. And him? What do you think? Just once I wish it could be a *female* partner putting the moves on a *male* associate, but that would never happen. Women have more sense. Besides, if she did, guaranteed, she'd be fired. So would he, but that's not the point. No matter how high we get, it's still a man's world, and you're kidding yourself if you believe otherwise.

When we got outside, I told Brenda, "Okay, spill it. What's wrong?"

"I don't want to talk about it, Sara, okay? I don't feel like hearing your negativity right now. It was my own fault anyway," she said with a loud sniffle, ready to cry again.

"What did Terrell do this time? I swear to God, I don't know what you see in that loser," I told her impatiently.

"See that's what I mean. You don't even know what happened and you automatically assume that it's Terrell."

"Well it is, isn't it?" I snapped.

"Sort of," she said in a small voice, her chin quivering. Taking a ragged breath she said, "We had a fight on the phone. He called all pissed off because I forgot to get his clothes out of the cleaners yesterday and he needed his stuff for work. I completely forgot and he had told me twice to pick the stuff up."

"Wait a minute. Doesn't he get off work around four? Why couldn't he pick his own damn stuff up?"

"He had a basketball game."

At my incredulous look, she rushed on with, "And I had told him I would do it. So when he went looking for his stuff today and couldn't find it he called up cussing me out and shit. Plus, he was pissed because

I didn't get a chance to go by the MAC machine and leave him some money before I left for work today."

"Your money or his?" I asked, knowing the answer when she refused to look at me, let alone answer me.

I had to press my lips together to keep from saying something that would hurt her feelings. I felt like slapping her myself and then shaking her and shouting in her face, "WILL YOU PLEASE WAKE THE FUCK UP?" But I didn't do either of those things. Instead, I gave her what she needed, a long, strong hug. I felt so powerless. How could I help my friend when she refused to help herself?

When Theo came to pick me up that evening I told him about it. He just shook his head. He had given up trying to talk some sense into Brenda. We both had.

When I told him about my other news, however, he was very happy for me. He said it sounded like a great opportunity, especially since the office would be so small. Less office politics, which he knew I was sick to death of.

Theo and I had barely gotten into my house when my landlord, Esteban, who lived across the street, came banging on my door. He was from Portugal, and sometime it was hard to understand his English. Such was not the case tonight.

"I'm moving back to Portugal in four months. I hate to do this to you, but I'm going to have to terminate your lease."

"What? What does your moving have to do with my lease?" I asked him, confused.

"I sold my house faster than I thought I would. Your place is the cleanest of all my apartments. My family and I will be moving in here in three weeks."

"*What?* You can't just move me out because you want my place. I have a lease!" I told him, outraged.

"A month-to-month lease. I have the option of terminating, as of the end of the month. That's in three weeks. I'm sorry, I hate to do this to you, but I have no choice. As I said, this is the cleanest of my places. The rest of my tenants are slobs," he said with an apologetic smile and shrug.

Theo came to the door and wanted to know what was going on. I ran it down for him and he asked Esteban, "Can't you give her more time than that? How is she supposed to find a place in such a short amount of time?

He just shook his head, shrugged and left. I sank into the closest kitchen chair.

"What am I going to do? I can't get that kind of money together in three weeks! What the hell am I supposed to do now?"

"I don't know Sara. I'll think of something. I'll see if I can find some place else for you," he said as he absently rubbed my back. He was standing behind my chair. He started to say something and his hesitation made me turn and look up at him.

"What? What were you going to say?"

"Well, there is one alternative. You could move in with me."

I looked at him like he was crazy. I wasn't ready for that kind of a move. I liked having my own place, even if it was a struggle to keep it.

"I couldn't do that. I have a cat, you have a dog," I said stupidly, grabbing onto the first thing I could think of.

"Well, yes, that could be a problem, especially since my dog hates cats. But if you can't find anyplace else, Sara, what choice do you have? Move in with one of your sisters?"

"Please," I said with a slight shiver. "I can't. None of them have the room, except for maybe Stephanie, and I'd live on the street first. We did that already in Pittsburgh. I will *never* live with her again. Shit! Shit! Shit! I hate this. I hate when other people have control over my life or me. Look, before we go that route, I mean me moving in with you, I have to at least see if I can find another place of my own," I told him, ignoring his hurt look. I think he was actually hoping that I would have to move in with him.

"If I can't find anything, then I will, but only temporarily, until I can save up enough to get my own spot, okay?"

"Sure baby," he said with a grin before kissing me.

Two weeks later, I was packing my stuff; to move in with Theo. I hadn't been able to find anything that I could reasonably afford. I was skeptical as hell about moving into Theo's house. I kept telling myself, it was only temporary, even though Theo had said that it was not. Thanks to Frankie's crazy ass, I was being forced to do something I really wasn't comfortable with.

The man just didn't know how to let it go. Every time I turned around, there he was in my face. He would show up at my job, at the grocery store, at the bank, at the Laundromat. It was getting to be sickening. Sometimes we would argue and sometimes I could just feel him watching me. He kept trying to tell me he was sorry and to please give him another chance. Not! I finally had to tell Theo about him, after he jumped in my face one night when we were coming home from the movies.

"Oh, so this is the mu'fucka you dropped me for, huh?" he said to me, ignoring Theo. With a contemptuous sweeping glance up and down Theo, he spat, just missing Theo's shoe.

"An old-head at that. What, you afraid you can't handle all this young stuff? Can't handle a real sho'nuff brother, a *black* brother," he taunted, spreading his arms out, profiling.

"Niggah, please. Why don't you take your triflin' ass home to your mama's house and get out of my face. I'm not playing with you Frankie. I told you to leave me alone. I'm sick of your stupid shit, okay? Get a life."

In a deadly quiet voice, Theo asked Frankie, "You got a problem, my *brother*? The lady said to leave her alone. I would strongly suggest you listen."

"Fuck you, man! This is between her and me. I think you'd better stay out of it," he shouted at Theo, getting all in his face.

"And I think you'd better leave before it gets ugly out here."

"Man, what is your old ass gonna do? Bore me to death? Please, dismissed," he said throwing up his hand in Theo's face and turning back to me.

Before he knew what was happening, Theo grabbed Frankie's hand and twisting it up and behind his back, brought him down to his knees as he applied pressure to his bent back thumb.

"I said, I think you'd better go, *my brother*. Now. I'd really hate to have to break your hand," he said tightly, applying pressure to Frankie's hand, causing him to howl in pain.

"Are you going to leave *my brother*, or am I gonna have to give you the ass-whipping your mother obviously neglected to do?" Theo taunted him; his voice deceptively low and calm. Finally, Frankie nodded, and after a moment, Theo let him go. No sooner had Frankie gotten up than he made the mistake of swinging on Theo. With a quick punch to the stomach, followed by a devastating blow to the jaw, Theo flattened him.

I stood by, wide-eyed in amazement, seeing a different side to Theo that I'd had no idea existed. He always seemed so calm and kind of reserved. *Still waters run deep.* My mother's words flashed in my mind unbidden. Well, she was right about that in this instance.

Frankie finally picked himself up off the ground, dazed and more than a little wary of Theo. However, as he limped off, he turned and snarled, "It ain't over Sara. Believe that." Then he hastened to his mama's car as Theo took two steps toward him.

After we got in the house, Theo said, "So do you want to explain to me what the hell that was all about? Who was that jerk?"

"Nobody," I mumbled. At his raised eyebrows I sucked my teeth and flounced into the living and sat down on my lumpy sofa with my head in my hands, trying to stop my delayed reaction to this newest drama. I was shaking like a leaf in a frigid breeze. Theo stood in the doorway, waiting for my explanation.

Looking up, I drew in a shaky breath, expelled it slowly, and told him, "Brenda introduced us. Funny, it was the same day I met you. He's Terrell's cousin. Guess that explains a lot, huh? Frankie was the one who came and got me when Terrell had beaten Brenda up so badly. He's also the one who got Terrell out of jail. That's when we had our disagreement, and I told him I didn't want to see him anymore."

"So you were seeing, what was his name, Frankie?" At my nod he continued, "So you were seeing Frankie and me at the same time?" he asked, frowning.

"No, not really. I mean I just met you both at the same time, and I didn't know where, if anything, either relationship was going. He was just a friend. Just like you were. I enjoyed talking to both of you and no, before you ask, I never slept with him."

"Well if you never slept with him, why is he tripping like that?"

"The hell if I know!" I answered irritably. "I guess his ass is crazy like his psycho cousin. He's been following me and bothering me for weeks. No matter what I say, he won't leave me alone," I told him miserably.

"Why didn't you tell me about any of this before, Sara?"

"I didn't want to worry you. I thought I could handle him by myself. He seems to be getting worse. It's like he's stalking me or something. Like he's obsessed."

"Well that does it. You can't stay here. It's settled then. You are going to move in with me and I don't want to hear anymore about it. And forget that dumb shit about it only being temporary. As you are fond of saying, the end."

I looked at Theo with raised eyebrows. Here was yet another side to Theo. Decisive and authoritative. Actually, I found it kind of sexy and stimulating. I hate a wimpy man. I'd been making so many decisions for so long by myself that it was almost a relief to have somebody else make them for me. Within reason, of course.

So here I was, packing up, anxious and nervous about where this new turn in my life was going to take me. Bethany was bouncing off the walls. She was excited to be moving into Theo's house. She had been there a few times and was excited to have a back yard, a big room and a quasi-big brother. She had told T.J., "Now I'll get to see you every day!" He had groaned at the thought.

Finally, after an army of Theo's nephews had helped to move me, my daughter and I were settled into his house. The one thing I had truly been sad about was that I had to give up my cat. I loved my Leah. That was her name. She had been a great cat and I had watched her give birth to a fine litter of kittens twice.

I remember the first time she was ready to give birth. I had invited the kids from the neighborhood in. I thought it would be a great learning experience for them. Especially the boys. That way they could see what a female went through to bring a new life into the world, even if it was just a kitten. You could tell by the way that Leah howled that she was in pain. I remember their eyes were big as saucers as they watched a healthy-sized kitten come out of such a little place. One after another, they watched six kittens being born. Afterward, they had all thanked me, saying it was the most awesome thing they had ever seen.

And when I had gotten really sick once and that asshole Keith left me to fend for myself, it had been Leah who had watched over me. I had sent Bethany to Zoe's house because I was simply too sick to take care of her. I remembered lying on the sofa, wishing I could die, burning up with fever, and Leah jumping up on my chest and gently stroking my face with her paw as she mewed in helplessness. Every time I got up and dragged myself to the bathroom, she was right on my heels. It was as if that cat knew how sick I was. Finally, I had called an ambulance to go to the hospital, and my mother came down to take care of Bethany. She told me later that Leah had run all over the house, crying, looking for me. I remember when I came from the hospital, how she had run and jumped into my arms almost as soon as I came through the door. And now I had to give her up. Theo thought I was crazy because I cried so hard when they took her away. I guess I'll never forget those eyes that stayed on mine as his niece carried her off. She looked like she was asking what had she done that was so bad that I was making her leave.

As for moving my meager things, it hadn't taken that much really. Most of my things I had sold to a second hand store because Theo's house was already fully furnished. Not that I really cared for what he had. I mean, his house was nice and all, just not my taste. After that first visit, I had really had chance to check his place out. And while most of it was okay, a lot his things looked a little, well, tired. Other than the new addition of the kitchen and family room, the house really hadn't been updated since he had moved in. He had told me once that he had bought most of the things in the house, without his wife's input. That would never work for me. If I don't like it, I'm not cleaning it.

Right now, my main concern was getting used to living with someone else. This was a new experience. Other than my sham of a marriage, the couple of times that I had lived with someone, they had moved in with *me*. So the rules had been different. This time, *I* was doing the moving in. I had no point of reference. As for running his household, how much of a problem could it be? I was used to running things the way I wanted them to be done and I saw no reason to change my mode of thinking. I mean, how hard could this be? I already had one child, so another wouldn't be that hard to deal with. Right?

And even though I'm giving up my freedom, I'm not in love, okay? Let's just get that shit straight. I care a lot for Theo, but hey, this is survival. The fact that he just happens to be an unbelievable lover makes it a whole lot sweeter. As far as I can tell, most of my heart is still safely under lock and key, thank you very much. And if you think there's more to it than that, you're crazier than I am.

Chapter Thirteen

"I'm glad your boss let you take a few days off, even though he's getting ready to make a move himself," Theo said, as we snuggled in bed.

"Me too. This way I got to use up some of my vacation time from the old firm before going to the new one," I murmured as I rolled on top of him.

"But right now, Mr. Watkins, Dave and the job are the last things on my mind. We are supposed to be celebrating my moving in, remember?" I tell him as I bend my head to tease his lips with my tongue.

I had the CD player in our room programmed to play a mix from Waiting to Exhale, R. Kelly's 12 Play, Joe, Toni Braxton and Jonathan Butler. I wanted music that would facilitate us getting our freak on. The kids were in bed and we were sipping on some chilled wine. I had made up my mind earlier in the day that tonight would be the night I would well and truly turn him out.

While he had been taking his shower, I had heated some body oil and slipped it under the bed. "Roll over," I command him as I slipped off his body. Reaching under the bed, I poured a little of the heated, scented oil in my hands and after putting the rest back under the bed, I climbed back on him, resting on the back of his legs.

Slowly, I massaged his back with the scented, warmed oil. As I worked my way down his body, he was practically purring in contentment. I continued with each leg and foot.

"Turn over," I said as I got more oil to massage his front, but not the one thing I know he's dying for me to touch. Everywhere but there. Again, I climbed on him, and begin kissing him deeply.

Theo tried to kiss me back and I pulled back, telling him, "The rule tonight, Mr. Watkins, is that you can't kiss me back. You can't touch me, until I say you can." With that, I again ran my tongue around his lips and in and out of his closed mouth, barely teasing his tongue. "Open you mouth, but just a little, and give me your tongue," I whispered, a hair's breath from his lips. When he put his tongue out, I slowly caressed the tip of it with my tongue before slowly drawing it into my mouth, softly sucking on it. I smiled to myself when I heard him groan and felt the evidence of his desire between our bodies. Sliding off his body, I turned to the night stand on my side of the bed and after picking up my wineglass, proceed to pour a small amount of the liquid from his chest to his belly button. I quickly began to lick the wine off him, moving lower and lower down his body. He tried to slip his hand between my legs from behind, but I removed his hand and silently shook my head no.

By now he was breathing heavily, especially when I came back up and twirled my tongue around his hardened nipples, sucking them like he does mine, while my fingers lightly skimmed his body and lightly rested on his thighs. Moving lower still, I swung over his leg and positioned myself between his legs, my fingertips lightly running up and down his thighs, kneading and massaging. Leaning forward, I gently fondle his sac as I kissed his thighs, letting my fingers inch up his penis.

"Baby please! You're driving me crazy!" he panted. I smiled as I softly blew kisses on the tip of his penis. As I look ed up his body, I could see that he had his eyes closed. That will never do. "Look at me," I commanded. Propping the pillows under his head, he opens his eyes which were a dark, glittering green. Looking him directly in his eyes, I slowly took him in my mouth. As he groaned and starts to close his eyes, I stop. When he opens them again, I continue to proceed to take him into my mouth inch by slow inch. I could feel him trying to move his legs to push further into my mouth faster and I shake my head no, forcing him to remain still.

Breaking our eye contact, I move up onto my knees so that I was directly over his penis making it easier for me to use my hand and my mouth to stoke him and move him in and out of my mouth. I continued to do this and slowly increased my speed. Every time that I felt that he's about ready to lose it, I would slow it back down and then increase it again. I eased him out of my mouth and leaning over him to my night stand, I let my breast gently tease his chest. I reached for my glass of crushed ice next to my wine. Taking a small mouthful, again positioning myself between his legs, I take him into my mouth with the melting ice. He almost comes off the bed and then moans deeply in his throat, as the cold melted water trickled to his balls. I quickly replace the cold of the water with the heat of my mouth. Instead of the ice making him soft, it makes him as hard as iron encased in velvet.

As I'm feeling his increased excitement, I can feel myself getting wetter and wetter. Some women find oral sex repulsive. I find it one of the most powerful aphrodisiacs. I mean think about it. You literally have him in the palm of your hand. You have all of the power to do with him what you will. You can bring him to the brink of release or you can just sweetly torture him. As I said, it's the ultimate power and I just love it!

Anyway, just when I thought that he couldn't take anymore, I suddenly swung over him and slid down his throbbing hardness.

"Now you can touch me," I tell him with a smile, as I felt my first climax.

His hands immediately began playing with my breasts that were swinging over his face like ripe melons, sucking on one nipple and then the other as I felt his hips thrusting his hardness deeply into me, causing me to come again.

"Don't move, Sara. Be still," he whispers as his hands still the movements of my hips.

"Look at me, Sara," Theo commands, while I was feeling his penis throbbing inside of me, causing me to shiver from the delicious feeling. Bringing my eyes into focus, I look down into his handsome face.

"I don't remember the last time I felt this way about anyone, Sara. I know you don't believe in love, but I do and I think I love you Sara." I was shocked. I didn't know what to say. Before I could answer, without warning he suddenly reversed our positions, and holding me by my ankles, spread me wide as he slowly pulled almost all the way out and then with infinite slowness, slides all the way back in. Now he's the one in control and I'm the one shaking and whimpering with an incredibly fierce need. As he proceeded to sweetly torture me like this over and over, he's talking much shit, like "Yeah, I know you like this don't you? Come on baby, cum for me. Yeah, just like that. That's what I'm talkin' about. You know you like all this good shit," urning me on so much that it's making me experience one climax after another, barely able to catch my breath in between.

Finally, in a moment so pure, so sweet, I felt the tears slipping down my face as an emotion almost forgotten swelled inside of me as we both hit that plateau at the same time. Theo gathered me in his arms, as I wept into his chest, unable to explain what was wrong with me. If I couldn't explain it to myself, how could I possibly explain it to him? I did, however, assure him that he hadn't hurt me in any.

At that moment when we had climaxed together, I had felt those words tremble on my lips, but I had bitten them back. Was that the reason for my tears, because I wanted to say them or because I couldn't say them?

So who really had gotten turned out?

Chapter Fourteen

Whew! Has it been hectic the last few weeks! First the move into Theo's and then the move into our new office space. Brownstein, Bromowitz & Klein, L.L.P. opened with a small party of friends and relatives. Strangely, Priscilla came by herself. However, I have to say the guys picked a nice brownstone on Locust Street, not far from Rittenhouse Square.

I knew Sandy Brownstein a little from our old law firm, but I didn't know Lee at all. He seems like a nice guy, even if he is a little quiet and tends to break out into song at the most unexpected times. He also likes to tell whoever he's talking to on the phone, "You da man!" a lot. He's funny, with a very dry, cryptic wit. Not bad looking, either, for a slim goody. I have also heard through the legal grapevine that as far as being a lawyer, he is a legal genius, with a mind like a steel trap. Dave says he has more money than God.

Sandy is the one I call Dapper Dan. He's always dressed to the nines, and being so thin, wears his clothes really well. Since he has salt and pepper hair, when he wears blacks, grays and navy blue, he looks really sharp. Very GQ. I like to give him complements so I can watch him blush. I think it's kind of cute. And he always smells so good. I don't know what the fragrance is, but it's one of those come-here smells. You know what I mean, the kind where you want to lean in and get a better whiff. Subtle. Very sexy.

Then there is my boss, David Klein. Dave looks like a football player. I think at one time he played for Temple University before blowing out his knees. He's tall, has a massive chest and arms, intense blue eyes, nice ass. Hey, I'm still a female, even if he's my boss. What am I suppose to do, not look? Please. Now, *he* was the man. He's the managing partner of the firm, which means that he has to watch the money, and make sure all the i's are dotted and all the t's are crossed. I've been working with Dave for years. I think we get along so great because we both have a sick sense of humor. His mother says that we get along so well because I treat him like a husband. I told her I treat him better because he signs my checks and I don't have to tell him I have a headache! And why not treat your boss like a husband. Whether it's at home or at work, you still have to do a lot of stroking. At least at work, I get paid for it.

And then there is Priscilla, Sandy's secretary. I don't even know where to begin with this one. First of all, if anyone is in need of an Oprah makeover, it's this chick. Lord, her hair and clothes look like something out of the 70's, maybe even the 60's. I guess no one ever told her that sometime in your life you are supposed to get your ends trimmed every now and then and that one really shouldn't use sponge rollers. And I guess no one ever told her it was okay to use the firm's dental plan either, judging from all the missing teeth in her mouth. That's probably why they put me at the desk near the door. Most of the time she's okay, but I find her kind of depressing. She wants everything in the office to be run the way she says. I asked Dave if she was supposed to be the office manager and no one had bothered telling me. He emphatically said that he was the only manager in there and to ignore her. But for the most part, for the time being, we seem to be getting along okay. I just miss all my buddies from the firm. I don't have anyone to chat with as I pass along in the hallway.

The good news is that I don't have to go down forty-some floors to get a cigarette. All I have to do now is go out the back door to the roof. It's actually kind of cool.

Things at home, however, have been a little touch and go. In the weeks since I'd moved in with Theo, it had been less than a smooth ride. Theo and I had argued about everything from leaving the toilet seat up to the dog chewing up my favorite pair of red leather pumps. However, for the most part, Bethany and I have settled into Theo's house quite well. Bethany loves her new school and has made friends with a few girls in the neighborhood who she walks to and from school with, and has even been to a couple of sleep overs.

There have been a few more episodes with T.J. and Bethany, though. Like when he marked up her favorite baby doll's face with indelible ink and the time he punched pinholes all over her Backstreet Boys, 'NSync and Sisqo posters. Theo and I had had a few words about that. I told him if she respected his room and stayed out of it, he should do the same with hers. Granted, we had moved into their house, but still, it was the principle of the matter.

T.J., bless his wicked little heart, was trying to make my life a living hell. I was used to a house being perfectly straight at all times. T.J., in a word, was a slob. Bethany knew better than to even *think* about going to school without making her bed. T.J.'s room was always a disaster area. Theo's solution? Close the door. Chile, please. Then there was the fact that T.J. was allowed to stay up as late as he pleased, make popcorn and leave the dirty bowl in the family room, or half eaten sandwiches or whatever other snack he felt like having or just generally do whatever the hell he pleased. I'm sorry, that just was not how I was raised. In my mother's house, you did as you were told, not what you felt like. And you'd better not think about shutting a door. Get real. It was either do as you were told, as in cleaning up your room, or when you came home from school, you'd find your window open and all of your stuff in the backyard. And Mandy didn't care if it was below zero. Then, not only would she kick your ass for not having a straight room, she'd kick your ass for making her waste her heat with the window being open all day, not to mention for making her have to go through that exertion. So that whole close the door shit was just pissing me off. Humph. Trust me, you never, ever, went out of my mother's house without having your bed military straight. You never left a dirty glass in the sink and you never, ever, left your towels on the bathroom floor. I was beginning to feel like the freakin' maid.

Then there was Chelsea, Theo's daughter. She didn't have a lot to say about us moving in, but I could tell she wasn't that happy about it. I think she's still trying to make up her mind as to whether or not she likes me. I mean we're only eight years apart in age. So it's not like I'm expecting her to treat me like some sort of stepmother or anything. I just want us all to get along. Surprisingly, she's taken a real shine to Bethany. And Bethy seems intrigued by her. With all that long hair Chelsea has, every time she comes over, all Bethy wants to do is play in her hair.

I also finally got a chance to meet Aisha, Chelsea's daughter. To my surprise, she doesn't look a thing like her mother. Everyone says that she looks like her father, whom Theo can't stand. From what I've heard about him, he doesn't sound like the nicest of people. Theo thinks that he's gotten Chelsea on drugs, and we're not talking about just joint either. But he loves Aisha to death.

Once Chelsea talked me into watching Aisha for a few hours while she had something for school to do. As I fixed her something to eat, she solemnly watched me as I moved around the kitchen. She has the oldest eyes I've ever seen on a child. Like she's been here before, as my mother would say. Anyway, when I fed her, she gave me the most beautiful smile. By the time Chelsea came back, we had bonded. Chelsea walked into the house, surprised to find Aisha all snuggled up on my chest, asleep. To my surprise, I was actually sorry to see her go home. Since that time, I have kept her a few times and I found that I enjoy having her around.

Now that I've settled into Theo's house, I was itching to redo it. Don't get me wrong, it's nice and all, but it is a little tired. It doesn't look like it's been updated in *years,* with the exception of the addition he added, and even that could use a little help.

As I'm sitting here sipping my rum and coke and looking around the house, I'm thinking about what I'd like to do to the house just to keep from exploding about yet another wasted dinner. I had gotten home again, and after busting my ass to try and make a decent dinner, the only ones to eat it were Bethany and I. Theo hadn't gotten home yet, so I didn't know if he wanted it either. Probably not. Lately he'd been dropping his brother at Carol's house since they worked together and his brother's car wasn't working, even though he had to actually bypass home to take his brother to Southwest Philly. By the time he got home, he was too tired to eat. So much for those romantic dinners we used to have.

"Theo, baby. We've got to talk. This is getting to be ridiculous," I told him as soon as he walked in.

"What is it this time, Sara?" he sighs. Damn. He sounded tired as all get out, but I had to get this mess off my chest.

"I'm tired of making dinner and the only people to eat it are Bethany and I. What, your son can't eat my food?" I asked, feeling pissed all over again that Theo's son refused to eat my cooking.

"He's just used to eating his Aunt Carol's food, Sara. Don't take it so personally," Theo sighed, obviously not wanting to get into yet another argument about his son.

"Well how else am I supposed to take it?" as I drain my glass and fix myself another drink.

"I come home every day and try to make something good and he walks into the kitchen, bypasses what I've cooked and makes a damn bowl of oatmeal rather than eat what I've cooked. But when we go to Carol's on Sunday, he gorges himself like he has eaten in a week, which he hasn't because he won't eat what I've cooked! Now your family thinks that I'm not feeding the boy," I sulked, puffing furiously on a cigarette.

I found that I was smoking a lot more since I'd moved in with Theo. I've been drinking a lot more too, but we won't talk about that. I can only deal with one drama at a time and right now, this shit was working my nerves. Sometimes I felt like I was ready to bolt. But where was I supposed to go with no money and now, no furniture?

"Give it time, Sara. Maybe you're expecting too much too fast. You have to give the boy time to adjust."

"It didn't take Bethany that long to adjust, and she's younger than he is."

"Exactly. She's young. What am I supposed to do, force him to eat your food? I can't do that."

"Goodness no. God forbid T.J. should be made to do something he doesn't want to do, like cleaning up his room, picking up a wet towel or doing his homework," I snapped.

"Look, don't worry about T.J. He's really not your concern, he's mine."

"Oh, so it's like that, huh? Fine. Do what you want," I told him as I stalked into the bedroom.

I knew what was going to happen next. We were going to have a huge argument and then he was going to bring up his wife. I swear to God, if I have to hear one damn more time about his sainted wife, I think I will either kill him or kill myself. Jesus H. Christ! You would think this woman was the Second Coming to hear him tell it. Every goddamn time we get into an argument I have to hear, "I never had to deal with things like this with my wife. She didn't take every little thing to heart. She was so much easier going. Why can't you be more like her?"

I'm sorry, I know it may be wrong, but I was beginning to hate this woman. You would think that they never had one argument in the twenty some years they had been together. First of all, her pictures are all over the house. All over the mantel in the living room. All over the table tops in the family room. There's even pictures of her and Theo on the chest of drawers in our bedroom. I was just about tired of every-where I looked, were pictures of somebody who looked like she was accusing me of something I didn't know I was guilty for. Getting it on with her husband, maybe? And of course, we'd argued about that too. I felt that since I was here, that he could at least take the pictures down in the bedroom. When we had first started sleeping together, before I had moved in, almost immediately afterward, he would tell me about *their* sex lives. Because of that, once during a particularly vicious argument, I told him that there was only room for two of us in his bed, and that I would appreciate it if he could keep her out of it because there wasn't room in it for all three of us.

He was beginning to make me think something was wrong with me until I learned from a very talkative relative that they used to fight like cats and dogs over Chelsea. Of course, I felt it my duty to bring that up to him and he always tried to dismiss it as so much groundless gossip.

After I stomped off into our bedroom, I decided to call my girl Lela in Maryland. I figured since she was so far away, she could be objective.

After chatting for a while, while she caught me up on everything happening with everyone down there, I laid everything out for her.

"So, what do you think I should do? Am I wrong?"

"Well, you know you can be a little overbearing, Sara. And you know how you're used to always having your way."

"I am not!"

"Yes, you are. Don't you remember how we used to fight because you always wanted to do everything your way?" she laughed. We had had some knock down, drag out fights. But I had loved her too much to let it stay between us. She was like a sister to me. She was also a lot calmer than I could ever hope to be.

"So what do you suggest I do?"

"Theo sounds like a really nice guy, Sara. Give it some time. Maybe you should back off a little bit," she gently suggested.

Grudgingly, I agreed to think about it, as we promised to keep in touch.

Later that night, long after I had gone to bed, I woke to Theo's slow caressing.

"I'm sorry, Sara. I'm just not used to sharing my responsibilities for my son. I didn't mean to hurt your feelings. Just give me some time, okay?" he whispered in the dark.

"Sure, Theo," I told him, letting his touch make me forget my hurt and disappointment. Later, as I listened to his soft snoring, I was beginning to realize that Theo's son would always be Theo's son. It made me sad to think about that, especially since Theo was starting to call Bethany his daughter, which she delighted in. It was so easy to think about me, Bethany and Theo being a family. I wanted us to be one, but I wanted T.J. to be part of that family too. My instincts were telling me that Theo, Chelsea and probably other family members were never going to let it happen.

However, I was still having a problem with learning how to deal with the here and now of everyday living together. A couple of days later, I called my other best friend, the one person I felt could give me the best advice; my mother. She said to me, "Why are you running again, Sara?"

"I haven't left yet, Mom. I'm just thinking about it."

"Same difference," she sighed.

I told her I didn't know what she was talking about.

"Yes you do. Every time thing seems to get a little complicated, a little hard, or like you might actually have to work for what you want, you run. Think about it. You ran from Ohio because you felt it wasn't big enough for you and Bethany's father. You ran from Pittsburgh because you felt it wasn't big enough for you and your sister. You ran from Washington, D.C. because you just couldn't deal with the men there, even though the best relationship you had was with Lela and her family. Now you've got this really good man, and you're ready to run from him because you can't run his house the way you want to. Because you can't always have your way. I think I did you a great disservice by spoiling you like I did. But you were my last one and I was tired. I wasn't as strict with you as I was with the other girls. Give it a chance Sara, before you chuck it, honey. Good men are hard to find."

Before I even realized I was going to say it, I spat, "How would you know Mom? Dad's no prize, you know!"

I heard my mother's indrawn breath and fully expected to hear a dial tone but instead for a few minutes, she was silent. Then I heard her sigh deeply.

"I guess you would feel like that, Sara. I'll admit, your father has been hard to live with sometimes, but my staying with him has always been my decision to make, Sara, not yours," she gently said. I could hear the sadness in her voice vibrating over the telephone line that connected us. I didn't really want to hear it. I had made up my mind a long time ago about the state of my parent's marriage. My mother was the most gentle person I knew. How she'd put up with a brute like my father had always been beyond me.

Interrupting my thoughts, she said, "But that's why I can see what a truly good man Theo is Sara. You are always so afraid that you are going to end up with someone like your father, that you not willing to give this man a fair chance. All I'm saying is, don't make the mistakes I did, Sara. After leaving Stephanie's father, I was so afraid to get involved with another man. A man whom I had been casually dating asked me to marry him. He was much like your Theo. He had his own business, was kind, gentle and treated me like a queen. His mother and I got along great. He even came from a very well-to-do family. And even though I had deep feelings for him, I turned him down.

"But why? That doesn't make any sense! Your life could have been so much better! Why did you turn him down?" I asked, curious. I had forgotten my own problems for a moment, surprised to get this unexpected glimpse into my mother's life. She had never talked about any of *this* before.

"You know your grandmother and I had always had a volatile relationship. She liked this guy, a lot. She always made such a fuss over him whenever he would come over. That was reason enough for me to walk away from him. She hated your father on sight. The more she talked down about him, the more attractive he seemed to me. I was old enough to know better, and I know that's no excuse. But she could always push my buttons."

"But your situation is totally different from mine," I protested.

"Is it, Sara? Your father really liking Theo has nothing to do with what's going on in your head?"

Okay. So she had a point. It did irritate the hell out of me how much Daddy seemed to like Theo. But that had nothing to do with what I was dealing with right now, I argued with myself. Or did it?

"All I'm saying honey, is to think first. Make your decisions carefully, and don't do something you may spend the rest of your life regretting," she said quietly. There it was again. I heard that slight catch in her voice, making my throat tightened with sadness for all my father had put my mother through. Pushing those thoughts aside, we chatted a little longer while I tried to make her laugh by telling her a funny story about something Bethany had done earlier in the week. Finally, I promised my mother I would think about everything and would call again soon as we said our goodbyes.

So I've been trying to be *mature* and deal with all the shit that's been coming my way, because deep down inside I know my mother is right. And frankly, I'm tired of going from relationship to relationship.

As my mother said, Theo, for all his faults, was a good man. He treated me with respect and devotion. He could be embarrassingly sweet. He treated my daughter like his own. He was gentle, but firm with her. She was beginning to go to him more often with her problems and woes than me, but I was okay with that. I was glad that they were building a solid relationship. However, it also made me realize that if I ever decided to bail on this relationship, it was no longer just about me. Bethany was getting old enough to also be affected.

This man had gone from being a no-name entity to being "Uncle Theo" and it was heartbreaking and heartwarming to see how her eyes lit up each night when he came home. Once she had said, "God saw that

T.J. needed a Mom and I needed a Dad, so He found a way to bring us all together."

Out of the mouths of babes.

Chapter Fifteen

However difficult the situation may have been from time to time for Theo and I, there was one area that we were united, and that was trying to get his niece out of her increasingly dangerous situation. It seemed like Terrell was kicking her ass for any little thing with increasing regularity. And no matter what anyone said, she defended him and she always went back. It was beginning to put a strain on our relationship.

Brenda had been missing a lot of days from work before I had left the old firm. I really wasn't that surprised after I left when I found out that she had been fired. Not only that, but I was becoming increasing worried about her bizarre behavior. Shortly before I left, I found out the reason for her strange behavior.

One day, right before we moved to the new office, she had rushed up to my desk with a small paper bag saying breathlessly, "Look what I just bought!"

When I looked inside, I saw a small glass pipe. I thought it was for smoking joint and said as much.

"No girl, it's for smoking cocaine. You know, crack."

"Have you lost your fuckin' mind?" I asked her incredulous, as I hustled her out to the hallway near the elevators so no one would over hear us.

"It's the bomb, Sara. I've never felt anything like it. And girl, when you're high from that shit, the sex is incredible," she gushed.

I know I was looking at her like she'd just lost her last marble. But she was my friend and I had to do whatever I could to make her see the light.

"Brenda, I'm begging you, please leave that shit alone. Terrell got you on that shit, didn't he?"

"So what if he did? He gives me everything I need, as much as I want and he's still paying all of my bills. Besides, I'm too smart to get hooked. All that shit they be saying in the news, it's just that, shit. Come on, Sara. You know I'm too strong to get strung out," she said confidently.

I was thinking that if she went out and bought a pipe, she was already strung out. And I told her as much. I also felt that I should bring up that she had missing a lot of days from work. Of course, she didn't want to hear it.

"Does your mother know what you've been doing, Brenda?" I finally asked her as a last resort to make her see what she was doing was wrong. I've always found that if you can't tell your mother what you're doing, there must be something truly wrong with it.

"Look, just because you're living with my uncle doesn't make you my aunt, okay? Keep my mother the fuck out of it, Sara. I mean it. It's none of her business. I'm grown, damn it, and it's not for you, Theo or my mother to judge what I do!" With that, she stormed off.

I could only look after her as she stomped down the hallway, her shoulders rigid, and shake my head as I slowly made my way back to my own desk. Should I tell Theo about it or keep it to myself? Brenda was correct in that she was grown, but I didn't want to see my friend become another statistic, either. For the rest of the day, there was no conversation between us. When I had to pass her desk, she made it a point to turn the other way. I was heartbroken that drugs and her loser boyfriend had torn our friendships to shreds.

When I got home that night, I couldn't stop thinking about Brenda and her predicament. As I found myself downing one drink after another, I couldn't help but to think what gave me the right to judge

Brenda's addiction, when I wasn't honestly dealing with my own? However, once again, I pushed those unpleasant thoughts away. I just wasn't willing to face that lady in the mirror. A few more drinks later, I was able to self-righteously convince myself that my drinking was no way nearly as terrible as Brenda's use of crack. I mean, it wasn't like I couldn't still get up and go to work the next day. I had never missed a day of work because of it, and really, I could stop any damn time I felt like it. So what if I felt like shit some days and it wasn't until after lunch that I would finally stop feeling hung over? By the time I got home, I was more than ready for that first numbing sip. But I wasn't an alcoholic, okay? I just happened to like the way it relaxed me after a hard day at work. So how come there was that small but insistent voice in the back of my head saying, *"who are you fooling?"*

That night I tossed and turned so much, Theo finally asked me what was wrong. I apologized for keeping him awake and mumbled something inconsequential to keep him from asking any more questions.

I had just gotten off the phone with one of my old firm cronies who couldn't wait to tell me all about Brenda being fired for missing so many days at work. But the thing that had really done it was her getting caught in the bathroom doing coke. At least, that was the rumor going around the firm. That made up my mind for me. I decided that when I got home, I had no choice but to tell Theo what was up with his niece. I felt bad for him. He already had nieces and nephews who were not allowed to come to his house because they were known drug addicts. Now he had to add Brenda to the list. I especially felt bad since she was the one who had gotten us together in the first place. Now I was supposed to tell her she was no longer welcomed in our house?

I couldn't help but to think about one of our last conversations together after she had dropped her bomb on me. Things had quickly deteriorated between us. For a while I had felt that with things being so bad between her and Terrell, I could no longer tell her anything good that was going on in my life.

Like how Theo had bought me a minivan so I wouldn't have to wait for him to come home if I wanted to go to the store or over Zoe's house. Not only that, with Bethany now involved in soccer, dance and gymnastics, I was always running her and her friends here and there.

When I had told Brenda about it she had snapped, "Well thank the hospital for killing his wife. That's how he got all his money, from suing the doctors and the hospital. Of course, he didn't see his way to sharing it with his *family*. Oh no, you just waltz right in there and get everything!" I had looked at her in shock. First of all, because I hadn't known anything about him suing anybody and second because I couldn't believe that she actually seemed to be *jealous*. After that, I stopped telling her anything about all the things Theo was doing for me. I wouldn't dare tell her about when he paid off all of my bills and put money in my credit union account. Or how he had bought computers for T.J. and Bethany so they wouldn't have to argue over who got to use it first. It seemed the easier my life got; the more she resented me for it.

When I got up the next morning, I decided that he deserved to know the truth. So instead of rushing out to catch the train, I asked him to drive me into town, even though I knew how much he hated rush hour traffic.

"Listen," I finally mustered up the courage to say, turning down the banter on the Tom Joyner Morning Show that was on the radio, "one of my old co-workers from the old firm called me yesterday."

"Oh yeah? That was nice," he said absentmindedly, his mind on the traffic.

"Not really. She told me some rather disturbing news. Brenda got fired the other day."

"For what?" he asked, a frown on his face as he glanced at me.

"Part of it was for missing so many days from work. From what I could gather, she'd been warned a number of times, but she kept calling out."

"Because of Terrell?"

"Sort of. Look, she told me something and I was hoping I wouldn't have to tell you this. I think she's been calling out partly because of him, but mainly because she's been using crack."

"*What? Aw hell no!* Don't tell me that shit! Do *not* tell me that she's stupid enough to be using that mess. She should know better than that. I mean, shit, her brother died from messing with that damn heroin. Maybe you're wrong, Sara."

"I'm not wrong, Theo. She showed me the pipe she bought and I tried to tell her to leave that shit alone. That was the other reason she got fired. She got caught doing coke in the bathroom."

"Get the fuck out of here! Oh shit! When did she show you the pipe?"

"Ah...a couple of weeks ago," I said in a low voice.

"Why didn't you tell me then? What the hell is wrong with you? If I had known sooner, maybe I could have talked some sense into her. I can't believe you didn't tell me something as important as that, Sara. Jesus H. Christ! What the hell were you thinking? Obviously, you weren't thinking. Shit! I can't believe this."

"Look, don't jump in my shit, okay? I tried to talk to her and I wanted to give her the benefit of the doubt. Besides, we have been dealing with our own raggedy shit, and I didn't think you needed anything else to worry about. Excuse me for trying to spare your feelings," I huffed, trying to bring my temper under control.

"Okay, I can understand that. But it wasn't up to you to think for me. But, you're right. Things have been, hectic, to say the least. Look, I'm sorry for jumping down your throat," he sighed. "My sister is going to freak when she hears this."

"I'm sure she is."

"Damn! I thought Brenda had more sense than that."

"So did I. But Terrell has made sure that he has her under his thumb now."

"I should have blown him away a long time ago," Theo muttered grimly.

I didn't say anything, but secretly agreed with him.

By the time we got downtown, we hadn't figured out anyway to help Brenda. Theo had finally concluded, "We can't help Brenda unless she wants to help herself."

True dat.

Chapter Sixteen

The problems with Brenda aside, I couldn't believe what a change Theo had made in my life. Of course we continued to have our squabbles, but by and large, things had never been better for me. However, I was surprised with people's reactions to my changed status, to my sudden good fortune.

Take Theo's house for starters. Although it may not have been where I wanted it from an interior designer's perspective, it was a hell of a step up from where I had been before. I was in a single house in Montgomery Township. My daughter was in an excellent school district. I thought my sisters would be happy for me.

The realty was a little less than I anticipated. With all the things that Theo was doing for and giving me, I couldn't help but to tell my sisters. It came as a supreme shock when I found out that they thought I was bragging and trying to rub their noses in my good fortune.

I had struggled for so long and had so little, that it seemed the only people happy for me were my parents. It was my mother who finally pulled my coat tails.

"Try not to tell your sisters everything that he does for you, baby," she had gently suggested.

"Why not?" I asked, completely not getting it.

"Well, they feel like you are just bragging, honey. I know you mean well, and you're excited about all the changes in your life, but you have to look at it from their perspectives."

"But I'm not bragging, Mom! I just can't believe the things this man has done for Bethany and me. I just wanted to share my good luck with them, that's all."

"I know, baby. But they don't see it that way."

I was so hurt that my sisters felt that way about me. It didn't feel right to have to guard every word I said to them.

However, my parents seemed to be really happy with everything positive that was happening for me. And even though they never asked for a thing, even with them, Theo had come through. Once when we were visiting them, my mother was complaining about how the refrigerator, which was the same one my uncle had bought my grandparents after a flood, still continued to leak from the next flood it had been in. So Theo went out and bought them a new one.

We took my mother to an appliance store on some pretense or another, and when she found one that she oohed and ahhed over, I found a way to distract her. While I did that, Theo paid for the one she had liked the best and arranged to have it delivered. When we got back to their house, I handed my mother the bill of sale. She went tearing into the living room and told my dad, "Phil, look at this! You won't believe what they just did."

"What the hell is this Mandy?"

"It's a receipt for your new fridge, Daddy," I told him, Theo and I beaming all over the place.

My father looked at it again, and I could see his hands shake and tears he couldn't hide rolled down his face. "Honest to Pete! Y'all didn't have to do that," he said, his voice shaking with emotion.

I couldn't help but to feel a little self-satisfied. Here was the daughter I had always felt he liked the least, who was doing the most for him. And a small part of me wondered if it would maybe make my father love me just a little bit more.

"I know we didn't have to, Pop. We wanted to," Theo told him, as he pulled out another piece of paper from his pocket. "Oh yeah, they're delivering the stove on the same day."

"What? What?" my mother said in astonishment as she sank into the nearest chair. Even I was surprised about that one. I threw my arms around Theo and kissed him, my eyes misty.

"Lord, Theo, the Lord is going to bless you, yes He is," my mother said as she got up and pulled his face down to give him a kiss.

My father jumped up and gave him a bear hug. He even hugged me with what felt like sincerity.

"Thank you, baby," I whispered to him, giving him a lingering kiss.

He just smiled and didn't say anything, basking in my parents' surprise and delight.

On the way home, I told him that I was really surprised to find out he had bought the stove also.

"I'd spend my last dime, just to see that beautiful smile on your face Sara," he said quietly. "Matter of fact," he continued, "I'd give everything I own to hear those words I want to hear and to make you happy."

That shook me. Who was this man, to do not only for my daughter and me, but now my parents? Who was this man with his heart in his eyes, ready to put it in my hands? And how could I continue to jealously guard my own heart and not give him the one thing he wanted from me?

"Why, Theo?" I cried, feeling panic-stricken.

"Because I love you Sara. I don't know any other way to explain it. How can I make you understand what you've done to my life? I loved my first wife, but she was the love of my life as a young man, a boy really. You are the love of my life as a man."

Shaking my head in the negative, I told him, "Don't, Theo. Please. Don't love me. I like you too much to see you get hurt. If you know what I know, you'll run the other way. I'm not what you need, and I'm not what you want. I can be such a bitch. You deserve someone a hell of a lot nicer than me."

"Why would you say that? You know what your problem is, Sara? You don't love yourself, so you don't think anyone else can either. And it's not just that you don't want to love. You don't think you deserve love. Usually when a person has such low self-esteem, it's because of the way they grew up. I've met your parents. I don't think it was your mother, she seems like she adores you. So it must be because of your relationship with your father. What did he do to you Sara?"

I was quiet for a very long time, as memories rushed at me. It seemed like I was always trying to get my father's attention. I had even mustered up the nerve one time to tearfully asked him if he loved me. He said he did, but for some reason it was never enough. He had said at the time that every day that he got up and went to work, he was showing that he loved me. But he never talked to me. He always seemed so removed from us. He never took the time to know *me*. When I was growing up, the only time my father was nice was during the holidays when he'd had his "snort" as he called it. Well, many snorts, actually.

And then there was how he treated my mother. How could a man who claimed to love me beat my mother? How could my mother continue to stay with him? What a horrible way to grow up, never knowing what was going to set him off. Constantly walking around on eggshells. That probably had a lot to do with why I'd always broken up with someone before they could do it to me. Or why I had no patience. If the relationship was looking raggedy, out the door they went. Or why I hated confrontations of any kind. Of course, that depended on who it was. I'd get up in a man's face quick, fast and in a hurry, if he came out of his mouth the wrong way.

But still, that never explained why my mother stayed with my father all of these years. Neither my sisters nor myself ever understood it. From what I knew of my mother's background, clearly she had grown up with no one to love her or make her feel special.

Her mother had worked as a domestic also, but was the kind that was a live in. So she had left my mother's care in the hands of relatives who had done nothing but abuse her and demean her. Every time she would tell me one of the stories of her childhood, I could always feel my heart breaking for my mother's pain. I would always picture a poor child just wanting somebody to love her for her; faults, freckles and all. My mother had said that her armor was her mind. Someone had once told her that people could take anything they wanted from you, but they could never take what was in your mind; so she'd become an honor student. She'd been crushed when the aunt who she was living with had told her it didn't matter how much she learned; she'd still be a nigger and that was all white people would ever see. I had always been so proud of the fact that my mother graduated from high school at the age of fifteen. She had wanted to go to college so badly. It was ironic that the mother, who had practically thrown her away, had ended up needing my mother. My mother had had to go to work to take care of her mother when she became too sick to take care of herself.

My mother had been briefly married to a man who let his mama do all of his thinking for him. Like my father, he had been a light-bright, damn-near-white, man. His mother had made quick work of destroying their marriage. He had never stopped being a momma's boy and had never gotten over how fine he thought he was. A few years later she'd met my father when they were both insurance agents. She had been his friend even when he went through losing his first wife to leukemia. Somewhere along the line, they moved from being friends to lovers, who eventually married.

I think my father really married my mother because he wanted a wife for his baby daughter, my sister Zoe. He mourned for so many years over his ex-wife, that I always wondered if he ever truly loved my mother. No wonder I was so fucked up. I think my mother stayed with my father because she had never gotten over the fact that she had another fair-skinned, good-hair man. They were the prizes back in the day, no matter what their faults were, and for some reason, my mother has never thought she was attractive. I guess because she had been told her entire life she was ugly because she had bright red hair and freckles as a child. I also think that when my mother found out she had been conceived as a result of my grandmother being raped, that she had always believed that she didn't deserve to be loved. My mother would always say that she thought I was so pretty, then turn around and call herself ugly. I would always tell her how could she be ugly when I looked exactly like her, without the freckles? No matter how hard I tried to give my mother some self-esteem, it never seemed to penetrate. Too many years of hearing negative things had ingrained themselves in my mother's psyche. On the other hand, when she wanted to get clean, Miss Amanda could turn it out! Girlfriend had serious style! When she got her glad-rags on, she would stand her full four-feet, eleven inches and you couldn't tell her shit. She *knew* she was cleaner than the board of health!

I tried to explain all of that to Theo, which was a first. I had never talked to anyone about how I felt. I didn't want to stop and think about what that said about our relationship, or about maybe how close I felt to him. I tried to explain that for most of my adult life, in my relationships, I had fluctuated between trying to please whoever I was with to telling them to go fuck themselves.

"Okay, I understand what you're saying. So, is that why are you're always pushing people away?"

"I do not push people away!"

"Yes you do. You said it yourself. When people fail to live up to your standards, you're quick to tell them where to get off. It's like you don't want to give anyone a chance to get close, that way they can't disappoint you or hurt you as much.

I've watched you do it with your sisters, even your own daughter. When she gets too huggy or playful, all of a sudden you get serious and chastise her for something stupid. Don't you ever see that crestfallen look on her face? And you're always picking at her to be perfect in everything she does. Poor thing. Nobody could ever possibly live up to your standards Sara. You put unnecessary pressure on yourself and everyone else. You need to relax more."

I wanted to argue with him, but to a certain degree, he was right. I did expect high standards from everyone. But I expected high standards from myself as well.

"Geez, I need a drink," I mumbled under my breath.

"About that. Don't you think you've been drinking an awful lot lately?"

"Probably, but I can only battle one demon at a time Theo," I sighed.

"You didn't seem like you were drinking that much when I met you. What happened?"

"Yes I was, you just didn't know it," I said with a nervous laugh.

"Why?"

"Why, what?"

"Why do you feel the need to drink?"

"I don't know, Theo," I said exasperated and a little sharper than I had intended. This was one subject I really didn't want to talk about. Told y'all I had a lot of baggage, remember? Anyway, I had known that sooner or later, this subject was going to come up.

After awhile I said, "I started when Keith and I split up. Actually, it was probably long before that. Whenever things seemed to be just a little more than I could handle. I come from a long line of drinkers. It's what we do to deal. What can I say? I'm a product of my environment. But when Keith and I split up, I had so much on me, all the bills and all the debt he had left me in, I just couldn't deal with it. I know that I have a problem, Theo, and I'll figure out a way to get out of it. Just let me work it out in my own way, okay?"

"But I don't understand, baby. I mean, I've done everything in my power to make you and your daughter's life easier. Why do you still feel the need to drink?"

Good question. If I knew the answer, I would have told him. How could I explain to him what I couldn't explain to myself? It also would have meant admitting things to myself that I wasn't ready to deal with.

Chapter Seventeen

Okay. This bitch in this office is starting to work my nerves. She picks at every friggin' thing I do. If I don't put the copy paper back, just so, she has something to say about that. If I ask for certain supplies, I never get them. Actually, that was no big deal. I just went out and bought what I wanted, including the in and out boxes on my desk. When Dave noticed the new boxes, he asked where they had come from. I told him I had bought them, the letter/mail holder and my own color block post it notes, along with my steno pads. He asked me why had I went out and bought all of my own supplies. While he's talking to me, he's looking at her like 'how come she has to go buy her own supplies?' I told him because it seemed like it was so hard for me to get anything I asked for. She was sitting there the whole time we were having this conversation. When he asked me for a receipt so I could be reimbursed, I just told him, "No, that's okay. When I go, they go." She sat there and looked stupid.

If I come back from lunch one fucking minute late, she's got a lot to say about it. If I go to lunch late because Dave or Sandy asked me to do something, she acts like I'm not supposed to get my full hour. But when she goes to lunch, she comes back up to a half an hour late. Of course, she always does that shit when Sandy or Dave isn't around. Or she'll order her lunch and *eat* while I'm at lunch, then take another hour for her lunch, effectively giving her two lunch hours. But all of that is piddlin' bullshit. It's her attitude that's working my nerves. I have never seen such a miserable person in my life. And will *somebody please* call the fashion police? Half the time she looks like she got dressed and did her hair in a closet with no mirror. I mean girlfriend is pretty damn ugly to start with, but her wrinkled clothes, tired hair and missing teeth don't help any either. Combine that with a miserable personality, and the result is one fucked up chick, okay?

I've also noticed lately that she's lost a ton of weight, sniffs a lot and always has her purse with her. When we first started there, she hardly ever used the bathroom, now she's in there all the time. I swear my arms are bigger than her damn legs. They look like strings hanging from her skirt. No shit. With what's been going on with Brenda, I'm beginning to think it's not a sinus problem, but a nose candy problem she has. That would explain the up and down mood swings. Hhmm. One thing I know about coke, some days you don't want to eat at all, especially when you're using. Been there, done that. But that's another story. Anyway, when you're not, you have a voracious appetite. Well, that's this chick. Some days she hardly eats anything but sweets or junk. Other times, she's scoffing full fledged three course meals. What's up with that?

I breathe a sigh of relief every day when 4:30 finally rolls around so she can take her depressing ass out of there. I breeze through the last half-hour, glad to be free of her demented ass.

Today, as soon as I got outside, I paused before continuing up the street to light my cigarette. When I turned around, who's standing in front of me but Frankie.

"Hey baby. Long time no see," he purred, sidling up next to me as I continued walking, trying to ignore his ass.

"Aw, come on, Sara. Don't be like that. Hey, how's the old head you dealing with? Excuse me, *living* with."

"How do you know anything about my living arrangements, Frankie?" I snap, baited into responding to him.

"I know plenty, and don't worry about how I know," he smirks.

"Why don't you get a life, Frankie, and leave me the hell alone? Damn!" I said in exasperation, tired of all this bullshit.

"Yeah, you tell that mu'fucka I'm going to fuck him up for what he did to me. Yeah, you tell him that," he says, like I never said anything at all.

"You know your ass is crazy, right?"

"Crazy like a muhfuckin' fox. Yeah. Believe that. Just tell him he better watch his back. Don't nobody take what's mine," he drawls, sounding too calm and sure of himself.

I, on the other hand, was anything but calm. "I was never yours, you asshole! Why can't you get that through that thick head of yours?"

"But you would have been if it hadn't been for him."

"No, I *might* have been if it wasn't for your stupid decision. Now, believe *that*." With that I walked away from him, praying that he wouldn't follow me. Before I went down the steps at Suburban Station, I turned around and saw him standing a few feet away, people swirling around him as he just stands there staring at me, with this crazy, maniacal gleam in his eyes. With a small shiver, I hurried down the steps to my train.

When Theo got home that night, I told him about Frankie's warning.

"Who do you think told him about you moving in here?" he asks before commenting.

"Who else? Brenda. She's mad as hell at me for not associating with her anymore. I also think she's jealous of how things have worked out for us and wants to put a fly in the ointment, so to speak," I sigh, disappointed that our relationship was no longer what it once was.

"But what are we going to do about Frankie?"

"I wouldn't worry about him. He's all talk, Sara. Please. I'm not hardly scared of that little chickenshit niggah."

"But he was in prison, Theo. He might be dangerous," I fret.

"So what's that supposed to mean? Hell, I've probably got a score of nephews who have been in prison. They bleed just like everybody else. Trust me. I'm not worried about him. I can take care of myself," he told me confidently, softly kissing my forehead before going into the family room to channel surf, totally unconcerned about Frankie and his threats.

I wasn't convinced. I think Theo was underestimating Frankie. I couldn't understand why his crazy ass wouldn't just let it go. Maybe I should introduce him to Priscilla and they could kill each other. Wishful thinking. Seriously though, it was like he was obsessed. I had seen a light in his eyes that hadn't been there before and I'd be lying if I didn't say that it had scared the shit out of me. However, I knew that the only way to deal with Frankie was to not let him see how scared I was.

Thank goodness it was Friday and I wouldn't have to worry about running into Frankie anytime soon, at least for the weekend. I didn't think he'd be stupid enough to show up at Theo's house, even if he did know where I was living. If Brenda told him where I was living, I hoped she remembered to tell him about Theo's rifle collection. Hunting deer and a crazy ass can't be that much different.

One thing I realized, it was nice to have someone to take my problems to. We may have our ups and downs, but the reality was that when the shit got sticky outside of our house, we faced it together.

I was beginning to think about the "L" word. A lot. For every argument we had, there were many more good times. Lord, he could get on my nerves sometimes. And then there were the times when it seemed that we were right on point, thinking exactly alike. And yes, he was still rocking my world. At this point, our sex lives were just fine, thank you very much. Even when I was mad at him, the sex was still all of that; the man had serious *skills*.

When we'd gone to my parents for Thanksgiving, however, I had learned that I had pretty good skills keeping quiet. First of all, I had been shocked when my mother had put us in the same bedroom. I had figured that Bethy and I would sleep together and she would put Theo in my grandfather's old bedroom in the back, next to the bathroom. When she had indicated that we were to share a bedroom, I had looked at her with wide, questioning eyes. She had just shrugged and said, "I was young once too, you know," with a small smile. Theo had laughed out loud, but I had felt distinctly uncomfortable until my mother told me to get over myself. Bethy had ended up pushing my father out of his bed and he slept downstairs on the sofa, near his precious television. Now he could watch television all night without my mother fussing. T.J., of course, had opted, to spend Thanksgiving with Carol. I had really wanted him to come, so that he and my parents could get a chance to know each other better. But, of course, what T.J. wanted, T.J. got.

Anyway, with Theo's midnight and early morning raids, I had found myself fighting hard to keep silent, so that my mother and daughter, who were right across the hallway, wouldn't hear us. It had only seemed to heighten the sensations.

I still hadn't told him the words, but I felt that he knew how I felt about him. It was becoming increasingly harder to think of my life without Theo in it. My parents, my daughter and my sisters all loved him, and I wondered if that was what was keeping me from admitting how I really felt about him. It was no longer just about him touching my body; he was also touching my heart. Those magical zaps were hitting harder, deeper and making the wall around my long frozen heart crack and melt faster than I had expected. And maybe that wasn't such a bad thing.

Chapter Eighteen

"I can't believe it's almost Christmas!" I told Zoe as we stroll around Willow Grove Mall on a Saturday afternoon. It seems like we had hit every mall in the area in the last couple of weekends: Montgomeryville Mall, Neshaminy Mall, Cherry Hill Mall, King of Prussia Mall and the granddaddy of them all, Franklin Mills. Some nights when I got home from work, Zoe would call and say that she heard that so and so store was having a sale on such and such and Bethany and I'd pick her and her five-year-old daughter Shanice up, and we'd be off and running. And let me tell you, it's hard as hell to do Christmas shopping when you have a curious ten-year-old and talkative five-year-old with you. Zoe and I were constantly running interference for each other if we saw a present for one of the girls while we were out shopping.

But it was fun to be shopping with my sister again. In the last few months, I had been feeling a little distance between my sisters and I; especially Zoe. We were the closest in age to each other, and I missed her company.

This afternoon, though, we had gotten a reprieve. Zoe's husband, Vaughn who was a cop, was off for a change and Theo had left the care of the body shop to his brother. We had left T.J., Vaughn, Zoe's sons Chris and Jonathan, and Theo in front of the big-screen in our family room hollering at some sporting event, happily munching on chips, pretzels, steak sandwiches, beer, and for T.J., Chris and Jonathan, soda. Bethany and Shanice were playing dolls in Bethany's room.

"Think we can finish up today?" I ask Zoe.

"Girl, I hope so. I don't think my feet can take anymore, especially after walking from one end of Franklin Mills to the other," she complained good-naturedly.

"Tell me about it. I felt like I had worked out I was so sore the next day. But I still haven't found that perfect gift for Theo. He keeps telling me not to get him anything, but you know I can't go out like that."

"Any ideas at all?"

"Nope. I don't think that there is a tool that he doesn't have. He already has a video camera, and he really doesn't need any clothes. He already has jewelry, you know, rings, chains, a gold link bracelet. That doesn't leave any options. So I'm stuck."

"What have you gotten him so far?"

"A cashmere dress coat, some wool slacks, a couple of sport coats, a few sweaters and a Napa leather three-quarter inch jacket and some towels. Oh, and a monogrammed Coach briefcase."

"Well damn, Sara! What the hell else do you need? Shit! A *cashmere* coat? You go girl. I'm scared of you," she said, sounding a little envious.

"Did you say *towels*? Why would you give him towels for a Christmas present?"

"A private joke. I hope he gets it," I laughed, thinking about the time I had struggled with his skimpy towel.

"You think that's enough?" I asked, changing the subject.

"Hell yeah! You win the lottery and not tell any damn body?"

"Well, no," I answer slowly, reluctant to tell her. I had forgotten that I had never told her about the account he had opened for me, with money I had found out, thanks to Brenda, had come from his settlement. When I had questioned Theo about it, he had told me not to worry about it. I had especially become curious when he started getting calls from financial planners. He did tell me that he had invested a healthy portion of it into stocks and such. Still, money had never seemed to be a problem anyway. Thank God for car accidents. Business was booming and he had said he was having one of his best years. So much so, he was meeting with an architect to discuss expanding the shop, since he had recently purchased the building next door to his shop. Hell, I could get used to this.

"So 'fess up. I know you're not making that kind of money from being no legal secretary to afford all of that. You're not doing anything Vaughn is going to have to arrest you for are you?" she joked.

"I doubt it since he's a Philly cop and we live in Montgomery County, dear," I answer flippantly. By this time, we were strolling around the food court.

"I'm starved. Let's get something to eat and try to find an empty table," I tell her looking at all the packed tables and effectively changing the subject. We split up and went to different eateries and met back in the middle, both checking out the table area, looking for an empty table. Finally, Zoe spotted one and said over her shoulder, "Follow me," as we wove in and out of tables.

When we finally sat down, there is a few moments of silence as we dug into our food, me with a charburger with bacon, cheese, fried onions and mushrooms with barbeque sauce, fries and bottled sparkling water; Zoe with a turkey club, chips and fruit drink.

I knew that Zoe was dying to start in on me again, so to forestall her I asked her, "Hey, did I tell you I got a Christmas card and letter from Lela?"

"That's your friend in DC, right?"

"Actually, she lives in Clinton, Maryland, a suburb of Washington. But yeah, that's her. She just got an unbelievable raise and her and her husband is having another house built."

"Wow! That's nice. I didn't know you two still kept in touch."

"Oh yeah! That's my girl. She's one of those really genuine people. I swear that there's not a malicious bone in that girl's body. I used to tease her about being so trusting and innocent. But for real, she's good people."

"You're lucky to have a friend like that."

"There were times when I was living down there that if it hadn't been for Lela and her sister, I don't know what Bethany and I would have done. Did I ever tell you, when Grandmother died, she gave me the plane fare to go to her funeral?"

"I didn't know that. She is a friend."

"Tell me about it. I don't think she knows how much I've always valued our friendship. She'll always be my sister-friend," I told Zoe with a smile, thinking about my friend.

For a few minutes, there was silence as we both devoured our food. I should have known it wouldn't last.

"So, are you going to tell me or what?" she started in on me again.

Sighing, I decided to just tell her. There really was no point in pretending I didn't know what she was talking about. I hated having to hide shit anyway.

"Theo put some money in my credit union account. He had a good return on some investments, and he was nice enough to share. End of story."

"Well damn! Investments, huh? I didn't think black folks had 'investments.' I knew he was tight, but I didn't think he was that tight! Investments. Well excuse the shit out of me. You go girl. I'm happy for you."

"Really, Zoe? Are you really happy for me?" I asked her, searching her face to see if she meant it.

"Of course, silly. You're my baby sister. I'll admit that I've been a little jealous. Hell, I wouldn't be human if I wasn't. But I remember that when I met Vaughn and he was doing all kinds of nice things for me, it seemed like you were just so happy for me. How could I feel any less for you?" she smiled at me.

"I'm so glad to hear that. You don't know how much I've been worrying that y'all was mad at me."

"Well I can't speak for the other two. But I think they're happy for you too. You know Gina's not about material things, and Steph, well, what can we say except Stephanie is Stephanie. As long as she's got her beer, she's a happy camper."

I thought that it was more than that with Stephanie, but for once I kept it to myself. Zoe and Stephanie were tight. What you said to Zoe was said to Stephanie and vice versa. I'd learned that the hard way.

"Yeah, well, whatever," I said, waving my hand slightly in the air in a dismissing motion, indicating that I didn't want to go *there*.

"You finished?" Zoe asked as she applied a fresh coat of plum lipstick to her lips. I could never figure out why my sister, who was so light, wore such dark lipstick. To me, the shade made her lips look bruised.

She continued with, "I'm pissed at Vaughn, so I think I'm going to finish putting a hurting on these charge cards." She got up and dumped her tray and mine of its contents.

"Why are you mad at Vaughn?"

"I found out he's having an affair," she stated matter-of-factly, as we strolled out of the food court.

"What? He's having a what? Vaughn?"

"An affair and yes, Vaughn. Some skeezer in West Philly."

"How did you find out?"

"You know my friend Patty?" At my nod, she said, "She knows the woman. This woman was going on and on about this great guy who she had been dating. Or should I say *doing*. Then she mentions that he's a cop. Then she said his name. When she said his name, Patty asked what his last name was. She didn't let her know how well she knew us, but she said if it was the same Vaughn Knight she knew, he was married. She asked the woman if she knew that he was married. She said yes, but it didn't bother her. She wasn't looking for a full-time thing anyway. As long as he continued to pay her bills and get with her a few times a week, she was content. So I figured my best revenge is to not leave Vaughn any extra spending money. I also reduced my hours at the hospital. He knows he *better* pay those bills at home first. I guess he must have forgotten who he's playing with!"

"Damn, girl. That's some deep shit. Vaughn? I just can't believe it. He seems like he adores you," I said, shaking my head in bewilderment.

"Yes, Vaughn. Will you stop saying 'Vaughn?' Sheeeet. This ain't the first time he pulled some shit like this. Y'all don't know the half of it. Everyone thinks that Vaughn is this great guy who likes to give awesome parties and cookouts. He can be a nasty motherfucker when he wants to be. You'd be surprised with the shit I've put up with over the years. But I got a trick for Mr. Vaughn. Humph. I can do him one better. The difference is, he'll never even know about my shit, unless I want him too."

I looked at my sister in shock. What rock had I been living under not to see all this going on? As we walked from store to store, purchasing this and that, I was trying to pick my jaw up. Zoe actually laughed at the expression on my face. Finally I asked her "How come I never heard about any of this? You and Vaughn had always seemed like the perfect couple."

"Because everybody doesn't feel the need to share every little thing going on in their lives like you do, Sara. I swear, you're like a bad refrigerator; you can't keep anything," she teased me.

I was insulted. Just because I liked to talk my problems out with my family didn't mean that I told them everything. There were some things I kept to myself I thought defensively.

"Oh don't look so insulted," she laughed, reading my mind. "You know you do. But seriously, you, like everyone else, always saw what he or she wanted to see when they came to our house. Vaughn is very good at charming everyone and making them think he's this great guy, with that 'aw shucks' act of his."

"Well, I damn sure bought it."

"Don't get me wrong. Vaughn is, for the most part, a good husband and father. He takes care of home and his kids. He just has a lot of shit with him that y'all don't know about. But I'm dealing with it in my own way. He thinks he's playing me? Humph. He's going to find out he played himself. Believe *that.*"

"I hear ya, sis. Gon' girl." What else could I say?

With a wicked gleam in her eyes, my sister hit the stores with a vengeance. If nothing else, her kids were going to have a *really* good Christmas! By the time we left the mall, we were both loaded down with bags and declared our Christmas shopping finished. I had even managed to find that one special gift I had been trying to find for Theo.

When we returned home, the guys were still hollering at the television set, but most of the food and snacks we had left were gone. However, the crowd had swelled, since a few of Theo's nephews had dropped by. Of course, no one had thought to turn on the tree lights or the lights around the house.

"Did the girls eat?" I hollered over the noise.

"Yeah, we had some hamburgers and fries delivered for them," Theo told me with a smile, his eyes holding mine briefly as I smiled back at him, before his attention was drawn back to the game.

"I saw that," Zoe laughed.

"Saw what?" I asked all innocent, trying to play it off.

"Guess it's going to be hot up in here tonight," she teased me.

Blushing, I told her, "Gon' girl," with a quiet, knowing laugh.

"So that's what love looks like. I'd almost forgotten," she teased.

"Love? What's love got to do with it?" I asked as we picked up the drinks I had fixed us. We looked in on Bethany and Shanice and satisfied that they were fine with Bethany playing a game of Shoots and Ladders with Shanice, we went back downstairs into the relative quiet of the living room. I put on the stereo on WJJZ before settling on the love seat opposite the sofa Zoe was languidly lounging on.

"Yes, love," she continued.

"I don't know about all of that," I said with a small frown.

"Oh come on, Sara! It's as plain as the nose on your face. At least to everyone but you."

"As you've told me today, you can't always believe what you see. Besides, I would have thought that you and Vaughn were the poster children for a loving couple. If y'all's shit could fall apart, what chance do I have?"

"Uh-uh, Sara. Don't go there. You can't base or judge you and Theo's relationship on Vaughn's and mine. Every couple is different, and that man in there loves you; I mean, really and truly loves you. And I think if you're honest with yourself, you'll admit that you love him, too."

"Maybe," was all I would say, as I looked out the front window. A sudden movement caught my eye, making me jump up and parting the curtains slightly, I just caught Franklin's mama's car slowly going down the street.

"Damn! I can't believe this shit. Theo's going to be pissed," I mumble.

"What's wrong?" Zoe asks, sitting up and watching me at the window.

"That idiot Frankie. I just saw him pull off down the street. He must have been parked up the street a little bit. This is getting ridiculous, Zoe. I don't know what to do. He's being a real pain in the ass."

"You really know how to pick them, Sara."

"Look, I don't need to hear that shit, okay? I know all of that already. If I ever forget, I'm sure y'all be happy to remind me," I snap.

"All right, forget I said that. He has a record, right? Maybe I can ask Vaughn to do something. He knows I'm mad about something, he just doesn't know what, so he's trying everything under the sun to keep me happy. Maybe him and some of his buddies need to give Frankie a little talking to, Philly cop style," she says meaningfully.

"Could he? Girl, I'm desperate. I just want him to go away."

"I'll talk to Vaughn about it," she assures me.

"Thanks, sis. I would really appreciate that," I told her gratefully.

Soon, all of Theo's nephews girlfriends, who had dropped them off, started showing up. By this time the game was over and it seemed no one wanted to go home, and we ended up having an impromptu party. We ordered out for pizza, cheese fried and more soda and then the card games started.

T.J. took the boys into his room and they all started playing Nintendo games while we adults played cards and talked much shit.

Later that night, as Theo and I snuggled in bed, we talked about how much fun it had been to unofficially host our first party as a couple. I could tell his family was still feeling me out, but by and large, I was beginning to feel more and more accepted.

After Theo made sweet, slow, love to me, and as I was drifting off, I fuzzily tried to define the feeling I was experiencing. I felt myself smile as I finally drifted off to sleep, having figured it out.

I was content.

Chapter Nineteen

It's Christmas day and all the presents have been opened, a fire is blazing in the fireplace in the family room and, much to everyone's delight, there is a gentle snow falling outside. It was looking like it was going to be a true white Christmas, a rare occurrence in Philadelphia. Smooth jazz is wafting around the house while the rich fragrances of butter, cheese, ham and turkey mixed with the earlier smells of apples, cinnamon and sweet potatoes continued coming from the kitchen.

"Mom, are the rolls done yet? The smell is killing me," I ask my mother, my mouth watering with the yeast and butter smell of her rolls baking in the oven along with a pan of macaroni and cheese. We had bought my parents down for the holiday, first, because I wanted them to see where I was living and second, because I hated the idea of them being up in Athens away from all the family. And speaking of family, in a moment of madness, we had invited everyone over for Christmas.

My mother, bless her, had the kitchen under control. She and Theo had started cooking last night. And since T.J. actually liked everything my mother cooked and certainly his father's cooking, I was pretty sure he wasn't going to eat just oatmeal today. With so many people coming, we had to start the night before. While Theo and my mother had been busy with the meats and some of the vegetables, I had been busy with my Christmas cookies. Surprise, surprise. T.J. had actually liked those too. Thank goodness Theo had an extra refrigerator in the partially finished basement. That area would also help with the spillover crowds. The plan was to throw all the kids down there. To facilitate that, there was an air hockey table, a pool table and an old television with a Nintendo already set up. For the little ones, there was a corner with dolls, trucks, push toys, etc., that I had picked up at the dollar store and discount stores to keep them occupied. Theo and I had worked frantically right after Thanksgiving to give the area a fresh coat of paint and we had put some inexpensive new furniture down there to make it like a second family room. If anybody knew how to make a space look good inexpensively, it was me. I had chosen to paint the basement in a soft cream color and then I had used a feather duster to apply a sage green and maroon pattern on the walls. Most people thought the walls were wallpapered at first. At any rate, there was finally a space where Bethany and T.J. could both enjoy together. At least when they were playing Nintendo together they weren't fighting and I do believe it was helping them to get to know each other. We had told them that it was an early Christmas present for *both* of them. So far, it had been working out.

"Sara, do you want me to put this next pan of macaroni and cheese in the oven?" my mother asked, carefully lifting a steaming pan out of the oven with butter and cheese still bubbling around the edges. After carefully placing the hot pan on the counter, she turned back around to the oven and pulled out a tray of golden brown homemade crescent-shaped rolls. One of these days, I was going to have to get around to getting my mother's recipe. I've never made homemade rolls in my life. What was the point when hers were so delicious? And I won't even talk about her sticky buns. Chile, please! Make you want to slap somebody they are so good.

"Yeah Mom. Actually, I think we can fit both of them in there now that you've taken the rolls out. Do you think three pans will be enough?" I asked, eyeing the three disposable silver roasting pans of macaroni and cheese, one of which my mother had just pulled out of the oven and the other two were still waiting to go in.

"I don't know dear. Are there that many people coming?"

"Oh I forgot. You haven't experienced one of Carol's Sunday dinners. Yeah. There will be that many people. Not only will they come and eat until they can barely move, but just like in our family, everyone will expect to be able to take a plate home. That's why I've been stockpiling aluminum foil and plastic bags from the grocery store. The best I can tell you is that when the food is ready, fix you and Daddy's plates, then get out of the way. You won't believe the stampede!" I laughed, not at just what I said, but the look of horror on my mother's face. Trust me, you had to have experienced a Watkins Sunday dinner to believe it. Having come from a very small family that had discreet sit-down Sunday get-togethers, it had been almost frightening as well as exhilarating to experience.

At one of Carol's dinners, the kitchen counters would usually be lined with the large silver pans, as well as any available space on the table, and sometimes pots would still be simmering on the stove. If everyone arrived at once, folks would come in, give a cursory greeting and head straight for the kitchen. Then it was utter chaos as everyone fought and jockeyed for a spot as you moved around the kitchen "dipping" up your plate, as the Watkins called it. You didn't "fix" a plate; you "dipped" up a plate up. Even the kids would get into the act. If you were at least age seven, you were on your own to fix your own plate. They would jockey for space right along with the adults, dodging elbows and hips as they fixed their own plates. Then it was a mad dash to get to the first available seat at the table or anywhere else you could find to park it. It was "*Soul Food*" taken to a whole different level.

For Christmas dinner, we were having three turkeys, two large roast beefs, four roast chickens, two pork loins, two ducks, half a dozen baked fish stuffed with crabmeat for those who didn't eat meat, mashed potatoes, macaroni and cheese, sweet potatoes, string beans, greens made up of collard, mustard and kale, shrimp fried rice, peas, cabbage and mashed potatoes and gravy. Not to mention regular salad, pasta salad and potato salad. Then there were the breads: fresh baked rolls, snowflake rolls, white, rye and wheat breads, all made in my bread maker. Whew! Chile, there was going to be some serious grittin' today, trust me. Then there were the deserts: Mincemeat pies, sweet potato pies, apple pies, peach cobbler, Angel's food cake, sticky buns and a variety of cakes. And no meal would be complete without washing it all down with the Watkins special, secret recipe iced tea.

"Honey, the snow doesn't look like its letting up any. Do you think it'll keep everyone from coming and we'll be stuck with all this food?" I asked Theo, worrying as I looked out the kitchen window. The snow looked to be coming down thicker and faster. Since a lot of his family had to come from Southwest Philly and Roxborough, I was worried they would decide not to come. I was dreading all the people, but I had worked like a dog getting the house ready for the holidays.

With Theo's blessing, I had turned the house into a Christmas wonderland. With the fragrant cherry and apple woods burning in the fireplace and the cinnamon candles burning, combined with the smells from the kitchen, the house felt and smelled warm and welcoming. Around every doorway were fresh greens woven with gold ribbons. Evergreens also adorned every banister, also with gold ribbons, but I had added small twinkling white lights. Gold, crystal and cream ornaments, with white lights graced the huge real tree in the family room. In the bow window in the living room, I had set up a Dickens style miniature ceramic village, complete with people, evergreens, and fake snow-dusted pathways lit with a warm glow. Around the entryway and around the fireplace and under the bow window, red and white poinsettias proudly displayed their beauty.

"You don't know my family. They never miss a free meal," he laughingly assured me.

"Gee, sounds just like my family," I chuckled. "Well, in that case," I continued, "I'd better get a move on getting ready. I look a mess and I will not have anyone catching me looking like this," I told him, looking down at my stained sweats.

"By the way, are you sure you liked your presents?" I ask him shyly as I briefly snuggle against his chest.

"Baby, I loved every one of them, especially the Billie Holiday framed poster. I thought the one I had of her in the gown and smiling was nice, but this one with her in front of a mike with a drink in her hand, is deep. It looks like the weight of the world is on her. Very thought provoking. It'll look great next to my other one. How did you know?"

"Lucky guess I guess," I beamed, basking in the warmth of his eyes.

"Did you like *your* presents?"

"Are you kidding me? My sisters are gonna die when they see what I got!" I laughed, then sobered when I asked him, "Are you sure this is what you want, Theo?"

"You mean even though you've never told me that you love me. Yeah, I'm sure," he whispered in his husky voice, lightly brushing my lips with a kiss as soft as a butterfly's wings. I felt a shiver as I looked into eyes that smiled into mine. A discreet noise behind Theo broke us apart. Looking around him, I blushed to see my mother keenly observing us with a small smile on her face.

"Did I hear you say you were going to change? I think I will too," she said as she removed her apron.

My mother and father are technically sleeping on the pull out sofa-bed in the family room but for dressing, they were using Bethany's room. After she gently closed the door, she turned to me with a smile on her face.

"I see you and Theo are getting along well. I'm glad. I told you before, I think he is a good man. You have chosen well, Sara."

My mother's compliments, while making me blush, made me feel slightly uncomfortable. While I like Theo for Theo, I was beginning to wonder if maybe I had chosen him more for my parents' approval than anything else. It was scary how much my parents liked him, especially my father. For years, my mission in life had been to piss Daddy off, not please him. Or had it? Could it be that somewhere in the back of my

mind I had figured out fucking up wasn't getting his attention? He figured it was the norm for me. So had I gone out and found somebody
that my father could finally approve of just to, dare I say, *please* him?
Squirming under her direct gaze, I say, "Yeah, he's nice. Things have
been calm lately."

"Good, I'm glad to hear it. I told you, you just needed time to adjust.
You'll see, things will settle down and you all will be just fine."

"From your lips to God's ears," I told her as I got up off the bed and
crossed the room to the door. Changing the subject, I said, "I'm going to
jump in the shower Mom. It's getting late and before you know it,
everyone will be here."

"All right, sweetie. I'll see you when you come back out."

After I closed the door, I paused for a moment, my back to the door, as
I let out a slow breath. Shaking my head, I moved down the hall to me and
Theo's room. Going through the bedroom to the dressing room between
the bedroom and the bathroom, I pulled open one of the wide closet
doors. Looking through my clothes, I pulled out a pair of black velvet
pants, a black velvet tunic top and my black suede ankle booties, laying
my clothes, bra, panties and stocking out on the bed and the shoes
nearby. Picking out a thick, long silver chain and some chunky silver earrings, I laid them out on my dresser before going to the bathroom for a
fast shower. I quickly dried off, dressed and threw my makeup on. While I
was dressing and making up, Theo had rushed in to shower and change.
He had chosen to wear a pair of gray linen slacks, a black crew neck wool
sweater and gray kid skin slip-on loafers. He had trimmed his beard and
after slipping on a thick herringbone silver chain and splashing on my
favorite cologne, Obsession for Men, stood back and let me admire how
fine he looked. Brother-man was looking good!

We finished about the same time and had barely gotten back into the
kitchen before the doorbell rang. Glancing at the clock as I went to the
door, I noticed that it was just a little after three o'clock.

After that first ring, it seemed the crowds kept coming and going nonstop. For a while it had been a joyful chaos with everyone exchanging presents and shouting to be heard over everyone else.

At one point in the day, Theo had tracked me down to a corner in the kitchen, quietly watching the ebb and flow of people in and out of the nearby family room.

"What's wrong, babe?" he asked when he saw the tears in my eyes.

"Nothing, Theo. It's just this is the most beautiful Christmas I have ever had. Thank you. Everything you gave me was so beautiful, but this by far is the most special gift ever. Your family and my family all here together. Thank you, thank you, thank you!" I told him as I kissed him all over his face.

"Humph, this ain't shit compared to that rock he gave you," Zoe said as she waltzed into the kitchen, having heard our conversation.

"Yeah, it is pretty awesome, isn't it?" I said as I held my hand out for the hundredth time to examine the one and a half carat solitaire brilliant cut stone with ten small round channel set stones, five on each side of the solitaire. I was fascinated with the sparks that flashed from it as I turned my hand this way and that. Pretty soon, a number of the women there had gathered around me to again examine my ring.

"So, did y'all pick a date yet?" Carol asked.

"She hasn't told me yes yet," Theo laughed.

"So what's she doing wearing the ring?" Stephanie asked, as they discussed me like I wasn't even there.

"I told her to try it on and see if she liked the fit," Theo told them, looking at me. I knew he was talking about more than just the ring.

"So? What's it going to be Sara? If you fuck this up, I'm going to kick your ass," Stephanie threatened, and not exactly playfully either.

By now, the whole house seemed to have gotten quiet and it seemed that everyone was waiting for my answer. I nervously looked around at all the expectant faces. Even my father had managed to separate himself from the football game on television as he came to stand behind my mother. Bethany was practically jumping out of her skin and T.J., who was trying to act like he really wasn't interested, had managed to work his way into the middle of the crowd to stand next to Chelsea. I could feel myself blushing to the roots of my hair. I looked at Theo and saw the expectant look on his face, even though he was fighting hard to play it off.

"Come on, y'all, give her a break. She'll tell me when she's ready," he said, trying to make light of the situation. But I still saw how his shoulders seemed to slump a little in disappointment.

"No, wait," I said, holding up my hand to keep anyone from moving or saying anything. "I'll answer now." Taking a deep breath, I moved through the crowd to stand in front of Theo. I stood in front of him, looking into his eyes, searching them, as I reassured myself that this was the right thing to do. I could tell he was holding his breath. Finally, I said, "Yes, I'll marry you Theo."

He let out a whoop and picking me up whirled me around and then planted the most incredible kiss on my lips. Suddenly, the room erupted into a cacophony of voices with everyone laughing, crying and congratulating us.

Chelsea, who had been somewhere in the middle of the crowd, finally came up to her father and me. I held my breath, waiting for her to say something that would spoil the mood.

"Are you sure this is what you want to do, Daddy?" she asked, searching his face.

"I wouldn't have asked Sara if I wasn't sure, Chelsea," he told her gently.

"Are you happy, Daddy?"

"Very happy, baby. I never thought that I would ever get over losing your mother. But I know she would have wanted life to go on for me. And I know that she would have been happy in my happiness. Please, don't spoil this, Chelsea," he told her, an edge to his voice.

For a pregnant moment, she didn't say anything. Then suddenly she hugged me and whispered in my ear, "If you hurt my father, you'll have me to deal with."

"I wouldn't expect anything less," I whisper back. When we break apart, we look at each other with tears in both of our eyes and for the first time, with a small nod, she gave me a genuine smile. Without words, I knew that I had just pasted a milestone.

"I can't believe it! She didn't fuck it up!" Stephanie exclaimed, prompting everyone in my family to laugh.

Later that night, after everyone had left, and the mess in the kitchen and elsewhere had been cleaned up, my parents, Theo and I sat around the family room. We were enjoying watching the Christmas tree lights as the fire warmly blazed while we listened to some soulful Christmas songs; a mix of R&B and jazz picks I had put on the CD player. Bethany and T.J. had long since retired to their own rooms stuffed, tired and happy with their Christmas haul. Santa had been *very, very* good to them.

"Sara, Theo, thank you both for such a lovely Christmas. We're both so glad we came, aren't we Phil?"

"Yup," my father nodded. Told you he was a man of very few words.

We all laughed and talked for a while about who had gotten what and how much everyone seemed to enjoy themselves.

Finally, I said, "I'm beat. Night y'all," as I got up and stretched, weary from the day's activities. After helping my mother pull out the sofa bed, and kissing her goodnight, Theo and I made our way to our own bedroom.

After our showers, and after one thing led to another, and another, Theo and I made love to the soft sounds of the music that played in the background. And as I climbed that stairway to heaven, of their own volition, the words 'I love you!' that I had been so afraid of, came tumbling from my lips. And this time, it was his tears that I tasted on my lips. And as I held this strong, gentle, wonderful man in my arms, I finally realized that besides my daughter, I held the world in my arms. My world anyway.

Chapter Twenty

"Oh my God. I can't believe this. Are you sure, Carol?" I heard Theo asking as I came into the kitchen. I had just gotten back from a fast run to the grocery store on Cheltenham Avenue, not far from our house. It was a bitterly cold February evening, and there was the possibility of a major snowstorm moving into our area. Although Theo kept the pantry well stocked, I wanted to pick up more snacks, soups and toilet paper, etc., just in case. I had also stopped by the video store and rented a bunch of movies in case we ended up being housebound for a couple of days. As I had pulled into the garage, the snow was just starting to drift gently through the trees.

Usually Theo did the grocery store thing. I hated grocery shopping with a passion, but since his knees were bothering him and he had been so tired when he came home, I had volunteered to go. Thankfully, I didn't have far to go and I hadn't had a drink yet. I refused to drive anywhere once I started drinking. I had a pet peeve against drunk driving. Hey, I might have been a lush, but I was a lush with principles, okay?

"All right, Carol. I'll call you back. Have you talked to Sadie yet? Well call me back when you get a-hold of her, okay? Fine. Talk to you later." he said as he put the cordless down on the counter instead of in its cradle.

"What's wrong?" I asked, alarmed when I had heard Brenda's mother's name.

"I can't believe this shit. It's just to fuckin' unreal!" he said as his hand slapped the counter hard.

"Theo, you're scaring me. What happened?" I ask again, starting to feel panic tighten my throat.

"It's Brenda. Oh God! I can't believe this."

"What? Jesus Christ, just tell me!"

Taking a deep breath, he exhaled and said, "Brenda is," he stopped, a sob choking in his throat.

"Brenda's what? Theo, please! Just tell me for God's sake!"

"Brenda is dead," he choked out, unable to hold back his tears.

For a moment, I just stared at him, not wanting to believe what I'd just heard.

"What? No! What? I didn't hear you right, did I? What?" Stop saying 'what?' over and over I thought stupidly to myself. I didn't want to, couldn't, believe what Theo had just told me.

"How? Was it drugs or Terrell?"

"Apparently, it was both. They got into a fight about some drugs and Terrell beat her to death."

"Get the fuck out of here! Where is he now, the son of a bitch," I spat. I was so angry that I could have chewed nails and shit bullets. I had tried to tell her sick ass to leave him and those drugs alone, but she wouldn't listen to me. Now she was dead. I know I'm feeding into my anger so I can forestall my grief.

"I don't know. Carol's trying to find out. She's going to call me back. Damn! I should have done more to get her out of that situation," he sighed, passing a weary hand over his face in an effort to wipe his tears away.

"You said it yourself, Theo. No one could help Brenda unless she was willing to help herself. I feel just as terrible as you do. I tried everything under the sun to make her see reason. I even went to see her after she stopped speaking to me. She told me to get out of her house and to leave her the fuck alone and let her live her life as she saw fit. There wasn't anything else we could have done."

"Yes there was, but I didn't want to take that step. I should have let Romeo dust his ass when he wanted to. You know 'Rome. He'd kill you as soon as look at you, then sit there and eat over your dead body. And he wasn't happy about what was happening with his sister. Neither was Jeff. I told him it wasn't worth his going back to jail. Now, I'm not so sure."

"You did the right thing, Theo. You know you couldn't have lived with that on your conscience. But you're right. There's gonna be hell to pay. Oh Lord. Terrell better hope the cops find him first. Now there'll be no stopping 'Rome or Jeff. Not to mention her other brothers, Steven and Jared. And you know your other nephews Willie and Darnell are just as dangerous and just as crazy as 'Rome. Shit! This could be some serious shit. It was bad enough when Terrell put her in the hospital that time. I thought ya'll were going to have an old-fashioned lynching then. Now, there's no telling what might happen."

"Tell me about it," he said as he hung up the phone from trying to call Sadie again.

"I don't know how my sister is going to survive this. Brenda was her youngest girl. Up until she started this drug shit, she was the one who always helped her mother out the most. Even then, Sadie said she was still trying to help her. As quiet as it was kept, I think Terrell was dealing. That's why Brenda always seemed to have so much money even with doing crack."

"I didn't know anything about that. Why didn't you tell me?" I asked, hurt that he hadn't told me.

"There was nothing to tell. I was just doing some checking. I was hoping to have him removed, legally, from her life. Now it's too late," he said, breaking down again.

As I gathered him in my arms, I felt tears slipping down my own face for my lost friend, my own grief finally overtaking me as it finally hit me that Brenda was dead. As we weathered out the storm inside, Mother

Nature picked that time to hit with a vengeance. Without notice, snow that had started slowly and gently had gathered strength and was now coming down so thick, you couldn't see across the street.

At that moment, the phone rang, and Theo snatched it up. I nervously puffed on my cigarette, only catching snatches of his side of the conversation. After he hung up, he grabbed his keys and pulled his black First Down jacket out of the closet by the garage door.

"Where are you going?"

"To Sadie's. She's finally home and Carol says she hysterical."

"Please don't go out in this weather, Theo. Look at it out there," I told him as I shivered in the doorway and we both looked toward the open garage door. Just that fast, the streets and sidewalks looked to be covered in almost an inch of snow.

"I have to, Sara. There isn't anyone else who lives as close to her. We're not that far from Mt. Airy; everyone else is in Southwest or Roxborough. It's only about ten or fifteen minutes from here. I won't be long, I promise."

"I understand what you're saying, and it makes sense, but I don't like it."

"I know baby, but somebody should be with her," he reasoned.

I knew he was right, and had it been any other night but this one, with the weathermen predicting it to be one of the worst snow storms in recent history, I wouldn't have been so worried. Even though I was freezing, I watched as the automatic door slowly closed. Then I slammed the door to the garage and raced through the house to watch him as he pulled out of the driveway and slowly backed out into the street. My one consolation was that Theo is an excellent driver and, thank goodness, he's driving the Lincoln Navigator, which is four-wheel drive.

An hour later, however, I was worried sick. I had called Sadie to give her my condolences and to see if Theo was there yet. She had told me she hadn't seen him before breaking down crying about Brenda. After I finally got off the phone with her, I tried Theo's cell phone. Of course, he didn't have it on. I was trying to fight the rising panic I was feeling, and I was ready to tear out to search for him. Of course, I didn't because I couldn't leave Bethany and T.J. home by themselves. Not in this weather.

For what felt like the millionth time, I looked out the living room window and noticed that the snow was almost five inches deep. The newscasters were telling people not to go out if they don't have to, and kept breaking into the regularly scheduled programmed viewing with updates.

Another half-hour passed, and then another. Finally, when the phone rang, I was almost afraid to pick it up.

"Hey baby," had never sounded so sweet. Sagging against the kitchen counter in relief, I snapped, "Where the hell have you been? Do you know how worried I've been?"

"I know, darlin'. But people just can't drive a little bit out here in this snow. Then I saw a very pregnant lady with a flat and I stopped to change it for her. I couldn't believe nobody would stop to help her."

"Well you could have called on the cell phone! I've been going out of my mind with worry, Theo."

"I keep forgetting about that damn thing, Sara. I told you, I'm still not used to carrying one. Anyway, I'm at Sadie's. I've gotten her calmed down, called the funeral home, gotten things underway and Beverly and Sandra just walked in, so I know she won't be here by herself. I'm on my way home, baby."

"Be careful, Theo. I hear the snow is suppose to change to freezing rain."

"Will do, sweetie. See you when I get there. Hey," he says before I could hang up, "love you, baby."

"I love you too, Theo. Now hurry home, Boo, so I can stop worrying."

Forty-five minutes later, coming in on a gust of cold wind, I finally breathed a sigh of relief. In anticipation of his coming home, I had started a fire, made some popcorn and when he walked in, jumped up and filled a snifter with some brandy to warm him up.

"How's Sadie," I asked when he finally settled down in front of the fireplace.

"Bad, baby, real bad. I had to get out of there. When Beverly and Sandy came in, it was terrible. Between the crying and the cursing, I couldn't take it. They didn't want me to leave, but I told them I had to get home before the weather got much worse. Sadie looked like she was ready to collapse. I can understand how she feels. A parent never expects to have to bury one of their children. She's already buried a son; now she has to bury her youngest daughter," he says with infinite sadness.

I quietly agree with him. I couldn't even imagine how I would feel if something happened to Bethany.

I don't think either of us got that much sleep that night. We just held each other and tried to console one another, trying to make it through the night. Somewhere around three in the morning, I finally drifted off into a fitful sleep.

A couple of hours later I got up after untangling myself from Theo, having given up trying to get any meaningful sleep. When he started, I told him to go back to sleep, and throwing on my favorite fuzzy-wuzzy, as I called my favorite housecoat, groggily made my way to the kitchen. I made a pot of strong coffee and after grabbing a steaming mug, sat down at the kitchen table near the patio doors, and felt the slight chill emanating from the not so great insulation curling around my ankles, causing me to shiver slightly and wrap my hands a little tighter around the hot mug. Theo's German Shepard, King, ambled over to me and put his head in my lap. After allowing me to pet him for a few, he walked to the door, then turned to look at me with those soulful brown eyes, indicating he wanted to go out. When I opened the vertical blinds and went to open the door, I was stunned to see the amount of snow outside. There must have been at least a foot and a half and it was still snowing heavily.

"I don't know how you're going to get through that snow, King, but I guess if you have to go bad enough, you'll figure it out," I told him as I eased open the door, then gasped from the frigid blast that whooshed in. After quickly sliding the door shut after King went out, I watched him through the glass and had to laugh at his antics. Apparently, this was a dog that liked snow. He hopped and jumped and played outside all by himself. He even dropped down and actually rolled around in the powdery stuff. Finally having had enough, he did his business and obediently came back to the door. I made him stand there for a minute as I ran to the closet by the garage door to get the towels Theo kept folded on the floor for his baths before letting him back in.

When he came back in, he stopped right inside the door as he had been trained to do and let me dry him off.

"Good dog, King!" I was impressed with how well he'd been trained. After wiping up the puddles from where he had stood, I got a fresh mug of coffee and went into the family room and after starting a fire, turned on the TV and sat on the floor, King beside me, all dry and fluffy now, with his big head in my lap.

"Well here's a sight I'd never thought I'd see," Theo laughed as he padded into the kitchen. Grabbing his own cup of coffee, he joined us in the family room.

"I thought you hated my dog."

"No, I hated that he chewed up my favorite pair of shoes. He couldn't chew up a pair of my Payless shoes. No! He had to go for the one pair of real leather shoes I had at the time. I think he was trying to get rid of me. I guess he's gotten used to me now and has finally accepted that I'm here to stay."

"If he snuggles his head any further in your lap, I might have to get rid of him myself," Theo joked, watching King with a mock jealous look.

"Is that a fact? Jealous of your dog, are you?" I teased.

"The way he's all up in your lap, yeah. I'm ready to push him off and take his place," he said sounding half serious.

We both laughed as I got up and went back into the kitchen to get another cup of coffee.

"You couldn't sleep either, huh? Have you looked outside yet? I don't think anyone is going anywhere today. According to 'Action News,' all the schools are closed. So are the banks and City Hall, which means the courts are all closed. I checked my voice mail at work already. I'm off today. Not that it mattered; I was going to call out anyway. With no sleep, by eleven o'clock, I'd have been done."

"If it keeps snowing like this, you won't be going to work tomorrow either. There's no question I'm not opening the shop today. I'll have to call all my customers who were supposed to pick up their cars and tell them they will have to wait until the roads open back up. Thank goodness I went over to Sadie's last night. Brenda's funeral is on Saturday, so all the roads should be back to normal by then."

"Any word on Terrell's whereabouts?"

"No, I called Sadie and Carol before I'd even gotten out of bed. Nothing. No one knows where he is."

"Damn! I hope the police catch that asshole. He's going to pay for what he did, and this time, he's not getting away with it." Theo nodded his agreement.

For a while we just sipped our coffee and flipped through the stations to hear all the latest updates on the snowstorm. After a while, we got up and started making a huge breakfast. I knew as soon as Bethany and T.J. smelled those onions and peppers in the home fries cooking, together with the scrapple and bacon, they'd soon be getting up. Sure enough, as I was slicing the cinnamon raisin bagels, they both came stumbling in the kitchen, still rubbing the sleep out of their eyes.

"Both of you, turn right back around and go brush your teeth and wash your face and hands. By the time you get back, breakfast will be on the table and the hot chocolate ready," I told them. Since T.J. saw his father at the stove, I knew he'd eat more than just oatmeal that morning.

Theo and I had solved the food problem. I let him to the cooking. Hell, almost everyone in his family were gourmet chefs, and I had finally gotten tired of all the fights. Every now and then, I'd slip in something that I had fixed. T.J. had grudgingly acknowledged that there were a few of my dishes that he liked better than his aunt's, such as my greens, fried chicken and he *loved* my cornbread. He also liked the way I made my buttered noodles. Still, he was a kid who kept a lot of things to himself. He was kind of standoffish. But I'd gotten used to it, and I think he was finally accepting my place in his father's life. There were still issues regarding him that Theo and I couldn't talk about, much less work out, but I was trying to deal with it. So far, the pluses in our relationship were still outweighing the minuses.

Over breakfast, Theo shared the unhappy news about Brenda. Both T.J. and Bethany took it very hard. T.J., of course, had known Brenda all of his life as his cousin. Bethany had known Brenda for the last few years as my co-worker and then friend before her foolishness had torn our friendship apart. Even then Bethany had still referred to Brenda as 'Auntie Brenda.'

"Why does everybody I know keep dying?" T.J. hollered, jumping up from the table and running to his room, trying to keep everyone from seeing his tears.

"Don't let him be by himself, Theo," I advised, motioning Bethany back in her chair, who had jumped up ready to run after T.J. in an effort to make him feel better.

"Let his dad handle this, Bethy," I told her.

Bethany helped me clean the kitchen up as we waited for either Theo or T.J. to come back. By the time we were done, neither had yet come back into the kitchen. I sent Bethany to wash up and get dressed, as I returned to our room to take a much needed shower.

I was sitting on my side of the bed lotioning up when Theo quietly slipped through the door. He passed a hand over his weary face but not before I saw the moistness there.

"What happened?"

"We talked. First about Brenda, and then about my parents dying and finally, about his mother's death. He would never talk about it before. I never saw him cry about it. For some reason, what happened to Brenda just seemed to open it all up for him. God Sara, it was awful. It just seemed to pour out of him. I felt so helpless to help him. But maybe

now he'll stop being so angry about it, and allow himself to start heal-
ing. I hope so. I don't think I could go through that again. I feel as
though it's all my fault. That if I hadn't been so immersed in my own
grief, I could have better helped my son deal with his."

"You dealt with it the best way you knew how, Theo. That's all you
could do. It might not have been the best way, but there's nothing you
can do about it now. At least he finally got it out. Hopefully, as you say,
he'll begin to heal. Maybe in the tragedy of Brenda, some good has
come from it."

The afternoon went quietly by, with phone calls to be made regarding the funeral, people that had to be notified. Other than occasionally
wandering in the kitchen for a snack, the kids stayed in their own
rooms, with Bethany for once, wisely, leaving T.J. alone.

That evening, when the snow finally stopped, thirty inches later, and
while Theo had the snow thrower clearing the drive and sidewalks, T.J.
and Bethany, putting their sorrow aside, played in the snow. Life, especially for children, does go on. While standing in the window watching
them, T.J. suddenly turned and looked me directly in my eyes. Instead of
turning away as he normally would, he stared at me for a minute before
he shyly smiled and waved. Surprised, I smiled and waved back, before
letting the curtain fall gently back into place. It had taken me by such
surprise that I sank into the nearest chair.

Suddenly, I grinned and laughed out loud. Getting back up, I
watched as T.J. taught Bethany how to make snow angels. For once, it
seemed that she wasn't getting on his nerves. Getting tired of that, they
started having a snowball fight and then they decided to gang up on
Theo. I found myself laughing out loud as I watched the three of them
play in the snow. It warmed my heart to watch them playing together.
Somehow, I felt that we had just turned another corner. That maybe this
place I always referred to as "the house" would finally become a "home,"
and at last, we could *all* try to be a family. Who knows? Stranger things
have happened.

Chapter Twenty-one

Saturday dawned cold and dazzlingly bright with the sun reflecting off the new snow. We had gotten just enough of a new dusting last night to cover the dirty snow that had been plowed from the previous storm. At least I had gotten two free days off from work. The clouds lazily drifted across an azure blue sky. The branches on the trees appeared to be encased in crystal as the sun filtered through them, turning them into natural prisms. It was an achingly beautiful day, and it seemed a mockery to be attending a funeral.

As we pulled up to St. James Church in East Oak Lane, I wondered if the church would be able to hold all the people I saw milling outside. Theo hadn't been kidding. His family was huge. I had only met a small portion of them.

"My family may not be as tight as when my mother was alive, but they do turn out for a funeral," he whispered to me as we were approached by yet another group of relatives. It seemed that every one of his brothers and sisters were there, along with every one of their children and their childrens' children. Then there were the spouses, partners and friends of all those people. Whew!

My sisters Zoe, Gina and Stephanie had even come. They had known Brenda for almost as long as I had. She had been to every party Zoe and Vaughn had and up until she had gotten involved with drugs, she had always been welcome at every family gathering. They had been as shocked as I was when they found out that she was dead.

The church ended up being standing room only. Luckily, we got in before all the seats were taken.

I hate funerals. I hated having to say goodbye to someone I knew, cared about or loved. I intensely dislike having to get in that line and file past the casket and having to look in that casket and know that I would never share a smile or a joke with that person ever again. I hated knowing I would never see that person's particular smile or hear the sound of their heartfelt laughter. I really resented having to hear the preacher tell me that this was really a celebration because that person was never going to have to suffer or worry or hurt again, that they had gone on to a better place. I hated watching that person's mother, father, sister, brother, child, husband or whatever publicly fall apart, causing me to feel their pain mixed with my own. And somebody would always get up and sing a hymn so beautiful that it would make me fall apart.

Today was no exception to my feelings about funerals. Especially when I had to walk past my friend's mother and hear her ask me in anguish, "Why? Why did this happen?" and all I could do was shake my head in bewilderment, choking on my own tears. And then having to turn from her and walk over to see Brenda who was only twenty-fuck-ing-six-years old laying in a casket, not looking anything like my beautiful, vivacious friend. Who was this skeleton with the fucked up hair-do and gray skin? And I'm racked with this incredible guilt as I frantically think that there should have been something, *anything* that I could have done to keep this from happening. I felt my knees buckling when I felt Theo's strong arms grab me and help me as I stumbled back to my seat as we cried our hearts out.

And when the preacher started with his rhetoric, I wanted to jump up and say "Shut up! Just shut the hell up! How dare you say she's in a better place? Her place is here, with those who love her and miss her!" But I didn't. I just felt myself dissolve into more tears that I was unable to control. Today, the hymn that did me in was *"I'm Going Up Yonder."* I didn't think I could take much more after hearing that song.

Then there is that last tradition that I hated the most. The having to watch the family put that cloth over the dead person's face and them usually going to pieces. Their tears always make my tears come. There is something almost barbaric in that custom. Maybe the Catholics have the right idea. They have a viewing for a certain time, then they close up the casket and that's how it stays. You don't have to sit through the entire ceremony staring at the person in the casket, nor do you have to endure that second walk by.

And we can't leave out the final heartache. Going to the grave site, and putting those flowers on top of the closed casket and then, depending on the graveyard, watching them lower it into the ground. And wouldn't you know it, one of Theo's nieces, who has this incredible voice, decided to sing *"His Eye is on the Sparrow"* as they were lowering the casket. It was all I could do not to jump up and run for the car. Zoe squeezing one hand and Theo the other is what got me through it.

By the time the funeral was over and we all headed to Carol's house for the repast, I felt drained. My head was pounding and all I wanted was a dark room and full glass of rum. Fuck the Coke. Just give me a full glass of Bacardi's so I can pass out quickly and put this day behind me.

After we get to Carol's and I got something to eat, I felt the tension between my shoulders start to ease up. Thankfully, somebody had thought to set up a mini bar on the kitchen counter. Two fast drinks later, and a larger portion of the tension had started to disappear. I finally felt like that elephant that had been sitting on my chest all day had finally moved its heavy ass somewhere else and I could finally take a deep breath without choking on my own tears. Two more drinks and I'm in full socializing mode as me and everyone else tries desperately to pretend that this is just another family dinner and not the last hours of a funeral.

My sisters stayed for a little while but soon left, whispering words of encouragement to me before leaving.

Some people were telling funny Brenda stories and occasionally, you'd see somebody reach for a napkin to wipe at damp eyes, followed by watery smiles. After awhile the conversation turned to everyone wondering where the hell Terrell had disappeared to. Among the family toughs, there was plenty of conversation about getting even. Theo put an end to those discussions when he noticed how upset Sadie was getting. She had just calmed down from her last bout of crying. She was still asking anyone who would listen why this had happened to her baby.

Thankfully, the time finally came for us to go home. When we arrived, I fixed yet another drink, hoping this one would be the one to knock me out. Theo and I had almost no conversation, each of us dealing with our grief. Gratefully I slipped into a rum-induced sleep after taking a quick shower.

For once, Theo didn't fuss at me about how much I'd had to drink. I guess he knew I wasn't up for it tonight and decided to leave me alone.

My last thought before going under was, *I fuckin' hate funerals.*

Chapter Twenty-two

"Lord this sun feels good!" I exclaimed, stretching on the chaise lounge I was lounging on, taking a deep breath of the salt laden air.

"I'm glad I finally bought that smile back to your face," Theo smiled.

"Oh, you did! In a big way, baby," I tell him as I take a sip from the reddish-orange fruit concoction with the yellow umbrella in it.

"I just can't believe you did this Theo. You are the sweetest man alive."

"I couldn't have my baby so down. A man's gotta do what a man's gotta do," he chuckled.

And he had done it in a big way. I'd been so depressed since Brenda's death, that Theo had booked us on a cruise. It had been almost two months since the funeral, but I hadn't been able to shake my blues. I have to admit, a change a venue was definitely working wonders for me. This was our fourth day out to sea on a week long cruise, and with all the pampering of the staff and watching the waves, my weary, bruised soul finally felt relaxed. I looked around at the packed deck and breathed another sigh of satisfaction.

My parents had graciously agreed to come down to stay with the kids while we were away. I had wanted to bring the kids with us, but Theo had insisted that we needed this time alone. Now I'm glad I had listened to him. I had needed to get away from everything and everybody. I had been trying to deal with my grief over my friend and trying to deal with that evil bitch at work. What made having this week off even better, when I went back to work, she was taking a week off. Two weeks without her silly shit. Hallelujah!

Thinking about that now, I said to Theo, "I don't know what's better, being on a cruise or being away from Evilleen." That's what I had taken to calling her behind her back, Evilleen or Pricillyass.

"I thought we weren't going to talk about that bitch. I told you, she'll get hers."

"Yeah, I know. Still, it just burns me up the way she acts. And all over a stupid copy machine! Jesus Christ, why doesn't she get a fuckin' life?"

"I can't believe she has a job after the way she talked to your boss. If that had been an employee of mine, she'd have been out the door that day."

"I don't know why they keep her ugly ass. Shit, she needs to be fired just for being so fucking ugly. Now, since they didn't fire her after the way she performed, she thinks she can get away with anything. Sneaky bitch. She does all kinds of underhanded shit when they aren't around to see it."

"Calm down baby. You're getting yourself all upset again and the purpose of this trip was to cool you out."

"Okay, no more talk about Evilleen. I promise," I swear, hold up my right hand, as we both laugh at my pet name for her.

As I settled back on my lounger, I couldn't help but to think that there was something to be said for letting the sun kiss your skin while the ocean breezes gently caressed it. It seems to heighten your awareness of your body. It certainly seemed to make me more sexually aware. Ever since we'd pulled away from the dock in Miami, gotten settled in and started to enjoy the trip, Theo and I had been insatiable. I couldn't believe it. We were drunk on lust. It was absolutely fabulous and just what we needed. Maybe those thong bikinis were helping after all. I had bought them for Theo's benefit, but they seemed to have caused a minor sensation on deck whenever I wore them. Being depressed did have its benefits. I had lost about fifteen pounds and if I do say so myself, I was looking pretty sharp. As the sun kept making me darker and darker and the swimsuits were brighter and brighter, the combination was the bomb! Theo had actually insisted that I put a towel over me when he found that more than a few men were admiring my ass just a bit too much. However, he really seemed to get off on seeing me like that.

"What are you thinking about?" Theo asked, looking at the smile on my face.

"I was thinking about last night. It's always been my fantasy to do it outside, but that exceeded even my wildest dreams!"

He just quietly chuckled in that self-satisfied way that men have when they know they've effectively rocked your world.

And Chile, let me tell you, he rocked my world *unreal*! After another fabulous dinner, a great show and some time in the casino, we had made our way back to our stateroom, albeit more than a little tipsy.

After a shower and changing into something more comfortable, him in a silk robe with nothing underneath, and me in a sexy peignoir set, we decided to sit out on the private deck from our room. Theo had gone all out for this trip, bless his heart. Anyway, he was sitting on his deck chair with me sitting between his legs, leaning back against his chest as we watched the waves and counted the stars. Soon, however, his hands began playing with my breasts, and he started kissing me along the side of my neck and swirling his tongue in my ear. As always, I was again amazed at the warmth of his hands as they gently caressed my breasts, causing me to shiver with need.

Slipping off the chair, I knelt in front of him as I untied the belt to his robe, happy to find him already in a state of arousal. Bending forward, I took him into my mouth and worshiped his hardness, sucking and teasing him unmercifully. Luckily, the way our balcony was situated, we had a fair degree of privacy. It wouldn't have matter anyway. I was beyond caring if anyone saw or heard us. I let my mouth and tongue lavish the length and breadth of him completely. I tried to convey how much I loved him in my praise of his penis with my mouth. I could feel him shaking beneath my hands as he fought to keep from climaxing.

Suddenly pulling himself from my mouth, he pulled me up and made me lay down on the chair, which he pulled out so the back could be adjusted so that I was almost laying flat, but not completely. Pushing my legs apart, he placed his mouth on my sex, his tongue tasting, teasing and tantalizing me, coaxing my honey from me. He pushed my legs up and open wider to better accommodate himself, as he teased my bud to its own kind of hardness. Over and over his tongue teased me, bringing me closer and closer to that place I wanted to be. Without warning, I came, trying unsuccessfully not to shout too loudly, as I felt myself soar and burst apart like a falling star. Before I could come down, he jumped up and pulling me up and making me get on my hands and knees, in one smooth thrust from behind, entered me, causing me to climax yet again. Over and over he thrust into me; fast then slow, fast then deliciously slow and then fast and furious again. And I felt myself climax again and again, each time better and more intense than the last, until he finally stiffened and in one powerful thrust, I actually felt him as he shot long and deeply inside of me, as we each shouted our glory. At that point, neither one of us was capable of controlling whatever may have come out of our mouths.

Thinking about that now, I felt myself blush and then I laughed out loud.

"What's so funny?" Theo asked, a smile on his face as he too remembered last night.

"I was thinking about how that couple had looked at us when we all came out of our rooms this morning. The wife looked disapproving, but was I mistaken when I saw her husband give you the thumbs up sign?"

"No, you weren't. For a minute I didn't know what he meant, and then I realized that they must have heard us last night. Damned embarrassing."

"Yeah right. You've been grinning all day!" I teased.

"Like I said. A man's gotta do what a man's gotta do."

"Well in the words of Lee Bromowitz, 'You da man!'" I laughed.

Looking around at the teeming deck, I asked, "think anyone would notice if I went down on you now?"

"You wouldn't dare! Would you?" he asked, not certain.

Laughing, I just shrugged my shoulders as I threw a towel over his lap, and scooting my chair closer, put my hand under the towel. Snaking my hand under the band of his swimming trucks, I fondled the sleeping giant.

"Sara! Stop, or I'll be forced to stay here until I can get up and it's almost dinner time." he chided, but he didn't make me move my hand. In fact, he briefly closed his eyes, enjoying the sensations I was giving him and I quietly laughed knowingly.

Suddenly, he jumped up, forcing my hand away from him, as he loosely wrapped the towel around him and bending over, he began shoving my sunbathing paraphernalia into my big yellow mesh bag.

Gripping my arm, he pulled me up and said shortly, "Let's go."

As soon as we got into our stateroom and he had locked the door, he threw me on the bed, ripped off my bathing suit and shoved himself into my ready wetness. My soft laughter of triumph was quickly replaced with moans of pleasure as he slammed into me over and over again until we both came with a shattering intensity.

We barely made it to dinner on time. I knew my glow came from more than just sitting in the sun most of the day.

The rest of the cruise was spent on shore leaves during the day, sumptuous dinners in the evening and earthshattering sex at night. Once, we went to the very top of the ship, a la *Titanic*, but instead of just standing their pretending we were flying, we were getting busy. Talk about a rush! We almost got caught that time and laughed and giggled like naughty school children all the way back to our stateroom.

The last night as I regretfully packed our bags, I wished that I could just sail away forever, going from port to port, exploring new worlds and cultures. Sighing, I realized that as pleasant as the cruise had been, eventually we had to go home. At least I had a lot of pleasant memories to sustain me through the rest of the cold winter months.

I also had a secret that I'd yet to share with Theo. I just hoped that he would be as happy about it as I was.

I was pregnant.

Chapter Twenty-three

I know, horrifying thought, right? With all that drinking I've been doing, what the hell was I doing being pregnant? Up until a day or so before the end of the cruise, I didn't know I was pregnant. Now what do I do? Normally, there wouldn't have been any thought or question. I would have immediately scheduled myself for an abortion. But my life had changed drastically since the last time I'd found myself in this condition. I'd be lying if I didn't say I was terrified. How was I going to handle morning sickness and drying out? It was just too mind-boggling.

But as scary as the thought was, I had quickly realized that I really wanted this baby. With all my heart I wanted this baby. I wanted a chance to do it again and, hopefully, do it right. Not saying that I'd done that bad of a job with Bethany, but you learn what not to do with the first one. At least this time I was fairly certain that this man wouldn't run out on me.

However, first I had to be sure that I was even pregnant. So the first thing I did when we got home was to schedule an appointment with my gynecologist. It was all I could do not to blurt it out to my mother when I got home, especially when she commented that something about me looked different. I just played it off and said it was because I was well rested. She'd just smiled and said, "Mm-hmm."

"What?"

"Nothing. I suppose you're right. It must be that you're so rested," she'd chuckled. "By the way, did I tell you I had a dream about fish? I guess because you were on a cruise, huh?" she asked, looking at me expectantly.

I groaned to myself. My mother only dreamed about fish when somebody in the family was pregnant. I started to say something but decided that this was something I had to deal with by myself first.

In the meantime, I was struggling on a day-by-day basis not to fix that drink every night when I first got home from work or whenever I got in from one of Bethany's practices. I was trying to find things to occupy myself, so I went on a cookie making binge. The kids were in pig heaven. I was buying cookie magazines and books like penny candy and living at the supermarket buying all the regular and exotic ingredients for my concoctions. Chile I was a cookie-making fool. I was even taking them to work because I had so many.

I noticed Theo watching me, and at first, he didn't say anything. Lord was I a bitch to live with! I felt so sorry for him. I didn't know if it was raging hormones or me trying to kick the bottle or a combination of both. Whatever it was, I was baking one minute, crying the next and biting his head off the moment after that.

And sex? I couldn't get enough of it. When I wasn't biting one head off, I was either sucking or riding the other one. Finally one night when I went to reach for him, he moved out of the way.

"Sara, what the hell is the matter with you? Jesus Christ, I'm not a fucking machine you know. Excuse the pun. What has gotten into you lately? Ever since we got back from the cruise you've been all over the place. At least emotionally. First you're happy and laughing and the next you're like this caged *thing*, swatting at anyone who gets within striking distance. I'm almost tipping around my own damn house because I never know what's going to set you off next. What's up with that?" He looked bewildered and hurt at the same time.

"I stopped drinking," I whispered, my chin starting to quiver, not wanting to look at him.

"So I noticed. What made you stop?"

I just shrugged my shoulders, struggling not to cry. I finally gave up as first one tear came and then another and another until I was bawling like a baby. Sighing he pulled me over as I proceeded to soak his tee shirt.

"It's just so hard," I told him, sniffing and snotting all over the place, as I sat and reached over to the night stand to grab some tissue to noisily blow my nose.

"I know, babe. But I also know you can do this. You can do anything you set your mind too. But I'm curious what made you just suddenly stop."

Even though I had vowed I wouldn't say anything until after my appointment, I was on the verge of telling him. I was pretty sure that I was pregnant since I had been getting sick almost every morning and sometimes in the evening when I would try to eat dinner.

Still I didn't want to blurt it out when my face was all blotchy, my nose clogged up and me probably looking like a wild woman. I wanted to get the kids out of the house, fix a nice romantic dinner (even if I couldn't keep it down), and tell him when I was looking sexy and fabulous.

"I just did, Theo. I don't want to talk about it, okay? I promise that I'll try to stop being such a bitch. Maybe as soon as my body gets itself together, things will go back to normal. I'm sorry I've been such a problem," I sniffled, feeling sorry for myself, as I laid down, turned my back on him and tried to go to sleep. I could feel him looking at me for a long time before he finally got up and went to take his shower. By the time he got back I was already asleep.

On the day of my appointment, I was as nervous as a cat on a hot tin roof. The doctor had already examined me and I was again dressed and waiting for him to come in with the results.

"Congratulations, Sara, you're definitely pregnant," Dr. Pagano said as he closed the door to the examination room.

I let out a loud whoosh of air, finally glad to know for sure.

"Do you know what you want to do, Sara? If you are going to termi-nate, I need to know right away. You're about ten weeks gone."

"Ten weeks! I thought I was only about six weeks pregnant."

"Nope, from the feel of your uterus, I would say ten weeks. Of course, I'll send you right away for an ultrasound. That will give us a more def-inite expected delivery date."

"Ah, Dr. Pagano, there's something I need to tell you. I've, uh, been drinking rather, um, heavily, actually very heavily, lately." At his frown, I rushed on, "But as soon as I thought I might be pregnant, I stopped. Could something be wrong with my baby?" I asked, embar-rassed and concerned.

"I won't lie to you Sara, that could be a problem. But I'm glad that you told me. Although there is no one test that can be done to check for Fetal Alcohol Syndrome or FAS as it is commonly called, there are a few things we can do to get a preliminary idea as to whether or not your fetus could be suffering from FAS."

"And what might those be?"

"Well, ultrasounds can check for facial features, and alpha fetal pro-tein tests can check for brain abnormalities."

"But what about an amniocentesis? Wouldn't that just tell us everything?"

"Not necessarily. An amnio can check for chromosome abnormali-ties. The most definitive tests will have to be done after the baby is born, Sara."

"But that might be too late! The alpha fetal protein test. How is that done?"

"That's done through blood work. I can take a sample today and have it sent out right away. However, I still want to schedule you for the ultra-sound; one, to determine your due date, and two, to see if the baby's size is smaller than it should be for how far along you are. That will also help to determine if there is a problem. In the meantime, there's no point in you worrying yourself to death. We won't know for sure until the results come back. I'm assuming from this conversation you are anticipating going full term?"

"Yes, I am. But if there is something wrong, I don't know Dr. Pagano. I'll have to talk it over with Theo."

"All right, Sara. Just give this to my nurse on the way out, and she'll set everything up for you," he told me as he gave me the prescription slips for the tests and for the vitamins he wanted me to start taking right away.

"Thank you Dr. Pagano," I smiled weakly, determined to think positively.

After his nurse made my appointments for the following week, I rode home in a daze. *Pregnant.* I just couldn't believe it. And how was Theo going to feel about this? He was nearing fifty; surely he wasn't going to want to start a brand new family. And if he didn't want to, then what was I supposed to do? I honestly don't know if I could go through another abortion. I'd already had four; each worst than the one before. Just the thought made a chill run through me.

Who could ever forget that what it felt like in that cold, sterile room? That Valium they gave you to relax you before you went into the operation room did little to relieve the painfully sharp pinch you felt when they numbed your cervix and then the pain and pressure as you got dilated all at once. And then them telling you to be very still as they inserted the long vacuum needle into you and you feel it probing deep inside of your uterus as it scraps and scraps and sucks that new life out of you. And if they have the tank within your vision, the suddenly seeing the blood and what you know is your baby rushing through the tube into a giant jar. And the pain you feel is more than just physical, as you feel the sudden unexpected rush of tears. At least the nurses seem to be kind and caring as they hold your hand and pat your shoulder and tell you it is going to be all right, when you know in your heart it's never going to be all right. Then being wheeled into a recovery room full of other women who avoid eye contact with you and the sounds of muffled crying. And the nurse coming in to check your pad to make sure you're not bleeding to death. And you convincing yourself that there really was no other choice, as you beg God to forgive you for what you've just done. I don't care how hard and tough you may think you are. You'd have to be totally inhuman not to feel some sadness. You might feel relief because a problem has been solved, but somewhere deep down inside, you wonder if God will ever forgive you for what you've just done, while you try really hard not to think, 'what goes around, comes around.' It made me think that I was living on borrowed time. I'd had not one, or two, but *four* abortions. I kept thinking that there was going to be some major cosmic justice coming. I just didn't know when or what.

No, an abortion at this point in my life, was not an option. Of course, if the test came back that there is something was wrong with the baby, would I have the courage to carry it to full term anyway? I wasn't sure. However, if the test came back normal, then I absolutely was going to have this baby, no matter what. I vowed to myself, that this time, even if I have to do it alone again, I will find a way to make it work. I felt that this was God's way of giving me a second chance. I wasn't supposed to get pregnant. We had been very careful, but somehow, here I was, almost three months gone. *The best laid plans of mice and men* flitted across my mind. In the end, it was God who decided what would be what.

As an overwhelming emotion hit me, I had to pull over to the side of the road.

"Hey you," I said to my stomach. "If you're okay, then soon we'll get to meet each other. I'm sorry I didn't know you were there sooner. I'd never have knowingly put you in danger. I'm sorry, baby. Mommy didn't mean it. But we're going to get through this. You and me kid."

Feeling better, I went to the market and picked up some lobster, shrimp and filet mignon for dinner. I also picked up salad fixings, potatoes and vegetables. I stopped by the florist and picked up fresh flowers for the table. I went by the mall and after practically standing in the doorway to make my purchase because the abundance of smells made me feel sick, purchased some beeswax candles.

Rushing home with my purchases, I called Zoe as I began preparing dinner. Thankfully, it was a Friday, which meant that T.J. would probably be going to Carol's house. After hinting to my sister that I had a special night planned, she finally agreed to let Bethany spend the night at her house. As much as I hate driving on the expressway, almost the minute T.J. came in the door, I had him pack an overnight bag and I hustled him to Carol's house. After dropping off Bethany and suffering through my sister's teasing, I jetted back home to finish dinner, set the table and before taking my shower, laid the wood in the fireplace for later. I then showered, lotioned up and as a final touch, I applied fresh makeup.

"Damn, what's all this?" Theo asked when he walked in, sniffing the air in appreciation.

"Don't worry about it. Go take your shower and put on something comfortable," I told him mysteriously, shooing him out of the kitchen. While he showered, I loaded the CD player up with George Benson, Alfonzo Blackwell, Jonathan Butler, Patti LaBelle and Santana. I tiptoed near the bedroom door, and opening it a crack, heard him when he turned the shower off. After rushing back downstairs, I waited a few minutes, then fixed our plates, lit the candles in the dining room and started the fire in the family room. As a last touch, I hit the 'play' button on the CD player.

When Theo came into the kitchen, I pulled him into the dining room, proud of the beautiful setting I had created. The table was done in cream and gold, with the fresh creamy tulips in the heavy leaded crystal vase I had bought earlier serving as the center piece. The candles created interesting shadows on the walls and the music was a seductive background.

"Damn, baby. To what do I owe all of this? Where are the kids?"

"T.J. is at Carol's and Bethy is at Zoe's house. As for what all this is about, well, in a way it's a thank you for putting up with my shit for the last couple of weeks. And it's also because I have something I want to tell you," I told him, my voice fading as a feeling of acute shyness comes over me.

"You've been doing good, baby. Really. I'm so proud of you. I know it's not an easy thing you're going through, let alone by yourself. You know my brother Arthur is an alcoholic and he always had to go away to rehab, then to the AA meetings. I don't know how you're doing it like this. But I want you to know that I'm here to help you every step of the way," he smiled into my eyes as he stretched his hand across the table. I placed my hand in his along with my heart and trust, even though he didn't know that.

Taking a deep breath I said, "I have some news for you, baby, and I hope you'll be as happy about it as I am." At his expectant, questioning look, I pulled my hand from his and got up from the table, walking over to the dining room window.

"I can do this, I can do this," I was mumbling to myself.

"Do what, Sara?" Theo asked as he silently walked up behind me and kissed the back of my neck, causing a shiver to slither its way down my spine.

"Tell me, Boo," he whispered in that husky voice I'd come to love so much, as he gently turned me around to face him.

"Look at me, Sara. It can't be that bad, can it?" he softly said as his lips brushed mine.

Gathering my courage, I whispered as if someone might overhear us, "I'm pregnant."

"Are you sure?" he whispered back.

Nodding my head I told him, "The doctor confirmed it today." For a long moment we just stared at each other. Suddenly, he whooped and picking me up, whirled me around in a circle.

"We're pregnant! All right!" he laughed and started raining kissed on my face, which made me start laughing and crying at the same time in relief. He *wanted* this baby, as much as I did. I'd never told anyone before about me being pregnant that was happy about it. I guess there was something to be said for being with an older man, huh? And since that came up, let me tell you; girl get you an older man. They spoil the shit out of you. I mean really, look how much my life has changed!

"When are you due? How far along are you? How did this happen? Are you happy about it Sara? You are going to have it, aren't you? Damn! Pregnant! All right!" Theo said, firing one question after another at me.

Laughing I told him, "Hold up, baby! Damn! I can only answer one question at a time. I don't know the due date yet until I have my ultrasound next week. I'm about ten weeks; yes, I want to have it. But here is the other thing I wanted to tell you. I have to have additional test to make sure the baby is okay.

"Okay? What do you mean, okay?" Concern was evident in his voice. By now he had finally put me down and going back to my chair, I slid into it, unable to meet his eyes.

"Sara, talk to me. Whatever it is, we can handle it together, Boo."

Finally looking up, I said, "I told Dr. Pagano about my, you know, drinking. So he felt it warranted further tests. To rule out Fetal Alcohol Syndrome. If there is anything wrong, Theo, as much as I don't want to, I'm thinking of terminating the pregnancy." I was praying to God that this baby would be healthy. I knew without a doubt that I couldn't deal with a less than healthy child. At least I didn't think I could.

"As much as I wouldn't want anything to be wrong Sara, and as much as I would want you to go to term, no matter what, I respect the fact that it is your body, therefore your decision. I guess there is nothing we can do until we learn the test results."

"I feel so guilty. This is all my fault. If I hadn't been drinking so much, this wouldn't even be an issue," I cried.

"No, it wouldn't," he said, sounding a little bitter, but recovering said, "but neither one of us expected you to get pregnant, either. How did it happen? We've both been so careful."

"I think it was Christmas night, when we got carried away with me accepting your proposal. Remember? I don't think we took the time to stop and use protection."

"Oh yeah, but what a night!" he grinned, then leered, wagging his eyebrows at me. Suddenly, his expression got serious as he once again held out his hand to me. Wordlessly, I got up and went around the table and sat on his lap, where we proceeded to feed each other our dinner. Soon however, it turned into something more as I sucked the drawn butter from his fingers and he the steak sauce from mine. In no time he had me bent *over* the dining room table, both of us moaning our pleasure before I made him stop and pushing him into the chair, climbed on him and rode him to glory.

We finally made it into our room, and the night was an emotional and sensation filled memory as Theo loved me in turns fiercely and with aching tenderness that made me laugh, cry and sigh with pleasure. And the dawn, painted with colors that in some era must have made Monet jealous, was just beginning to steal its way into our bedroom before we finally fell into a satiated, exhausted sleep.

Before he fell asleep, Theo kept saying, like a mantra, "It's going to be okay, babe. Everything is going to be okay."

From his lips to God's ears.

Chapter Twenty-four

"You did very well, Ms. Livingston. You can call your doctor in a couple of days for the results," a nondescript lab tech was telling me as I sat up on the examining table. I had already had the ultrasound and he had just finished performing the amnio. We were still waiting for the alpha fetal protein test results. From what the technician had said, the ultrasound looked normal. The baby was the size it should be and even the head size appeared to be normal.

I drew a shaky breath as I looked at Theo who had been with me for both tests. At least we knew the baby was certainly active! That child had been all over the place during the ultrasound. However, when it came time for the amniocentesis, I freaked when I saw the size of the needle they had to use. It took all of Theo's powers of persuasion to make me go through with the test. Then after you see this thing that looks like it comes from Dr. Death's Chamber of Horrors, they have the nerve to tell you to stay *perfectly* still. Like you don't want to jump up when you feel that needle going through your belly button that they say is going to pinch a little bit. A little bit my ass! That bitch HURT, okay?

But thankfully, it was over. Now we had to go through the next torture. Waiting. Until we knew for sure, we weren't telling anyone about the baby. After all, there was still the chance that there wouldn't be any baby. Don't ask me how I'd made it through these past through weeks without taking a drink. Only the memory that it was my drinking that had put me in this torturous place helped to keep me sober.

At least I had stopped biting everyone's heads off. However, it had done nothing for the morning sickness that seemed to have kicked up a level or two. Chile, every morning I was praying at the porcelain god. I think I had dropped about fifteen more pounds and I looked better, shape-wise, than I had in years. I remember my mother always saying that a woman sometimes had the best shape of her life when she was pregnant. I guess so if you can't keep a damn thing down!

It was the middle of winter and if Theo cooked before he went to work, he had to put on his coat and open all the patio doors, garage door and front door to get any and all smells out of the house. Otherwise, the minute I got home, I was rushing for the bathroom and emptying anything that was left in my stomach from lunch. When I could eat lunch. I can't wait for this to be over because I'm starved! All I dream about anymore is food and eating as much as I want and keeping it down. I swear this is God's revenge on every woman suffering through morning sickness, He's somewhere up there laughing His ass off. He has a sick sense of humor, and I think He's still pissed at Eve for disobeying Him.

Right about now, I'd like to kick Eve's ass myself.

However, bless Theo's heart. He's there every morning with a damp, cool cloth for my face, which he tenderly bathes and leads me back to bed to lie down until I can get myself together to get up for work.

Now, as he helped me to get re-dressed, we avoided speculating about the tests. Neither one of us wants to think that anything could be wrong. In the few days since confirmation of my pregnancy and these tests, I think we have both gotten very used to the idea of being parents again.

"The technician did say that the ultrasound test looked good, right? I did hear her correctly, didn't I?" I asked Theo again for the fifth time.

"Yes, Sara. See I told you everything would be okay," he says again like he hasn't said the exact same thing four times before.

"Let's get out of here, I have a surprise for you," Theo rushed me, a mysterious smile on his face. The smile however, does nothing to mask the worry I see around his eyes that he's trying to hide from me.

After we left Abington Memorial Hospital, we headed up Old York Road. It was about eleven o'clock in the morning, and at least I didn't have to worry about rushing back to work since I had taken the day off. I'd had no idea the tests would be over that quickly. Anyway, after a while I noticed that we're in the Ambler/Horsham area and Theo had pulled into a new home development.

"What are we doing here?"

Theo just shrugs and gets out of the car. "I was passing by here the other day and wanted to bring you back to look at the model. I know how much you love looking at them."

"Especially since we are getting ready to do some more work on the house. Great way to get ideas," I told him with a smile as we walked up to what would normally be the garage but had been transformed into the office.

"I see you came back!" a perky lacquered blond said to Theo, smiling toothily at him.

"Yeah, I wanted her to see the house," he answers.

"Well just help yourselves. Take as long as you'd like," she gushed.

"I wonder how many cups of coffee she's had," I whisper to him on our way out the set of doors next to the door where we came in, to take the path leading to the front door, making him laugh.

"The landscaping is nice even though it's winter and there are no flowers; I like the way the flowerbeds are laid out and the boxwood and Japanese maple trees that they do have in," I comment as we walk up the half-circle, brick front steps, to the oval-shaped, frosted leaded glass, front door.

When we opened the front door, we were in a generously-sized two story foyer with a huge brass and crystal chandelier and golden oak hardwood floors that extended into the living room, dining room, study and on into the kitchen. I briefly looked into the living room, which was done in shades of sage and moss green with cream and the same soft greens in the furniture. The dining room had a smaller version of the chandelier, and was done in basically the same shades as the living room. However, the walls which I thought were papered, upon closer inspection I noted they were painted in a large harlequin design, with each diamond outlined in a thin line of gold. Back out in the hallway, I peeped into the very masculine looking study, noting the floor to ceiling bookshelves, along one wall, stained to resemble cherry wood, behind the antique, leather-topped desk. There was also a closet along the wall in the hallway, between the study and the powder room. Walking back through the dining room, I inspected the kitchen. The kitchen was huge with forty-two inch top cabinets, some glass fronted, a salmon, black and cream speckled granite topped center island with a cooktop that had been extended to accommodate four wrought iron-backed, padded burgundy leather-seated bar stools, and opened on one end to a breakfast room and beyond that, a family room. What I really liked the best about the area was that between the breakfast room and the family room, was a stepped wall with a see-through fireplace that could be viewed in either the family room or the kitchen/breakfast room area. In addition, the wall, instead of just being a straight wall, was cut out into a series of three steps that served as display shelves. Where the hallway was leading from the kitchen into the dining room was a split staircase. When you walked up to the first landing, you could either continue up or go down another set of stairs that emptied into the foyer. On the far side of the kitchen, there was a small hallway with a pantry, that led to the laundry room, a walk-in closet and the steel door to the garage.

Going up the backstairs to the second floor, I saw two nice sized bedrooms on one side of the house with a bathroom in between. As you walked toward the master bedroom, you could look over the balcony area either to the foyer on the right or into the breakfast/kitchen area on the left.

The bedroom next to the master bedroom, called a princess suite, had its own bathroom. The master bedroom was huge, with two generously sized walk in closets. It also had a sitting room to one side that was furnished with two cream, celery green and black plaid, silk club chairs, a stripped love seat, with small, fringed accent pillows in green, cranberry and cream, was done in the same hues and sat opposite a built-in entertainment center finished in washed oak. The windows in the sitting room, as well as the bedroom, were swaddled and swagged in the same silk as the love seat, casually tied back and allowed to puddle on the floor. Even though the furniture was large, dark and heavy looking, the overall effect was one of airiness and space.

The sumptuous bathroom had two sinks set into cream marble, a Jacuzzi tub big enough for two, glass enclosed shower, linen closet and the toilet was in its own little room they called the "water closet." The entire bathroom was in cream and taupe marble with gold accents. The swagged topper over the window above the bathtub was the same pattern as the chairs in the sitting room.

"This house is nice, Theo. The rooms are all perfect. Did you see the two rooms with the bathroom between? It would be perfect for the baby and Bethany and the room with its own bathroom would be nice for T.J. And I love this bedroom! It's huge! And the decorator must have been thinking about me. These are all my colors," I told him as I looked around at the soft greens and creams with touches of cranberry. "I don't know if I could get used to all this white carpet though. Especially with the kids and now with a baby? Could you see what this would look like in a few years?"

"Just replace it. No big deal," he said. "Other than the carpet, do you like the house?"

"Of course, you know what would work? You know those large Aubusson rugs I've been drooling over? They would work great in this house and help to save the carpet," I commented, not really listening to him, as I continued to slowly move around the master suite again. I kept sighing over the size of the closets. To have one where I could walk into it and not have to fight everything in the floor or on the rack.

"Sara!" Theo said, pulling me out of my musing.

"Hhmm?"

"Well, do you like it or not?"

"Like what?"

"The house! Damn, weren't you listening?"

"Oh! Well, yeah. What's not to like? It's brand new. Hell, who wouldn't like it?"

"Did you see the size of this lot? It's about an acre. Plenty big enough to put a pool in. And the deck is actually a decent size. Most model homes have those teeny-assed decks. But I like the size of this one, and even though it looks like wood, it's made out of that new man-made material that is suppose to no maintenance and won't rot," he said as we made our way back down to the kitchen.

"I hadn't noticed. But now that you mention it, yeah, it is a nice size," I tell him as I look out the French doors in the breakfast area that lead to the deck.

"Well, what do you think?" he asks me.

"Think about what?"

"The house. If it was available, would you buy it?"

"With what, my good looks?" I scoffed.

"Seriously, Sara. If it was available and the money was available to buy it, would you consider it?"

"With or without the furniture? Cause the furniture is slammin'," I say as I sink into one of the overstuffed, moss-green chenille chairs in the family room. This room also had a built-in entertainment center on the other side of the wall from the kitchen, next to the fireplace.

"However you would like it, with the furniture if you want."

"Well, in that case, yeah, I would love it if it came with the furniture, it was available and I had the money. Like I said, what's not to like?"

"True dat. Feel like looking at some other models?"

"Sure, why not. At least it keeps my mind off other things. Why are we looking at houses anyway? I thought we were going to just renovate the house you already have."

"I wanted to see what was out here and what the market was like. If I sold my house, added in what the new renovations would have cost, it may be easier just to buy a new house, one that already has four bedrooms and the extra bathroom."

"Oh. Makes sense I guess. I just don't know if I will have the energy to pull a house together by the time the baby gets here."

"Hhmm. I see your point. Well, you won't have to do much. Just tell me what you want done and I'll see that it gets done the way you want," he smiled at me.

By this time we had pulled up to another development sample. From the houses that were already in, I could see that, although they were nice, the lots appeared much smaller. After another toothy salesperson, this one brunette, we went through the house.

The first disappointment was that it was your basic house, which is okay, I suppose. I mean that's what it would look like if you'd had it built, but it wasn't a finished model. That aside, I noticed that some of the downstairs rooms were comparable with the first one we looked at, but the kitchen was a lot smaller. So were the bedrooms. All of them, and it only had a master bath and a hall bath.

Next we looked at two more developments and their sample homes, and both were the bomb! However, the prices were also through the roof. Theo suggested going back to look at the first one we had seen. I didn't know what for, other than to enjoy its ambiance. But since he seemed to be in a 'let's pretend,' kind of mood, I figured I'd humor him.

When we went back, this time I remembered to look at the basement, which was already partially finished with a small mini kitchen, an open area furnished with a sectional grouped around yet another fireplace, and another room that was set up like a billiards room. There was even a full bathroom down there. Once again, however, we were sitting in the family room, like we were at home or something.

"This house is really comfortable, don't you think?" he asked me, again.

"Yeah it is. I could get used to this," I said as I went into the kitchen and ran my hands over the granite countertop on the island.

"What if we bought something like this? Would that be okay with you?"

"But I thought you were getting ready to expand the shop. Could we afford something like this?"

"Let me worry about that Sara. If this is what you want, then this is what we'll get. "

"How come you never want to discuss finances with me? You wouldn't tell me how much your case settled for, or how much the shop renovations are costing, and now, how we can afford a new house. What's up with that?"

"I'm just used to handling the money matters by myself, that's all," he said, sounding a little defensive.

I was trying not to catch an attitude. I mean, damn, the man had just said he was willing to buy me a new house, so I guess I should be grateful. But I've always handled *my* money and I like to keep a handle on things. They have a way of coming back to bite you in the ass. Keith had taught me that when he left me with all his debts. I had trusted him and look what had happened. After that, I was always cautious about mixing my money matters with anyone else's. Speaking of which, I told him, "Theo, I don't have any kind of money to contribute to this project. I'm just a lowly secretary you know."

"You don't need money Sara. I told you I'll take care of everything."

"But then it would still be just *your* house, not our house, much like now." I didn't like that one bit.

"No, it'll be our house because both of our names are going on the deed, so what's the problem?" He was starting to sound a little impatient. We still hadn't left the house and as I was about to answer him, Toothy Smile came in.

"So, is everything okay? Did she like your surprise?" she asked Theo who was shaking his head like he was trying to shut her up.

"What surprise?" I ask suspiciously. After looking confused for a moment, Toothy made a hasty exit.

By way of answer, Theo threw me a set of keys.

"What's this?"

"Keys."

"Well I can see that, Theo! Don't be such a smart ass. Keys to what?"

"Keys to this house."

"To this house? But I don't under...*OH MY GOD! NO YOU DIDN'T! NO YOU FUCKIN' DIDN'T!*" I screamed as I jumped up and launched myself at him, almost knocking him over as I kiss him all over his face. Then like a rocket, I was off, racing around the house looking at everything again, only this time, I know it's ours. Somewhere in the distance I heard a car door slam and glancing out of one of the bedroom windows, I saw Toothy leave.

Racing back down the stairs, I ask Theo, "Where did she go? Are we allowed to be in here with her gone?"

"I would imagine we can stay as long as we like since we own it. I saw it right after Christmas when you agreed to marry me, Sara. I had put a bid in which was accepted, but didn't find out until we got back from the cruise when we could move in. I was going to tell you the same night you told me you were pregnant. I knew I had made the right decision, but with all the other things going on, I decided to wait before telling you. All that has to be done now is to add your name on the paperwork and for them to convert the garage back. I told them to leave it as it was so when I bought you here, you'd think it was just a sample. I had to pay a pretty penny to have her here today, but when I found out when your tests were, I thought that this would be the perfect time to bring you here. I hope it's made you feel better, baby."

"Oh God yes, Theo! It's like an omen, you know? What a wonderful thing you've done!"

"You're not mad that I bought the sample? That you won't get to decorate it your way?"

"Oh I can still do that, but I won't have to do much. For the most part, the house is exactly as I might have done it. Hell, this just makes my life easier. I hope the kids like it. Oh Lord, that means we are going to have to transfer their schools. And is there a train station nearby? How am I going to get to work? And what about the other house? I guess we'll have to put it on the market. How much was this house again? Did you buy it with the furniture? Wait. If you haven't sold the other one yet, how can we afford this one? Jesus, I just unpacked from the other move. Lord I hate packing. But who cares? *I GOT A BRAND NEW HOUSE!*"

Theo was laughing at me with all my questions that I really wasn't expecting to be answered. But he attempted to answer me anyway.

"The kids can stay where they are until the end of the year. We'll transfer them next year. I'll just drop them off every morning on my way to the shop. Yes, there is a station nearby where you can park and ride to 30th Street Station. As for the old house, I was thinking that I'd give it to Chelsea." I could tell he was waiting for my reaction.

"I think that's a great idea! We could leave the furniture and most of the stuff we don't want to take. The yard is a great size for Aisha; we could have a swing set installed before we leave, and I know how much Chelsea loved her Mom. Maybe she would feel closer to her there. It's a wonderful idea, Theo. Can you afford to do that, though? Don't you need the money from the sale of that house to help pay for this one?"

"No. This one is already paid for. Did you forget that I got a big settlement, Sara? I didn't want another mortgage. By the way, we move this weekend." At my look of horror he assured me, "I've already hired a moving company. You won't have to do a thing. Since this house is already furnished, and I'm going to give Chelsea the other one, it's not that much to move. Really just our clothes and whatever other stuff you want to take. Everything else, we are going shopping for today."

"Like what?"

"Pots, pans, dishes, whatever. It's your decision Sara, so you'd better look around carefully and figure out what it is you need. Oh, and yes, it came with the furniture."

"Well *damn*!" What else could I say? I got busy assessing what it was that we needed from the kitchen to the bathrooms, but the whole time, I couldn't get that grin off my face.

"Can we go get the kids out of school, Theo, so they can see the house?" I couldn't wait to see their reactions.

"Later. Right now, I think we should 'baptize" our new home, Sara," he said, his voice husky, as he picked me up and sat me gently on the island, like I was a piece of priceless porcelain, fragile and to be treasured, where he proceeded to kiss me breathless. Pretty soon, things got hotter and hotter and each new position meant a different room. Even the stairs was fair game. I didn't even notice until much later the rug burns on my knees and back.

Afterward, we rushed home to the old house to take a shower and get a change of clothes. I'm sorry, but I'm not going out to shop anywhere without washing my ass first. I could never understand when you watch movies or television shows, how they show people having buck-wild sex, then get up, get dressed and never wash their funky behinds. What, they think no one else can smell the funk on them, because trust me, unwashed sex is funky as hell. You be smelling like you want to be by yourself!

By the time we got done, the kids were already home. We even went and got Chelsea and Aisha and took them to show them our new home.

Bethany and T.J. were thrilled with their new rooms. Chelsea looked a little put out until we told her that she was getting the old house, debt free. Then she was just as excited as we were. She was happy to get out of the cramped apartment where she had been living in the Logan section of the city. Finally, Aisha would have room to run around in, not to mention the big backyard for the spring and summer months.

It was decided that we would move out on Friday and she could move in on Saturday. That decided, we all went shopping, and I even asked her opinion on some of my purchases and she shyly asked me to help her make the old house her own by helping her to redo some of it in her color choices. For the most part, she wanted to leave it like it was, but she wanted to redo the master bedroom and her old room that would now be Aisha's room. Theo generously offered to assist in the cost of redoing the two rooms for her. Then she was grinning from ear to ear.

Theo and T.J. went to sit out in the open court area of the mall while Chelsea, Bethany and I went racing from store to store, depositing our goodies with Theo and his son. Soon, they were surrounded by bags. When we finished, we all decided to shoot down to our favorite place to eat, Warm Daddy's in Center City, with its incredible soul food menu. We were all so pumped up that we laughed and joked through the entire meal, and for that moment, we felt just like a real family.

Since Christmas, things had improved greatly between Chelsea and me. The same could be said with my relationship with T.J.

Theo and I had decided not to say anything about my pregnancy until we knew what the test results were. It was hard as hell not to blurt it out. I wanted to tell them so badly, but if there was a serious problem, there was the possibility there would be nothing to tell. I didn't want to think about that at the moment, however. I was just too happy with Theo's wonderful surprise.

But somewhere in the back of my mind, I just knew the other shoe was going to drop, I just didn't know when or what it would be.

Chapter Twenty-five

"I'm sorry I can't give you a more definitive answer, Sara. The alpha fetal protein test was inconclusive. Had it been high, it might have indicated spina bifida or other malformations; low would have indicated a possibility of Down Syndrome or other chromosomal problems. However, these tests often have inconclusive results. Many abnormal test results are falsely abnormal and do not accurately indicate a problem with the mother or the fetus. However, the ultrasound came back normal. The amnio came back marginal. There *could* be damage and then again there might not be. As I told you, the only true test results can be gotten after the baby is born."

"Well what are we supposed to do now, doctor? How am I supposed to make a decision based on that?" I asked, overwrought.

"I can't answer that for you. I'm sorry, Sara. This is a decision you and Theo will have to make," he said as he excused himself from his office.

Fuck! Fuck! Fuck! Just what the hell was I supposed to do now? The silence in the room was deafening as I stood up and turned to look at Theo. Neither one of us knew what to say. While the test didn't say for sure that there was something wrong with our baby, it also didn't say it wasn't. We hadn't counted on this. We had hoped to know for sure one way or the other.

We got as far as the car. Theo stuck the key in the ignition and then slumped over the steering wheel.

"Now what?" I asked, dazed and confused myself.

Sitting up, Theo turned to look at me. "Forget all the bullshit, Sara. Imagine for a moment that this is a normal, healthy baby and you are having a normal, healthy pregnancy. Would you want this baby?"

"Of course I would. But it's not that simple, Theo."

"Yes, it is. Either you want it or you don't. Do you want to go through another abortion? And think about this. If you have an abortion at this point, since you are now past twelve weeks, they would have to slice it up and pull it out in pieces. Is that what you want?" At my slight shiver and negative shake of my head he continued with, "then I guess that's it. I guess we'd better get ready for a new baby." With that he turned the key in the ignition.

And just like that, the matter was settled. I didn't want to think about my baby being sliced and diced and he's ready to accept whatever God sends to us. I just hope there is more strength of character in me than I think I have to deal with a child who may not be perfect.

At any rate, I could now at least tell our family the news. I couldn't wait to tell my mother. As soon as we were able, we were planning on bringing my parents down for a visit. I hoped it would be soon because right about now, I really needed my mother.

My sisters were still reeling over my house. They couldn't believe it when they saw it. They were really going to be shocked when I told them about being pregnant. Their reactions had been mixed when they came to the house after we moved in. But, by and large, I think everyone was pretty happy for us. I couldn't wait for my parents to see it. I could just hear my mother saying, "Chile dear, I never thought one my children would end up living like this," as she clucked her teeth and shook her head, but I know that she would still be happy for me.

Hell, I was still in a daze about the house myself. Every time I walked in the door, I was amazed that my name was on something this gorgeous.

So Theo and I planned to have a family Sunday dinner and make our announcement. We had decided for the time being, however, that we would not tell them about the possibility of there being a problem. We had no problem sharing our joy. Our worry was entirely private.

Before telling the family, though, we felt we should tell our children. It went about as expected. Chelsea and T.J. were kind of quiet at first and, of course, we had to practically scrape Bethany off the ceiling. She'd been bugging me for years to have another baby, and when Theo and I had gotten together, she really had been dropping hints. However, once she became aware of Chelsea and T.J.'s underwhelmed reactions, she tried to calm herself down.

T.J. finally shrugged like it was no big deal. Chelsea just had to point out that her father was too old to be a new father. He got right in her world though. He told her, "Hey, you don't like me telling you how to live your life. What gives you the right to tell me how to live mine? Yes, I'm your father and I'll always be your father. But I'm a man too. Now, whether you like it or not, I happen to love this woman right here and I already love this baby. So you liking or disliking it is not going to keep it from being born. So I suggest you just used to the idea. You got that?"

"Yeah, I got that. Sara, you know I don't mean any harm. You know I don't have any beef with you anymore. I've come to accept you in my father's life and I'm glad that he has somebody. But surely you understand it's just a little hard on me. It's like my mother never existed. First he gets a new woman, then a new house and now a new baby. It's just a lot to absorb in so short a time."

"I do understand, Chelsea. But you have to understand, we never planned on having any children. This just happened. We thought we were being very careful. And I don't mean any disrespect to your mother, but life, my dear, does go on. I didn't know your mother. It's not like I set out to come between them. I met your father almost a year after she died. All I know is the life we are living now. And we want you to be part of that life along with T.J. and Bethany. This baby will be related to all of you. He will be everybody's brother."

"He? You already know it's a boy?" T.J. asked.

Smiling, I nodded in the affirmative.

"All right! Finally! I won't be the only boy!"

"Have you picked out a name?" Chelsea asked, finally smiling.

"We think we like Ian Charles," I told her.

"Ian. I like that. Very strong sounding," Chelsea smiled. Picking up her glass of soda, she said, "To Ian! Our new brother!"

I breathed a sigh of relief as Theo squeezed my hand under the table. That told me that he was relieved also. Having gotten through that, the rest of the family would be a breeze.

The next day, when my sisters came for dinner, they circled around me in the kitchen as I was busy trying to make sure that everyone had gotten enough to eat.

"Okay, what's up, Sara?" Stephanie asked me.

"I have no idea what you're talking about, Steph."

"Oh come on. This was practically a command appearance. You wouldn't have insisted that everyone be here unless something was up. I mean we've already seen the house. What, you just wanted another opportunity to show it off?"

"No, Stephanie. And I'm sorry you think me wanting my sisters to share in my good fortune is showing off," I snapped. I swear to God, Stephanie could try the patience of Jesus Christ Himself.

"Come on, Steph. Chill, okay?" Gina told her.

"Well what's up, Sara? You've been looking like the cat that swallowed the canary all day," Zoe added.

"There is something, but you'll have to wait like everybody else."

"Hey, we're your sisters. We should know first," Zoe objected.

"Okay, I'll tell you. Theo just expanded the business and we are celebrating its success."

"Bullshit! Do we look that stupid?" Stephanie asked.

"Do you really want me to answer that?" I couldn't help asking, laughing at the look on her face.

Gina choked on her glass of water, bursting out laughing when Stephanie rolled her eyes at her and sucked her teeth.

"You were always such a smart ass, Sara," Stephanie snapped, as she stomped off to the basement to harass the kids playing down there. After Gina left, still laughing her ass off, it was just me and Zoe.

"Well?"

I just smiled and shook my head.

Sucking her teeth, she left the kitchen, as Theo came in from the garage area.

"I think we need to make our announcement soon. I've been quizzed by almost everyone trying to get the inside scoop," I told him laughing and lightly kissing his neck.

"If you keep doing that, they will be asking where we went off to."

"Sorry, but I just couldn't resist. Do you think we should do it now that everyone has eaten?"

"Might as well get it out of the way. Then they can go home and the real fun can begin," he leered at me.

"Oh you!" But I still felt my pulse quicken.

After he had gotten everyone's attention, he said, "I'd like to welcome Ian Charles Watkins into the family!"

"Who's Ian Charles Watkins?" somebody asked.

"Oh didn't I say who that was? Gee, I thought I did," Theo said, messing with them. Pulling me next to him, he began to rub my stomach and said, "Did you hear that Ian? They don't know who you are. This, my dear family, is Ian Charles. My soon to be born son!"

First there was a stunned silence and then pandemonium. The men were grinning and slapping Theo on his back like he'd done some great, special thing and the women in the family immediately began talking about a baby shower, asking when I was due, how I was feeling and all the things women do when they hear about a new baby.

My sisters were totally shocked because they knew I had vowed to never have another baby. When they questioned me, I could only sheepishly shrug my shoulders and mutter, "Shit happens." Zoe had been quietly watching me. After awhile, she made her way next to me.

"I'm happy for you sis, but I get the feeling there's more to this story."

I looked at her in surprise. "Why would you say that?"

"I don't know. There's something, a sadness or worry I see in your eyes. What's the deal, Sara? You're my baby sister and I probably know you better than anybody. What's up?"

"I'll tell you later," I told her as one of Theo's nieces came up to me with her congratulations.

A while later, I told my sisters to go up to our room and when I came in, they all looked at me expectantly. I could tell that they had been discussing me among themselves. And even though Theo and I had agreed to keep the problems to ourselves, I needed to share my worry with my sisters. Our mother lived so far away, I needed to unburden myself with my family. I thought about what Zoe had said about me needing to share every little problem with my family, but this time it was different. I needed to know what they would think if I had a child that was less than perfect. So I told them, simply and bluntly.

Zoe was the first to speak up. "Damn, Sara. How are you and Theo dealing with this shit? I don't know if I could."

"Well so far, none of the tests have come back saying conclusively that the baby might have a problem. So we've taken the attitude that he's fine. We have to believe that or I think we'd both go crazy."

"Come sit down, Sara," Stephanie commanded. She was sitting on the side of the bed. Warily I approached her. Sitting next to her on the bed, she just looked at me for a long time. Then she abruptly pulled me into a fierce hug, and we rocked back and forth as both of us started to cry. Soon, Gina and Zoe were on the bed and we all cried and had a group hug.

I realized that no matter what problems I may have with my sisters, in true times of need, they would always be there for me. That only made me cry harder. Of course, the ever practical Zoe was the first to break the circle and go into the bathroom to get everybody tissues to get their faces together. Once we got ourselves together, my sisters told me, "You know we're here for you sis. If you believe this baby is fine, then we're behind you. But if it's not, we will not love him any less than any of our other nieces and nephews."

"Thanks y'all. I really needed to know that. Now I can tell you. Do you know that Theo bought this house for me to take my mind off all of this? That was the real reason we moved."

"Damn! I wish he had some single brothers," Stephanie joked, looking around my bedroom. "I love this furniture in here. Did this come with the house?"

"No. Theo had found this antique furniture in a shop in West Oak Lane. He took me by there on the pretense of looking at a sofa for Mom and Dad. I turned a corner and there it was. I fell in love with it the minute I saw it. I found out later that he had seen it earlier in the week and he liked it but wanted to be sure I did before he bought it," I said, running my hand over the dresser that was part of a nine-piece antique French Provincial bedroom set that included an elaborate head board, foot board, dresser, a chest of drawers, two night stands, dressing table and two mirrors. I absolutely loved this furniture, especially since it was a soft moss green with gold accents and went so well with the cream and taupe diamond patterned walls and off-white carpet in here. Under the bed I had an antiqued Aubusson carpet in soft sage green with taupe, rose, and cream colors.

"In any case," Gina is saying, "we can only hope for the best and we will be here for you Sara, no matter what."

"Thanks, sis," I tell her with a watery smile, grateful for their support.

When we go back downstairs, we find that a lot of people had already left. After my sisters made their plates up (don't they always!) they soon left also, but not before giving me reassuring hugs and kisses.

Later, when Theo and I finished making love, we discussed our families' reactions to our news, and decided that for the most part, it went

well. We also decided that we are going to have to come to some agreement on a wedding date. I would have preferred to wait until after the
baby is born because soon I'll be starting to show and I think it's tacky to
be in a wedding dress pregnant. However, I did want a traditional wedding in a church in some kind of pretty dress. Especially since the first
time I had gotten married at City Hall, during my lunch break. Seriously.
I got married on New Year's Eve, kissed that idiot Keith and went back to
work. I really wanted it to be special this time, which is why I felt we
should wait until after the baby was born and I had hopefully gotten my
shape back. Theo, however, didn't want to wait. He wants us to get married before the baby's born. Actually more like right now.

Like Scarlet, I decided I'd think about it tomorrow as I drifted off to
sleep.

Chapter Twenty-six

I would really like working here if it wasn't for this sistah of Satan. When I come in and I say good morning, she doesn't even have the breeding, good manners or home training enough to respond. Thankfully, I was raised better than that. *My* mother always said that 'breeding tells.' *My* mother always said 'manners will get you where money won't.' Apparently, some folks were raised in a barn.

I mean if you can't even say a simple freakin' 'thank you' when somebody says "God bless you," when you sneeze shows you have total lack of breeding and manners. That was this chick. Chile, please. The worst part was I didn't even know what she was mad at me for. The only thing I could figure out was that she hated my boss, and therefore, by association, she hated me.

Maybe it was the color thing. You know some of us are still caught up in that light versus dark issue. Like we don't have enough going against us, we have to still be holding that shit against each other. Personally, I have never been like that. I don't care how light or how dark you are. But some of us are still color-struck. How can you hold it against me because I was born light-skinned? Give me a break. Stupid, right? I never said she was playing with a full deck. Maybe she was just getting on my nerves because I was pregnant.

I still hadn't shared my news with my bosses. I wasn't exactly sure how to tell them. I certainly didn't want her to know. I had been trying to be civilized. I went out of my way to avoid confrontations with her. Finally one day I had had enough.

The morning started off simply enough. As usual, I came in, spoke and she didn't even grunt out a response. Talk about your lower life forms. Anyway, I had printed out something and when I went to get it off the printer, which was next to her desk, she had snatched all the papers out at one time. I'm standing there with my hand out so she could give me papers. Instead, she went right over my hand and threw the pages in a bin we had for print jobs. I guess I should have been grateful that this time she put them in the bin. I suspected on a few occasions, she had picked my work up with hers and had simply thrown it in the trash. There had been a few times when I *knew* I had sent something to the printer only when I went to get it, it wasn't there.

Anyway, I had been violently sick that morning and I wasn't in the mood for *anybody's* shit. So when she didn't just hand me my papers, I went the fuck off.

"What, you can't even give me my papers now, Priscilla? Damn, talk about being trifling!"

"Oh, you're so lazy now you can't walk over to pick up your papers?"

"No, I'm not lazy, but I was standing *right next to you*. How trifling is that that you had to pass over my damn hand to throw the papers in the bin?"

By this time, Sandy is in, standing at her desk, hearing this whole exchange. I could see his lips getting tighter and tighter. I didn't care. I mumbled loud enough for him to hear, "Fuckin' bitch!"

The rest of morning passed in icy silence. Other than my radio, it was so quiet in our area you could have heard a mouse piss on cotton. But the shit really got raggedy when I went out to get my lunch and came back.

I had gone to my new favorite eatery, Wolf's Market, where they have the most incredible grilled chicken sandwich on olive bread with grilled red peppers and caramelized onions. Chile, that sandwich is the bomb.

My other favorite place is Flip's Café. They have the best bread in the city for their hoagies. Instead of the usual gooey stuff you get at hoagie shops, theirs in nice and crunchy. Their sandwiches are so good that a famous comedian who is a native of the City and a famous Temple Alum, actually called the owner once to order sandwiches for a football game.

Anyway, it was one of those days where it felt like my lunch might actually stay down. So I'm tasting this sandwich before I even get back, thinking about grabbing my book and doing some serious grittin'.

When I got off the elevator, I noticed that the door to our conference room was closed.

"Is Dave in the conference room?" I asked Evilleen. She just ignored me. "Well, is he?" Instead of answering me, she threw her nose up in the air, made this snorting noise and sucked her teeth.

"That is so rude! I can't believe how friggin' ignorant you are," I snapped.

"If I am, I got it from *you!*" She growled. Gee, maybe I needed to call a priest to perform an exorcism the way she growled that one!

"Excuse me? I have no idea what in the hell you're talking about. All you had to do was answer the damn question, Priscilla."

"I don't have anything to say to you Sara," she snapped.

"Whatever," I replied giving her my hand to talk to. I knew how much that always pissed her off.

In response, she gets up and walks in front of my desk and then proceeds to *threaten* me with physical violence. Actually, what she said was, "We both know you ain't all that tough."

"You think so, huh? Well guess what, you keep right on thinking that, okay?"

"Yeah, well, we can do this!"

"Whatever." The hand again. I think that was what might have made her lose it.

Breathing hard, and practically pawing her foot like a bull before a red flag she hissed, "Bring it on! Bring it on!"

I'm looking at this pitiful bitch like she's just lost her last bit of sense along with that last non-decayed tooth in her head. Maybe the sizzling grease from her last press and curl had finally fried her brain. This was not happening. What *mature, grown* woman threatens another co-worker with physical violence in a law office? Does this sound like a person playing with a full deck? Obviously, the lights are on, but nobody is home and the premises have been vacated for a while. This goes well beyond having *issues.*

Okay, I had two choices here. I could get up, go into Lee's office and get his Louisville Slugger and proceed to start whaling on her skinny ass or I can take it to Dave. I opted to take it to Dave. Mama didn't raise no fools, okay? I burst into the conference room and in a most distressed voice, told him that she had just threatened me.

"What did she say to you?"

I told him what was said, on both our parts. His lips got tight.

"What am I supposed to do now? Just what the hell am I supposed to do?"

"You're not supposed to do anything," he sighed.

"Can I eat in here?"

"Sure, go ahead." But as I'm trying to eating, stewing in *my* pissivity, I noticed he was turning that really interesting shade of red he gets when *he's* good and pissed off. Suddenly he jumped up and stalked out of the conference room. When I got back to my desk, I noticed that she wasn't at her desk, and then I heard loud shouting coming from Dave's office. After awhile, his door was snatched opened and she stomped by my desk to hers. When the phone suddenly rang, it was Sandy, who asked for Priscilla.

"I don't have to be *aggravated by anybody!* I don't have to put up with that bullshit from anybody, especially *her!* After this morning she should have *known* better than to say anything to me!" After slamming down the phone, grabbed her purse and left. Around three-fifteen, Dave came out of his office and asked me where she was.

"I have no idea. I thought she had went to take the rest of her lunch, but she never came back." I was so upset, I called Theo on his cell phone and he came all the way from Montgomeryville, where he was picking up supplies, to pick me up from work.

"Sara, you've got to calm down. You know this can't be good for the baby."

"I just can't believe that shit happened. I mean, isn't it a little sopho-moric? Isn't that the kind of thing you do in *high school*? Jesus H. Christ. Mature, *stable*, grown women don't go around threatening co-workers do they? That is so ghetto!"

"As your mother says, breeding does tell."

"True dat."

Chapter Twenty-seven

"Hey girl. What's going on? Vaughn told me you called and you sounded funny. Is the baby okay?"

"Yeah, he's fine, Zoe. I was just calling to tell you about the trip I went through today at work," I told my sister. After I got done running it down for her, she said, "That bitch! She must not know who she's fucking with, right? Shit. I'm ready to come down there my damn self!"

"Girl, I'm not even going to trip about it. She made herself look totally stupid in front of the partners today. I already talked to Mom about it. She told me to let go and let God. I'm trying to girl, but it was all I could do to maintain myself today. But you know Mom raised us better than that. I wasn't sinking to the ghetto fabulous level, okay? Besides, in a split second, I weighed the options, and decided taking the defensive would be far better."

"What do you mean?"

"Think about it, Zoe. Who came off looking sillier? I keep telling you, some battles are like a chess game. Guess what? Checkmate!" I laughed.

"I hear you, sister-girl. You damn sure put her in check. She's lucky you didn't slap the black off her. But I don't know; if it had been me, I would have put my foot up her ass and worried about thinking it through later! You always did take Mom's rules to heart."

"Yeah, and you always ignored them!" We both laughed as we thought about how we were so different, yet so much alike.

"I also remember on more than a few occasions, you gave the rest of us a run for our money. Shit, you could almost kick my ass and I used to fight and beat *boys* when we were kids. So, are you going to work tomorrow?"

"Hell yeah! Like I'm going to let a lowlife, no breeding, no mannered, can't-have-a-good-hair-day-if-she-tried, cheap-ass clothing, hoopty-driving bitch keep me from my job! Chile, please!"

"Damn, Sara! Does she look that bad?" Zoe was cracking up.

"Worse! I was being kind, dear. She wouldn't know a piece of designer clothing if it came up and slapped her." I quipped.

"Girl, you are too much with your shit. Up until a few months ago, neither would you."

"Oh, I knew; I just couldn't afford them then. At least not retail. But if Mom didn't teach us anything else, she damn sure taught us how to have a sense of style. And that's one thing we *all* have in common, even Steph."

"As you always say, true dat."

"So, moving onto another subject, how are things with you and Vaughn?"

"Please. I don't even want to talk about that. Fine, I guess. I'm maintaining my happy homemaker image. But remember that guy we met a couple of weeks ago at the mall? I'm meeting him tomorrow for drinks."

"Get out! You don't mean that young stud, do you?"

"Yeah, that real chocolate, baldheaded brother. His name is Antonio. He might be young, but he sure talks a good game."

"Just be careful, Zoe. You don't want to do this just to get even with Vaughn."

"The hell I don't! Like I told you, he played himself. Another thing Mom always says is don't get mad, get even. Like what you did today. You kept a cool head, didn't go off, but you got even. Who did the shit fall on, you or her? Humph. Checkmate."

"But that was different, Zoe. You're talking about a marriage here. Why not just confront him and get it all out in the open?"

"Cause we've been down that road before. I don't feel like hearing the rhetoric again. That it doesn't mean anything. Or that he's ended it already. That he really loves me, while he's crying those phony crocodile tears and looking at me with those big puppy-dog eyes. I'm tired of it. I'm tired of the lies, the promises and most of all, being hurt. I really tried with Vaughn to make it work. Well, I'm sick of being constantly shit on and taken for granted. He thinks because he's made life so comfortable for me that I'll take whatever he throws my way. *Wrong.* Brother better get a clue. Until I can figure out what my next move is going to be, this is where I have to be. But that doesn't mean that I can't do something with somebody else that makes me feel good about *me*."

"I am so sorry Zoe. I wish I could do something to make things better for you."

"Yeah, well . We can't all have your fairy tale life, Sara." She sounded a little bitter and it stung, but I decided to pretend that I hadn't heard it.

"Guess what? I think I felt the baby move today." I told her changing the subject again.

"Must have been gas, you goose. You can't feel the baby move until you're about five months pregnant. Don't you remember?" She was trying to let go of the bitterness herself. I could hear the false joviality in her voice. But it was a sister thing you did when you wanted to move past the moment and not hurt the other one's feelings.

"I remember. Maybe I'm having an exceptional child who is advanced beyond the norm," I laughed, glad the moment was gone.

"Yeah right. Girl, let me go. Chris and Jonathan are upstairs trying to kill each other. I swear those boys are enough to drive me crazy sometimes."

"Okay sis. Catch you later," I told her but doubted she heard because she was already screaming at her sons before abruptly hanging up the phone.

I had been talking to my sister on the phone in my room. When I went downstairs to clean up the kitchen from dinner, to my surprise, I found it already done. I looked around the kitchen in amazement. They had done a damn good job. I could even hear the faint hum of the dishwasher, already going through its cycle. When I walked into the family, I found T.J. and Bethany grinning from ear to ear, obviously proud of their handiwork.

"Thanks you guys. I appreciate the help. I just hope y'all will be this helpful when the baby gets here."

"I will, Mom. It'll be like having a real live baby doll," Bethany piped up.

"Let's see if you still think that when's he's screaming his head off or you catch a whiff of one of those messy diapers. And lucky you, T.J. He'll just be on the other side of your bathroom." I laughed at the horrified look on his face. We had decided that since we were having a boy, Ian and T.J. would have the rooms divided by the bathroom and Bethany ended up with the bedroom with her own bathroom since she was now the only girl. Since there was already a full bathroom in the basement, we were in the process of adding another bedroom in some of the unfinished space. With a mini kitchen down there, it made for very comfortable guest quarters. There was the general area of the finished basement and also the other room that served as a pool room, complete with pool table, cue sticks and club chairs. We had also put one of those huge screen televisions down there. The men tended to congregate down there when we had company, while the women stayed in the kitchen/family room area. When the kids had friends over, they usually took them down there also.

"Did you both finish your homework?" At their affirmative nods, I told them, "Yeah? Well go get it and let me check it." Since the move, things had gotten much better with T.J. and I. Taking matters into my own hands, I treated him no different than Bethany and I had stopped taking a hands-off attitude with him and wouldn't let him get away with giving it to me. There had been some initial resistance, but things had settled down quite nicely. Now when I asked about homework, I got a response instead of a shrug or sullen look. Once he understood that I expected him to do his homework and to participate in his classes and would accept no less, he had finally started to get with the program.

I had also insisted on structured hours. Theo used to let him stay up as long as he wanted. I don't think so. That had been a huge battle. But bit by bit, I had gotten my way. The results had been slow in coming, but there was a marked improvement in his grades and his attitude. The biggest change, however, had been with him and Bethany. Suddenly they had become as thick as thieves. When they had started making friends in the new neighborhood, and her little girlfriends would come over, I noticed that she was introducing him as her brother. I heard him do the same thing with his friends and their friends just accepted it as fact. Since Theo and I were getting married, we had started investigating his adopting Bethany, which she was just thrilled about.

After I finished checking their homework, and sent them up to their rooms, I went looking for Theo. I found him in the study, working on his company bills, the glow of the computer screen lighting one side of his face. I quietly stood in the doorway as I watched him write out the checks and put each entry in the computer. When he finally noticed me, he smiled and beckoned me to come in and sit on his lap.

"You look tired, baby. Why don't you call it a night? You can finish this stuff in the morning, can't you?"

"Unfortunately, I can't. I'm working on payroll and I need to get this done tonight."

"Why don't you hire an accountant to do that kind of work for you? We have one who comes in once a week to do all of that. I could get his business card from him and he could come to either the house or shop once a week and take care of all of this for you."

"I don't know, Sara. I've always handled my business myself. I'm not sure I'm comfortable with turning that over to somebody else. It's like handing a gun to somebody and saying 'here, rob me.' I've heard some horror stories from people who lost everything because they trusted somebody else to handle their money."

"Well he must be pretty trustworthy. I mean these are lawyers and they don't seem to have a problem with him."

"I'll think about it baby," he said as he nibbled on the back of my neck. "Hey. How's my son today? That mess at work didn't bother him today did it?"

"Naw. Ian's just fine, aren't you baby?" I asked my stomach as I placed my hands over Theo's that were already rubbing my stomach.

Sighing, I told him, "This is so scary, Theo. I feel like maybe I'm a little too happy. I just have this feeling, this premonition, something awful is going to happen. I've never been this happy or secure. It almost doesn't feel right. Like I don't deserve it or something."

"That's silly, Sara. You just didn't have the right man in your life."

"No, I didn't have the right life!" I laughed, then getting serious, I tried to make him understand what I was feeling. "I've decided not to worry about what may or may not be wrong with our baby. We will deal with it when he gets here. But I have decided that no matter what, he's my child and I can't do anything else but to love him and care for him. If he has special needs, then we will deal with that. But that's not what scares me. It's all of this," I gestured around the room. "Who would have ever thought that I'd have a house like this or even a man like you. Why me? Why have things worked out like this for me, and Brenda, who introduced us, is dead? It doesn't seem right."

The room was silent except for the soft whir of the computer fan for a while before Theo quietly started to speak.

"When I met you Sara, I thought you had the saddest eyes I had ever seen. I thought for a woman so young, you had so many bad things that had happened to you. Remember when I first met you how you used to always say 'what's love got to do with it?'" At my nod, he continued, "Well I decided to show you that love has everything to do with it. I wanted to show you that not every man out here just wanted to use you and leave you. I wanted to give you everything that you never had, and to make your eyes happy eyes, not the sad ones I first saw and to bring a smile to that beautiful face. I wanted to give you so much love, security and happiness that you would never want to leave me. I told you before, I'd give you my last dime, just to see that smile. I never wanted any more children either. And then I met Bethany and I just love her to death, and I began to wonder what it would be like for us to have a baby. And when you told me you were pregnant, it was one of the happiest days of my life.

I love you Sara Livingston, and I want you to be my wife, my friend, my lover and the mother of my children. I want you to be happy at last and to enjoy what we have, both materially and emotionally." With that he turned me around and kissed me so passionately, it should have burned the house down.

Getting up from his desk, he led me upstairs to our room, careful to shut and lock the door behind us. He undressed himself and then me and led me into the shower, where he proceeded to torture me by soaping up his hands and sensually washing ever inch of my body, lingering over my breast and between my legs. Returning the favor, I did the same for him, feeling him lengthen and harden in my skillful hands.

After rinsing and toweling off, he led me to the bed and gently pushed me down on my back. Putting his hands on either side of my head, he leaned over the bed and gave me another body drugging kiss before trailing kisses down over my neck to my aching, pregnant-sensitive nipples. His tongue lazily stroking them made them even more sensitive but actually seemed to make them feel better, even when they tightened and seemed to extend, begging for more attention. As he slowly sucked one into his mouth, it made me cry out from the pain-pleasure he was giving me, before blessing the other one in the same fashion. Slowly he made his way down my body, licking, kissing and sucking until he was kneeling in front of me. Pulling me to the edge of the bed, he placed my legs over his shoulders as his tongue founds its way unerringly to the very core of me, which was already wet in anticipation. He teased and tempted me, bringing me to the brink of a climax over and over again, but never letting me have the satisfaction of climaxing, until I was begging and pleading with him to stop torturing me. I was literally shaking from head to foot and sounds I didn't know I could make were coming from me as I clutched at the bed linens, writhing in his hands that played a symphony I didn't know I had in me. Finally, blessedly, I felt him spread me open as his tongue did strange and wonderful things to me that made me see stars when I finally climaxed, as I at least had enough presence of mind to put a pillow over my face to muffle my scream of pleasure and release. I was still riding the aftershocks when I felt the head of his penis as it slowly rubbed at my opening before slipping inside and I sighed, removing the pillow from my face so that I could look into his eyes. I welcomed his fullness in my body. I could feel myself squeezing and stroking him with each slow, beautiful thrust of him. Over and over he would pull out slowly, and then quickly thrust back into my body, grinding himself into me and pulling out again. And I could feel myself becoming mindless in the pleasure he was giving my body. And through it all, we stared so intently into each other eyes, that it seemed that even though there was an intense physical thing going on, it was much more psychological. It was almost as if we were trying to get into each other's heads, and that only seemed to make the physical even more intense.

And I watched in amazement as his green eyes became darker and darker, and his face became tight with his strain not to succumb, as if he never wanted it to end. And as I climaxed I laughed my joy, not realizing until I tasted the salt on my lips that I was crying too. I looked at Theo in amazement as he said my name hoarsely before I felt his climax slam into my cervix, causing me to climax again. And the whole time, his eyes ever left my face. He collapsed on me and we both struggled to get our breathing back to normal. It had just been too intense. I have never felt like I had connected with somebody on a higher plane before. I'd heard about it, but never believed it. Now I knew what it was to truly be connected to someone. At that moment, I felt so much love and tenderness for Theo, I don't think I could even try to articulate it. Obviously, he had felt the same thing, because when he was finally able to speak he said, "Whoa, what was that?" As he gently brushed his lips over mine.

"I have no idea, but I liked it!" I smiled against his lips.

"Me too. I love you, Sara-girl. Oh God, how I love you!"

"I love you too, Theo," I told him as I snuggled in his arms. And as happy as I was, I still felt that something was wrong somewhere. It was just a feeling that I couldn't seem to shake, no matter how hard I tried.

Chapter Twenty-eight

"Hello, Sara, long time no see," a familiar voice said.

I turned around slowly, unwilling to believe my hearing. "Keith. Obviously it hasn't been long enough."

"Damn, you lookin' good, baby. How are you, *Mrs.* Horsestetter?"

"It's Livingston, Keith, and you damn well know it!" I snapped. The last person in the world I thought I'd run into at the Montgomeryville Mall would be my ex-husband. Okay, so technically, he was still my husband. But since I hadn't known how to find him, I had filed for a no-fault divorce and had sworn in Court that I didn't know where he was. Now his sorry ass was standing in front me. I wondered if this would muck up my divorce. God, I hoped not.

"My daddy would be offended," he said, trying in sound hurt.

"Oh, did you finally figure out who he was?"

His face tightening in anger, he said, "That's not funny, Sara. I see you're still a bitch."

"And I see you're still an asshole. I guess that makes us even, huh? And speaking of being an asshole, where's my fuckin' money, Keith?"

"What money? I don't know what you're talking about."

"The money you cleaned out of my bank account, you shithead. You really left me in a bind. So where is my fuckin' money?"

"Gee, Sara, I think you must be mistaken. I have no idea what you're talking about."

"Yeah, right. Look, I have to go, Keith. It hasn't been nice seeing you."

"Wait a minute baby. Why the rush? Damn, you're looking good. You picked up some weight?" He was checking me out from head to toe. I have to admit, I was looking good today. I had on my brown leather pants, a cream-colored silk angora sweater and brown leather blazer jacket with some smooth brown suede pumps. As a finishing touch, I had a thick brown and cream plaid chenille scarf tossed around my neck. I was totally into texture this season. As yet, I wasn't really showing yet, but my ass and my breasts were fuller than the last time he had seen me.

"It's called getting good lovin' Keith, and with a dick I can actually feel."

"Now see, why did you have to go there, Sara? Damn. And here I was ready to take you back."

"Take me back? What makes you think I would want your sorry ass? *Please.* We both know our marriage was a mistake of monumental proportions. Give me your address, Keith. I want to end this shit and move on with my life, okay? I want a divorce."

In a moment of rare honesty, Keith said, "You're right Sara. We never should have gotten married. All bullshit aside, how are you really, Sara?"

I looked at him suspiciously, feeling the frown that marred my features. He was looking so sincere, like the man I had fallen in love with and married. I knew from experience, though, that for the most part, it was an act. Keith was just trying to find out what was going on in my life so he could figure out how it might benefit him. In the next sentence, he confirmed my suspicions.

"I mean look at you. Damn, you're wearing all this expensive-looking shit and look at that rock on your finger. How can you be engaged when you're married to me? Is that why you want a divorce so badly? You've already got another one lined up. What's in it for me to let you go?"

"You know, Keith, I can get a divorce without your help. We have been separated for more than three years. I can get a no-fault divorce. I just thought it might expedite things if you cooperated."

"Not if I contest it, you can't. And I will, baby, unless you make it worth my while."

"Oh for Christ's sake! What the hell do you want, Keith? Money? How much will it take to get your ass out of my life?"

"Let me think about it. Give me your number and I'll call you with the figure."

"Oh, I don't think so! What, do I look like I have "fuck me" written across my face? Been there, *done* that! Please. You've forgotten who you're playing with. I don't have to give you shit, but I'm willing to think about it if you will let this thing go more smoothly. Give me *your* number or you don't get shit."

"Damn, Sara, when did you get so hard?"

"After you. Now give me your number and get the fuck out of my face Keith." After a moment's hesitation, he pulled out a card and scribbled his number on the back of it.

Glancing at the number, I frowned when I realized it was a suburban area code and exchange.

"You're not living in the city anymore?"

"Naw, I had to get away from some of the drama. Besides, I'm working out this way, so it's less of a hassle being close to my job."

"*You* have a job? Humph. That's only until you can find some woman to sponge off of, which will only last until she gets tired of your bullshit."

"Give me a break, will you? Damn. I've been on this job for almost a year now."

"That's an eternity for you. Anyway, I'm out. As I said before, it *hasn't* been a pleasure seeing you." With that, I turned and walked away from him. See, I knew something was going to come along and spoil things for me. But Keith was just a minor bump in the road. I wasn't going to let anything spoil what Theo and I had. I'd do whatever was necessary to get my divorce and get Keith permanently out of my life. Asshole.

I tried to finish shopping but Keith had ruined the outing for me. I finally gave up and after calling Theo on my cell phone, I told him I was on my way home.

I had just gotten in my van when the driver's side door was snatched open. I thought at first that it was Keith trying to be funny. I was just opening my mouth to curse him out when Frankie shoved his way into my car. Pushing the door button, Terrell jumped in on the other side behind me through the sliding door.

"What the fuck do you think you are doing?" I screamed at him. Turning to Terrell, I was ready to tear into him when I saw the gun in his hand. Ignoring him, I turned to Frankie and said, "What is this shit? What? You're trying to scare me? Okay, I'm properly scared. Now get the fuck out of my car," I sneered. I was too fucking angry to be scared.

"You're not scared, Sara. Not yet. But you're going to be," he said in this deadly calm voice. "Give me the keys."

"I'm not giving you shit! Have you lost your fuckin' mind? You can just kiss my ass, okay?" Then I heard the click of Terrell's gun and felt the coldness of the barrel as he placed it along the side of my face.

"Give him the fuckin' keys Sara. Don't make me have to shoot your ass and leave you here," Terrell threatened. Okay. Now I was scared. These two niggahs were crazy. I handed Frankie my keys. He started the car, backed out of the parking spot and started driving around the mall, trying to find the exit.

"Damn, Terrell, your breath stinks! When's the last time you brushed your teeth? I guess not since you killed Brenda, huh?" I taunted him, frantically looking around, hoping to see mall security.

"Shut the fuck up! Just shut up! I didn't mean to kill her. It just happened. She came at me first. She was so strung out, she didn't know what was up."

Turning around in my seat I hissed, "and who got her strung out? *You*, you sorry son of a bitch! You got her like that. And when you couldn't control her, you beat her," I spat, glad to have a chance to tell him what I thought of him.

I was stunned when I realized that he'd back-handed me as we exited the mall and turned onto Route 309. I was furious and more than a little scared when I realized, the metallic taste in my mouth, was blood. I decided it might be better to leave him alone. Turning to Frankie, I said, "Oh, so now you're going to let your cousin manhandle me, huh? What, you couldn't handle me by yourself? What do you want with me Frankie?"

"You're going to give me what I should have gotten a long time ago."

"What the hell are you talking about?"

"You know what I'm talking about, Sara. You've been giving it to that old mu'fucka you living with. Now you are going to give me some." Terrell gave an ugly, menacing bark of a laugh.

I felt a cold chill run down my back. If I wasn't scared before, I was terrified now. How was I supposed to get out this? I couldn't let him know how scared I really was. I had to act like I believed he was just making idle threats.

My mouth dry, I told him, "Frankie, you don't want to do this. Come on, Frankie, you know you're better than this. Why would you put your parole in jeopardy? You're too smart to do some dumb shit like this." I was praying that I could get through to him. I didn't want to tell him about the baby; I instinctively knew that would only enrage him more. He just let out this insane sounding laugh. "Still tryin' to be the tough girl, huh, Sara? Nobody walks away from Frankie Santiago. Nobody."

"Tell her, Frankie, man. We gonna pop that pussy tonight! Yeah, let's see if you're as big a freak as your girl Brenda was," Terrell growled in my ear, caressing the side of my face with the barrel of the gun. He and Frankie just laughed.

I realized then that I had made a horrible mistake. I had underestimated Frankie. I should have paid more attention to that crazy gleam I had seen in his eyes the last time he had accosted me. This was that bad feeling that I'd had. I had thought it was seeing Keith, but that was nothing compared to this. I knew something was going to happen, but I had foolishly ignored my radar. I had begun to believe the hype; I had bought into the fantasy that I was just another suburban housewife going about her daily life. Forget the fact that I wasn't technically a wife; still I had bought into the fantasy that me, Sara Livingston, could be happy.

My only chance now, I realized, was to try to keep my purse with me. As long as they didn't discover my cell phone, maybe I could call for help.

Frankie turned right onto Stump Road and pulled into a new housing development. Throwing the car into park, he killed the lights and pushing the door open, he hauled me out across the driver's seat and proceeded to drag me toward a wooded area ringing the development. I inanely thought, 'Theo and I looked at the model here,' as I stumbled along the unseen path he was dragging me along. Suddenly I lost my footing and I fell on a sharp rock, flat on my stomach and I swallowed a scream as I felt a searing pain in my stomach. I rolled away from the rock, but before I could get back up, they fell on me. Terrell pried my arms apart, which were clutching my stomach, to hold them over my head with one hand before kneeling with all of his weight on both of my wrist, the gun at my head with his other hand. Frankie clawed at my pants, dragging them off me, along with my panties. I felt the cold dampness from the ground slowly seeping through what was left of the clothes I still had on and it was all I could do not to lift my behind away from the cold ground. I didn't want the movement to be construed as an invitation. I watched in horror as he undid his pants and let them drop, as his engorged member sprang into view. He was long and thick, and for a moment he fondled himself, before falling on the ground and prying my shaking legs apart and then forcing himself inside of me. My scream of pain echoed in the cold, silent darkness around us. I watched helplessly as Frankie moved in and out of my dry body, each thrust more painful than the last, as it felt like I was being torn apart inside. I felt the tears as they sprang to my eyes as he shoved my sweater and bra up and painfully pinched and twisted my sensitive nipples and breasts. I could barely hear the obscene encouragements that Terrell was giving him over the frantic beating of my heart as he too began clawing and pinching at my breast with his one free hand. However, he still had enough presence of mind to keep the gun firmly planted against my head. Finally, I felt Frankie when he emptied himself as he shakes and grunts over me.

Almost as soon as he got up, Terrell and Frankie switched places and had it been different circumstances, I would have mocked him for his lack of a dick. Instead, I just pray for him to finish his business and leave me alone. Thanks to Frankie, I wasn't as dry inside, so it wasn't as painful. His body odor is making me sick and it's all I can do not to throw up all over him. Thankfully, it doesn't take him long, before he stiffens and he too empties himself in me.

He got up and after adjusting his clothing, said, "Yeah, bitch, you don't have a lot to say now, do you? Do you? What a lousy fuck!" he sneered as he viciously kicked me in the stomach and then again in my face. I screamed from the pain I felt and I barely heard Frankie say, "Oh shit! What is that all over her legs?" Bending down, he smears something off my thigh and then walks over to a break in the trees and holds his hand toward the light of the pale winter moon. "Shit! I think she's bleeding. Come on, Terrell. Let's get out of here. I think I hear something in the woods. Maybe some wild animal will finish her ass off." Before leaving he bent down, and moving very close to my face, said, "If you tell anybody who did this to you, you're dead. Do you hear me? I mean it, Sara. And if I can't get to you, I'll kill your daughter. Do you hear me?" Numbly I nodded my head yes, terrified for a new reason.

I couldn't believe it when they jumped into my van and with the back fish tailing, they sped off, the taillights quickly dimming in the oppressive blackness. Trying to feel around for my purse, my breath was cut off from the unbelievable pain I felt that made me double over, clutching my stomach. I felt that if I could just get to my cell phone, I could call Theo and he would make everything right again. However, I quickly found that too much movement caused too much pain. I think I must have passed out for a while because when I finally came too, I could barely move and when I did, I could barely stand the pain. As I lay on the cold, hard, damp ground, gasping like a fish out of water, feeling the frigid air sear my lungs with every indrawn breath, I began to shake when I heard footsteps approaching where I was, balled up in pain. *Oh God, they've come back!* Feeling around on the ground, I frantically searched for something that would aid me in defending myself.

"Sara? Oh my God. Are you all right?"

"Keith?" I hoarsely whispered in amazement, barely recognizing his voice, as I squinted at the dark figure above me, his face obliterated by shadows since his back was to the moon. Who would have ever thought that I would be happy to hear my almost ex-husband's voice?

"What are you doing here? Oh God, Keith, please, you're going to have to help me. I'm afraid I'm losing my baby. Please, Keith, help me!" I choked out as I doubled over with another pain.

"You're pregnant? Oh shit! Okay. Okay. Hold on. Let me go get my car. I'll be right back. Oh Jesus, there's so much blood," I thought I heard him say as I passed out yet again.

Chapter Twenty-nine

Damn it's cold in here. Especially my arm. It feels like I've got ice water running through it. And for God's sake, what is that aggravating noise? That beep. Beep. Beep. Beep. Who's crying? And why does it feel like I've got a mountain of bedding between my legs? Why did Theo turn the heat down so much? And when did we get a bed that sits up at an angle?

I slowly opened my eyes, waiting for them to adjust before I looked around the room. This isn't my bedroom. Where the hell am I? *Oh my God.* I remember. Frankie. Terrell. The rape. Keith finding me. My baby. Is my baby okay?

"What happened to my baby?" I cried out, feeling my stomach.

"Sara. You're awake." Theo came into my line of vision, wiping his eyes and looking like ten miles of bad road. He looked like he hasn't slept in days.

"Theo? Is the baby all right?" I anxiously search his face, knowing before he can answer that Ian is gone.

Drawing a shaky breath he answers, "He's gone, honey. You lost him before you got to the hospital. The police are holding your husband until you can make a statement."

"Keith? Keith didn't do this to me. Keith helped me. I not suppose to tell. They'll kill my daughter. Ian's gone? No, that can't be! No, Theo, there must be some mistake. Are you sure?" But I know he's telling me the truth from the anguish I can see in his eyes. I know I'm not making sense, but I can't help it.

"I'm tired, Theo. I just want to sleep," I tell him, turning my face away, willing the drugs slipping into my bloodstream to take me away again. I can't, *won't*, deal with this now.

"Sara. Baby, let me help you through this. I'm so sorry I wasn't there to help you." I can hear the anguish in his voice, see the tears on his face, pulling me back into unwilling consciousness. I want to, but can't, comfort him. I can't comfort myself, let alone anyone else.

"Who did this Sara? Please, baby. You have to tell me."

"I can't. I told you. They said they'd kill Bethany if I told."

"Sara that's crazy! Nobody's going to get to Bethy. I promise. Please, baby, tell me who did this."

Still I say nothing. What can I say? It happened to me. I want to cry or scream my anger and frustration, but it's become lodged in my throat like yesterday's oatmeal, congealed into silence. To many words, too much movement will make me heave and heave, maybe into forever, until I'm dead too. But I can't die. I have to live to protect Bethany. I'm afraid for my daughter. I want Theo's arms around me. But I feel frozen in place; frozen with fear deep in my heart. I can't move, or cry; or even speak. I just want to be left alone. My poor Ian. Ian Charles. Ian Charles Watkins. Such a strong sounding name. I wonder who he would have looked like. I had hoped that he would look like Theo with his hair and those beautiful green eyes. Now we'll never know. He was left in some wooded area, where he slipped from my body, helpless to save himself and me helpless to save him. *I'm sorry, baby.* I am so sorry. I feel a tear slip from my eye but quickly dash it away. Tears can't help me now. They can't give my baby back. They can't make the rape unhappen.

"Sara, there's someone here who really wants to see you, baby."

"I don't want to see anyone. Make them go away." I mumble.

"Sara? Oh baby, I'm so sorry. I wish I could make all your hurt go away." my mother cried, the tears freely flowing down her face. I envied her tears.

"Mom? How did you get here?" I ask stupidly.

"Zoe came and got your father and me. Poor man, he's been worried sick about you. We've been staying at the house to help Theo with Bethany and T.J. They've been worried and scared to death. We didn't know what to tell them. Theo finally decided that they deserved to know. Of course, he didn't tell Bethany that you had been raped. We felt that she was too young to know about such ugliness. They really want to see you. Poor Bethany has cried herself to sleep every night since this awful thing happened."

"Days? How many days have I been here?" I'm confused. I thought they just bought me in a few hours ago. My mother is standing there with her hand over her mouth, tears running down her face, horrified to realize that she may have said the wrong thing.

Putting his hands on my mother's shoulders to reassure her, Theo tells me, "You've been out for almost five days, Sara. The doctor said that you had a slight infection and were running a high fever. He also said the shock may have made you shut down for a while, until your mind could deal with it all."

"Did you say that Keith was being held? How did he find me?"

"He said that he had seen you earlier in the mall. When he came out, you were getting into your car when he saw two men force their way in your car. Concerned, he decided to follow you, but then some other cars got between your car and his. It caused him to miss the street where your car turned, forcing him to go further down the road until he could turn around and come back. He said he would never have found you except when a van went by him like a bat out of hell, he recognized it as yours and when he didn't see you in it, he went back the way the van had come. He said it took him awhile to find you and then he flagged down another car to get help. Since your blood was all over him, the police suspected him of causing the rape and telling the story of the other two men to cover himself. However, there is the fact that your car is gone."

"You mean they haven't found Terrell and Frankie? They're still out there?" I can feel panic taking me over, closing my throat, making it difficult to breathe. Again, I felt the bile rising, and again, I choked it back down.

"What if they figure out I'm in the hospital and come back to hurt me again?" Then I realized what I'd just said as I clapped a hand over my mouth.

"Terrell and Frankie did this to you? Those sons of bitches are dead! I swear to God, Sara, they are as good as dead."

"Theo, no! They said they would kill Bethy if I told. Please promise me you won't do anything. They can't know that I told. Please, Theo. I can't bear the thought of losing my daughter too! Has anyone seen them lately?"

"No one knows what happened to them or your van. The police in both Montgomery County and Philadelphia are looking for the men that did this. They wouldn't dare come here, baby. Don't worry, they can't hurt you any more."

"You don't know that!"

"Yes, I do, because I'm not leaving your side, Sara. Trust me, Sweetness," he gently pleads, trying to calm me down and reassure me that I'm safe. Noticing my mother's distraught face, I tell her, "Mom, you look tired. Theo, take my mother home so she can get some rest," I fret, more concerned with my mother. In actuality, I can't deal with her either right now, and for the first time in my life, I don't want my mother around me. For my entire life, whenever things have been bad for me, I always went to my mother, and a part of me wanted to now. However, there was something in me that was making me shut down and just wanted everybody to please, just leave me alone.

"I'm okay, honey. I just want to stay with you for a while," she says, fussing over me, adjusting my pillows and bedding. I just want to shout, 'Stop it please!' but I don't want to hurt her feelings.

"I'm fine, Mom. Really. Go home and get some rest. Give Bethany and T.J. my love. Tell them I'll see them real soon, okay?"

"If you insist, Sara. I'll go home and make them a real nice dinner," she says with false cheerfulness. I know I've hurt her feelings, but I can't deal with that right now.

"Thanks, Ma."

"I don't want to leave you, Sara. Let me go call somebody to come take your Mom home. I'll be right back."

While Theo was gone, I forced myself to have conversation with my mother, who again told me that Zoe had bought her and Dad down. Whenever the conversation veered too closely to what happened, I'd bring up something else. Finally, she got the message that I didn't want to talk about it.

With relief, Theo came back into the room and got my mother to take her home since he couldn't find anyone to pick her up. At long last, I was alone. I waited and waited for the emotion to hit me so that I could cry. Nothing. I felt like I was screaming on the inside, but I couldn't get it to come out. I finally fell into an exhausted sleep, only to be awakened by the nightmare of reliving my rape. When I woke up, I was shaking and soaking wet from my sweat.

I felt an overwhelming need to shower, in the hottest water I could stand, but with this damn I.V. attached to me, I didn't know if I could go into the shower. I located my call button to the nurse's station, and buzzed it over and over again before somebody finally answered my call.

"Is everything all right, Ms. Livingston?"

"Have I been examined yet, for, you know, evidence?"

"Yes, you were examined and samples were taken when you first arrived in the Emergency Department, Ms. Livingston. I believe pictures were also taken."

"Can I take a shower with this thing attached to me?"

"Oh yes, once I attach it to a mobile unit. Do you feel well enough to get up? Do you have to go to the bathroom?"

"Yes, I do. I also want to take a shower."

"But it's two o'clock in the morning!"

"And your point?"

"Well, it's just unusual for a patient to want to take a shower at two o'clock in the morning. Wouldn't you rather wait until the morning?"

"No, I would not. Now are your going to fix this damn thing so I can go to the fuckin' bathroom or am I going to have to piss in the fuckin' bed or what?"

"There's no need to be rude, Ms. Livingston!" she said, turning seven shades of red. "I don't think you should be thinking of taking a shower. I think you should wait until you speak with your doctor in the morning."

"And I think you need to mind your damn business. Now unless there is a medical reason why I can't take a shower, I'm taking one. Now either get this damn bag on a mobile unit or I'm ripping it the hell out of my arm!"

In my heart, I knew I should listen to this nurse and there was no need to be so evil about the whole thing, but I felt like a woman possessed. Even though I realized someone must have given me sponge baths, it wasn't enough. I had to try to wash off what they had done to me. And I had to do it *now*.

Realizing that she wasn't going to dissuade me, the nurse left and came back, tightlipped, with a mobile unit to put whatever they had dripping into my vein on, mumbling under her breath the entire time. Painfully, I got out of the bed and made my way to the shower, careful to avoid looking in any mirrors. I didn't want to see the horror that I knew was my face. At least not yet.

It's a wonder I didn't give myself third degree burns with the water being as hot as it was. I scrubbed and scrubbed myself, over and over, trying in vain to remove the feel of Frankie and Terrell from my body. I was horrified when I looked down and saw the bruises that were still on my body. I finally realized that although I was squeaky clean on the outside, I could do nothing to remove the feel of them on the inside, short of cutting my vagina out. After trying to dry myself off and put on a clean pair of panties and my pad, I was finally forced to buzz for a nurse when I noticed that my blood was going back up the tube instead of the drip going into my hand.

Sucking her teeth in disgust, she came in and helped me to put on my panties and pad and then a clean hospital gown, assisted me back to bed, horrified at the red splotches all over my body from the scalding water.

"I told you this wasn't a good idea, Ms. Livingston. Now you've raised your hand too much and we are going to have to find another vein to put your I.V. into." Finally, after changing the location of my I.V., none too gently, she left me. I was just starting to drift off when Theo came in.

"Hey. How are you feeling?"

"Better. I just had a shower. How are the kids?"

"They're okay, anxious to see you though."

"What are you doing here this time of the morning? Visiting hours are over."

"I've been here every night since they bought you in Sara. The doctors and nurses finally gave up trying to make me stay home."

"Hhmm."

The room was quiet and I was almost asleep again, when he said, "Do you want to talk about it, Sara?"

"No, I don't Theo. I just want to be left alone, okay?"

"Okay, baby. I won't push you. I'm here if you need me, Sara."

"I know."

"Ah, I hate to bring this up, but I, ah, was thinking of having your mother help me to clear out the nursery before you come home."

"*No!* Leave it. I want to do it myself."

"I don't think that's a good idea, Sara."

"I *said*, I want to do it myself! Leave the room alone. I mean it, Theo. Just leave it the hell alone!"

"Sara, why would you want to torture yourself like that? Honey, please. Let me take care of it for you."

"No, goddamn it! Just leave it the way it is," I snapped.

He looked so hurt, but I couldn't help it. I felt it would make things that much worse to go home and find the room I had fixed up as the nursery stripped, like Ian had never existed. I just couldn't face that. If we had to strip that room, I wanted to know where everything went.

Changing the subject, Theo said, "Ah, Dave called. He said to take as much time as you needed to get better."

"Humph." The last thing on my mind was my job. At this point, I could care less about the damn job. I didn't give a flying fuck about the job. I could always get another job, but I could never get my baby back. I could never get *me* back. Even I realized that Frankie and Terrell had taken so much more from me than just my baby. The Sara Livingston I had once been was gone. I didn't know who I was suppose to be now. Everything had changed. The only constant was that I was still Bethany's mother, and right about now, I didn't think I could even handle that. And if I didn't know who I was supposed to be, how could I be Theo's wife?

Chapter Thirty

"We're home!" Theo said with false cheerfulness. I stretched my lips into some semblance of a brief smile as I walked into the house. All I wanted was to go to bed. However, that was not to be the case. It seemed my entire family was there as well as a strong showing of his family. Damn! All these people were the last thing that I wanted to deal with. Why were they here? What were they thinking? Didn't they understand that all I wanted was to be alone? Shit! I didn't feel like being brave and putting on a good face. I didn't feel like trying to make anyone feel better.

"Goddamn it, Theo, why are these people here?" I hissed, not caring about the hurt look on his face. "What an asinine idea! I just want to go to bed. I'll tell you what. Since this was your bright idea, you deal with them. I'm going upstairs." And with that I walked upstairs, waving everyone off when they tried to talk to me. Let him deal with them. I didn't care if they thought I was rude or not. I just wanted to be left alone.

I let out my breath when I got upstairs to our room. Quietly shutting and locking the door, I lay down across the bed, not bothering to take my clothes off. Lord this bed feels good after being in that awful hospital bed. At least, here at home in my own bed, I feel safe. The police, incompetent idiots that they were, still hadn't found Frankie and Terrell. I know it was being unreasonable, but I didn't even want to go out of the house while they were still on the loose. I had just known, after I gave the police my statement, that they would be picked up.

Apparently, Frankie had vacated his mama's house. The idiots hadn't even found my van.

I wasn't even sure I wanted the police to find them. I wanted to find them myself, or at least some of the male members in my family or Theo's family. I wanted justice. Street justice. Beat you within an inch of your life justice. Slice off your dick and shove it down your fuckin' throat justice. Going to jail was too easy. I wanted them to suffer, like I'd suffered. I wanted them to feel such unbelievable pain. I wanted them to pray for death as I ripped off their balls and shoved them down their fuckin' throats. I wanted to take that gun Terrell had held to my head and shove it up their asses and pull the trigger, justice. Barbaric thoughts, but they were what got me through my days.

At least here at home, I also wouldn't have to deal with that annoying rape counselor. She was starting to get on my last damn nerve. How many ways can you say you don't want to talk and just want to be left alone? I finally had to curse her ass out before she finally got the message.

I heard a soft knock at my door. I was about to say "Go away," when I heard a timid, "Mommy? Mommy, can I come in?" I jumped up from the side of the bed and throwing open the door, I scooped my daughter into my arms. Her warm body felt so good and I remembered what she felt like as a baby. The thought almost made me cry. Almost, but not quite.

"I'm so glad you're home, Mommy! I missed you so much! I'm so sorry about the baby."

"Ian, Bethany. His name was Ian," I gently corrected.

"Ian. I'm sorry I'll never get to see him or play with him. Are you okay? What happened to your face?" she cried, noticing my still swollen jaw and black eye.

"As well as I can be right now, Bethany. As for my face, the doctor said it will be fine in a few days. I fell on a rock, baby."

"Well, I'm glad you're home. We've all missed you, but especially Uncle Theo. I heard him crying one night, Mom," she whispered, sounding scandalized that a man would cry.

Before I could comment on that she asked, "Why did you lose the baby? I thought you were okay. I asked Uncle Theo and he just got upset and wouldn't tell me. Will you tell me, Mom?"

"These things just happen sometimes, Bethy. There really is no explanation other than it just happened, baby." I didn't want to tell my daughter the real reason. She was too young to know about such ugliness. A sudden noise made me look up and when I did, I found T.J. in my doorway. Without hesitation, I held my other arm out and he flew across the room to give me a fierce hug. He never said a word, but his arms around me said it all as I felt his slight trembling. He understood and he was genuinely concerned about how I was feeling.

"I'm so sorry Sara, about what happened to you. Are you okay?" he said, tears in his eyes.

"Thank you, T.J. I'm fine, baby. I'm just glad to see you both again," hugging them close enough to me to feel T.J.'s slight shiver.

I think he had an idea about what had happened, because he looked angry and distressed. I'm sure he had overheard some of Theo's angry telephone conversations with other male members in his family. I had been told that there was an all points bulletin out on Frankie and Terrell within the family. Since they lived all over the good City of Philadelphia, there was a pretty good chance of somebody spotting them somewhere. Theo's family lived from Southwest Philly to Chestnut Hill; from downtown to the Greater Northeast. Somebody, somewhere, was going to find those two fuckers and God help them if the police didn't find them first.

And so went my days, living in this limbo. I drifted from room to room when the kids were in school and Theo was at work. We had argued vehemently about him going to the shop. I had finally convinced him that I was fine at home alone, once he took my parents back home. Faithfully, every morning after he left, I would put the alarm on. I felt quite safe then. I liked being home by myself. I didn't have to pretend to be fine and put on a happy face.

I avoided my sisters like the plague. My conversations with my mother were short and stilted. I wouldn't even talk to Lela. Any information any of them got, they got from Theo. Other than Bethy, Theo and T.J., I methodically cut myself off from everyone. I couldn't deal with anything or anyone. I didn't want to feel everyone's pity and sympathy. T.J. and Bethy walked around on eggshells, afraid of upsetting me. Suddenly, it was Theo and not me who checked their homework and sat around with them in the evenings. Almost as soon as they got home, I excused myself and holed up in our bedroom. Half the time, I forgot to even cook dinner. Theo, bless his heart, never complained once. On more than one occasion, his sister Carol sent full dinners up to our house. At least they ate. Me, I had no appetite. Theo had to practically force food into me. For once in my life, I was actually thin. What exercise and diet couldn't do for my hips, depression had. I didn't care. Nothing mattered to me anymore.

At one point, each of the partners called me and no sooner than I hung up the phone, I forgot my conversations with them. I did remember, however, that Dave hinted that they wished I would come back to work, especially since Priscilla had gotten fired for refusing to do their work unless they paid her more money. So they were going through a series of temps from hell. I felt bad for them, but it wasn't my problem. I just couldn't go back and deal with the office bullshit. What the fuck did I care about a statute date when my baby was gone? Or how many reams of paper we had or filing this motion or that brief. It all just seemed like so much superficial, pathetic bullshit. Please. None of it seemed to matter. Theo had told me that I never had to go back if I didn't want to, so I didn't give a rat's ass about it. I liked my boss, a lot, but I just couldn't deal with any of that bullshit right now. Dave was a really great guy. But how could he understand what I was going through right now? How could he understand my grief, my fears? I was no good to myself or my family. I would really be no good on my job. I didn't care about anything or anyone.

I had other things to think about. Like what was I going to do the first time Theo approached me for *that*? You know, to make love. I missed the comfort of his arms, but I couldn't stand to be touched. I felt like I was smothering every time he tried to hold me. I could see he needed my comfort too, but I felt powerless to help him. I knew he was grieving too, and again, there was nothing that I could do for him. I wasn't dealing very well with me. What the hell could I do to help him? He kept begging me to let him in, to let him share my pain, but I couldn't. Maybe if I could cry, scream, shout, to let it out, maybe I'd feel better. But I couldn't, wouldn't even allow myself that.

I kept thinking that I must have really done something bad or evil for God to punish me like He had. And I kept racking my brain trying to remember the one thing that I had done that was so bad that warranted what had happened to me. But try as I might, I couldn't pin it down to one thing. Maybe just being a lifelong bitch was my sin. But life had turned me into the bitch that I had been. Theo, however, had softened my edges. Maybe that was it. Maybe I had just been too damn happy and it had been my reality check. Maybe it was my punishment for all those other abortions. I hadn't wanted any of them, so when I had wanted one, it had been taken from me. Maybe it was finally that Divine Retribution that I had feared for so long.

But I was afraid to question God to closely. My mother had always taught us that you never, ever question God and his reasons for things happening to you. But I was tempted. Oh so tempted. Tempted to rail and curse and hate Him for what had happened to me. Why? Would somebody just tell me why, that's all I wanted to know. And what? What sin had I committed that was so bad that my baby had to pay the price for it.

And then there was the nursery. Every day, I stood outside of the closed door, trying to make myself go in. Over the weeks I had even gotten my hand on the knob, only to let it go like it was a hot poker. So every day, no matter how hard I tried, I walked away from that door.

Before I knew it, six weeks had passed and I had my check up with Dr. Pagano. He said I was fine and I could resume sexual relations whenever I wanted. Actually, I was fine at four weeks, but I didn't tell Theo that. Unfortunately, he was with me at the check up and heard what Dr. Pagano said.

On the ride home, we were both quiet. I didn't want to talk about it at all. Finally, Theo said quietly, "I won't ask you to do anything that you're not ready to do, Sara. I hope you know that."

"Are you sure?"

"Absolutely. You should know by now, I'm a very patient man."

Instead of making me feel better, it made me feel worse. He was such a good, loving man. He really did deserve better than me. I felt I owed it to him to at least try. On the other hand, he did say that he wouldn't press me. So maybe I should just take him at his word and wait. Yeah. That's what I'd do. I hadn't felt this nervous about sex since I'd lost my virginity. But after a rape, isn't the first time almost like being a virgin? At least in the sense that you don't know how you're going to feel, or even if you can go through with it.

Not only that, I wondered how Theo could still want to sleep with me. I had convinced myself that he didn't.

I remembered once we'd had a conversation about cheating. I had asked him if he could ever take back his wife or his woman if he found out that they had cheated. He had said he couldn't. When I asked him why, he had used an analogy to explain. He had said, "If you had this beautiful, delicious piece of cake, and a roach crawled on it, would you still want it?" I had said absolutely not. "Well, that's how I feel about my woman sleeping with another man. Why would I want her when some other man has crawled on her?" Not one, but two had crawled on me.

For the first time in a long time, I seriously wanted a drink. I was thinking that maybe if I got really drunk, it would help me to be more relaxed. But did I want to compromise my sobriety for that? Was it worth it? I didn't know what to think anymore.

When we got home, the kids were already home from school and soon we were busy with homework and dinner. During that time, I was able to put tonight out of my mind, but too soon, it was time to go to bed.

After taking my shower and putting on my night gown, I slipped into bed. Theo wasn't long behind me. He still slept the way we had before, in the nude. It had only been since the rape that I had started sleeping in night clothes. Before that, I had enjoyed sleeping au naturel. I was on my side of the bed and Theo on his. The small space between us felt like a continent. Neither of us could seem to fall asleep. I was looking at the wall next to me, he, the ceiling above.

"This isn't going to work, Sara," his deep voice floated to me in the darkness. I heard him sigh, as he moved and I could tell that he was now sitting on the side of the bed.

"I'm sorry, Theo. I'm just not ready."

"I know. I just wish you would at least let me hold you. I miss you in my arms, Sara."

I didn't say anything for a while. I was trying to make up my mind; I could do that much at least.

"Okay," I finally whispered.

"Are you sure?"

"Yeah, I'm sure."

I could feel the bed move once again as he laid back down, again on his back with the arm nearest me stretched out. I slowly rolled toward him, and for a moment, it really did feel good to be in his arms, and to smell that smell that was uniquely him. But as our combined body heat started to co-mingle, it started to get warmer and warmer and I started to feel suffocated. I was fighting my panic, telling myself that this was Theo, that I had nothing to be afraid of. Breathe, I kept saying in my head, but instead of it relaxing me, it was making it worse.

Finally, with a strangled noise, I pulled away from him and sat on the side of the bed, taking in great gulps of air. I was *thisclose* to jumping up and taking a hot shower. Not wanting to face Theo anymore, I grabbed my pillow and a blanket and snatching our door open, flew down the back stairs to the family room.

Without thought or control, I had a drink in my hand and down my throat before I could stop myself. I barely tasted the first one. The second one quickly followed the first. By the time I realized what I was doing, I was horrified. I looked at the glass I held in one hand and the bottle I held in the other, not even remembering picking them up. I threw them both against the fireplace wall, not even feeling the pieces of glass that bounced off, slicing through my night gown and cutting my arms, hands and face. That had felt so good, I threw another one and another one.

"Sara! Stop it! Jesus Christ, you're going to cut yourself all up," Theo thundered. I turned around to look at him in amazement. He'd never raised his voice like that to me. Behind him, I saw Bethany with her hands over her mouth crying and T.J. just looked scared. I looked at the debris around my feet and saw the liquor running over the bricks of the fireplace wall. And then I felt my tears running down my face and realized that finally, at last, I was crying.

"Go back to bed, you two. I'll take care of her. Go on now," Theo told them and the tone of his voice brooked no argument. T.J. put his arm around Bethany and led her back upstairs.

"Don't move, Sara. Let me get a broom, or you'll cut your feet to ribbons.

I couldn't seem to stop crying. Even as I stood there among that debris, even as I watched Theo clean up around me, I cried.

When he was finally able to reach me, I collapsed against him as he led me over to the sofa. He wouldn't let me pull away this time, and when I looked at him, I saw that he was crying too. And for the first time since the rape, we mourned our baby together. I finally let him in to share my pain and was finally able to share his.

"Feel better?" he asked with a smile in his voice, when my tears had turned to sniffles and hiccups.

"Actually, I do. I feel like a dam just opened up and I was able to let a lot of the poison out. But there is still the matter of us."

"True. Why did you leave like that Sara?"

Shrugging my shoulders, I just looked away, sighing.

"Come on, baby. Talk to me. We're finally making some progress. Don't shut yourself off from me. Tell me what's wrong," he pleaded as he rubbed my back.

I finally turn around and tell him in a low voice, "You can't possibly still want me, Theo. Not after what's happened."

Frowning, he asks, "Why would you say that? Don't you know how much I love you, Sara?"

"That was before. You can't now. You said so yourself."

"When? I never said that!"

"Yes, you did. Remember I asked you once what you would do if your woman cheated on you? You said you could never forgive her or take her back. You said you wouldn't be able to sleep with that person who'd let somebody 'crawl' on them. Well, two people did it to me. So how could you possibly want me?"

"Oh, Sara! That's not what I meant. I meant if you went out and deliberately slept with somebody else. I meant an affair. Honey, this was beyond your control. You're not to blame for what happened to you! How could you even think I would hold that against you?"

"I don't know. I just did. Are you sure, Theo?"

"I'm positive. Come on, Sara, give me some credit." He seemed hurt and offended that I would think that, but he *had* said it. What else was I supposed to think?

Suddenly yawning, I realized that I was bone tired, and not wanting to talk about it anymore, I told Theo I was just too tired to deal with it right now.

"Are you staying down here, or are you coming back upstairs, where you belong?"

I thought about it for a minute and decided that I really did prefer sleeping in my own bed. At my hesitation, he told me, "I won't bother you, Sara, if that's what you want. But I would feel better with you being upstairs. I don't like the thought of you down here by yourself."

"All right, Theo. I'll come back upstairs if it'll make you feel better," I told him as I put my hand into his outstretched on. When we reached the top of the stairs, two doors immediately opened and two worried faces looked out us. Theo went to talk to T.J. and I went to Bethany.

"Is everything okay, Mama?" Lord, she was worried and scared. Bethany only called me Mama when she was really upset about something.

"Better than they've been in a long time, honey. I'm sorry I scared you like that. I didn't mean too."

"It wasn't just tonight, Mama. You've been different for a long time. Ever since you lost the baby and after, you know, what happened to you. You seemed like you were, I don't know, somewhere else and like you didn't want to be bothered with me anymore," she told me, her eyes filling up.

I hugged her to me, realizing for the first time, I had done more than just shut myself away from Theo. I also realized that she must have heard what had happened to me and knew what it meant. My child wasn't supposed to know about such things as rape. At least not yet. I felt guilty that I had made my innocent child feel so unwanted. That hadn't been my intention, not when she meant so much to me.

Hugging her fiercely to me I said, "I'm sorry, baby! I didn't mean to hurt you, but I had to get my head together, I guess. I didn't know losing the baby would hurt so much. But I'm better, I promise. Things will be different. You'll see."

"Can you stay with me for a while, Mommy? I've missed you. I've missed our pajama parties we used to have, and how we used to pig out on ice cream and stuff and tell silly stories. Will you stay with me until I go to sleep?"

"Sure baby, I'd love too," I told her as I laid down with her in bed, turning off her bedside lamp. She promptly snuggled up next to me, and I heard a contended sigh before she drifted off to sleep. Theo cracked open the door and I waved him away, giving a helpless shrug and smiled. He smiled back before quietly closing the door. I knew he understood. Before long, I drifted off to sleep, me and my daughter helping each other get through the night.

Chapter Thirty-one

"Look Lieutenant, it's been weeks. Why haven't they been found yet?" I can't believe these incompetent assholes. After all this time, you would think they would have some kind clue where Frankie and Terrell were.

"I understand your frustration, Ms. Livingston. We're doing all we can to apprehend the suspects. We've been working around the clock on this, but you have to realize, this is a big city and there are crimes every day. The police are doing everything they can. And by the way, you have some powerful friends in high places. Believe me, we understand that this is being monitored very closely. It's in our best interest to apprehend these two."

"I don't think you do understand, Lieutenant. I've been trapped in this house for weeks. I'm afraid to leave my own home. Do you know what that feels like? No, of course you don't. You've never been raped. I want something done and I want something done *now*!" I snapped. At least my temper was coming back.

"Yes, ma'am. We'll keep you informed of all developments."

"You do that," I said as I slammed the phone down. *Damn*! Still no sign of those assholes. The police and I had been going back and forth like this for weeks. Early on, I had called Dave, who called somebody in City Hall, who called somebody in the Mayor's office. That's why he'd said I had friends in high places. Sometimes it was good to know lawyers. Since the ones I worked with were very involved in city politics, it had come in handy for putting pressure on the police. Unfortunately, it hadn't yet yielded any positive results.

The sudden ringing of the door bell interrupted my thoughts. After carefully looking out the sidelight windows, I opened the front door.

"I hope I got the right stuff you wanted," Chelsea tells me as she passed me some bags before picking up the rest.

"I'm sure you did just fine, Chelsea. Thanks for your help. I wish I wasn't such a baby. I should have gone to get this stuff myself."

"Don't even worry about it. We all understand. Shit, I'd be just like you if it had happened to me. Humph. Glad to be of help. Check this stuff. If it's not right, I'll take it back to Home Depot but I have to do it quickly because I have to get home myself. Rita has Aisha and she'll be bringing her back home soon."

"Oh, okay. Sure. Let me see, paint, brushes, rollers, stencils, yeah, it looks like you got everything."

"Is that the right shade you wanted?"

"It's perfect," I told her after prying open the paint can. The color inside is a smooth, creamy, pale butter yellow. After trashing the family room, I'd decided to paint and stencil it. Theo had told me that he'd do it, but I want to do it myself. And I want to have it done by the time he got home. Getting my purse, I gave Chelsea back the money she had spent picking all this stuff up for me.

"Okay, girl. I'm out. I have to be home when Rita gets there, with a hot snack or I'll have to listen to her mouth, and I ain't in the mood today. Ever since I kicked her sorry-ass son to the curb, she's been riding my shit. She's lucky I even let her see Aisha. Shit. Gettin' on my damn nerves!"

I couldn't help but to laugh and shake my head. Chelsea is the oldest, fussiest, *young* woman I've ever met. She bitches and moans a lot, but I've found out that she is really a big softy. Before leaving she looks at me hard and says, "You're doing better aren't you? Something about you looks different."

"I finally cried."

"Good! It's not good to keep all that bottled up inside. It'll eat you alive. I know. I did it when my mother died. Finally one day I snapped and after that, it got easier. You sleep with my father yet?"

"Chelsea! That's none of your business!"

"Well did you? Shit, I'm a woman. I know it can't be easy after what happened to you. At least you're lucky. You've got my father, who's a very patient man. A lot of men wouldn't be. So did you?"

Looking down I mumble, "No. I can't." When I look up, I see such a look of compassion in her eyes, it made me catch my breath and almost at the same time, both of our eyes filled up.

"Hell, Sara, every woman has been raped in one way or another. We've all had to give it up when we didn't really want to. Only we didn't call it rape, we called it forceful persuasion. Granted, the way you were raped is every woman's nightmare, but you'll get through it. You'll see."

Hugging her, I thanked her and walked her to the door. After she left, I grabbed a cup of coffee and thought about what she said.

I remember when I was fourteen and there was this guy whose name I can no longer recall. I really liked him a lot and he came over to my house one hot summer day. First of all, I wasn't supposed to have anyone in the house when my parents were at work, but I let him in anyway. We were sitting on the sofa, listening to music when we started kissing. He started to feel me up. Then he put his hand in my shorts, under my panties. As I felt his hand, his finger really, moving into my vagina, I tried to stop him, but he was so much bigger and stronger than I was and the more I tried to stop him, the more he was determined to finger-fuck me. I finally slapped the shit out of him and he almost hit me back. Jumping up from the sofa, I ran into the kitchen and got a knife and told him to leave. Just as he was leaving, my friend, who lived next door, came over and I started crying hysterically. She wanted to know what was wrong and I finally told her. After a while, I put it out of my mind, but I never forgot it.

And how many dates had I been on where I'd had to give it up when I didn't really want to? *Forceful persuasion.* I'd never thought about it like that before, but on more than one occasion, I had been raped. Just because I knew the person didn't make it any less so. How many times had it happened because I had been afraid of being hit like I'd seen my mother being hit? So many thoughts and feelings started coming at me at one time, I was forced to sit down.

I thought back to that awful night and wondered if I should have fought more. But Terrell had been holding that gun to my head. I had just wanted it to be over. Had all that had happened to me before made me fight less, or was it the fear I had felt in trying to protect my baby? In the end, I still had lost; myself and Ian. No. When I fell on that rock, I knew then that there was a chance I would miscarry. I had acted the only way I could, with the least resistance in an effort to save my baby's life. If Terrell hadn't kicked me, he might have survived. And I felt another layer of guilt lift from my shoulders. Ironically, in the background, I had been playing Lauryn Hill's *The Miseducation of Lauryn Hill.* When one of the extra cuts on her CD, "*TellHim,*" came on, suddenly I was focused on every word. It bought me almost to my knees, especially when I heard, "*tell Him I need Him, tell Him I love Him, and everything is gonna be all right.*" It was almost spooky and prophetic at the same time. I played it over and over, willing the song and God to give me the strength to pick up the shattered pieces of my life.

Jumping up, I got busy. Covering the furniture, moving things out the way, I poured the paint and started with my project. Before I knew it, I had the first coat done. Having one of those painters that feeds the paint into the roller made the job go very quickly. Soon I had the second coat on and I stood in the doorway, admiring my handiwork.

An hour later, after a hearty lunch of soup and a sandwich, I started my stenciling. I had chosen a simple pattern of some ivy leaves and pale pink and maroon flowers. I had just cleaned everything up and put the furniture back in place when Bethany and T.J. came home from school.

With the family room having beige, raised diamond patterned Berber carpet, a beige, mossy green and cranberry striped/patterned sofa and moss green chenille overstuffed armchairs, the pale butter walls made the room seem more warm and cozy than the beige walls we'd had when we moved in. No doubt about it, painting is the easiest way I know to give a room a whole new look. It's cheap, fast and easy.

"Hey, this wasn't this color this morning!" T.J. noted. "I like it, looks nice, Sara."

"Dag, Mom, did you do this all by yourself?" Bethany asked, looking around the room with a big grin on her face.

"Yup, sure did."

"Go Mom!" she laughed.

"Think Theo will like it?"

"I love it," he said, surprising me as he came to stand behind me and admire the room. "Damn baby. I need to hire you out. We could make some money. You've got skills!" He said, kissing my cheek.

"What are you doing home so early? I haven't even started dinner," I asked, shocked to see him before eight o'clock at night.

"I missed my family. Can't a man come home early if he wants too?"

"Hey, no arguments from me," I laughed, actually glad to see him. For so long, I'd been avoiding everybody, I realized with a shock, I was glad to have my family around me.

"This looks really nice Sara," he said quietly, with something in his voice I couldn't quite catch.

I just grinned, proud of myself.

"There's that smile I love so much," he said softly only loud enough for me to hear, kissing me before I could turn away. I touched my lips, surprised that I hadn't wanted to turn away. I was even more surprised that I had liked the heat of his fleeting lips on mine.

"Did I hear you say you haven't started dinner? I guess not since I don't smell anything. Besides, I can see why not. You've been a busy lady today. How about we go out to dinner?"

"Oh, I couldn't do that! Why don't you all go? I'll fix a Hungry Man dinner or something."

"No, either we all go or none of us go. Come on, Sara. You've got to get out of the house sooner or later."

"I don't know, Theo. I don't know if I can."

"Please, Mommy? Please? Come on. Tell her, T.J. She just has to come."

"Come on, Sara. Please?" T.J. asked, looking at me with those puppy dog eyes.

"Oh, all right. I guess I'll be fine since I'm with all of you."

"Yes!" Bethany and T.J. whooped, giving each other high fives as they ran to get their coats.

"Are you sure you're okay with this?" Theo asked, concerned.

"You'll be there, Theo. I'll be fine. I mean I did leave the house to go to the doctors. I can do this. Where are we going?"

"How about TGIFriday's? You know how the kids love it there and T.J. loves the Mississippi Mud Pie.

"That'll work. Let me run upstairs and try to pull myself together. Tell the kids to take their coats off. I'll be right back!"

With that I raced upstairs and washing up quickly, I got all the paint off my hands and face and throwing on some makeup, I pulled on a pair of navy blue velvet leggings and a sky blue silk and angora cable knit oversized turtleneck sweater. Grabbing my navy blue suede jacket and stepping into some navy suede ankle boots, I threw on a thick, long silver snake chain, some silver hoop earrings, my sterling silver tank watch and then I was ready to go. I had been living in sweats or a housecoat for weeks. I had to admit that the clothes did make me feel a little bit like my old self. The sweater that had been a little tight on me only weeks before, now hung on me. Even the blazer was a little loose, but it couldn't be helped. I guess I was going to have to go shopping soon to get some clothes in size or two smaller.

When I came downstairs, at first no one said anything, they just gawked.

"Now that's *my* Sara," Theo grinned. T.J. and Bethany applauded.

"Dag, have I been looking that bad?"

"Yup!" Bethany said with no hesitation. "It's been *ages* since you put on any makeup, Mom, let alone one of your sharp outfits. You've been in a housecoat for *weeks*.

"Well honeys, the DIVA is back!" I teased, laughing, a joyous sound that hadn't come out of me in weeks.

We had so much fun that night. I caught up with what the kids had been doing and all the family gossip. I felt bad that I had missed so much. It's funny how life can pass you by if you let it.

"So there's this girl who's *soooo* in love with T.J." Bethany was saying. "She's pretty, but I don't like her. I think she's stuck on herself."

"Shut up Bethany! *God*. You are such a blabbermouth."

"Well she is. You should see her Mom. All the boys around the way like her and T.J. just drools whenever he sees her. I think she likes him because he's on the basketball team. That must be it, cause we all know he's ugly as sin," she teased.

"Yeah, well, I don't see you volunteering any information about your boyfriend."

"Which one?" she came back with.

"None," Theo told her. "You're way too young to be thinking about a boyfriend, Bethany. There'll be plenty of time for that," he told her before I could open my mouth.

"Uncle Theo!"

"Uncle Theo, nothing. I'm not playing Bethany. Don't let me hear any more of this boyfriend foolishness."

"Yes, Uncle Theo," she told him, albeit mutinously. I looked at him in amazement. He'd sounded so much like her father should have, if he'd been involved in her life. I let it go. I was glad that he was there to take up the slack. Bethany was getting to an age where she needed the influence of a father figure. I was glad that it was a man such as Theo.

The rest of the meal passed in pleasant and playful banter, and I suppose to anyone who walked by our table, we looked like the typical

American family: mother, father, an older son, who looks like dad, a younger daughter, who looks like mom. And while we were there, I enjoyed the perception. More than one woman walked past our table and smiled and nodded at me. I guess I looked like the woman who had it all. If they only knew.

When we got home, since it was a Friday, everybody hung out in my newly decorated family room. We had the fireplace going, a movie on cable, and we popped some popcorn when we got the munchies. And I realized for the first time in God knew how long, I felt safe, warm and dare I say, happy. Bethany and T.J., after valiantly trying to fight sleep, soon succumbed. Theo and I let them sleep before nudging them awake and sending them staggering to their beds.

After yawning repeatedly ourselves, we decide to call it a night. After taking my shower first, I fell into bed so exhausted from the day's activities, I didn't even realize that I had forgotten my self-imposed armor, my night gown.

I remembered, however, when I awoke in the middle of the night and found myself practically covering Theo. As I moved my leg, which was flung across him, I felt his hardness as it dragged against my moving leg. I also realized that he was awake, barely able to draw a breath. When I placed my hand on his stomach to push myself away, I heard his sharply indrawn breath. In the dark and in my haste to move, I accidentally brushed his hardness with my hand, and I heard him groan. I hesitated before wrapping my hand around him. I heard him groan again, this time in need. Surprisingly, I felt a response in myself. Continuing to fondle him, I begin to kiss his neck, having moved my leg, but still snuggled up next to him. Things went on like this until Theo rolled me over on my back. Unbelievably, I felt the moistness between my legs. Theo positioned himself between my thighs, too far gone for any foreplay. I believed that I was ready for him. As he slowly penetrated me, I could feel myself stiffening in panic. As he began to thrust in and out of me, I realize that I can't feel anything. *Nothing.* And as I realize that, I felt my body just dry up.

And his moving over me was causing me to go into a serious panic. Get off of me. GET OFF OF ME! "GET OFF OF ME!" And then I realize that I've actually said it out loud. Oh dear God. I thought I was ready. I thought I could do this. Stricken, Theo, scrambles to the other side of the bed, still erect, and there is nothing I can do for him.

Jumping up from the bed, I raced to the shower, and for what seemed like forever, I let the hottest water I could stand cascade over me. I finally got out, dried off and put my robe on. With dragging feet I slowly went back into our room. I was shocked to see that the room was empty. Switching on the light, I looked around our bedroom and in the sitting room, wanting to be sure that Theo was, indeed, nowhere to be seen. Walking into the hallway, I looked over the balcony into the breakfast room/kitchen area. Nothing. Looking over the other side, I looked around the foyer/study area. Still no sign of him. I went downstairs to make some hot chocolate and checking around all the rooms, I found that he wasn't anywhere down there either. I finally looked in the garage and saw that his Navigator is gone.

Lord, what have I done? I hadn't meant to react like that. Now I had forced the poor man to go God knows where in the middle of the night. Padding into the family room, I put the stereo on low and was shocked when I heard Maxwell playing. It made me think about the first time Theo and I had made love.

After that first time, it had become a favorite CD for background music when we were gettin' busy. Right now, however, it was the last thing I wanted to hear. I was just getting up to turn it off when Theo said, "Leave it on. Maybe it will help you to remember that I love you and that I would never hurt you." I turned around, startled to see him in the doorway. I hadn't even heard him come in, so lost in my own thoughts and memories.

"Where have you been? I was worried when I couldn't find you anywhere."

"I just went for a drive. I thought about checking into a motel or something, but then I decided we needed to talk, Sara."

"Yeah, I guess we do." For a while neither one of us said anything.

"I don't know why I did that or why it happened," I told him, frustrated that I couldn't articulate what I had been feeling.

"I wanted to make love with you Theo, I really did. But then I realized that I couldn't feel anything. It was like from the waist down, I've become numb, paralyzed."

"I see. Is it because you still think I don't want you?"

"No, I don't think so."

"Then what is it?"

"I don't know, Theo! Damnit, if I did, don't you think I would tell you?"

"Then it's because of the rape, isn't it? Having sex makes you feel like you are being violated again, doesn't it? And that's why you're numb. You probably feel that if you make yourself *not* feel, you can't be hurt. Am I right?"

"I don't know, maybe."

"Well, what if we left the lights on so that you could see that it's just me, Sara? Not Frankie or Terrell, just me, Theo, the man who loves you with all of his heart. Please baby, let me help you with this," he begged me, wanting me to open up to him. I just couldn't. I wasn't ready.

"I just need time Theo. Just give me some time," I tell him wearily.

Chapter Thirty-two

Today is the day. I'm finally going to do it. It's been more than four months since I lost the baby. And almost every day since I've been home from the hospital, I have stood in front of this door. So I've made up my mind that I'm not going to walk away today.

Spring had long since arrived in full, glorious bloom and I have cleaned and aired out every room in the house but this one and now it's the beginning of summer. In another week or so, Bethany and T.J. will be on summer vacation. This room has been shut up for far too long. Ever since I quit my job, I've been like a woman possessed around the house. Not one corner has escaped my attention. The house is so clean, you could eat off the garage floor. My closets are so neat and organized, they would make Martha Stewart weep.

Taking a deep breath, I grasped the door handle and forcefully pushed it open. I was startled at how bright it was in there. Sunlight was pouring in the two windows which overlooked the front of the house. Although the filmy cream curtains I had hung there did filter the light, it is still quite bright in the room. I slowly walked into the room and turning in a small circle, looked at the room I had so lovingly decorated. The walls, between the cheerful animal alphabet border at the top and middle of the wall, are a soft mint green. The bottom half of the wall is pearl white and green narrow stripped paper. The carpet on the floor is the same off-white as the rest of the house. The crib, dresser, changing table and chest of drawers are all washed oak. The valance and glide rocker are the same prints as the stripped wallpaper. The window seat is upholstered in the same print as the border, with a lot of stuffed animals nestled in the corners waiting for little hands to lovingly play with them. The crib is all dressed, and the coverlet turned back in anticipation of a small, warm, sleeping body or one laughing and playing with his many crib toys and gadgets. The mobile hanging over it is still and silent, its soothing music never to be heard in this house.

Walking over to the window seat, I sank down and cradled a stuffed elephant in my arms, trying to stop the violent trembling that has taken over my body. I felt myself rocking back and forth as this ungodly keening noise, that started low and increased in volume is ripped from deep inside my empty womb. I'm crying so hard that I realized I was about to be sick, and jumping up and running into the bathroom, I just made it before I was violently sick on my stomach. And I heaved and heaved until there's nothing left to bring up. After splashing cold water on my face and rinsing out my mouth, I slid to the bathroom floor, trying to get myself together. Taking deep breaths, I slowly pulled myself together, forcing myself to stand on shaking legs.

I wanted to run out and shut the door again, but I made myself stay. I realized and understood that I had to go through this before I could start to heal. For the first time in a long time, I really wanted my mother. Only, she's not here, so I know I have to do this by myself. Resolutely, I went back into the room, and after I picked up one of the plastic trash bags I had dropped from my numb fingers when I first came into the room, I surveyed the room again.

Taking a deep breath, I went through the room and began filling the bag with all the stuffed animals. Once that's done, I tied the bag up and picked up another one. This time I filled it as I snatched open drawer after drawer, scooping up the contents and dumping it into the bag, not allowing myself to linger over all the beautiful clothes, gowns, diapers, pajamas and other baby paraphernalia I had purchased.

I cleared the top of the dresser and chest with one swipe into the bag. I pulled the bed linens off and not bothering to fold them, I stuffed them into another bag, along with the long silent mobile. Dragging the bags down to the garage, I rummaged around Theo's tool box until I found what I needed. Racing back upstairs, I broke the crib and the changing table down and dragged them to the garage also.

Marching into the kitchen, I pulled out the yellow pages and I called the nearest Salvation Army and told them if they can come today, right now, they can have all the furniture and clothes, but only if they are here within the hour.

Less than an hour later, I'm ushering them into the house and directing them to the room to get the furniture, which they are delighted with. They've gotten really picky and unless they think it will sell, they will no longer take whatever anyone is offering. Then I had them take the stuff out of the garage, and after rummaging through the bags, they agreed to take that stuff too. They could tell the things were brand new and after settling on a ridiculous price for tax purposes, they happily haul everything away. I probably could have used the dresser and chest of drawers, but I don't want any reminders of what their original intended use was for.

After the movers left, without a thought I grabbed my purse and keys and I'm halfway to Home Depot when I realize that I'm out of the house by myself. A hysterical giggle escaped me before I made myself stop and look around to see if anyone else in the cars around me was looking at the crazy lady in the van. Thankfully, no one was paying me any attention.

Pulling into the parking lot, I parked my car and practically raced into the superstore. In record time I picked out paint colors and had them mixed. I usually take forever trying to pick out just the right shade of paint. Not so today. I picked out a color called Spiced Paprika. While the paints were being mixed, I picked out a room sized area rug that will actually complement the off-white carpet in the now defunct nursery.

The area rug is a sort of ethnic/abstract design of browns, beiges, creams, burnt orange and black with occasional touches of red. After arranging to have it delivered, I purchased the paint and left. My next stop is Pier One Imports at Five Points. I buy a brown woven full size rattan bed, dresser and end tables. I spotted a funky green wicker chair and decided to buy that too. Spotting some mission style stained glass-shaded metal lamps, I added those to my purchases. I also picked up some animal prints, African masks and some wrought iron candle holders and some of the fat vanilla candles I liked so much. I also bought a set of sheets, and an animal print coverlet. I found a fabulous piece of material that I bought to go around the window. Finally satisfied that I had enough to get me started, I again arranged for delivery and loading everything else into the van, I raced back home.

After cursing like a sailor, I struggled to get all of the old border and glue off the walls. When that was finally done, I pulled out my trusty painting machine, and I made short work of repainting the room. Even though the color is darker than the palette I usually work with, I like how it makes the room look. Since the room has two big front windows, plenty of a light comes in, keeping the room from being depressing.

I had just finished getting the material around the windows to my satisfaction when the Home Depot truck pulled up. I had them bring the rug up and roll it out. Now I'm glad I paid the extra money to have it delivered today. Same with my stuff from Pier One. One truck was pulling off as the other one was pulling up.

Three hours later, I was satisfied with my handiwork. Anyone looking in this room now would never know it had once been intended as a nursery. Now I had a very nice guest room. With the one in the basement, we now had two guest rooms. At the very least, with T.J. getting older, it would make a great suite. I was pleased with the afrocentric flavor I had going on in here now. I think I surprised myself. Considering how fast I had bought everything, it all worked. Quite nicely, thank you very much. Thank goodness for Theo's gold charge cards! I was even thinking of redoing T.J.'s room to go with this room. Maybe I would make this his room and redo his as a sitting room. Once he left for college, it would be a great guest suite.

For the first time in months, the door to this room was finally open. As nice as the room looked, though, I still felt a little bit sad. However, I realized that it was something that I had to do, and even though I was sad, I felt like another weight had come off me. That closed door had represented more than just hiding away the nursery. It had been keeping a part of me closed off too.

In the last couple of months, Theo and I had attempted to make love on more than a few occasions. And no matter how hard I tried, I still can't feel anything. I've been to the doctor and he has emphatically ruled out anything medical. So it's all in my head. Maybe I just needed to open up *my* door.

Sighing, I wearily cross the hall to our room to take a much needed shower. When I got done, I decided to lie down for a few minutes before going downstairs to take something out for dinner.

I must have fallen asleep because the next I knew, Theo was sitting on the bed, gently rubbing my naked back. I stretched and snuggled further into my pillow. Cracking one eye open, I was surprised to see that the room was almost dark. I was also surprised to notice that his rubbing my back felt good. Damn good. Since my head was turned away from him, for a little while longer I pretended to still be asleep while I enjoyed his warm hand on my back that was inching its way down to my behind. As his fingers trailed over my cheeks, an involuntary groan of pleasure escaped my lips and I felt my hips starting to slowly writhe of their own volition. This really felt good. Should I let him know I'm awake or pretend to still be asleep? If he thinks I'm awake, he'll stop, afraid of my rejection. So I continue to pretend I'm asleep, just to see how far he'll go. Now he's gently rubbing and squeezing my ass and his hand is moving closer and closer to the apex between my legs. I wait in breathless anticipation to feel his finger slip between my nether lips and

I'm shocked by the contact when it does. I'm even more shocked to realize that I'm actually wet. When I move my hips, his finger slips inside of me and we both freeze. Slowly I squeeze my muscles around his finger and he begins to move his finger in and out of me. To my joy, I realize that I can feel it and it feels so good in fact that I want more. Theo's breathing has gone from normal to a hoarse sounding rattle. Poor man. I finally take pity on him and turning over, I forced him to stop. Sitting up in the bed, I could see that he thinks we have failed again and he looked so hurt, then surprised when I wordlessly reach over and undo the button on his pants before pulling his zipper down.

"Are you sure?" he whispered in that husky voice I love. I just nodded my head and laid back on the bed, spreading my legs wide and opening my arms.

"Hurry!" I urged him, laughing at his haste to rid himself of his clothes, but when he entered me I stopped laughing and released a long, slow moan instead. Theo immediately stopped, afraid that I was in pain. I shook my head, silently telling him not to stop. When started to move again, slowly at first, it felt so wonderful, that I was finding it hard not to shout how good it felt. Theo must have known that I was concerned that the kids were home because he said breathlessly, "They're not here." Aw shit, it's on now! Chile, it's a wonder my neighbors *three* doors over didn't hear me! Talk about gettin' buck wild? Please, we made a whole new definition. I don't know who was making more noise; me or him. But what a joyful noise! Too soon, it was over, but not before he made sure that I had been satisfied. The next time, it was much slower and sensual. The time after that, intense. The one the next morning, sweet, gentle and memorable.

When we finally got up, we were by turns, silly and giggling like two teenagers, and then serious, with long loving looks and kisses passing between us. It felt so good to be back to us. At least for a minute.

While we were fixing breakfast, I finally asked, "By the way, where are the kids?"

"Bethany wanted to spend the night over Zoe's house and T.J. is, where else, over Carols."

"Lucky us, huh?"

"I'll say, with all that noise you were making. Would have been damned embarrassing if they'd been home," he teased.

"Me?! Ha! You weren't doing too badly yourself, Mr. Watkins. Sounding like a moose in pain," I laughed.

"And how would you know what a moose in pain sounds like?"

"I don't, but if I did, it would be that noise you made," I tell him as I demonstrate, making us both crack up.

"I was coming to tell you how much I like what you did with the room, Sara. I'm telling you, baby, you've got talent. You really should think about starting your own design business."

Blushing in pleasure, I say, "You really think so?"

"I know so! You know, one of my suppliers was telling me that his wife is redoing their living room and she's really having a hard time. He swears she's color blind. They've done nothing but fight since she started the project. Why don't I have him call you and set up an appointment for you to take a look? Maybe he'll hire you to do the job."

"I don't know, Theo. It's one thing to decorate for my taste, but it's something altogether different when somebody is paying you."

"Yeah but everybody in your family, and now mine, is always asking you for design advise. And they usually take it too. So you must know what you're doing."

"True. Okay, tell him to give me a call. It can't hurt to look, right?"

"That's the spirit! You'll be fine."

"Oh wait, that means I'll have to go out by myself."

"Didn't you go out yesterday by yourself?"

"I was on a mission. All I could think about was getting that room done. That was different."

"So think of this as a different mission."

"Why haven't the police found them yet?" I suddenly asked in frustration, totally changing subjects.

"I don't know, baby. I'm sure we'll hear something soon. But in the meantime, I think we've got some lost time to make up for, Miss." Pulling me into his arms, he started nuzzling my neck. Lifting me up, he sat me on the island, much like the first time we made love in this house, with the same tenderness and fragility, and we were engaged in some serious tongue play when the phone rang. Sighing, we broke apart as Theo answered the phone.

"What? No shit! Aw man. Okay. Yeah. We'll be right there."

"What is it? Is something wrong with one of the kids?" I didn't know what to think was the matter.

"They got them."

"What? Got who....oh shit! Really? Are you sure? Who was that?"

"That was Vaughn. They picked them up some time this morning. We have to go to the police station to make a positive identification. It's over, baby. They finally got those bastards. From what Vaughn hinted at, I don't think they are going to enjoy their time in jail. There are a lot of guys in jail who don't like rapists."

"Like I give a shit! I hope somebody named Bubba decides to make Frankie his bitch. Same thing for Terrell."

By the time we got to the police station, it looked like a lot of our family members were there. My family for what had happened to me; Theo's for me and Brenda. Of course, Brenda's mother was also there. I hadn't seen her since the funeral. I was shocked at how much she had aged since then. She looked old and defeated. I suppose losing two children can do that to you. The police were keeping a watchful eye that things didn't get ugly. Everybody was being cool, though. As soon as Vaughn saw us walk in, he came over and he and Theo walked a few feet away for a private conversation.

I could see Theo gesturing with his hands and Vaughn shaking his head no, making Theo stiffen and gesture some more. I had a pretty good idea what was up when some of Theo's nephews noticed and joined in the discussion.

We watch as Vaughn gestures to another cop who came over and listened then shook his head. Theo and some of the other men get into a heated discussion with the second cop. All of them look pissed. Vaughn shrugged his shoulders helplessly and called me and Brenda's mother over. They explained that we had to make a positive identification. Theo went with me and Brenda's mother.

When the police led them in, I stared through the glass at their mangled faces. Somebody had gotten to them before the police had. However, some of their bruises looked fresh. For all their wounds, they didn't even look sorry, or ashamed or anything. They just looked hard and I wondered what I had ever found attractive about Frankie. I felt myself shivering when it looked like he was looking through the mirror right at me. I moved closer to Theo's warmth and assurance. Wordlessly, like he felt my apprehension, he pulled me into his embrace, his steady rubbing my back in concentric circles doing much to calm my sudden fears. Drawing a shaking breath, I confronted Terrell and Frankie's belligerence through the mirrored glass.

"Are these the two men who raped you Ms. Livingston?" one of the officers asked me matter-factually.

"Yes, that's them," I choked out, squeezing Theo's hand so hard, it's a wonder I didn't break it.

"And could you identify the man who beat your daughter, Mrs. Bodell?" he then asks Brenda's mother.

"That's the bastard right there," she snapped, seemingly beyond tears, just angry as all hell, as she pointed at Terrell.

"Thank you ladies. Someone from the DA's office will be in touch. You can all go home now."

"Thank God it's over, Sara," Zoe told me as we walked out of the station.

"It'll never be over, Zoe. As long as I can remember what I've lost, it'll never be over," I told her, trying to keep myself together, shaking my head sadly.

"I know, sis. I just mean, at least you don't have to be afraid anymore. You don't have to feel like you're trapped in your house."

"True dat."

I gave my sister a hug in the parking lot before we got into our respective cars.

"What happened to them? Why did they look so beaten up like that?"

"I don't know, Sara," Theo said vaguely. "Vaughn just said they 'resisted' arrest. However, he did say that they were in very bad shape when they found them. Somebody called in with an anonymous tip about where they could be found. Who cares who found them before the police did? The important thing is that they are now in custody."

I couldn't believe it. In a way, Zoe was right, it was over. What does it matter that I'll probably have to spend hours in a courtroom, or worse, that I'll have to get on that stand and tell everybody what happened in gory detail? In the end, they're going to jail. I'm finally free. All I can do is sit there, crying, and at the same time, grinning my ass off!

Chapter Thirty-three

"Do you, Theodosius David Watkins, take this woman, Sara Nanette Livingston, to be your lawfully wedded wife? To have and to hold, through sickness and health, for better or worse, richer or poorer, till death do you part?" Reverend Chapman asked.

"I do," he answered clearly.

"And do you, Sara Nanette Livingston, take this man, Theodosius David Watkins, to be your lawfully wedded husband? To have and to hold, through sickness and health, for better or worse, richer or poorer, till death do you part?"

"I do," I answered through my tears. I've been crying through the whole ceremony, but they are tears of happiness this time. Before I knew it, we were walking back up the aisle listening to the applause and cheering in the packed church.

It was a beautiful, sunny September Saturday. It's also the day our baby should have been born. Yes, he would have been a Saturday's child also. Ironic, huh? Theo and I had decided to marry on this day, the day Ian should have been born because although we were not celebrating a new life, we were celebrating a new beginning. Only a few members of our families knew the significance of the day. For the most part, we'd decided to keep it private.

What a beautiful wedding it had turned out to be! I had chosen a gown of antique gold satin with seed pearls around the scooped neckline and scattered down the bodice. My bridesmaids were Bethany, Gina, Stephanie and my friend Lela from Maryland. My matron of honor was Zoe. Their dresses were tea length, A-line dresses in fall shades: warm yellow, maroon, burnt orange, and moss green. Zoe's dress was antique ivory. Theo's nephews Craig, Bruce, Robert and Zoe's husband, Vaughn, were the groomsmen. T.J. was his best man and he looked so handsome in his tux, trying to look so grownup. I thought I would truly become undone doing the ceremony when I had glanced at him and he had given me the most beatific, understanding smile I had ever seen. It had been all I could do to keep it together. As for the wedding, I had tried to keep everything simple, yet elegant.

I kept watching Zoe and Vaughn, though. I hoped that Zoe wasn't too uncomfortable. Two days before the wedding she told me she and Vaughn were splitting up. She was actively looking for a house to rent. She expected that she would be moving out by the following month. They were trying hard to be civil. When I asked her why, she said she had fallen in love with somebody else and was sick of Vaughn's shit. When she had found out that Vaughn was having her followed, that had been the last straw. I suspected that she had fallen in love with her young buck. From the little she had told me, he was rocking her world.

After Frankie and Terrell had been arrested, our lives had finally started to get back to being normal. Thankfully, the DA's office had put the case on the fast-track status. We had painfully endured the trial, my tearful account of the events and finally, had watched with satisfaction as they were carted off to prison. I had almost become physically ill when I first saw the pictures the DA presented of me. Pictures that I had no recollection being taken when I had first arrived at the hospital. They had been blown up to show every detail of what they had done to me. I had refused to see them when we had met with the Assistant District Attorney and her paralegal. In court, I had no choice but to look along with everybody else. It had taken all the strength I could muster to force back the bile that had risen in my throat. However, I had to jump up and run for the bathroom when they showed the pictures of Brenda and what Terrell had done to her. I hadn't realized until then just how much the undertaker had done to make her look as normal as he had.

Terrell got more time than Frankie because of killing Brenda. It just happed that one of Theo's nephews was serving time and he promised to make life a living hell for them.

And even though I felt that I had pretty much recovered physically from the rape, I was still experiencing occasional nightmares. Then too, there were still sometimes in the middle of our lovemaking I would panic and have to make Theo stop. Finally in desperation, I had talked to my doctor. We decided that therapy wouldn't hurt and I noticed that the nightmares were finally starting to occur less frequently, as well as my feelings of panic during lovemaking. I knew it was something I would never forget, but with help, I was learning to deal with it. Theo walked with me every step of the way. I don't think a lesser man would have been able to cope.

As soon as my divorce from Keith had become final, Theo and I had spent the summer planning this fall wedding. In between wedding plans, I was busy doing design jobs. After I had done the one for Theo's friend, it had seemed to just take off. Now I was getting almost more business than I could handle. I was still working, but finally, this Saturday's child was happy with the way she was making her living.

I had been so busy trying to handle everything, it seemed like I turned around and suddenly, it was our wedding day. And now, it was time to party!

We had managed to get a room at a country club in Wallingford because another wedding had been cancelled. The room was huge, but it was what we needed since we had more than two hundred people in attendance. Even my old bosses, with their wives, had come and I was really glad to see them there.

Theo and I chose "*I Wanna Know,*" by Joe, as our wedding song. It was perfect. Our other song we requested was "*The Dance*" by Dave Koz, sung by BeBe Winans because of the words "*And now, I'm glad I didn't know the way it all would end; the way it all would go. Our lives are better left to chance. I could have missed the pain, but I'd have had to miss the dance.*" We could have done without the pain of my rape and losing our baby, but would we have gotten to this place, this closeness, without the struggle we went through? And would I have walked away from Theo had I known all that we would have to go through to get to today? Not a chance. I found myself thinking back to the beginning, right before I met Theo when I foolishly believed that I didn't need love. What's love got to do with it? And I realize, understand and accept now, it's everything!

I had been so lost in my thoughts, I didn't realize that a tear had slipped down my cheek until I felt Theo gently brush it away. When I looked up at him in surprise, he just smiled into my eyes in understanding and softly kissed me, to the delight and applause of our guests.

My parents couldn't stop grinning and had a ball. They stole the show when the D.J. played an oldie and they did their famous bop. I've always loved to watch them dance. After so many years, they looked like Fred and Ginger; they were so in sync with each other and for a minute, I could forget some of the ugliness of their relationship. For now, they were what they seemed: the perfect parents rejoicing in their daughters wedding.

During the toasts, Stephanie stood up and said, "To my sister, Sara: You didn't fuck it up!" making everyone laugh.

Everyone had a good time and we partied like nobody's business.

Theo and I were going on another cruise for our honeymoon, but we weren't flying out until the next day. For tonight, we had a room at the Four Seasons. Our suite was unbelievable. Hell, I could live here. We had our bedroom, a living room, and a mini kitchen. It was all that!

After getting undressed, showering and spraying *Amarige* perfume all over myself, I fell back on the bed with a happy sigh. Ironically, the

Temptations, *I Promise* was playing in the background. WDAS must've been on.

"Happy sweetheart?" Theo asked as he joined me on the bed, smiling down at me, a glass of nonalcoholic champagne in each hand. After lightly touching our glasses, we both took a small sip. I placed my glass on the nightstand next to the bed, as did Theo.

"Very! It was nice, wasn't it?"

"Yeah it was. Everyone had a good time."

Gathering me into his arms, Theo suddenly said, "God, I love you, Sara," before giving me one of his body-drugging kisses. I felt myself floating away on the sensations he was generating.

Pretty soon though, there was no more conversation as we begin to communicate in another language. As always, I'm amazed at the heights Theo takes me to, sometimes making me weep with how wonderful it feels. And as he loved me, moving slowly and sweetly against me, in me, around me, I whispered to him, "Will it always be like this?" I know I don't have to explain to him that I'm not just talking about making love, but about *being* so loved.

After softly kissing my forehead, my closed eyes, my cheeks, and finally my lips gently, tenderly and then slowly and sensually slipping his tongue deeply into my mouth, causing me to gasp with the sensations he's making me feel, he answers fiercely, yet lovingly, "Always!"

About the Author

Gayle Jackson Sloan is a native of Philadelphia, Pennsylvania. She attended Philadelphia College of Textiles and Science, where she studied interior design. She is currently a legal secretary for a small, but prestigious, Philadelphia law firm. She is currently busy working on her second novel, tentatively entitled "*Wednesday's Woes.*"

Printed in the United States
977000007B